REJECTS
PARADISE

Cover Design: Covers by Aura
Photographer: Valua Vitaly
Proofreading: Danielle Stansbury
Editing: Heather Fox
Editing & Formatting: Sheridan Anne

To my nan who I lost while writing this book.

The past few years were hard and filled with pain. I know that couldn't have been easy, but you held on for as long as you could and for that, we thank you. You're in a better place now and I know that one day we will meet again.

I will miss you every day until then.

June 7th, 2020

CHAPTER 1

Thick smoke billows inside Dominic's car, threatening to suffocate the five of us and if we weren't having so much fun, we'd probably be worried. You know what they say about hotboxing a car ... actually, I've got no fucking clue what they say about that but when the opportunity presented itself, I wasn't about to say no.

What can I say? I like to live on the wild side, and if tonight is going to be my last night with my boys, then you'd better believe that we're going to fuck shit up.

I pinch the joint from between Sebastian's fingers and ignore his irritated protests as I bring it to my lips. "Hey, what gives?" he demands, reaching for it, only to miss it by mere inches.

I grin wide, my eyes glistening with laughter and I relax back on Elijah's lap. "Too slow, Sebastian," I tease, rocking the joint back and forth between my fingers. I wink, loving how easy it is to torment him. "Though, that's always been the way with you when it comes to me."

Sebastian rolls his eyes and flops heavily into the backseat. "Screw you," he says with a soft chuckle, his eyes scanning over my body. "I could have had you if I tried hard enough."

Dominic scoffs from the front seat and my eyes slice toward him to find him staring out the window. Both he and Kairo stare adamantly out the windshield watching the newbie dickheads of his father's gang fuck up their deal in the park.

Sebastian's hand swipes toward me, stealing my attention away from Nic. I pull the joint back, narrowly avoiding it being swiped from between my fingers. I grin back at him. "Just like I said. Too slow."

Sebastian groans and I laugh. He's one of my best friends and though he's the biggest flirt I've ever met, there's never been anything between us. He's like a brother to me, the best kind of brother and I hate that I have to move away from him. Apart from Dominic, leaving Sebastian is going to hurt the most. It's going to be an excruciating kind of pain, but when it comes to my crew, all it would take is a single phone call for the four of them to drop everything and come running.

"What's the big deal anyway?" I question, studying the sharp lines of his handsome jaw. "It's not as though you don't have four more of these bad boys hidden in your pocket or shoved halfway up your ass."

He ignores my stab and rolls his eyes. "You know damn well that

I don't give a shit about you getting high. I'll fucking welcome it if it means a shot at tasting that sweet pussy before you go, but you and I both know that the problem is Nic kicking my ass for letting you take it. Not to mention, he's currently scheduling a second beating for that comment about your pussy."

I laugh as Dominic grunts from the front. I keep my gaze locked on Sebastian. "If Nic has a problem with it then he can grow some balls and speak to me about it instead of messing up your pretty face. Black and blue aren't exactly your colors."

Sebastian groans as Elijah's arm tightens around my waist, over-protective at the thought of me and Nic having it out. We're both passionate people, and seeing as though angry-sex is off the table, that only leaves one other option and we all know it wouldn't be pretty.

"Go to hell," Sebastian chuckles, unable to keep the smirk off his face.

I laugh. "I did. It was full so I came back."

Kairo shakes his head, keeping his eyes trained out the front windshield, somehow able to ignore the thick smoke in the car. "I always knew you were some kind of devil."

Dominic scoffs, his eyes flicking up and meeting mine through the rear-view mirror—dark and way too intense. "More like an angel in disguise."

My stomach clenches and for a moment, it's too hard to look away. That is until I remember how he crushed me six months ago. Even still, with that pain sitting heavy on my chest, I can't possibly pull myself away from him. I love him and I always will. Nic is my world, he's my best friend and the man who saved me from myself. I'll just never be stupid enough to let him into my bed again.

Kairo starts murmuring beside Nic, knowing damn well that he's the one Nic is going to send to fix the newbies fuck-up. I silently thank him for the distraction. Nic is too much. He's intense and knows exactly what it takes to make me the happiest girl in the world, but he also knows how to take it all away.

I lean back against Eli's wide chest and finally bring the joint to my lips. I inhale deeply, closing my eyes with the hit.

Fuck, yes. This is what I've been needing ever since my mom delivered the heartbreaking news that we were leaving Breakers Flats. It still hasn't hit. It's been four long days since she told me the news and I've been refusing to come to terms with it.

I don't want to leave this place. This is my home. It's a complete shithole and filled with all the wrong kinds of people. Any normal person would be jumping for joy at the thought of leaving here, but not me. It may be a shithole but it's my shithole—gangs and all.

My eyes flutter open as I get comfortable against Eli and I instantly start cursing myself for making such a stupid mistake. Not the getting cozy with Eli part, but the opening my eyes thing as I find Nic staring right back at me. Only this time, it's not the same intense heaviness from before, this is the pissed off alpha bullshit that he usually pulls on the guys—the one that tells me he's just moments from spanking my ass, and not in a good way.

Before Nic and I got together a year ago, that look would have had me running, but when I realized that he'd fallen madly in love with me, things changed. Since then, he's had a little trouble keeping me in line, and I have no problems assuring him that tonight is going to be one of those nights.

It's my last night here in Breakers Flats and I intend on going out with a bang.

Nic doesn't look away and I hold my ground. There's been a strain on our relationship ever since I walked in to find his cock buried between the legs of Carmen Saunders. He knew he fucked up and he's been paying for it ever since. His shot was blown. I'm not the type to hand out second chances, but it doesn't stop him from trying.

Despite all of that, I still love him. He's the one I go to when I've had a bad day, he's the one who wiped my tears after my dad died, the one who held me and told me it was all going to be alright. He's my protector, my world, and my heart. Leaving him is going to kill me.

Leaving my whole crew is going to kill me but it's a necessary evil. It's a decision I hate, but one that I completely understand.

Without this move, mom and I are up shit creek without a paddle. This is our last shot.

I keep my eyes locked on Nic's dark ones and curl my lips into a little 'O.' I flick my cheek, keeping a straight face and watch the smoke puff out of my mouth in perfect rings knowing it's bound to drive him over the edge.

His eyes darken. He hates it when I smoke. Apparently, it's unladylike but what the hell would he know about being a lady? Besides, I happen to know for a fact that Nic Garcia loves it when I act like anything but a lady. It's been a while though. If it didn't hurt so bad, I might have even caved and given him a goodbye screw.

Dominic gives up and breaks the connection, snapping his gaze back to the park as the newbies somehow manage to let their deal go even further south.

All four of the boys groan. If this shit gets back to Nic's father, they're all going to go down for it. I slip off Eli's lap and drop into the center of the backseat, leaning forward into the front, wanting to watch the epic fail as it plays out.

My elbow drops down onto the center console, and I don't miss the way Nic moves his arm over, pressing his warm skin against mine, giving me shivers at his touch.

I concentrate out the front, trying to ignore the feelings swarming through my body.

The newbies are performing their very first drug deal. I remember Sebastian's. He was a good boy before the Black Widows corrupted him. He practically shit his pants. If it weren't for Kairo, we probably never would have seen Sebastian again. He's come a long way since then.

The newbies are meeting with a bunch of rich kids from some town that losers like us couldn't even dream about, and to say it could be going better is an understatement. They should have been better prepared and done their homework.

I'm not surprised when they hand over the goods before taking the money, only to watch the rich kids make a run for it.

Sebastian and I shake our heads as Eli groans beside me. "For fuck's sake," Kairo mutters under his breath.

The newbies start running after them, knowing damn well the consequences of losing that money. We let them sweat it a bit and watch the fuckers race through the park but when one of the little turds pulls a gun, Nic groans.

"Go," he orders with a ferocious snap. The Black Widows cannot afford any more shit on their doorstep. Nic's dad, Kian, is only one step away from being locked up for the next thirty years. If this shit falls on him, it's game over.

Kairo, Eli, and Sebastian move like lightning, knowing an order when they hear one. These guys might be best friends and brothers, but there's a clear boss among them and that's a line no one wants to cross. They're all good to fuck around and stir shit up, but when Dominic Garcia means business, they know.

Their doors are thrown open and the car instantly empties of the thick smoke. I go to move after the boys but Nic's hand snaps out and clenches down around my wrist. "Not you."

My head snaps back around and I hear "Good luck, pretty girl," muttered by Kairo just moments before the door is slammed with a solid thump.

The three of them chase after the newbies and rich kids while I look longingly after them. "Come on, Nic. For old time's sake."

"You're only going to make things worse and I can't have your mom banging on my door at three in the morning demanding that I cough up the cash to bail you out again."

I roll my eyes and sink back into my seat with a frustrated groan. "That happened once."

A cocky grin spreads across Nic's face as he turns in his seat to look back at me. "Come on, you know I'm not about to let you get messed up in the Black Widows business. You need to graduate from high school and go to college. You're better than this. It's part of the reason your mom is getting you out of here."

I stare back at him, meeting his heavy gaze. "The likelihood of me graduating and going to college is about the same as your father getting through the next few years without doing any jail time. It's never going to happen."

He shakes his head and watches me as though he's watching a misbehaved child. "You need to have more faith in yourself."

"And you need to get a grasp on reality," I throw back, more than ready to have the same fight that we've had a million times before. "Look around you, Nic. I'm a Breakers Flats girl—born and bred. There's no good for me out there. I'd be lucky to find myself a guy who doesn't hit me and keep a job long enough to afford a roof over my head."

His gaze drops for just a moment before meeting mine once again, the fight in his eyes now completely gone. He wanted to be that guy who gave me a future. He would have left his father's gang and given us a real shot at a life together, but that's not going to happen now. He would have made such a great husband. You know, in a few years, considering we would have made those few years without accidentally popping out a baby. It was bound to happen had we stayed together any longer. That's just the life we have around here. Hell, it's the same life mom had with dad until he was murdered four short months ago.

Nic reaches into the back and his warm, calloused hands take my waist just seconds before I'm hauled through the car. "Come here," he says a second too late before I'm straddled over his lap and staring back into the darkest eyes I've ever had the pleasure of seeing.

"What are you doing?" I question as I try to scramble off his lap toward Kairo's vacated seat, but his grip only tightens. If Dominic Garcia wants me on his lap, then that's exactly where I'm going to be. No question about it. Nic always gets what he wants.

I give in and relax into his hold, and seeing that resignation, he eases his grip on my waist. Nic tilts his chin, looking up and meeting my eyes, and in seconds I know what this is going to be about.

His hand comes up and brushes over my cheek, his knuckles rough against my skin but I can't focus on it. All I see are his eyes, desperately trying to pull me in. God, why does he have to look like this? Dark, scruffy hair, stubble over his sharp jaw, and a face tempting enough to have even the strongest of women breaking. He's sexy as sin and it's not fair. I can't resist him. Add the bandana and the tattoos covering his body and I'm a goner. But when he flashes that cheesy as fuck grin my way, I melt.

"Don't go, Ocean," he murmurs, his heart breaking before my eyes and slowly killing me from within. "Stay here with me."

My hands fall against his strong chest as I lean in and softly brush my lips over his. "I have to," I tell him. "Mom is all I've got left. I can't let her go alone. She's my only family."

"Ouch. That hurt," he grumbles, twisting his arm to show off his tattoo that reads 'No friends, only family.'

I let out a small sigh. "Come on, Nic. You know that's not what I meant. You and the guys are everything to me, but this is my mom. I have to do this. What am I going to do in Breakers Flats without her? The bank has already taken our home. We lost the car last month, what else do we have to give? We have no other choice."

"You can stay with me," he insists, his eyes searching for something deep within mine. "I'll get another job until you finish school and you know the boys will pitch in where they can. Come on, O. Tell me you'll stay?"

I shake my head, hating the traitorous tears that begin welling in my eyes. "I can't do that to you," I whisper, my hands dropping to find his. I lace my fingers through his. "You've already got so much going on with the Black Widows. Not to mention when dear old dad goes down, all that shit is going to land on your shoulders. I'm only a distraction to you and it's no secret that your mom hates me. It wouldn't work and you know that just as well as I do."

"O, please, don't do this. Don't go. We'll make it work."

"Don't make this harder than it needs to be. There's nothing here for me. If I stay, I'm going to end up pregnant to some sleazeball Black Widow whom you're just going to kill anyway. Nothing good could come from me staying here."

Nic releases my hand and curls his around the back of my neck, pulling me in and pressing his forehead to mine. "I know, but that doesn't mean that I like letting you go. It was supposed to be you and me."

"You ruined that, Nic."

"Believe me, I know."

I let out a heavy sigh and drop my face into the crook of his neck as his arms curl tightly around me. I only have a second before I break, and I can't have him see me cry. I want to be stronger than that.

Why does this feel like the end of something incredible? This hurts more than when he cheated. It's like I'm closing the book on a story that wasn't finished being written, a story that hardly got a chance to shine.

My tears begin soaking into his shirt as I slip my arms up around his neck. "You'll come and visit, right?"

His fingers trail over the floral tattoo on my shoulder and my heart twists, clenching until it's almost impossible to breathe. Why did I have to get *that* tattoo? "Just try and keep me away, Ocean. Nothing could keep me from you."

"You know I love you, right? If things were different …"

"I know," he says, pulling me back so he can see my face. His thumbs rub under my eyes, wiping away the tears. "I love you too, O. You're always going to be my girl, but you need to quit this crying. You know your tears have a way of bringing out the worst in me."

My bottom lip pouts out and I feel like such an idiot for getting so worked up. "Please don't beat up any of my boys."

He presses his lips into a tight line and gently shakes his head. "I can't make any promises."

I roll my eyes knowing he's only teasing, though I should be worried for Sebastian after those comments he made earlier. On second thought, maybe he isn't kidding. It's an emotional night for us all and these guys usually talk with their fists. I wouldn't be surprised if someone ended up in the emergency room.

I let out a heavy sigh and let him pull me back in. "Just no broken bones, okay?"

"Okay," he promises. "That I can do."

CHAPTER 2

What kind of rich, privileged bullshit fuckery is this?

The big iron gates slide open to reveal the most luxurious mansion in Bellevue Springs. I've never seen anything like it. Not even the mansions that surround us are as ostentatious or douchey as this, yet I can't stop staring at it. It's simply magnificent.

It looks like a modern version of a Victorian manor home with beautiful white pillars evenly placed across the wide span of the mansion. It's absolutely stunning, something out of a fairy tale, and those stairs … holy hell. There are three levels of stairs just to reach the front door.

Where the hell are we? This place is ridiculous. My home back in Breakers Flats wouldn't even fit the front gate inside of it. Not that we exactly have a home anymore. Those fuckers at the bank made sure of that. There's nothing quite like watching your home and everything you've built being taken away.

This place is ginormous. We don't belong here.

"We're definitely not in Kansas anymore," mom mutters under her breath.

I shake my head, agreeing with her completely. We've been here a whole thirty seconds and haven't even heard a gunshot yet. I can just imagine the security team sitting on the other end of these cameras, turning up their noses at what they see before them.

This isn't going to go well, but unfortunately for us, this is the only hope we've got. We've already lost our home, our car, and our dignity. What more do we have to lose? If we were to stay, we would've been on the streets, begging for food. Nic never would have allowed that to happen. He would have taken us in, but mom's pride would have held us back, not to mention, her fear of putting us one step closer to his father's gang. The last thing she wants is to see her little girl get mixed up with that. If only she knew just how close I really was.

When this opportunity landed on our doorstep, we had no choice but to scoop it up with both hands, hoping it didn't slip through our fingers. The eviction notice from the bank was already on the fridge and quickly creeping up to its 28-day deadline. We only had a few days left.

"Are you sure about this?" I question as mom and I step over the boundary line to the massive Carrington estate. This shit needs its own area code.

"Of course I'm not," she says, looking as though she's ready to break into tears. "But it's either this or working for those Black Widow thugs, so I chose the lesser evil. You don't belong in either of those worlds just as I don't belong scrubbing rich guys' toilets. Your father would be rolling in his grave if he was looking down on us right now."

I let out a heavy sigh. She's right. We don't belong here or there, but sometimes you do what you have to do just to get by. The people here wouldn't understand something like that. These are the kind of people who were born with silver spoons in their mouths and money overflowing their gold-trimmed pockets.

If I were the one who had to make the decision, I would have taken the gang option. At least that way I would have been close to the boys and close to dad's grave. Not to mention, someone needs to keep an eye on Sebastian. He's only one bad screw away from an STI.

My four boys. They're the four loves of my life. Well really, Nic is … was, but the rest are all fighting for second place. Though if I'm completely honest, Sebastian might have that second place. He and I share a special, unbreakable bond. He's just as protective of me as I am of him, but not in that crazy, eye-rolling way that Nic is.

I miss them already and it was only a two-hour drive in an Uber. They were there to wave me off, hangovers and all. They're my crew. They're the only reason I was able to make it through the past few years. Being a teen in Breakers Flats isn't easy. You either win or you lose, there's no in-between. At least for me, I had my boys and they've always had my back.

Now, I have nothing.

I guess that's not entirely true. I can always call them and I know they'll drop everything and come running. They're going to make four beautiful women really lucky one day.

Fuck. That thought sends a sharp pain sailing through my chest. The day that Nic finds the girl of his dreams is going to crush me. I won't handle it well and if she even thinks about hurting him, I'm going to fuck that bitch up.

I put it to the back of my head as Mom and I make our way down the long-ass drive. I can't step into this place crying about my old life. I'd be the laughing stock.

I can't stop gaping up at the mansion. Every step we take makes the place seem so much bigger. I can't believe people really live in homes like this. Back where I'm from, the amount of money spent on a home like this could house hundreds of people, even thousands.

"Do you think these people have staff to wipe their asses?" I question under my breath, wishing we still had our car. Carrying all our luggage and precious possessions down this ridiculous drive is really starting to weigh me down. I keep myself in good shape, but seriously ... there are some things a girl just isn't capable of doing. I guess I should be thankful that the driveway isn't an extra mile or two longer.

Mom grins before trying to smother it. She's doing her best to keep her spirit high. "They do but they call them bidets and they squirt water up into your ... you know," she says, popping her hip to indicate her ass.

I gawk at her, my eyes bugging out of my head as I suck in a deep gasp. I stop walking just so I can stare at her. "Up into your asshole?"

Mom sputters out a laugh and tugs on my arm, pulling me along. "Shhhh," she scolds, glancing around to make sure there's no one out here listening in on our absurd conversation. "You can't be saying stuff like that around here. These people aren't going to understand your humor."

I shake my head, still reeling with the thought of this bidet thing. "That wasn't humor. That was disgust."

"I know," she groans as we pass the massive abstract water fountain in the center of the circle drive, a water fountain that could possibly be bigger than the home mom and I were just kicked out of.

We reach the grand stairs that lead up to the front entryway and all conversation about how rich people wipe their asses comes to a stop. We both stare ahead. I can't believe we're about to walk into this place. People like mom and I could only dream about visiting a place like this, let alone living in one.

"It's now or never," I tell her when we've hovered around the bottom step for long enough.

Mom lets out a heavy sigh and nods her head. "Okay. Let's do this."

With that, we start making our way up the three flights of stairs and I find myself counting.

One, two, three ... sixty-six.

Sixty-six fucking stairs just to reach the front door. Who the hell needs this shit in their life? Mom is practically in a hot sweat. I'm surprised there isn't an escalator to get up here. My old school didn't even have thirty stairs over the whole campus. It's like a work out just getting this far. My ass is going to be hella toned if I have to walk this shit every day. I can only imagine what the inside of this place is like.

Every disastrous thought about the stupid stairs disappears as Mom reaches forward and presses the golden button for the doorbell.

This is it. My world is about to collide with another and I'm not sure that I'm ready.

I expect to have to wait at least a few minutes for the door to be answered but within a matter of seconds, there's someone there, pulling the door wide open.

A man appears before us in an expensive-looking suit and nods his graying head in greeting. "Good morning," he says in a flat tone before looking over us with distaste. "May I help you?"

Mom's eyes flick to me and I watch from the corner of my eye as she raises her chin, not liking the way this man is looking down on her. Though, she should be used to it, just like I am. This is the way anyone superior to us has always looked our way. "Hello. My name is Maria Munroe. I am here for the live-in housekeeper position."

Understanding flashes in his eyes. "Ah, you're the new maid," he says as his eyes flick toward me. "And this is?"

Mom's brows furrow before quickly glancing my way again. "This is my daughter, Oceania Munroe. It was put in my contract that she would be staying here with me. Mr. Carrington assured me that it wouldn't be a problem."

The old man who I'm starting to assume must be the butler looks over me, his eyes scanning from top to bottom and I see the same assumptions that I get from every adult—trouble.

I grin, catching his eyes and confirming exactly what he already knows to be true. I'm going to be more trouble than his fancy-ass can handle and if these rich pricks insist on treating me and mom like trash, then I'll show them just how much trouble I can be.

Fuck, I can't wait. I'm just begging for one of them to try and start shit with me.

"Yes, of course," the butler says, squaring his jaw and silently reminding me who's the boss around here. I swallow back and bite my tongue. He's not my boss but he's going to be Mom's and I can't fuck this up for her, no matter how much we don't belong. I can make trouble another way. "That's no problem at all. Her enrollment at Bellevue Springs Academy was finalized just a few hours ago."

Mom smiles as my eyes bug out of my head. A private school? What the fuck is that about? I'm not going to fit into a private school and I guarantee that mom can't afford the fees that go along with that.

I study the side of her face and watch as she focuses extra hard on the butler, refusing to look my way. She knows what I'm thinking and I don't doubt that she's trying to avoid having this conversation in front of this douche canoe.

Sir Douche Canoe waits a moment, watching me in silence, waiting for me to reel in my dramatics before allowing us to step into the Carrington mansion. When he deems I'm acting respectfully enough, he nods politely to my mom before scowling at me. "Follow me."

He turns on his heel and instantly begins stalking off, leaving us to scramble behind him. "Leave your belongings. I'll have Carlos take them to your rooms."

Mom and I look at each other in relief before quickly lining our bags up against the wall of the oversized foyer and hurrying to catch up.

"Um, Sir," I say as I listen to the repetitive sound of mom's cheap heels clicking against the expensive marble floors. "Your name?"

He doesn't turn around, just keeps forging ahead through the huge mansion, hardly giving me a second to catch my bearings. I'll have to explore later. "My name is Harrison Whitby. I am Mr. Carrington's personal butler and head of staff. Any questions, inquiries, or comments go through me. Mr. Carrington is a very busy man."

"Yes, Sir."

"You may call me Harrison, however in the presence of the Carrington family, I will be addressed as Mr. Whitby."

Mom nods despite Harrison not looking her way. "Understood."

Harrison leads us through the mansion and I quickly glance around, taking in the multiple huge staircases, the gold trim on the railings, and the stone statues. This place is fit for a king, but while it's the most impressive thing I've ever seen, it's also incredibly quiet. It's kinda eerie actually.

We're led down a long hallway and through a door at the end. As we step over the threshold, it's suddenly a whole new place. There are people everywhere, a busy kitchen is in full force while people scramble around. Women in maid outfits are walking in and out of a huge laundry room while others are busily refilling a tea and coffee cart.

It's only eight in the morning so I'm assuming they're busily preparing for the Carringtons' breakfast. Though, if this is the effort taken for breakfast, I'd hate to see how crazy it is in here for a dinner party. It has me wondering just how many Carringtons there are. This is a lot of fuss if it was just for one. I mean, what the hell is wrong with simple jam on toast?

Harrison finally stops in the center and I don't miss the way the other staff's eyes linger on me and mom. He turns back to us and gets started on mom's introduction, leaving me to go along for the ride. "This is the staff quarters where the majority of the staff spend their time. Lunches and breaks are taken in here and never in the main part of the house. You were hired as a live-in house-keeper, so feel free to take your breaks in the pool house which is where you'll be residing with your daughter."

He starts walking again and we hastily follow along, desperately trying to keep up with his pace. "This is the main kitchen area where all meals are prepared. The Carringtons' personal kitchen is not to be used under any circumstances. That is reserved solely for the family. The same goes for bathrooms, laundry, and dining areas." Harrison looks toward me. "You will not be permitted access to the main house unless invited by the family. Your time is to be spent in the pool house or the staff quarters. However, if you are to be in here, you must not be a nuisance. Is that understood?"

"Understood," I say with a sharp nod, feeling a slight twinge in my gut. I was kind of hoping to go exploring.

"Unfortunately, our previous live-in maid has fallen ill and is still clearing her things out of the pool house. It looks like she could be a few more days. However, Mr. Carrington has been kind enough to offer you both a room in the main house, provided you remain respectful to house rules. You will both be allowed access to the yard when you're not on the clock. The tennis courts and pool are open for your personal use. However, you are not to invite guests over to the pool house unless they have been accepted and added to the approved list of house guests." He focuses his stare on me but it comes off as more of a warning. "If they are not on the list, they are not welcome."

I hold back a scoff. I have a feeling that rule is going to be broken. Many, many times. My boys won't stand for that bullshit and I can guarantee, they sure as hell won't be approved to be on any list.

Harrison focuses his full attention on mom before pointing out a lady in the kitchen who's leaning over the counter with a massive schedule spread out before her. "This is Maryne. She is in charge of your schedule. If you need a day off or have any issues, you will discuss it with her."

Upon hearing her name, Maryne looks up and gives us a welcoming smile and I instantly like her. She's the first person in this place who hasn't looked down on us and something tells me that she knows a little about what it's like to grow up the way we have.

Maryne gets back to work as Harrison walks over to a door. "Alright, I will give you a brief tour of the estate, and then you'll be handed over to Maryne who will set you up with your uniform." He looks down at me. "She also has all the documents you'll need for your schooling."

I nod and follow him out of the staff quarters as he leads us right into the middle of the mansion.

I stop and stare, most likely mimicking the gobsmacked expression on Mom's face. This place is insane. Hell, I don't even know what area of the house I'm in. It could be a living area or it could just be one of those filler spaces rich people like to decorate. I don't know but it's fucking awesome and it's clear as day that an award-wining interior designer was the one who made this happen. No normal person would be able to put a place like this together so flawlessly. I'm in awe.

I don't get a chance to think about it further as Harrison begins leading us through the place that is going to become my home for the foreseeable future. Who knows how long I'll be here. If this guy is a douchebag, mom and I will be planning our escape as soon as we can. Not that we can afford that luxury.

We pass the second ballroom, and I'm listening to Harrison explain the grand parties that the Carringtons host when a familiar man comes walking out of one of the many living areas.

Charles Carrington. Billionaire businessman and CEO.

CHAPTER 3

Charles Carrington looks like he shits money.

I know nothing about designer brands, but I know the suit that covers his tall frame is worth more than anyone from Breakers Flats could earn in a year. He's got that tall, dark and mysterious thing going for him, and I'm not ashamed to say that he's a bit of a silver fox. There are grey hairs perfectly styled by his temples and kind, tired eyes that stare at the ground, deep in concentration.

The google search I did in the Uber on the way here did him no justice. It told me he's divorced and has three kids. A son and twin daughters. Apparently, the daughters went to live with the mother after the split, but his son stayed behind to live with Daddy Warbucks. I don't know how they can do that. If I had siblings, I couldn't stand to be separated from them. Family is everything.

I didn't really look into the son but considering I'm going to be living with the guy, maybe I should have. His name is Colton Carrington. CC just like his father. That's such a rich guy thing to do. I bet Charles' father's name is Connor or Colby or something like that. Hell, his twin daughters are Casey and Cora.

I was too occupied with the man whose home we were moving into. I couldn't find any dirt on the guy so I guess that's a good thing but these people can't be trusted. They can afford the best lawyers in the world to cover up every tiny little thing. When Harrison mentioned that we'd be in the pool house, I have to admit, I was kind of relieved. Mom and I will have a little space to call our own, a place where we can be ourselves and relax.

Harrison clears his throat and Charles' head snaps up, his eyes bugging out in surprise. "Oh, how rude of me," Charles chuckles, taking us in. "I didn't see you there. I'm onto my third meeting of the morning. Forgive me."

Wow. Third meeting before 8 am. I'm not going to lie, I'm kinda impressed. No wonder he's so successful.

Mom and I smile politely because we honestly have no idea what else we're supposed to do in this situation. "That's perfectly fine, Mr. Carrington," mom says almost as though she belongs in this world.

I give her a mental high-five. Nailed it.

Charles gives a welcoming smile and strides toward us, holding his hand out to mom. "You must be Maria Munroe? It's a pleasure to meet you." Well shit. I wasn't expecting the guy to remember her name. Guys like this never remember little details, especially when it comes to people like us. "I was hoping my last meeting wasn't going to go over, it would have been nice to welcome you in myself."

Mom nods and takes his hand before giving it a firm shake. "The pleasure is all mine, Mr. Carrington. This is my daughter, Oc—"

"Oceania," he cuts in, turning to me with a proud smile, one that doesn't send chills down my spine like I'd been expecting. "Of course. How could I forget?"

"Hello, Sir," I smile. "Please just call me Ocean. My father was the only one who ever called me by my full name."

Understanding dawns in his eyes and for a moment I wonder just how much this guy knows about us, then mentally kick myself. Guys like this would have a full file on us with background checks hidden in his office somewhere. "Of course. Ocean it is. I just got off the phone with the dean of Bellevue Springs Academy an hour ago and finalized your enrollment. You're good to start fresh tomorrow morning."

Rich guy say whaaaat?

"You did?" I question with a grunt before reeling it in and reminding myself to be polite. "I'm sorry, I just … I guess I didn't expect you to have done that yourself. You seem like a very busy man. Thank you."

He winks and gives me a knowing smile but I can't help but feel a slight edge to his gaze. "You know what they say. If you want a job done right, you do it yourself. Besides, the dean owed me a favor." He chuckles for a moment before continuing. "I have twin daughters roughly your age and I firmly believe a good education is the foundation of a successful future. Especially for young women of the world today. You already have so much to compete against with men being handed their futures on silver platters."

Well, shit. I think I like this guy. I wasn't expecting that.

"I … yes. Thank you. I really appreciate it," I tell him, feeling like an idiot for stumbling over my words. Why do I feel so moronic around this guy? He probably thinks I'm a fool for not being able to get a sentence out without stuttering, but there's something so intimidating about him. Maybe it's his success compared to my complete lack thereof or perhaps it's the way he seems to tower over me, silently screaming that I'm a nobody.

I don't get why he's being so nice. It's weird … off-putting. No one is nice for the sake of being nice. It's simply unheard of. He either wants something from me or my mom, or there's some kind of ulterior motive. Why should he care about my education? I'm just his new maid's daughter.

My mind begins reeling with distrust and questions when he steps back and waves his arm out, smiling at my mom. "Shall we? I have half an hour to spare. I'd be honored to complete the tour and get to know you both a little better."

Mom gushes and I roll my eyes. It's one thing for him to show manners but showing that he cares about the wellbeing of her daughter has captured her heart in one easy swoop.

We're in trouble here.

Don't get me wrong, Mom may be a stickler for rules and

boundaries, but she's no stranger to a little crush. I can't imagine her falling for someone so soon after dad's murder, but she's going to be fawning over this guy as though he walks on water.

Charles nods to Harrison and without even a blink, Harrison excuses himself and I openly gawk with how well trained he is. He's like one of those police dogs who obey their master wholeheartedly. I feel like someone needs to ruffle his hair and remind him what a good little boy he is. It's going to be entertaining to watch.

Charles turns to mom while walking through yet another huge living space. "I'm assuming Harrison filled you in on the pool house situation?"

Mom nods. "Yes, Mr. Whitby was very thorough with his introduction."

"Please, no need for formalities around here. Just Harrison is fine. He's fond of formalities but I prefer things a little more relaxed, especially for you two. You're going to be living here now. You should think of yourselves as family rather than staff."

"I'm sure that will come as we get to know you."

"Good," he says. "I'm pleased."

He goes on to show us the house and after ten minutes of walking around, I realize that we're barely halfway through. "This is the main kitchen and living space where you can generally find myself and my son if I'm not working. Otherwise, I will be in my office."

Mom and Charles remain at the entryway but I walk on through, absolutely astonished with what I see. A beautiful open living space, still with the marble floor the whole way through. There's no sneaking around this place unless you're wearing a pair of socks. Every step would be heard.

I make my way through the kitchen first, skimming my fingers over the cool counter. Naturally, it's marble, just a shade lighter than the floor but equally as stunning. "This is incredible," I say, glancing back over my shoulder at Charles.

He grins proudly and follows me into the kitchen. "You haven't seen the half of it," he chuffs like a kid in a candy shop as he strides toward a cabinet and opens the floor to ceiling doors. He steps inside the cabinet and my brows furrow.

What the hell is he doing?

I walk over to the cabinet and peer inside only to find it's not a cabinet at all but a secret door that opens into a private bar. "Holy hell," I whisper, taking in the massive array of choices behind the bar, the mood lighting, and the seating area. "This is freaking awesome."

Charles nods, also looking around. "We had it installed last year though I don't use it as much as I would like to."

"Well, you're a busy man."

Charles' eyes come back to mine and he watches me for a long second before nodding. "Yes, indeed I am," he says, walking out of the private bar and gently closing the doors behind him. "Come along. If you're fond of our bar, then I can only imagine how you're going to feel about our living area."

My eyes flick back toward the living area that he's referring to and I'm stumped. It looks exactly like the rest of them. Well, that's not exactly fair. They all have their own individuality but they all follow the same sleek, modern awesomeness.

I walk with him and mom's curiosity gets the best of her as she follows along.

We take the two large steps down into the sunken living area and as we turn the corner and pass the couches and coffee table, we find a massive indoor pool.

"Holy … fuck me in the ass."

"Language," mom scolds under her breath, her face flaming with embarrassment as Charles bellows out a laugh.

The pool is shaped somewhat like a beach, shallow at one end with sunbeds fixed in the water. I've never seen anything like it. The parties you could have here would be incredible.

Charles digs into his pocket and pulls out his phone before pressing a few buttons and watching the show. The back wall splits in half and begins to fold away, revealing the rest of the pool, half indoor and half out.

"No way," I breathe, gawking at the way the pool seems to go on forever. I think it falls off the very edge like a waterfall. I cannot wait to explore all of this. I feel like Alice in Wonderland … or maybe someone who's just been thrown into a fairy tale that wasn't meant for her. "That's amazing."

Charles grins proudly before pointing up, and it's not lost on me how he's so happy about his accomplishments. Maybe he really is just a nice guy. Not that I've had the pleasure of meeting many billionaires in my life, but I'm assuming things like this are usually lost on them, but not Charles. He still gets a kick out of the little things, and the fact that he's proud of what he's created here is a big sign that he's not the douchebag I assumed he was. Though, looks can be deceiving. I'd be a fool to judge too quickly.

My eyes shoot to the ceiling to find it made of glass, only after pressing yet another button on his phone, the ceiling completely opens up.

Mom's jaw drops as I stare in wonder.

I can only imagine what my boys would say about this place. Nic would just nod, acting as though he's not impressed. Sebastian would already be in the pool. Eli would be staring just like mom is while Kairo would have disappeared long ago, searching out Charles' safe.

The cool morning breeze begins gushing in and Charles is quick to start closing up his epic living space. "Don't get me wrong. It truly is a sight to see it all open, but when the chill gets into the house like this, it takes nearly all day to heat it up again."

"I can only imagine," mom says, her brows up in her hairline, still amazed by what she's witnessing here.

Charles glances down at his watch before his eyes bug out of his head. "I have to run. Let me show you to your rooms and then I'll leave you to explore."

"Of course."

Charles picks up his pace and mom and I are quick to follow behind. We walk back through the living space and up the opposite side of the kitchen from where we entered.

Charles waves off to the left. "This is the media room where Colton likes to hang out when he's actually home. The home gym is just … uh-huh. There he is now." Charles says, making me glance up. "Colton," he calls.

My head whips around, following Charles' line of sight. A man is walking out of a room wearing only a pair of grey, low hanging sweatpants with his shirt carelessly thrown over his shoulder.

His back is to us and damn, it's a nice back. Strong and defined with a sheer layer of sweat coating his tanned, sun-kissed skin. His shoulders are wide and damn, he's tall just like his father. His back stiffens at hearing his name and I don't miss the way every muscle in his back clenches, a clear cut sign of tension. Though, I can't seem to give a shit about it. I'm more intrigued by the idea of seeing his eyes. I bet he has eyes that could melt a woman's clothes straight off her body.

Fuck me. This guy … if his front is anything like his back, I'm in trouble.

I should have prepared myself. Why didn't I look into Colton Carrington when I had the chance? I feel like such an idiot. He's going to throw me off. I can feel it. I'm about to make an ass of myself. Nic would be so ashamed.

Colton begins turning and my gaze instantly drops, unable to help the curiosity pulsing through my veins. I need to see him before he no doubt realizes there's company and he pulls his shirt over his head. He's too far to see all the ridges of his strong body but I'll make do.

My tongue rolls over my lips and I hate how obvious I'm being but I can't help myself. All my boys have bodies like this but the idea of checking any of them out— apart from Nic— is simply outrageous and kind of disturbing.

It's like slapping a big juicy steak on a plate and telling me not to drool. Impossible.

Please be ugly. Please be ugly.

He turns slowly or maybe I'm so focused that the moment seems to be happening in slow motion. All I know is that one second, I'm staring at the most defined back I've ever seen and the next, I'm watching the way his abs crunch with each step he takes toward us.

My greedy eyes scan over his tanned skin and I briefly wonder if he's some kind of exotic being or if he just forgets to slather on the sunscreen when outdoors. Either way, he's the most delicious shade of olive brown. My eyes scan over his body. His chest is wide, just as I knew it would be—strong and demanding the attention of the room. I make my way down and start counting.

Two, four, six, eight … yum.

I count every visible ridge of his abs as my eyes travel in the direction of the hard 'V' shape of his torso. Nothing about his body is over-the-top, but still, all of the sharp lines and curves dipping into his low hanging sweatpants have me panting for just another few inches of skin.

Shit. I need to get laid. It's been way too long. I should have taken Nic up on his offer to take me home last night. I would have made a million bad decisions but at least I would be satisfied and not standing here staring at some guy like he's about to tear my clothes from my body and destroy my pussy in the best possible ways.

What is it with guys and grey sweatpants? It's like they know it's a woman's kryptonite. The way men feel about women throwing it back is the way I feel about them in grey sweatpants.

Shit. *Get a fucking grip, girl.*

Remembering that I'm going to have to face this guy every day for the next who the hell knows how long, I snap my eyes up.

Fuck. He's just as pretty as I hoped he wouldn't be and he's staring right at me with a set of hazel eyes that are going to be my undoing.

Brown, messy hair, hazel eyes, and skin that screams to have my nails digging into it.

I'm in trouble. Real fucking trouble.

Don't screw the boss' son, Ocean. Close those damn legs, whore. Do not sleep with the boss' son.

His eyes begin narrowing and my spine stiffens as chills sweep through me. My heart begins racing and my flight or fight instinct kicks into high gear.

My hands curl into fists by my side and within moments, I realize that I already hate this guy. I don't even need to talk to him to know that he's a rich, arrogant asshole who's in love with his daddy's money, connections, and reputation.

Colton's eyes drop to my body, shamelessly scanning over my curves and taking in my thick, black hair. If I hadn't just done the same thing to him I'd say something, but at least when I checked him out, I did it with desire. The way he looks at me … ugh. I don't know if it's disgust … maybe repulsion in his eyes, but it instantly puts me on edge. He looks at me like I'm trash, or as if I'm nothing. He looks over my clothes, turning his nose up at the holes in my jeans and the fake, knock-off handbag tucked under my arm.

Maybe keeping away from the boss' son won't be as hard as I had thought.

"Colton," Charles says, demanding his son's attention.

Colton slowly turns toward his father but his eyes don't leave mine until the last possible second, and when they do, my breath catches in my throat. I struggle to calm my rapid pulse and the need to high-five him in the face with my fist.

I let out a shaky breath, repeating over and over again in my head that mom and I really need this, at least until I finish high school and can start paying my own way.

"Father?" he questions, his voice deep, bored, and demanding, crashing against my chest like an invisible force.

Charles goes on as though his son didn't just destroy me with one look. "This is Maria and her daughter, Ocean. Maria will be working here as our new live-in housekeeper. Could you show them to their rooms upstairs? I have to attend a business call."

Colton doesn't get a word in before Charles is looking back at us. "It was a pleasure to meet you both. Feel free to roam around the house and explore. There are a few more treasures you're bound to come across. There's a library on the upper floor that the twins had stocked with all of their favorite authors. I'm sure you could find some enjoyment there."

Charles doesn't wait for a response before rushing away and leaving us with a scowling Colton. I can't help but notice that everything Charles has said to us has been a complete contradiction to everything Harrison had said and for some reason, it's getting me excited about all the ways I could mess with the guy.

Colton's eyes come back to mine, making the excitement fade away, and before I have a chance to tell him what I think, mom steps in. "It's a pleasure to meet you, Colton."

He glances over mom and I'm surprised to see some sort of respect in his eyes. He's lucky because if he had looked at her the way he did to me, I would have shown him my favorite kind of crazy.

Without another word, Colton turns on his heel and begins stalking off. "Follow me," he throws over his shoulder in a tone that suggests he has a million better things to be doing.

Mom and I share a look and it's as though we can read each other's minds. She's not sure about this kid and the feeling is mutual. She sends me a silent warning to keep away from him and I nod, completely on board.

Getting mixed up with the boys in the Breakers Flats Black Widows is one thing, but getting mixed up with a rich boy is something else entirely. A Black Widow would use me and leave me brokenhearted, but a rich boy would humiliate me and leave me completely destroyed. They're both dangerous. I guess it's a question of which kind of danger gets me the hottest.

Right now, I'll be fine without either.

Colton reaches a massive staircase and skips up the steps two at a time, leaving me and mom to scramble behind him. He stops by a door and turns to watch us as we hurry to catch up. His long, thick fingers curl around the door handle and he swings it open. "Maria, you're in here," he says, not missing a beat before turning and continuing down the hall.

Mom stops by the door and peers into what will be her room for the next few days as I follow Colton, knowing that if I miss which room he says is mine, I'll probably end up sleeping in the hallway.

With one big stride, he steps over to the opposite side of the hallway and comes to a stop by a solid wooden door. He turns while curling his hand around the handle, his earthy eyes coming to mine. "Your room."

The door swings open and I go to step into it, but the prick steps right into my way, cutting me off. His eyes drop once again and I know without a doubt that he's judging me. "Don't get too comfortable, Jade. You won't be staying long."

I raise my chin, taking this for what it is—a challenge. He'd be smart to learn now that I'm not the kind to back down from anyone's bullshit, especially not from some rich, entitled prick. I don't care about his muscles, his good looks, and dreamy eyes. When someone has thrown down a challenge, nothing else matters.

My eyes narrow on his and I square my shoulders. "You don't scare me, Carrington. Where I come from, the people come packing a lot more than what you've got. You're nothing but an entitled prick who likes to play with daddy's things."

"You don't want to try me, trash."

I push up onto my tippy-toes and let my lips brush past his. I lower my voice to the softest whisper. "Watch me."

I bring my hand up and give him a hard shove back, creating space for me to walk past. I step into my room and grab the door, more than ready to slam it in his face. I only need him to back up one tiny little step but something tells me that's a harder challenge than it ought to be. "And for the record, the name's Ocean."

Colton's tongue shoots out over his bottom lip, right where my lips had brushed over his. He stares at me for a second, almost shocked that I had the nerve to stand up to him. I raise my brow, impatiently waiting for him to say whatever douchey comment he needs to say before fucking off.

"You and your mom, you're both trash," he says slowly, pronouncing each word as though I'm incapable of understanding his message. "You don't belong here. You won't last more than a week."

A breathy laugh pulls from within and I grin up at him, feeling my eyes shimmering with excitement. If he thinks his comments are going to scare me away, he's got another thing coming. He's got the wrong girl. "Tell me, Colton. Are you a dick to everyone, or am I already so far under your skin that you need to aim all your bullshit at me?"

He laughs, rubbing his hand over his wide chest. "You're nothing, Jade. You don't have the power to get under my skin. You're some cheap whore from who the fuck knows, living it up as though you're playing Cinderella. I see chicks like you every fucking day and it's pathetic. Don't get me wrong, I'm not going to say no when you offer to suck my dick for a few bucks, but you won't be getting shit out of me or my family."

Wow. He's so pleasant. Daddy Warbucks must be so proud.

"You need to scrub up on your people skills," I laugh, entertained by his tough-guy act. "Not sure if anyone has told you, but they're really fucking lacking."

"There's nothing wrong with my people skills. It's my tolerance to trash that needs work."

A wicked grin spreads across his face and not a second later he's gone, leaving me staring at the empty doorway, unsure of what the fuck had just happened.

CHAPTER 4

My door hardly has a chance to close behind me before mom is there, stepping into my massive room and glancing around. "Wow," she says, taking it all in. "These rooms are …"

"I know," I say, still looking around while pretending that I'm not at all fazed by the cocky prick who just vacated my doorway with a silent promise of running me out of here.

What does he think is going to happen? Is he going to pull out all his douchiness and force me to leave, or does he just assume that mom and I don't have what it takes to make it in this cut-throat world? If that's the case, he doesn't understand who he's messing with. Mom and

I have had to grow a thick skin living in Breakers Flats. We dealt with dickheads like this daily—usually before breakfast.

Mom walks deeper into my room which is when I notice my luggage is already here and I have to admit, I'm amazed by how quickly that happened. The staff here are seriously on the ball.

I make my way over to the massive floor to ceiling windows and peer out with mom coming to stand by my side. "This is insane, isn't it?"

"It is," I agree, looking out to see the very edge of the pool, only to realize this isn't the same pool that I'd been drooling over earlier, but a secluded, more private one. There's a building beside it and my brows furrow as I point it out to mom. "I wonder if that's the pool house."

She moves in closer and looks down, pressing her lips together. "Maybe," she says with a shrug. "Who would actually know? This place is huge. It's going to take me a while to learn my way around here."

"Right."

"I wasn't quite expecting the Carrington mansion to be quite so ..."

She stops, lost for words and I give her exactly what she's looking for. "Intimidating?"

"Yeah," she agrees with a soft chuckle. "Charles was lovely. Nicer than I had expected and very handsome too."

I roll my eyes. "Shame his personality didn't rub off on his son."

"Yeah," mom sighs. "I caught that. Are you alright? Colton didn't seem to take a liking to you. I wasn't fond of the way he was watching you."

"It'll be fine," I assure her. "I can handle guys like Colton

Carrington. He doesn't scare me."

Mom's hand falls to my shoulder and she forces me to turn and face her. "Are you sure? I can have a quiet word with Charles if you'd prefer. After all, you have to live with the guy now. I can't have you getting in trouble or stressing about what he might do. You have school work to think about."

"Mom, seriously. It's fine. I can handle myself. Dudes who think their dicks are huge just need a woman to help remind them of their place in the world. Speaking of school, were you ever planning on telling me that I was enrolled in some prissy private school?"

Mom shakes her head, letting out a heavy sigh before giving me a caring smile. "I worry about you sometimes."

"Seriously? That's all I'm going to get? Why is Charles paying for me to go to school? At least, I'm assuming he's paying for it because there's no way we could afford it."

She groans and I can see from the look in her eyes I'm not about to get a response, though I can't tell if it's because she doesn't want to explain the answer or because she doesn't know it. "Can we talk about this later?" she questions. "I need to get back down there. Just tell me if I need to be doing something about Colton?"

"No," I say with a frustrated huff, giving in. I've got all day to find answers and if she won't explain it to me, then I'll have to figure it out on my own. "I might be 5'2 but my attitude is 6'1."

"I know," she groans. "That's the issue."

I laugh and step away from the window only to have mom come with me. "Are you going to be alright if I go back down and meet with

Maryne?"

"Of course," I tell her, knowing how eager she is to start training for her first day tomorrow morning. "I was going to check in with Nic and look around a little."

She sighs and I know exactly what's coming. "I really wish you'd take a little space from Dominic. It's not a healthy relationship."

"Not this again, Mom," I groan, watching her make her way across my new room and stop by the door. "Nic is my best friend."

"I know this … I just think it'd be good for you to find some new friends who don't have gang affiliations. You know that boy is going to end up taking over for that troubled father of his. It's only a matter of time."

I let out a sigh. She's right but it's not going to be the same. "Nic's not like Kian. He's never hurt me."

"Yeah, that's what I thought until you caught him with that Saunders girl."

"Mom …"

"Look," she cuts me off. "What's it going to hurt to talk to a few girls at school tomorrow and try to make some friends? I know Nic has a good heart despite his downfalls, but whether you like it or not, he's heading down a bad path … a troubled path that I don't want you getting involved with. That goes for all those boys of yours and besides, they're too old for you. You could do with some friends your own age."

Realizing she isn't going to back down here, I let out a sigh and nod. "Fine. I'll try and make some friends but you know I don't mesh well with girls. They're too bitchy. And for the record, Nic is only twenty-one, it's not like he's *that* much older than me."

She gives me a scathing look and reaches for the handle. "Four years is a lot at seventeen," she tells me. "But try with the girls."

With that, she's gone.

I stand awkwardly in my room for a few drawn-out moments, not sure what the hell I'm supposed to be doing. What does a poor girl in a rich world even do apart from cleaning up after slobs?

My legs are itching to take me out of this room and explore the estate but something's holding me back and it's pissing me off that I don't know why. Seeing as though it's not Harrison who I want to avoid seeing, that only leaves one option and it infuriates me that he's already managed to get under my skin. Though I'd bet what little I have left that the dickhead is currently moping around his castle with me on his mind. I know I'm under Colton's skin, it's just a question of what it means to be there.

I find myself walking circles around my room, taking it all in. A massive king-size bed with about as many pillows as there are staff in this circus, a massive walk-in closet which I wouldn't be able to fill if my life depended on it, and a private bathroom. The walls are white, the bedspread is white, the furniture white, and even the curtains are all white. It's so clinical but in a modern living kind of way. Certainly not my style.

I don't doubt that I'm going to fuck it up. I can't be trusted not to spill my midnight snacks everywhere. At least it's only for a few days before we're moved down into the pool house and a step further away from the prince of darkness.

My phone vibrates against my ass cheek and I slip it out of my pocket, smiling down at Dominic's name. "Well, well, well, I've hardly been gone three hours and you're already calling me," I say, answering the phone as I flop down onto the too comfortable bed.

"Shut up, I had to make sure you made it there alright."

"We did …"

"And?"

"And it's just as bad as I thought it was going to be. Everywhere I look, there's a sign of how much money they have to waste. There's a fucking indoor pool and you can press a few buttons and it somehow becomes an outdoor pool. The whole ceiling opens up, Nic. It's crazy. There are secret rooms, private bars, and a butler with his head shoved so far up his own ass that he probably eats his own shit for breakfast. Not to mention, the guy has a douchebag son who's in serious need of an ass-whooping."

"Yeah, I know," he says dangerously.

"Right … wait. How do you know the guy is a douchebag? I don't even think I told you where I was going."

Nic scoffs and it turns into a deep chuckle. "You really think I was going to let you walk out of Breakers Flats without knowing exactly where you were going and who was going to be around you?"

My eyes practically roll into the back of my head. "Why am I not surprised?"

"You're my girl, O. I'm always going to be looking out for you. No matter what."

"I'm not your girl anymore, Nic."

"Don't start with me, babe. I just watched you walk out of here. I'm not about to listen to you reminding me of how I fucked it all up."

I scoff, fighting a grin. "You fucked it up real bad."

"Cut the shit, Ocean," he says with a sigh before getting back on track. "Just do me a favor and stay out of Colton's way. The guy is bad news and I don't want you getting caught up with him."

"Seriously? It might already be too late for that," I laugh, picturing the way Colton is probably fuming to daddy about their little house guest. "But what kind of bad news could he be? Surely he couldn't be any worse than you or the boys."

"Just … stay away," he says with that familiar annoyance when having to deal with me, but deep down I know he loves it. He lives for this shit. Keeping something from me 'for my own good' is one of his favorite pastimes and because of that, I know he's not about to give me what I'm looking for.

"You realize I'm currently living in the same house as him. Staying away from the guy isn't exactly going to be that easy when I'm sitting across from him at the breakfast bar."

"Ocean, I'm being serious."

"So am I. What's the big deal? He's just some arrogant rich dude with a chip on his shoulder."

"He's bad news, Ocean. He's not like the guys you're used to dealing with who get put down and stay down. Guys with money, they keep coming back until they win. It's a game to them. Something to keep them entertained until the next thing comes along. I know you, O, and you're going to see this guy as a challenge, and being the girl that comes from nothing, you're going to be his most exciting game yet. I don't want that for you."

"I can handle myself," I tell him, feeling as though I'm having to repeat myself after having a too similar conversation with mom. Only with mom, she gives up a lot easier. "I'm not a child who needs protecting anymore, Nic. I'll be fine. You don't need to worry about me."

There's a short silence and when he finally sighs, his voice is low and filled with emotion. "You won't be fine, Ocean. I'm going to lose you to that world."

"That'll never happen," I whisper.

He goes quiet again and just when I start thinking that maybe he'd ended the call, his velvety voice comes murmured through the phone. "How are you really doing? No bullshit."

I press my lips together and give him my honest truth. "Dead inside but I'm caffeinated."

"That bad, huh?"

I close my eyes, not wanting to keep looking at the plain ceiling any longer. "I miss you guys. I don't belong here. Neither of us does. Mr. Carrington has already taken it upon himself to enroll me in some fancy private school so unfortunately for you, It's not just Colton you have to worry about, but a whole school filled with rich pricks."

"The fuck?" Nic grunts. "What's his game? Why does he give a shit about your schooling?"

"I don't know but I don't like it. I'm kind of hoping it's just some way to look good in front of his rich friends. You know, maybe they have a club and he'll get a badge for taking us in and giving the poor girl a better life. Maybe I'm just a charity case."

Nic chokes back a laugh. "Trust me, nothing in that world is ever going to be that simple."

"Yeah, I had a bad feeling about that."

"Alright, babe. I'm out. Dad's out of town for the day so I'm playing boss man today."

"Shit. Don't fuck anything up and get yourself killed."

I can practically hear his smile through the phone. "Can't make any promises. Bye, O."

Nic ends the call, and the second his voice fades away I'm left missing him so much more. I don't know how it's even possible, but somehow he seems so much further away than he did ten minutes ago.

I drop my phone to my stomach and just lay for a minute, but that minute quickly turns into ten and then thirty.

My stomach grumbles and the need to pee creeps up on me and I recall that after the third coffee I had this morning, I failed to actually eat anything.

I pull myself up from the bed and drag my feet across the floor to the bathroom. I guess a private bathroom is one of the few bonuses around here.

I push the door open and find myself gawking. What the fuck is that?

I walk over to the toilet, warily keeping my eyes on the second toilet that doesn't exactly look like a toilet. It's kind of more like a urinal but not ... wait. Is this one of the bidet things mom was talking about earlier?

No fucking way.

I find myself laughing and as I drop my pants and sit on the toilet, I stretch my foot up to the little lever on the side of the bidet.

Water squirts up into the sky and my eyes bug out of my head.

No. Hard fucking no. I'll pass. This thing really does squirt water up into your asshole. What's a girl supposed to do? Squat over this thing and voluntarily get ass raped by pressurized water? Hell to the mother fucking no. I'd rather clean my ass with a scourer than participate in this ass witchery.

I bet Colton has one of these and I bet he loves it. He probably lives for getting fucked over by inanimate objects.

I finish in the bathroom and find the nerve to open my bedroom door. Feeling like a complete idiot, I peer up and down the hallway, making sure there's no sign of Colton Carrington before venturing out into this big house. I don't understand my hesitation. Twenty minutes ago when he stood at my door, I practically screamed from the rooftops that I could handle his bullshit. I practically dared him to try his worst yet here I am ready to scamper away at the sight of him.

Don't be such a fucking wet blanket, Ocean. Pick up your balls and march your firm ass downstairs for something to eat. Besides, what are the chances of running into him in a place like this? There must be over one hundred rooms in this mansion, not including the pool house, steam rooms, or stables that are no doubt somewhere on this property.

My eyes continue scanning as I make my way downstairs and

when I finally come into the kitchen, I feel like I can breathe again. No sign of him. I'm safe. But now the bigger challenge is finding my way around this kitchen.

I start opening cabinets and pulling open drawers until I find everything I need to make a sandwich. It takes way longer than it should, but the bread is fresh and that's a positive in my book.

I get busy, feeling like a fraud in this big place.

I so don't belong here. It's comical just how vastly opposite this world is to mine.

I busy myself making a sandwich, trying—and failing—to lose my thoughts in the task. That is until a voice calls out at the opposite end of the kitchen counter.

"Well, well, well. Who's this you've been hiding?

My head whips around to find a man-boy staring at me from the other end of the kitchen. His eyes are dark, and traveling up and down my body as though I'm some kind of meal. It's not like the way Colton had looked at me earlier, this is different … darker, and I don't like it. What I don't like more is the douche canoe standing behind his shoulder smirking at me like he's about ready to start playing his twisted little games.

The kitchen is so big that the two of them are far enough away for me not to feel uncomfortable, but if the fucker with the dark eyes even thinks about taking a step toward me, I'll be reaching for the knife I'd planned on using to cut my sandwich.

Colton laughs, his smirk making it come out like a scoff. "She's no one," he grumbles. "The help."

That word makes it sound like an insult and it instantly has me wanting to high-five the fucker in the face with my fist. He knows damn well that I'm not the help.

Colton's friend replies, his lips pulling up into a grin as his tongue pokes out and runs along his bottom lip. "The help is hot," he says hungrily.

"Who's fucking hot?" A chirpy voice comes from somewhere that is not here. My eyes flick around, wanting to know exactly where this third guy is and if he's going to be a threat to me. The guy appears a second later, striding excitedly out of the media room. His eyes come to mine and while they also travel up and down my body, he does it in a much less creepy way. This guy, he's just picturing me naked while the other was imagining all the ways he could fuck me.

"My, oh my, the help really is hot," the guy says, walking right up to me and taking my hand. He gives it a gentle kiss before letting it drop to my side. I'm about to prepare for an ass-kicking when Colton lets out a soft groan and I decide that this guy can kiss my hand as much as he wants if it's going to annoy his friend. He gives me a wide grin before respectfully taking a step back. He throws back over his shoulder. "Where have you been hiding this one?"

Colton rolls his eyes. "I haven't been hiding her anywhere," he says as though the suggestion is offensive to him. "She's new. The bitch is free game for all I care."

The creepy friend's eyes seem to light up as the new guy whips his head back to me, smiling brightly and showing off some of the brightest blue eyes I've ever seen. For a moment, it's startling. Where

I'm from, we don't see many blonde-haired, blue-eyed kids. We're all dark; hair, eyes, and personalities.

"I'm Charlie Bryant," he introduces politely, throwing me off as polite was anything but what I was expecting. He looks back at his friends. "Obviously you've met Colton, and the dickhead watching you like a predator is Jude Carter."

Jude. Huh, rhymes with rude. I can remember that.

Charlie continues. "Spencer is getting around here somewhere but he disappeared half an hour ago. My theory is that he's fucking one of Carrington's maids."

"Right …"

"You busy? Want to chill?"

Colton's booming demand comes flowing from behind Charlie. "No. We don't fraternize with the help."

I pick up my sandwich from the table, leaving all my mess behind as I stride toward Colton, keeping my eyes locked on his hazel ones. "Which is it, dickhead? I'm either free game or the help that can't be fraternized with. I mean, if you're going to attempt to insult me, at least get your insults straight."

Charlie laughs behind me. "Oh, damn. Colt. She's got you there."

His eyes heat like molten lava, glaring heavily but Jude straightens beside him, dangerously staring down at me as though he's ready to tear me in half. "Do you have any fucking idea who you're talking to, trash? That's Colton fucking Carrington. You'll learn some fucking respect."

I step in closer, proving that I'm not scared of their bullshit despite how my heart is thumping wildly within my chest. "He'll get my respect when he does something to deserve it. Right now, he's just the same trash that you three dickheads see me as."

Jude's jaw clenches and he goes to step into me but Colton slaps his hand up against his chest, holding him back and Charlie's laughter seems to grow. "Holy fuck, dude. Someone needs to take a chill pill."

Smirking up at the dickheads, I bat my lashes. "And it'd be even nicer if someone choked on it."

They stare at me as though they can hardly believe what they're seeing and I take the opportunity to step around them. I casually start making my way toward the living area as though that confrontation hadn't just rattled me to my core.

I'm going to pay for that. Colton is not going to roll over and accept that I just disrespected him in front of his friends. Hell, I also disrespected his friend too. Not Charlie though. He seems cool but I won't make up my mind about him yet. After all, he was probably just looking for a quick fuck.

There's no denying it, Charlie Bryant called me the help and as long as that continues, he'll be considered the enemy, just like them.

CHAPTER 5

My alarm screeches through my new bedroom and I peel my eyes open to remember it's Monday morning.

School.

Fuck. I was hoping the night would swallow me whole and I'll wake up again on Friday afternoon. There's nothing worse than being the new kid at school. I've never stepped foot into a private school but I'm assuming they're all the same. Bitchy girls and jock dudes who think they're God's gift to earth. Add the bucket loads of cash they all come equipped with, and I can guarantee that today is going to be one of the worst days of my life.

Being the new girl at school is going to be like having an automatic target on my back. The fact I don't come from money or that Colton will no doubt be calling me 'the help' is sure to be an absolute mess.

Yay for bullying, right? Wrong.

To be completely honest, I don't know how much of it I'll be able to handle. At my old school, I was feared by the other students. They all knew the company I kept and they respected me. They knew I was more than capable of fucking them up if my boys didn't. They were either kind or stayed the fuck out of my way. These private school privileged dickwads are different, they're going to judge me by what they see. None of them know me, and just as Colton had pointed out, I'm free game.

It's going to be a disaster.

I haven't even stepped through the gates and I'm already certain that there won't be anyone like me, not even close. No one in the whole town is going to understand what it feels like to lose your house, or how humiliating it is having to beg strangers for food just so you and your mother could eat that night. They won't know the feeling of having cold showers in the dark because the gas and electricity had been turned off.

Hell, the parents of the kids at this school are probably the same bankers and CEOs who took it all away from us. They don't care about the little people. They care about lining their pockets, and it doesn't matter who they have to squish to make it happen.

I wonder if this school will break me. I've never had to endure the pain of bullying before but from what I've seen, it can be brutal. I'd like to think that I'm strong enough to laugh as other people's bullshit sails off me like water off a duck's back, but when it's constant and comes from people who are higher up in this world, I'm sure it's going to get me right where it hurts.

I'm not looking forward to this.

I finally silence my alarm and pull the blankets up over my head. I wonder what kind of trouble I'll get in for missing the start of school. Would it be shrugged off like it was at my old school? Am I looking at getting detention, or is this the serious kind of bullshit that goes down in movies? Though one thing is for sure, Charles Carrington won't be happy.

We all sat around the dinner table last night and shared a meal together. It was awkward as fuck. Colton sat, ate his dinner in three seconds flat, and then left. So with him gone, it wasn't as bad, but it was still weird. I wonder if Charles ever invites his other staff to eat with him or if we're special because we're going to be living here. I hope he doesn't think this is going to be one of those big happy family situations, because if so, I'm out. I didn't sign up for that bullshit.

The pool house can't come soon enough.

The sound of someone barging through my door assaults my ears, and if I wasn't certain that it was mom I probably would have flown out of my bed and demanded some privacy.

I groan and murmur under my breath. "In three … two … one."

The blanket is torn from my body and thrown across the room, leaving me shivering on the bed. "Up and at it," mom says in a singsong tone. "Time to get ready for school. I thought you'd be up and ready by now."

"Just ten more minutes," I plead, wondering why I even bother.

"Nope. Up. You heard Charles at dinner last night. This is important for him. The dean at Bellevue Springs Academy owed him a favor and he had to pull strings to make it happen. You're not going to embarrass me and disrespect the effort he went to. Now get up. I want to see you in your uniform. Maryne had it pressed for you last night."

I fly up out of bed and stare at mom who happens to be wearing her own uniform. "Uniform?" I demand. "You didn't say anything about a uniform. I've never worn a uniform."

"It's a private school, Ocean. What were you expecting?"

I gape at her and watch as she makes her way across my room and opens the walk-in closet. She returns a moment later with a white blouse that dons the BSA crest on the breast pocket and a grey pleated skirt that looks like it needs to be hemmed.

I let out a heavy sigh. It could be worse. Much, much worse.

"Fine," I groan, trudging across the room and taking the hanger out of her hand. I hook it over the bathroom door before taking note of mom's blue uniform and apron. She looks like a hotel maid and from the look on her face, she's not thrilled about it.

"How's it going?" I ask, remembering her mention that she was starting at six this morning. Considering it's almost eight, I'd dare say she's had enough of a test run to know if she's going to like this position or not.

Mom shrugs. "It'll do," she says. "The other workers are nice …"

"Except Harrison," I cut in, recalling his scowl as he watched mom and I relax over dinner while he worked around us.

"Harrison is just one of those old guys you have to get used to. He's harmless."

I roll my eyes and make my way over to my bag of clothes. I start rifling through, looking for some underwear and a bra that won't show through the white blouse. "I think this is going to be a good thing," mom continues. "It's good pay and assuming you can keep out of trouble, there's no drama."

I give mom a blank stare.

"You're right," she says. "Trouble has a way of finding you."

"What did you expect when you accepted a job in Bellevue Springs. It's not exactly our scene. The two of us stick out like sore thumbs. You might as well have stuck a sign to my back saying that we don't belong."

"I know, honey. It's going to be alright. Once they get over the fact that you're the new shiny toy, it'll all calm down."

I raise a brow. "Promise?"

Mom's lips press into a tight line and I roll my eyes. She never makes promises she can't keep, even if it means letting me down.

"I better get back to work," she tells me. "Promise me that you'll be showered, dressed, and fed by 8:30. Harrison mentioned that the bus stops by here around then. You can't miss that bus, got it?"

"Yeah, yeah," I say, zipping up my suitcase. "I won't be late."

"Good. Now, come and give your mom a kiss. I would have liked to see you off for your first day but I'm not exactly in a position to be asking favors just yet."

"It's okay," I say, falling into her arms. "I can manage. Besides, I don't think having my mommy drop me off is going to help me fit in with the other kids."

"Good point," she laughs, pressing a kiss to my cheek. "Now get a move on."

The next half an hour flies by and before I know it, I'm racing down the stairs and desperately trying to make the stupid coffee machine work. I mean, how hard is it to do it the normal way? Why do rich people insist on having fancy machines for everything?

Giving up, I hurry into the staff quarters and let out a relieved sigh when I see the tea and coffee cart still in the same place I saw it yesterday morning. I hurry over to it while feeling Harrison's disapproving glare on my back. I won't even begin to try and understand why I've deserved his glare this morning. It could be several things; my running through the house, my wet blouse from where I accidentally dropped it on the bathroom floor, could even be the way I've rolled my skirt up so it's not hanging around my knees. Really, it's probably a bit of them all.

I get my coffee sorted while hearing his disapproving tone. "You're going to miss your bus."

"Would that really be the worst thing?" I shoot back.

Harrison doesn't respond, he just keeps going about his morning pretending as though I don't exist. I don't know why it makes me feel as though I've won something, but it does and I love it.

I walk out with my coffee in hand and my head held high. If today is destined to be a shitty day then the least I can do is start it off with a good coffee.

I somehow make it to the front door and groan as I push my way through it. I forgot about the driveway. I'm definitely going to miss my bus.

I wonder how Charles would feel about me taking one of the many cars that no doubt line his garage. I know he's been all sorts of hospitable, but my chances aren't great. It's a big jump going from letting me crash in one of his many spare bedrooms to allowing a seventeen-year-old with questionable morals drive one of his prized possessions.

I start walking.

It's times like this I really miss having a car or a crew of boys who lived off being my hero.

I get about halfway down the drive when a loud rumble echoes through the silence. I can practically feel the ground vibrating beneath my feet.

I glance back over my shoulder to find a sleek, brand new Lamborghini Veneno Roadster in charcoal with orange trim and my world explodes. My panties disintegrate, my lady bits clench and gush, while my jaw hits the driveway in awe. It's so fucking sexy.

That's my freaking dream car and it's currently gliding toward me. Maybe I've died and gone to heaven because there's no way in hell that this car would be coming at me like this. It's slow and torturous and I don't even give a shit that it's most likely Colton Carrington in the driver's seat.

I stare, and I stare good because I'm bound to fuck this thing up for me and mom sooner or later and I'll be damned if I leave this place without taking in every single inch of this car. I wonder how quickly

Colton will kill me if I lick it as he drives past?

The Veneno inches past me so close that I could probably jump on the hood and hitch a ride to school if I was stupid enough to pull a stunt like that.

I ball my hands into fists trying to control the urge to touch it. I'll slip into the garage tonight and have a proper look while Colton isn't around. Maybe I'll even slip into the driver's seat and rub one out just to add salt to the wound. Okay … maybe that's taking the obsession just a little too far.

When the Lamborghini comes to a stop and the window drops down, my back straightens. I should have known the dickhead wouldn't wait until school started to begin his torture.

His hazel eyes instantly meet mine and I thank all the heavens above that I've at least had a few sips of coffee to get me through this. Colton's heavy gaze drops and I watch as he takes in my uniform with a sick smirk.

What's his deal? He's acting as though he's never seen a chick in uniform. Hell, it's the same fucking uniform that he's wearing. Minus the skirt of course.

"What the fuck do you think you're doing?"

My brows furrow and my eyes slice toward the front gates. "Um … what does it look like I'm doing? The bus is going to be here any minute."

"Bus? What fucking bus?"

Is this guy daft? "The bus to school, dickhead. Harrison told my mom that it comes around this time every morning."

Colton laughs, his lips pulling up in amusement. "Look around you, Jade. Do you really think this town uses public transport? Most of the kids I know would rather die than be seen on a fucking bus. Harrison was fucking with you. I haven't seen a bus around here for … actually, never."

"The fuck?" I screech, my jaw clenching as I picture Harrison back at the house peering through the window and watching me make a fool of myself.

"Shocker. You must have pissed him off." I start walking again and groan as his car inches forward, keeping up with me. "Get in."

My head swivels around to look at him. Is he insane? Surely he must remember the day we had yesterday. You know, the part where he called me trash and I called him on his bullshit. "You're fucking kidding me, right?" I laugh, imagining what thrilling conversation we would have while being stuck in a confined space together. Though, conversation is probably taking it a little too far. More like throwing insults back and forth.

"Get in the fucking car, Jade."

I shake my head. "So you can tell me I'm trash a little more? No thanks, I'll pass."

"It's a twenty-minute walk. You're going to miss attendance."

"What do you care?"

"I don't," he scoffs. "You can go back to the good for nothing shithole you came from for all I care, but if you don't show up at school on time, it's on my ass."

I stop walking and his car comes to a stop. I narrow my eyes at him as it all becomes clear. "Daddy put you on babysitting duty."

"Trust me, there's a big fucking difference between babysitting and making sure the help doesn't embarrass the Carrington name. Now get the fuck in my car before I make you."

I throw my hands up and groan before finally deciding he's right. Not about embarrassing his precious family reputation but about being late for the first day. It's not a good look, and mom will kill me if she learns I was late.

I stalk around to the passenger side and do my best not to drool over his car. It's always been my dream car, a dream that will never come true, but now knowing that this douchebag owns one, it's suddenly less appealing. That is until the beautiful scissor door pops open and raises high above my head.

Holy fuck.

My hands shake. I'm about to sit in a 4.5 million dollar car. Only eight of these were put into production, and there's one right here in front of my eyes.

Are my shoes clean? Did I sit in anything? Should I throw my coffee away?

Come to think of it, what kind of psychopath allows their eighteen-year-old son to drive such an expensive car? I'm not surprised that he owns it, but surely it would be sitting up in some sort of fancy showroom with laser beams protecting it. I guess when you have the kind of money these guys have, not even a rare car is enough for them to use restraint.

I get into the car and realize that I'm holding my breath. What is wrong with me? Hell, my eyes are brimming with unshed tears of happiness. I need to get myself under control before I give Colton any more ammunition to use against me.

I place my bag down on my lap, not wanting it to dirty the floor of the car and then reach for my seatbelt, assuming that Colton is a shitty, reckless driver.

The door closes automatically and I think I come a little while studying the black interior and the orange trim that flows throughout the whole car.

It's simply stunning.

My seatbelt has hardly clicked into place before Colton hits the gas and I feel my soul leave my body. The engine rumbles through the car and I feel it beneath my seat, doing all sorts of yummy things. Is it wrong to be so turned on right now?

I adjust myself in my seat and don't miss the way Colton's lips curve into a slight smirk. That smirk is enough to have me twisting myself so I'm mostly facing out the window, not wanting his presence in the driver's seat to ruin this joyride for me.

Apart from the sound of the engine, there's absolute silence. No shitty conversation, no insults, no comments about me being the help. Nothing, and for once I'm actually happy to be here. I have no doubt that could change in only a matter of seconds.

Colton drives like some kind of professional. He's fast, smooth, and effortless and I hate myself for being so attracted to it. In fact, it makes me hate him more. What is it about the way that men handle cars that's so damn attractive?

He pulls up out the front of the school and it takes me all of two seconds to notice that something isn't right.

"Wait," I say, realizing that Colton isn't making a move to cut the engine and get out. Shouldn't he have stopped in some kind of underground, guarded student parking lot for rich kids? "This is wrong … all those girls. They're not in the same uniform."

"I can see that," he says, watching the girls pour in through the front gates and looking somewhat confused.

"Where are all the guys? It's just chicks."

"Because it's a girls' school. You didn't know that?"

"How would I have known that? I don't exactly spend my days googling schools. Why do I have a different uniform? I'm going to look like a fucking idiot."

"You don't need a uniform to do that, Jade. You're already there."

"Fuck you, Carrington," I say, looking back at him, only as I do, my eyes scan over the massive sign stating that this is Bellevue Springs Private School. "You brought me to the wrong school, dickwad. I'm enrolled at BSA."

Colton's face scrunches up and his eyes flick down to my uniform as if finally realizing that it matches his. "Bullshit. Dad did not enroll you at my school."

I roll my eyes and look back out the window. "Apparently, he did."

"Suit yourself," Colton groans before hitting the gas and leaving Bellevue Springs Private in our dust. He flies down the road and within the space of sixty seconds, he pulls into the parking lot of BSA.

Damn. We're here.

The parking lot is filled to the brim with Aston Martins, Ferraris, and Lamborghinis, though none quite with a price tag to compare against the Veneno's. These are the kind of cars you'd expect to see in a Fast and Furious movie, locked up in an Abu Dhabi penthouse. My dad was a car guy and taught me everything he knew. It was his dream to be able to have cars like this and because of that, the dream rubbed off on me.

This parking lot is as close to heaven as me or my dad would ever have gotten.

Colton parks in a designated spot right near the front and I roll my eyes. I wouldn't be surprised if he's the shining star here. He probably has all his teachers in his back pocket. All the girls probably drool over him and the guys, I bet they all want to be his best friend. It's amazing what being the son of a billionaire can do for you.

Colton gets out and starts making his way up to the front gates of Bellevue Springs Academy while I peel myself out of his car. The second my feet hit the ground, the scissor doors start moving back into place and I have to give it to the guy, at least he waited until I was out to start closing the doors.

I hear the subtle beep of the car locking and with no other choice, I start making my way up to the school, following miles behind Colton glaring at his back. The least he could do is walk with me to the front gates and point out the student office so I don't have to aimlessly wander around making an ass of myself.

My stomach starts swirling with nerves.

I hate this.

I don't want to be the new girl. I want to fit straight in, endure my classes, and get my ass back home. Preferably to the pool house.

I reach the gates and despite the school not starting yet, there aren't any students lingering around, only the ones who are just arriving. They all must hang out somewhere together. Maybe inside by their lockers or in the cafeteria. At my old school, everyone would loiter around the front of the school, not bothering to walk through the gates until the very last moment. Though I have to admit, not walking through a metal detector first thing in the morning is kind of nice.

I walk under the massive archway that has 'Bellevue Springs Academy' in massive gold-plated, metal letters and the school crest on either side. I find myself studying it. It's kind of cool for a school crest. You know, it's got all the usual things but instead of the usual letters or school motto in the center, it's a lion who looks scary as fuck. Not to mention the crown on top kind of gives it a badass feeling.

Maybe I'll like this school after all. I can get down with a bit of badass.

Colton disappears up ahead and I realize that I'm left to navigate this massive school on my own. I keep walking straight, hoping I'm going in somewhat of the right direction. A student starts coming my way, dressed perfectly in his uniform, complete with his blazer and looking like the arrogant fuck that I'm assuming this school is littered with.

As he gets closer, his brows pull down and I roll my eyes. No doubt this is the look I'll be getting all day. It's the new girl look, the one where they assume they can work me out in a matter of seconds, the one where he's racking his brain trying to recall what inner circles he might know me from. It's the one where he assumes he's superior and silently reminding me that I don't belong.

"Excuse me," I say before he passes.

The guy stops and I have no doubt that it's the manners that his parents would have hammered into him that pulls him up. "Yes?" he questions, his eyes cold and irritated to be disturbed.

"Could you point me toward the student office."

"Student?" he questions with a grunt that puts me on edge. "Don't you think you're in the wrong place?"

My impatience gets the best of me and I reel in my hands that are getting twitchy by my sides. "Can you tell me where the student office is or not?"

The guy chuckles to himself and shrugs his shoulders before pointing back from where he just came. "Third door on the left."

With that, he's gone.

I start making my way down to the office and make quick work of introducing myself to the woman behind the counter. I hand over my documents that Charles had made sure I filled out last night and after quickly scanning through them, she puts a big red stamp at the top and staples them together.

"Here's your school handbook. You are to read that and memorize the school code. You will be asked at random to recite the code and there will be consequences for students who fail to do so," she says, sliding a handbook across the counter with the letters BSA printed on the front of the expensive leather. "Your class schedule is inside with a map of the school. Now, I'll let Milo take it from here."

Milo? Who the fuck is Milo? Did I miss something? I swear, I was listening the whole time.

"Milo," the woman calls out. "New student orientation, please. A full tour of the school grounds and directions to morning classes."

"Got it," comes a voice from behind her.

A student appears from behind her and she hands him over all of my paperwork. He scans over it as he starts striding toward me and I can't help but notice his impeccable manicure. I wonder if he bats for the other team?

Milo steps out from behind the counter. "Hey, man, I'm ... FUCK." His eyes bug out of his face. "You're a chick."

The fuck? Surely he's seen the opposite sex before. What's his deal? My brows furrow in confusion as I watch him take me in. "Congratulations. You're a dude."

"I ... ummm. I'm sorry. It's just ... you can understand my confusion, right?"

I glance back at the woman behind the counter but apparently she couldn't give two shits about helping out my confusion as she dives back into her work. I look back up at Milo. "Help me out here. What's going on?"

"You realize where you are, right? Bellevue Springs Academy."

"Yeah ... so?"

"Bellevue Springs Academy for *boys*."

What the fuck? My eyes drop down to my uniform, remembering just how different it was from the girls at Bellevue Springs Private earlier this morning. This isn't a mistake.

Charles fucking Carrington enrolled me in an all-boys school.

Fucking perfect.

CHAPTER 6

Eyes track my every movement as I silently wish for the ground to open up and swallow me whole. This is fucking insane. What kind of arrogant asshat enrolls a girl into a boys school? But on top of that, what kind of dean accepts the request, especially when the chicks school is just a thirty-second drive down the road?

I've never been so humiliated. No wonder that guy was giving me a weird look this morning. There I was, assuming that he was thinking he was superior or wondering what my pussy tastes like when in reality, he was probably wondering what the fuck I was doing walking the corridors of his all-boys school in the same fucking uniform.

Damn it. I can only imagine what kind of bullshit is going to come from this. I knew it wasn't as simple as being enrolled in school and being sent off for a good day. There's always more to the story when you're an arrogant billionaire with strings to pull.

I was played like a fucking puppet. Not even a heads up about the humiliation I was about to walk into. I can only imagine what kind of torture I'm going to get from the guys here. On the plus side, at least I won't have to deal with the girls' bitchiness every day.

The only positive that's come out of this so far is seeing that look on Colton's face this morning when I told him what school I was enrolled at. I didn't understand his confusion and frustration at the time but now I do, and just knowing how my being here is going to grate on his nerves everyday kind of makes it worth it.

What is with my sick need to get under his skin? I only met the turd yesterday morning and already my desire to make his life a living hell is quickly taking over my mind.

I try to put the thought to the back of my mind. After all, I'm about to walk into the lion's den. Did Charles not even consider what this place is going to be like for a girl? Especially a girl like me? A girl who isn't even close to being on the same level as these guys. I mean, come on! I know I talk a big game, but when there are hundreds of rich boys all staring down at me, picturing me naked on my knees in a dirty supply closet, things couldn't possibly go well.

"So, what's your deal?" Milo asks me as he starts leading me through the school, taking me on the tour that I'd rather not be on, especially considering the way everyone is gawking at me. It's as though they've never seen a chick before. I feel like I need a sign above my head in flashing lights stating 'Yes, I am a chick, and yes, that means I have tits and a pussy under this uniform. Now that you're certain, QUIT FUCKING STARING!'

"I don't have a deal," I tell him, keeping my eyes forward and scanning over all the bodies I pass, taking a mental note of who I think is going to be a problem. For the record, I haven't found too many yet. There are a few guys mentally undressing me, a few curious glances, but so far none who look like they're about to organize a gang bang and not let me in on the secret until it's already too late. What would it matter though, these guys are the type to just pay off some fancy lawyer and make it all go away.

I'm in big fucking trouble here.

All I can hope for is that these guys party with the girls down the road as much as they physically can. I'm hoping those chicks are as slutty as they come and help these guys get their rocks off as often as possible. The last thing I need is unwanted sexual attention from these dimwits. It's hard enough trying to keep Nic at bay, let alone a whole school of horny dudes.

I wonder how Nic is going to feel about this? No doubt he's going to text me this afternoon wanting to know how it went at my new fancy private school. This is going to make his blood boil. I can only imagine how it's going to go down and it's not going to be pretty.

Milo scoffs beside me and I remember that he's in the middle of trying to start a conversation. "No offense girl, but you definitely have a deal. Your nails look like they haven't been seen to in months, your hair is in need of some good loving, your tan actually looks real, and you reek of poverty. You're not from around here and there's no way you could possibly afford the fees for this school. You have a deal and it's a big one, so spill. What's going on?"

"None of your damn business," I say, my already shitty mood plummeting to ground zero.

"Okay, I get it. You're on edge. I would be too being in your position. I mean, this is either some shitty prank, or someone really has it in for you, but closing off and being a bitch isn't going to get you anywhere around here. The guys won't let you get away with that kind of attitude. You're making the target on your back even bigger."

I let out a groan. He's right, and I freaking hate that he is. "How the hell am I supposed to act then?" I question, eyeing down some dickhead who leers a little too long. "Every fucker I pass is looking at me like I'm his afternoon snack."

"Just ... I don't know. Play nice."

"I'm not exactly known for playing nice."

"Yeah, I'm getting that vibe," he says with a smirk. "Look, while this school is filled with all sorts of privileged douchebag jocks, there are a handful of good guys."

"I'll believe it when I see it."

Milo shrugs his shoulders, looking as though he doesn't care about the point he's making enough to actually try to convince me, so he moves right along. "So, Ocean Munroe, who's your mommy fucking to get you enrolled in here?"

My mouth drops open and I come to a stop in the hallway, grabbing

Milo by the scruff of his shirt and demanding his full attention. "Don't you ever talk about my mom like that."

Milo laughs and pries my fingers from his shirt. "Chill out, babe. I'm just asking the question that every fucker here is going to assume. Let's face it, we've already worked out that you're not from around here, but the question of how you got here still lingers. A girl like you only gets places in this world if it comes with favors."

My eyes narrow to slits as we keep walking. "I resent that."

"I'm not trying to be offensive," he clarifies. "It's just the way things are around here so you can either get on top of the rumors now or let them get out of control. But I can guarantee that by lunch, the whole school is going to be talking and they're going to go with the version that makes you look like a cheap whore."

For fuck's sake.

"Fine," I groan. "I just moved here from Breakers Flats with my mom. She's Charles Carringtons new live-in housekeeper. Part of the deal was that he took care of my education, but I assumed he'd just stick me in whatever cheap public schooling system you guys have around here. This whole private school shit isn't exactly my style."

When Milo doesn't respond straight away, I turn my gaze up to meet his only to find him gaping. "Umm … are you okay?"

His brows shoot up. "Girl, you're living with Colton Carrington?"

I roll my eyes. "Geez, thanks for the reminder."

He seems to go somewhere far, far away for a slight moment and it's damn clear that I'm not the only one affected by the startling good looks of Colton Carrington. "Damn," Milo mutters under his breath.

"What I wouldn't give to be the salami in that guy's sandwich."

I scoff out a grunt. "You're into Colton?" I laugh. "Damn, I know you rich kids are fucked up but surely you have better taste than that."

Milo's eyes go wide as his head whips around to me. "Holy fuck, I just said that out loud."

"Umm … yeah?" I ask as he frantically starts looking around at the students passing by, but while they're all looking this way, none of them are paying any attention to him, they're all enthralled by their shiny new toy.

"Fuck. You don't think anyone heard?" he questions, his voice low. "I'm not exactly out of the closet here."

"Bullshit," I laugh. "My gaydar pointed you out from a mile away. How could you still be in the closet?"

His eyes swivel away. "It's complicated," he says, his voice taking on a strange, hurt tone. "Around here, being gay isn't accepted. We're born to be upstanding citizens of the community and then one day take over our father's businesses, marry and have children who will then do the same. I go against the grain and not to mention, this is an all-boys school. If even a whisper of my sexual orientation was to get out, I'd have the shit beat out of me every fucking day."

My mouth drops. "Are you kidding? In this day and age?"

"Yup. These guys are old money. They're set in their ways. They don't listen to what the rest of the world is telling them. All that matters is pleasing their grandaddies and hoping they don't fuck anything up before they're given access to their trust funds."

"You speak as though you're not one of those trust fund babies."

"Oh, I am," Milo says, a grin spreading wide over his face. "And I wouldn't have it any other way."

I shake my head but for some reason, I can't help laughing. There's something about this guy that I like. I don't know what it is, but I feel as though I can trust him. He's still one of them but he knows a little something about being different in a man's world and for that, he has my respect.

"Are you ready for this?" he questions after we've completed the whole loop of the school.

"Ready for what?"

"The last thing on your tour is finding your locker and this is where everyone is going to be. You thought those hallways were bad, just wait until you walk in here."

My eyes bug out of my head as he starts turning the corner. "Really?"

Milo nods as we take one final step, putting us at the head of the corridor swarming with man-boys. "Welcome to hell."

Within seconds, the corridor goes silent as hundreds of pairs of eyes turn my way. "Oh, shit," I mutter under my breath.

"Yup. Let's go. The longer you stand here looking like a deer in headlights, the weaker they think you are."

Fuck.

I force my feet to move beneath me, feeling like I'm not just walking into the lion's den, but as though I'm strutting right into it and pissing all over the lion's territory. My eyes bounce around and I do my best to appear as though I have my shit together, but the fear begins to rattle me.

I shouldn't be here. I should be chilling with the chicks, getting bleach thrown over me, and listening to girls claim I'm a slut for living in the Carrington mansion. Chicks are predictable, but dudes ... nope. I've spent years trying to work out Nic, Eli, Sebastian, and Kairo, but still to this day, they're a mystery and now I have a school full of mysteries staring back at me.

I hear their comments as I pass.

"Fresh meat."

"Who the fuck is this?"

"Dibs."

Milo steps in closer to my side, his tall frame brushing up against mine. "Ignore them," he murmurs, glancing down at my papers in his hand and nodding off to the left of the corridor. "Here. Locker 367."

Milo and I step into my locker and he scans the paper once again for the code. "I give it about three seconds before the rumors start," he tells me. "Prepare yourself."

I hardly have a second to respond before a heavy shoulder slams into the locker beside me. "So, you're the famous Jade I keep hearing about."

I groan knowing this guy could have only heard that name from one place. I turn to face the guy as Milo grunts behind me. "You've got the wrong chick, Spencer. This is Ocean. She's starting today. Don't be a douche."

Ahh ... so this is Spencer. The moronic fourth friend who had disappeared while Charlie was trying to get in my pants. I can only imagine the kinds of things Colton has told him about me.

Spencer's eyes flick up to Milo over my shoulder and the look he gives him is nearly enough to chill me to the bones, but it doesn't hold that same deadliness that Colton's glare does. "Fuck off, Milo."

Milo scoffs. "Yeah, right. Like I'm about to leave her with you."

Spencer rolls his eyes and as they drop back to mine, I can't help but take him in. He's just as charmingly attractive as the rest of the guys around here but there's a certain level of douchiness to him, and I can't work out if it's there because he's team Colton or if the guy is simply just a dick. What I do know is that he has some wicked jawline action going on, mixed with his mousy brown hair and tall, ripped frame, I don't doubt that he's a heartbreaker. You can just tell he's all about the games.

"Well, well," he says, pursing his lips into a smug grin. "If it isn't the illegitimate love-child of Charles Carrington."

Okay. I was expecting all sorts of shit to come from today but I can guarantee that wasn't one of them. My mouth drops open. "Excuse me?"

His brow shoots up. "Oh, you're going to take the denial route. That's cool. I had you pegged as a tough bitch who'd face it front on. Apparently not."

"I don't know what the fuck you're talking about. I'm no one's love-child."

Spencer scoffs, his eyes sparkling with excitement. "You know, I always took Charles for being the clean-cut type, but your mom must really have something special about her to get him to admit to your existence and move you in. No wonder Colt has his panties in such a twist. I'd have the shits too if my inheritance just got reduced by billions. It's bad enough he has to share it with his bitch twin sisters, but now you too."

All I can do is stare. "Did Colton say that?"

Spencer laughs as people start to crowd around, wanting to know exactly what's going on so they can run home to their country club mothers and tell them all about it. This bullshit is going to spread far and wide.

He shakes his head. "As if he'd admit to that. He didn't have to tell me, it's fucking obvious. Why else would Charles move you into his home? Carrington has strict rules about fraternizing with the staff and though Colton calls you the help, we all know it ain't true. You're staying in the main house, aren't you? If you were 'the help' you'd be out back with the rest of the leeches."

I hardly have a second to respond before he continues. "Did you get the DNA results back yet?" he questions before shaking his head at himself. "Obviously. Charles wouldn't have moved you in if he hadn't, right? Fuck. No wonder Colt's been so fucking pissy. This is hilarious."

"Dude," Milo cuts in, but Spencer is on a roll.

"You know," he says, leaning in closer, his eyes becoming hooded as he looks me up and down, laying on the charm way too thick. "Charles Carrington has an empire bigger than anyone else on this side of the country, just your inheritance alone is going to outweigh any one of the pricks here. You and I could make a deal. I know you're trailer trash but stick with me and I can make you a presentable young woman of society. We could get hitched and combined with my inheritance, we'd be unstoppable."

What. The. Actual. Fuck?

I laugh at him, loving how his eyes darken at my mockery. "You've got to be kidding, right? You know, I really am just the help. At least my mom is. We're just waiting for the old live-in to move out of the pool house."

"Yeah, right. Like I'd believe that." Spencer laughs, taking a step back with his hands buried deep in the pockets of his expensive uniform slacks. He winks and it's lethal. "Offer still stands, babe, but if I were you, I'd be taking on the Carrington name. It'll open all sorts of doors."

With that, he walks away, taking his confidence with him, a confidence that is so strong that it has me questioning my sanity. His theory makes sense but it couldn't be true. Why else would Charles have gone to this effort though?

I spy Colton down the end of the hallway, and as if sensing my gaze his eyes snap to mine, a deadly glare full of hatred. Maybe Spencer is right. Maybe Charles is my father and my dad … no. I refuse to believe it. My dad and I were like peas in a pod. Not to mention, I have his dark hair and sea blue eyes, though mom's genes are pretty damn strong too.

I fall back against my locker, zoning out and ignoring the whispers that continue to surround me. I knew today would be weird, but illegitimate love child and marriage proposals before 9 am wasn't exactly what I had in mind.

I feel a devilish grin pulling across my face only to realize my eyes are still locked on Colton's. He tears his away and I hear the slam of his locker door all the way up here before he stalks off with Jude on his six.

A chuckle pulls from within and a strange excitement begins to pulse in my veins. I can only imagine what other bullshit today is going to bring, and for some oddly fascinating reason, I can't wait.

Bring it on Bellevue Springs Academy, you can't break me.

CHAPTER 7

I sprint up the stairs of the Carrington mansion, taking them two at a time. I'm going to piss my fucking pants. Surprise, surprise, Bellevue Springs Academy doesn't come equipped with female bathrooms. I've had to hold it all day long. If I was a betting woman, I would have used the guy's bathroom during class but I'm a smart woman, and I know a losing bet when I see one

I would have been alright if my maybe half-brother wasn't so douchey and had offered me a ride home, but apparently his babysitting duties finished as soon as I was in school and had made it before the bell. Stupid prick. I'd do anything to get my hands on him and tear him limb from limb.

It was the longest twenty-minute walk of my life. There's something about the way you have to walk, squeeze, and clench all at the same time that's somewhat humiliating. By the time I reached the long-ass driveway and had to wait for someone on the other end to open it up, I was as close to dying as I'd ever been before.

I fucking ran. I wasn't going to make it.

Tomorrow morning, I'll be getting there early and speaking to the woman in the student office. Surely she can work something out for me. I mean, I doubt she holds it all day long. Maybe I could share with her. On second thought, she was a bitch. I doubt she'd offer up her bathroom to a desperate student.

I slam through my bedroom door and race to my bathroom. I've never been so happy to be in a skirt in my life. By the time I reach the toilet, my skirt is somewhere around my head and my panties are dangling around my ankles, threatening to send me toppling over and smacking my head into the toilet seat. God, that'd be a great story for paramedics.

My ass drops to the cold toilet seat and my world suddenly feels so much brighter.

Holy hell. I will never put myself through that same torture again. That was horrendous. I don't think I've ever been envious of a penis in my life but right now, knowing a man can just whip it out and take a piss wherever he wants is kind of lucky, while also fucking disgusting.

I finish up and as I'm dragging my panties back up my legs, I can't help but notice the bidet. "What the hell are you looking at?" I grumble, feeling as though it's staring at me, daring me to squat my sweet ass over it. "It ain't ever gonna happen, buddy."

I get my panties back into position and pull my uniform off before dumping into the dirty washing hamper and striding back out to my room.

I find my door wide open and curse myself for being so careless, especially now that Jude is hovering in the doorway, staring at my nearly naked body. "You need something?" I grumble with distaste. This guy has been giving me the creeps ever since I met him yesterday, not to mention, he stares all the time. It's fucking weird.

His eyes travel over my body as though I've purposefully walked out of the bathroom in my underwear just for him. He steps over the threshold of my room. "You wanna fuck, don't you?"

I freeze for a moment as he grabs the back of my door and goes to slam it shut. Shit. This isn't a position I want to be in. "Get the fuck out of my room," I say too loudly, hoping there's someone around who can hear me.

"Come on," he says, the bang of the door making me jump. "I've seen you watching me all fucking day. You want me. Just say the word and I'll give it to you."

"You're fucking kidding me, right? I haven't been watching you. You're delusional. I wouldn't fuck you even if you were the last man on earth."

His eyes darken as he starts making his way toward me. "Then I guess we're going to have to do this my way. Better prepare yourself because I like it hard."

My door swings open and I jump while Jude's eyes slice around to the door with venom. Colton stands in my doorway looking bored as hell, his gaze heavily on my body and filled with lust and for a moment, my panic worsens.

His eyes drag lazily over my breasts and stomach before coming back to mine and when they do, they're filled with disgust. "Put some fucking clothes on," he snaps. "What are you trying to achieve? Hoping to get knocked up by one of my friends and get your dirty claws into their pockets too?"

"Fuck you." I stride across my room to my luggage bag only to realize all my clothes are gone. Knowing mom, she would have snuck in here during school and put them all away. I slam the lid back down and make my way to the walk-in closet, pissed off that now they both have a perfect view of my ass in my Brazilian cut panties.

"Both of you get the fuck out of my room," I say, looking out through the closet door, aiming my glare at Jude. "Thanks for stopping by, but I'll have to decline your offer. Unfortunately, I'm not in the mood for being raped by some dick who probably doesn't even know what a fucking G-spot is, let alone what to do with a vagina if he ever got one. Which by the way, I'm sure is never."

"You fucking bitch," Jude spits, coming at me, making fear rattle through me as my hands shake by my side. I'm all for putting on the tough girl act, but deep down, I'm fucking terrified.

Colton's domineering voice comes shooting through my room, demanding attention. "Jude," he says in a tone that sends shivers spiraling down my spine. "Get the fuck out of her room. You know the rules about fucking with the help."

Jude pauses almost like Colton's tone had pierced right through him, anchoring him to the spot, the same way an alpha would to his pack. Jude glares, his eyes promising payback before spinning around and facing Colton. A silent message passes between them and a moment later, Jude is gone, leaving Colton standing in my doorway, staring at me with the same disgust.

"Feel free to walk your ass out any time now," I snap at him.

"How about a thank you for saving your ass?"

"How about not inviting rapists into your home, dickhead? I shouldn't have to thank you because it shouldn't have happened in the first place. I wonder what daddy dearest would think if he knew all his staff were at risk because of your bad decisions."

"You're fucking impossible."

"And you're a fucking over-privileged asshole who thinks the world owes him something. News flash, it doesn't. Without your buckets of cash, you're just like the rest of us. Now please, get the fuck out of my room so I can change."

Colton scowls one more time before finally stalking away, making sure to slam the door extra hard as he goes. I let out a heavy breath and start pumping my hands, trying to make the shaky feeling go away as I race to the door and flick the lock.

That was too close. I knew I could sense creepy vibes from the guy but I was way off the mark. I never thought in a million years that I'd be unsafe in this house. How fucking stupid was that? From now on, I'm playing it smart. I can't have that happen again because next time I might not have Colton there to save me.

I hurry back into my closet, feeling way too vulnerable to be walking around in my underwear despite the door being locked. Who knows what other ways into this room there are. After all, the house is filled with secret rooms and passageways. I'm kind of excited to go hunting for them, but now I don't exactly feel so safe to do it on my own. Perhaps I can convince Milo to come exploring with me.

Milo was great today. He stood by my side at every chance he got. He introduced me to a few of his friends who most likely won't try to rape me in a supply closet and I was grateful. Though to be honest, they were kind of nerdy and panicked at the thought of speaking to someone who came fully equipped with tits and a vagina.

I think Milo and I could be good friends. He seems like the girlfriend I've never had while also giving me all the benefits of having a guy friend. Have I mentioned how much I despise having girlfriends? They're so … needy. Ugh. I hope I wasn't like that to my boys.

Having Milo and his friends to talk to made the day a little more bearable and helped me to tune out the whispers, comments, and rumors. By the end of the day, I think the rumors were that I was Colton's fuck-buddy sister and there was some disgusting incestual thing going on. Yet among those rich people, the rumor didn't seem as scandalous as I had imagined it'd be. Back home, if someone suggested that, people would be hurling in gutters, gasping, wide-eyed and horrified. Here, they're more like 'Yeah, okay. It happens' and it makes me wonder if it's a common rich person thing who all have similar skeletons in their closets, or if it has more to do with wanting to idolize Colton Carrington so bad that any indiscretion can be excused.

What I do know is that I got to witness the second the illegitimate half-sister bullshit rumor caught up to Colton, and it was amazing. His response from across the room was enough to confirm what I already knew—we're definitely not related. What it also did was prove just how much my being here is affecting him. I've taken over his home and now his school. Nothing is safe.

My phone rings from somewhere and I grab the first shirt I see and a pair of sweatpants before rushing around my room trying to find it.

I end up back in the bathroom, scrambling through the dirty washing hamper for my school skirt and manage to pull my phone out just moments before the call rings out. I see Nic's name across the screen and my day starts getting better again.

I press accept and hold the phone to my ear as I try to dress with one hand. "Hey," I say with a heavy sigh.

"Hey to you too. Where the hell have you been? I was expecting your call ages ago."

"Sorry. It's been a shitty day. I'm only just now getting a second to myself. What's going on? Been busy?"

Nic goes silent and I can imagine his face scrunching up. He does this every time he's been working for his dad. This is his desperate attempt to try and shield me from the horrors of his day. I can only imagine, but right now I'm wondering if those horrors seem half as bad as mine. "Yeah, been busy," he finally says in a short, factual tone, not wanting to elaborate. "How's your fancy new school? Did they have you filling out college applications and putting you through etiquette classes."

"Screw you," I laugh, falling back onto my bed and looking up at the ceiling. "If anyone needs etiquette classes, it's you. I don't think I've ever seen someone with worse table manners."

"What happened?" Nic questions, his voice taking on a no-bullshit tone. "Why are you avoiding my question?"

"I'm not avoiding it."

"Ocean. Quit bullshitting. What happened at that school?"

I let out a heavy groan and smoosh my face into the too soft pillow. "It's a boys school. He enrolled me in an all-boys school."

"The fuck?" Nic roars.

"Yeah. That's what I thought. It's fucking humiliating. The guys all leer at me as though they've never seen a set of tits in their life, but I guess for some of them they haven't. Not to mention Colton and his friends are absolute dickwads. I just had one of his friends try something in my room. Luckily Colton walked by and put an end to it."

"What's the fucker's name?"

"Chill, Nic. You're not coming to Bellevue Springs to fucking kill the guy. Your father would fuck you up if he knew you were getting involved in this rich kid bullshit."

"Fucking watch me, O. I don't give a shit what my dad says or does. Did he put his hands on you?"

"No. I'm fine. Really. Stop worrying about it. I just need to be more careful. You know, lock my doors and shit. It'll be fine now that I know who to look out for."

"Babe ..."

"No. Don't start with me, Dominic. I already feel shitty enough being away from home, you're just going to make it worse. Besides, I might have met a friend today so it's looking up. I mean, it can't get much worse, right?"

"What friend?"

"A guy at school."

"What's his name?"

"For fuck's sake, Nic. His name is Milo and he's more inclined to climb into bed with you than me."

I hear a soft exhale through the phone and I shake my head at his moronic ways. My four boys will never change. They're always so protective of me. Sometimes I love it and other times … well, other times it makes me want to strangle them and dismember their corpses.

Okay, that might have been a little far but my point has been made. I couldn't live without them though. They're as much my family as mom is.

"So … this Milo guy? He's alright?"

"Yeah, I guess. I mean, I only met him today but he seemed okay. He stayed with me so I wasn't left to fend off the wolves by myself. He's kind of nerdy and he's a teacher's aid. I guess it doesn't get much better than that. He won't hurt me. He even offered to drive me to and from school so I don't have to ride with Colton."

Nic goes silent for a moment and I know he's deep in thought. He doesn't like this whole trying to protect me from far away thing, but reminding him that I don't need his protection isn't exactly going to go down well. He finally scoffs but it comes out as more of a breathy chuckle. "Milo is a stupid name anyway."

"Are you serious?" I laugh. "You have the maturity level of a doorknob."

"Like you're one to talk," he says with a smile in his tone before everything suddenly turns serious. "I miss you."

My chest starts to ache. "Miss you too, Nic."

"I don't mean because you are far away and living with those rich pricks. I miss us. You and me together. We were so good."

"I know that's what you mean but I can't do it again. You crushed me." I let out a heavy sigh, feeling the weight pressing down on my chest. "I don't know if maybe I just need more time to forgive and forget or if I'll never be able to try again. I don't know but every time I even think about the idea of you and me, all I see is the image of Carmen riding your dick and it hurts so damn bad. I just … I'm sorry. I don't think I can get past it. At least, not yet."

"You're my girl, Ocean," he tells me in that same no-bullshit tone. "You know it's going to be me and you. We're meant to be together. I know you feel how right it is."

"There's a difference between it feeling right and actually being right."

"Babe, come on. I'll try harder. I swear. I saw how much the Carmen bullshit hurt you. I could never do that to you again."

My voice falls to barely a whisper as I struggle to get the words past the lump building in my throat. "You see, that's just the thing Nic. When you're with the love of your life and you've found the woman of your dreams, you shouldn't have to try. The need to cheat wouldn't be there, not even the temptation because I would be all that you need."

"You are," he murmurs.

"I'm not, Nic."

"You know I would go back and change it if I could. I hate that I hurt you."

"I know you would."

There's a comfortable silence between us as the heaviness of our conversation sinks in and with every passing second, it becomes easier to breathe. It was six months ago, yet it still hurts so bad. It was a betrayal that I wasn't prepared for. I hadn't even considered it especially from someone who loved me the way Nic had. I thought he was my end game.

"Alright, girl. Dad's calling. I gotta go. I love you."

"K. Love you too," I say before ending the call and letting the phone drop to my chest.

I miss him so much already. I didn't think it would hurt this bad. I miss them all. The boys finished high school a few years ago but every afternoon they were there, unless Kian had them on a job. They would either pick me up from school or show up at my now non-existent home. My afternoons were always full, but right now, I've never felt so alone.

As if on cue, the text messages start rolling in.

Sebastian - Wanna fuck? ;)

Kairo - What's the fucker's name?

Eli - How tall is this guy? Stocky or skinny? Just working out what size rock I'm going to need to sink his body to the bottom

of the ocean.

It all becomes clear. Nic didn't have his dad calling. He needed to call the boys to start research on Jude and in doing that, explained what's been going down this afternoon. That fucker. The boys are going to be relentless now and if I don't start responding, it's only going to end up with them on the Carrington's doorstep. I can only imagine the look on Harrison's face when he opens the door to find my boys. Fucking priceless.

With a heavy sigh, I get busy replying to Sebastian.

Ocean - Hell yeah. Only if you hit it hard and fast. You know I like it rough!

Next up, Kai.

Ocean - Figure it out yourself. I'm not helping you guys. Tell Nic to back off. I've got this.

Then finally, Elijah.

Ocean - When you work it out, minus the weight of his dick. That'll be gone by the time you guys get to him.

Their responses start rolling in and suddenly the heaviness of Nic's phone call starts easing off my chest.

Sebastian - Wait. What? Are you for real?

Kairo - Come on, pretty girl. Just let me hurt him a little.

Elijah - That's my girl.

I spent the rest of my afternoon starting on the shitload of work my teachers gave me to catch me up to the rest of my class while texting with my boys. I know this was all Nic. After instructing them to find out what information they could on Jude, he would have told them to blow up my phone so I couldn't think about it. Though, considering I didn't say which of Colton's friends barged into my room, I'd be smart to assume that Nic now has background files on Spencer, Jude, and Charlie. It shouldn't be hard for him to figure out which friend it was.

At some point, mom shows up at my door and after unlocking it, she just stands there, watching me with my pile of books. I can't say it's something she's ever seen from me before but at the same time, I have this weird need to prove myself at this school. To them, women are nothing, just a hole to stick their dicks in each night. Right now, I'm proving them right.

I need to stand up for all womankind at this school and show them that we're a force to be reckoned with. I won't be failing my exams, I won't be behind the guys, and I sure as hell won't shy away.

It's after 9 pm by the time I come falling back through my bedroom door. Mom wanted to stay down in the staff kitchen, learning every aspect of her role so it was just me at dinner with Colton and Charles. Awkward as fuck doesn't even begin to cover it.

Dinner was dangerously silent. I felt that if I had said a single word, they would have ended my life on the spot. So instead, we just ate, not without the casual scowl from Colton of course.

Not wanting to head back to my room so soon, I stayed down in the kitchen and helped mom a bit. It probably didn't do me any favors with my 'the help' image, but fuck Colton. I'm not going to allow his insults to stop me from being a decent human being just because he insists on being a lousy one. I even think I might have scored a few brownie points with Harrison, but with the extra help, the job was done quicker than I'd hoped and I was sent back upstairs to finish off my reading for English.

With Colton's friends well and truly gone for the night, I don't bother going to the lengths of slamming the door and locking it behind me, instead, I settle in front of the TV. It doesn't take long for me to realize my mistake as my door swings open.

A pissed off Colton Carrington stands in my doorway, looking all sorts of lethal. "What the fuck are you doing in here?" he demands, his eyes narrowed and making me realize that maybe I was being a little louder than necessary.

"What do you care?"

"I care because your insufferable ranting and thumping is making it impossible to even hear myself think."

"Think? Really? Wow. I didn't know you were capable. Congratulations."

Fire burns in his eyes and my back stiffens as he welcomes himself into my room. "What's your fucking problem?" he asks, walking right up to me, his eyes like lasers burning holes into my skin.

"You're kidding me, right?"

"Look at you," he says, running his finger over my shoulder, lightly tracing over my tattoo before slipping his fingers beneath the thin spaghetti strap of my cotton pajama top. "You're nothing, and yet you think you have the ability to fly." His chest presses up against my back and my breath catches in my throat as his fingers trail down my arm, leaving a rush of goosebumps in their wake. His fingers on my skin are like burning torches, leaving behind only destruction. I have to get him out of here.

"You need to leave."

"No, Jade. This is my home. You need to leave." His voice is like velvet whispered against my ear, his breath brushing across my skin like butterfly wings. "Go back to the shithole you came from and leave mine alone."

"I didn't ask for this."

"Then leaving shouldn't be a problem."

"I'm not going anywhere."

His other hand comes up and trails down the side of my body until he stops at my waist, squeezing gently and making me jump. "I know you want me, Oceania," he murmurs, using my full name.

I scoff. "In your dreams, asshole."

He continues as if I hadn't said a single word. "I see the way you watch me when you think I'm not looking, I feel your eyes on me. I can feel your desperation. You want to feel me all over you. You want to taste me, feel me pushing inside of you." His words have me falling into a trance and I find myself pressing my ass back into his crotch, his very hard crotch, but his next words are like having a bucket of ice-cold water tipped over my head. "You want me to make you scream so you can forget your pathetic existence. But guess what? I'll never touch you. You'll never be good enough for me, for my friends, for my town. You're nothing."

I turn in his arms, looking up into his deadly hazel eyes. He keeps his hands on my body as though he thinks his touch is some sort of torture. "You've got it all wrong," I say, sliding my hand down his stomach and over the front of his pants until I feel his hard length against my fingers. He sucks in a tight breath and I resist jumping up and down in victory. "I couldn't give a shit about getting in your pants because you have nothing to offer a woman except money bags and a big cock, apart from that *you're* nothing. Women see you as a one fuck and leave type. A playboy with nothing to offer. No woman would ever stick around for more with you. In fact, I doubt you would even recognize a real woman when you saw one."

Colton's eyes narrow and I curl my fingers more securely around his cock, slowly working my way up and down his hard length despite his pants being in the way. He might act like nothing gets to him and that I'm a nobody he wouldn't even consider touching, but the truth of the matter is that I have him by the balls and he hasn't stopped touching me since he stepped into my room.

"You are right about one thing, Carrington. I will never sleep with you. Not because I'm not woman enough for you but because you're not man enough for me. You live off Daddy's good fortune and wouldn't know anything about living in the real world and making something of yourself. I wonder where you'd be if you didn't have Daddy to bail you out every time."

"You know nothing about me."

"On the contrary, I know far too much."

My grin finally starts to spread across my face and I give his cock a light squeeze. I raise up onto my tippy-toes, feeling his fingers tighten on my waist, steadying me. My lips hover by his ear and I nip the bottom of his lobe feeling victory with how he caves under my touch.

"I win, Colton. You keep coming at me, over and over again and each time, I'll keep biting back harder. You can't go to war against someone who has nothing to lose."

His eyes come to mine and our lips are a breath away. His arm curls around my back and with a hard tug, he pulls my body in flush against his. "If it's a war you want, Jade, don't be fooled, you'll fucking get one and I can guarantee that you'll lose."

My lips brush against his, not as a kiss, but just because we're that close. "Do your worst, Carrington."

Without warning, his lips crush against mine and I swallow a gasp, unable to pull myself back. His tongue dives into my mouth and I find myself kissing him back until suddenly he's gone and my door is slammed behind him.

What in the ever-loving fuck was that?

I'm left standing in my room, my breath coming in hard, sharp pants as my lips swell from his kiss. I fucking hate Colton Carrington but at the same time, I've never been so excited. Bringing him down is going to be the best thing I ever do.

CHAPTER 8

"Holy shit," Milo howls with laughter, grabbing my arm and pulling me to a stop. He spins me around and points out the parking space beside Colton's to reveal none other than Jude Carter with two black eyes, a broken nose, and his arm bandaged.

"Oh, no," I groan. They found him.

"What?" Milo questions. "Who found him?"

My eyes bug out. Crap, I didn't realize I'd said that out loud. "Uhh ... no one," I rush out.

As if hearing my voice from all the way across the lot, Jude spins around, his eyes zoning in on mine and getting darker by the second.

He starts storming toward me and my heart rate picks up.

"The fuck is his problem?" Milo grunts, gripping my arm tightly and stepping his large body protectively in front of me as though I need his help. I haven't told him what happened last night, and I doubt I ever will. Maybe I should let him in on one little secret; I'm not some little bitch who can't handle her own problems. Hell, maybe that's a little something I need to remind Nic of as well.

To Milo's horror, I step out from behind him. "Let him come," I tell Milo as he gawks at me. "I can handle my shit."

"Do I even want to know what happened to him?"

"Trust me, it's better if you don't."

Jude is only a few car spaces away when Charlie and Spencer rush in and step in front of him. Jude starts swinging punches, but in his state, he doesn't land a single blow. "'Get the fuck off me," he spits at his friends.

"Back off," Spencer growls low.

"Let me at the fucking bitch. I'm going to kill her."

Charlie gives him a hard shove back as the rest of the students loitering around the parking lot begin to gather around, wanting in on the action. "No chance in hell, bro. Colt's gonna have your ass for this."

"I don't give a fuck what he says. Look what she fucking did to me."

Spencer scoffs. "The cops said it was a random attack, Jude. She's just a chick and a small one at that. She couldn't inflict this kind of damage on you even if she tried."

"I fucking know that," he roars, "but it doesn't change the fact that this was her. Let me through."

I grin, meeting Jude's eyes over his friends' shoulders. "Yeah, let him through. Maybe then we can share with everyone what kind of bullshit you tried on me yesterday." Gasps are heard as Milo's hand flexes on my arm and it's clear that I don't need to explain for them to know what went down. "Oops," I say, my eyes going wide and my hand flying to cover my mouth. "I think I've said too much."

Jude starts thrashing against his friends' hold. "I'm going to end you."

I suck in a sharp hiss through my teeth. "Oh, big mistake right there. Rule one of committing a crime, you never say that shit in front of witnesses. Witnesses equals jail time. It makes you look guilty, but then, what does it matter, right? You *are* guilty."

Charlie's head whips around and he gives me a flirtatious smile as he struggles against Jude. "Hey, girl," he says with a sexy wink, reminding me just how startling his blue eyes are. "Looking good. How are you doing?"

I give him a beaming smile knowing it must be driving Jude insane. "I'm good. How are you?"

"I'm doing alright. Maybe we could have lunch together today?"

"Sure, I'd love that."

"Great. Listen, babe … you're not fucking helping the situation."

Spencer lets out a groan, slamming his fist into Jude's stomach. "Calm the fuck down," he says as the familiar purr of Colton's Veneno sails through the parking lot. "Colt's here, man. He's going to have your ass for this. He warned you last night, she's *his*. You're not to touch her."

"The fuck?" I laugh as students start panicking and racing away, clearly not wanting to get involved in something that has to do with Colton. "*She* ain't anybody's, especially not *his*."

"Babe," Charlie says, looking back at me with the sickly-sweet smile again. "I mean this in the best possible way, but do you mind fucking off now?"

I let out a groan but as the bell sounds, I give in. "Okay, but only because you're pretty."

He winks, and with that I allow Milo to start dragging me away. "Okay," he says slowly as I glance back to see Colton getting out of his Veneno, looking around with hard eyes and wondering what the fuck he just missed. "You have some explaining to do and you have about thirty seconds to do it."

I stand before my health teacher, Coach Sylvester, as he slams a sports uniform into my chest wondering how the hell I've managed to make it to the middle of the day, but more importantly, how the hell I ended up having to do PE. I was not born for this shit. I'm a fuck around and have fun kind of girl, not the put my body through grueling workouts for nothing kind of girl.

"Here, hurry up and get dressed. I don't take too kindly to students who don't come prepared for their classes. You should have had your sports uniform ready to go when you looked over your class schedule this morning. You've wasted enough of my time."

What the hell is his issue? I wonder if now's a good time to let him know that I'm not exactly the type to check my schedule every morning either. I'm more of a wing-it kind of girl.

The rest of the class begins making their way over and passes behind us as they start heading for the locker room. "Okay, so where the hell am I supposed to get dressed?" I ask as Milo holds back to wait with me in case he's about to be called to show me where to go.

Coach Sylvester's eyes narrow and he looks at me as though I'm stupid. "Where do you think you're supposed to get dressed?" he grunts, pointing toward the locker rooms where the rest of the boys just filed in. As his words reach them, they all stop and look back at him with questioning, excited glances. "Get in there, get yourself ready for my class, and stop wasting my time."

I gawk at him while the rest of my class watches on, Colton being one of them. "I'm not getting changed in there with the rest of them," I snap.

"Yeah, Coach. That hardly seems fair," Milo adds. "Or I don't know … legal."

Coach Sylvester glares at Milo. "What's fair is treating all my students as equals. If the boys have to get dressed in there then why should she get any special benefit? One school. United. Equal," he finishes, adding the school code to bring home his point.

"Come on," Spencer says behind me and I turn around to find my future wannabe husband, leaning against the gated doors of the locker room with his arms folded casually over his wide chest. "I promise I won't bite."

"I might," a guy I don't know adds as I feel Colton's intense stare shooting into my back like a laser beam.

Milo steps in closer. "This is fucking insane," he insists. "This is a sexual harassment case waiting to happen."

"One school. United. Equal," Coach Sylvester replies. "If she doesn't like it, she can leave and she'll receive a fail for physical education. What's your pick?"

My jaw clenches. This is fucking humiliating. Surely there has to be some kind of law against this. I'm only seventeen, still a minor while some of these guys are eighteen. I really don't give a shit if they see my body. I have nothing to be ashamed of but that doesn't mean I exactly want to go flaunting it around and stripping myself of privacy.

"What happened to all that gender equality you girls are always going on about?" Spencer questions. "Here's the perfect chance. If we have to use the locker room and get dressed together like sardines, then you can too. If you girls want to be like the boys, well, come on in baby."

I scoff, turning a sharp glare on him as I feel the rest of the class watching on with interest, some with excited gleams sparkling in their eyes while the others look nervous to be involved with this bullshit. Colton though, he just looks bored and it's as clear as day that he's not going to do anything about this. Why should he though? As of last night, we're at war.

"Shoving me into a dirty locker room with you fuckers is not gender equality. That's taking a massive step back from equality but of course, you wouldn't understand that because you're a man. What you're trying to achieve is just another privileged jerk taking advantage of a female who's backed into a corner. If you really want to see a set of tits so bad, you have a phone. Look them up on porn hub because you won't be seeing mine." I turn back to Coach Sylvester. "And for the record, Milo is right. This is a sexual harassment case against a minor waiting to happen, and I can guarantee that your ass will be the one to burn for it."

Coach Sylvester clenches his jaw before grabbing a set of keys from his back pocket. He unthreads an old key from the chain and shoves it into my hand. "You have three minutes to use the staff bathrooms. A second later and you fail my course. As for today, you're going to sit out and look pretty. You've wasted enough of my time. You won't be slowing down my game with your girly bullshit."

With that he turns his back and stalks away, leaving me gaping after him as the guys chuckle and stalk back into the locker room.

"Are you okay?" Milo questions, his voice filled with concern and looking just as shook as I feel.

I nod my head, watching after Coach Sylvester with venom. "Yeah … I, um … yeah."

"I can't believe that dick thought he could get away with that," he says, his tone filled with malice.

My eyes drop, unsure what I should be feeling. I'm an odd mix of humiliated, proud, upset, and disappointed and the feelings combined are messing with my head. I guess I expected more from the teachers.

Not even the teachers were that low in Breakers Flats. There were certainly some shady ones but for the most part, they just wanted to see us do well and get out of Breakers Flats. I guess I assumed there was a higher standard here. Maybe teachers who had our backs no matter what genitals are hiding beneath our pants.

"Yeah," I tell him, completely agreeing as I hold the uniform up to him. "I guess I'll go and get dressed for my afternoon of sitting on the sidelines being a good for nothing girl who's only going to slow the game down."

"Shit, Ocean," Milo sighs. "Give me two seconds to grab my shit. I'm coming with you and I swear, I won't even peek at your titties no matter how curious I am."

A smile pulls at my lips and I thank God for Milo in this very moment. Without that ridiculous comment, I fear I would have broken down in tears. "Curious?" I laugh. "What's there to be curious about?"

He looks back at me as he makes his way to the locker room door. "You can't tell me that if some chick had her vag out on display; lips, clit, sausage warmer and all, you're not going to peek, at least a little?"

I think about it for all of three seconds before knowing that I would. Everyone would, it's natural human curiosity. Everyone wants to know what someone else is packing. Hell, if Jude bent over in front of me right now to showcase his stinging ringer, I sure as hell would look even though it would most likely scar me for life.

"Yeah, that's what I thought."

Milo disappears inside the locker room and just as promised, he walks back out a moment later with his bag on his back, and an encouraging smile ripped across his handsome face. He leads me toward the staff bathroom and for the comment that prick of a coach made, I fully intend on keeping the key.

Milo and I duck inside the bathroom and I'm honestly surprised. It's fancy as hell. There are three showers in a connecting room, toilets with doors rather than just stalls like the guys have, and not to mention a fancy as hell dressing area complete with hairdryers, straighteners, and towels that look more expensive than mom's old car.

"Well, shit," Milo says. "At least we now know why the fees are so damn high."

I scoff under my breath and make my way into one of the toilets and close the door behind me. I deal with business and make quick work of getting dressed. The sports shorts coach gave me are about four sizes too big and droop under my knees, but it'll have to do. There's no way I'm going to back out. I'm showing my face on that soccer field and I'm doing it proudly.

I pull the drawstrings as tight as they will go and tie my shirt at the back so I look at least a little cute. My long boy sleeves get rolled up and before I know it, I'm good to go.

Milo and I walk out of the staff bathroom and pick up our pace as we hear the rest of our health class down on the field already playing.

We get down there a moment later and Coach Sylvester's eyes instantly come to mine with a heavy scowl. "Take a seat, Oceania," he demands, pointing to the grassy field by his feet. I groan under my breath at the use of my full name while Milo mutters an "Oh, shit," under his breath.

I walk right past the coach and into the center of the field. The boys instantly stop what they're doing with loud protests for me to get out of their way. I roll my eyes and as the soccer ball is discarded and rolls out in front of me, I pick up my pace, hoping I can still do this.

My foot kicks out and the instep of my foot collides with the ball, sending it soaring through the sky. I watch with a smirk as it sails exactly where I want it to go.

Coach Sylvester's eyes widen a fraction before the ball slams hard into his chest and a loud grunt is pulled from within. I silently thank Sebastian for teaching me his little party trick all those years ago and make a mental note to tell him all about it.

I hear the chuckles of the guys around me and of course, I feel one set of eyes that are staring heavily into my back. I raise my chin and keep my gaze locked on the douchebag with the ball between his hands. "Just because I am a girl it does not mean that I am lacking. It does not mean that I am going to slow the game down, and it sure as hell does not mean that I deserve any less respect than the rest of the dickheads out here. Got it? Because if you don't, we're going to have a big fucking problem."

His eyes narrow on mine and there's silence around the field for far too long. Finally, his chin lowers and the heavy scowl fades in defeat. "It's your funeral," he murmurs, and just like that, the game picks right back up without another word being said.

Two hours later, I stand under the hot stream of the showers, knowing damn well that this shower is better than the ones the boys are currently suffering through. Hell, they're probably cold and on timers.

I clean myself off, not wanting to get out. I'm not one for physical fitness but I'll be damned if I show weakness in front of those boys. I pushed myself harder than I've ever pushed myself before and made sure that I kept up with them for the whole two hours. My body is going to hate me for it when I wake in the morning but seeing the glisten of respect in their eyes was worth the pain.

A noise catches my attention and I stand a little straighter only to hear the familiar sound of feet scrambling through the bathroom followed by a wicked laugh. The door slams heavily and I jump.

Fuck, fuck. FUCK. That's not good.

Shutting off the water, I grab my towel and wrap it around my body before rushing out of the shower. Everything is gone. They stole my uniform, my underwear, my sweaty sports clothes, even my shoes, and socks. My bag is gone with my phone so I can't even call for backup. All I have is the towel around my body.

How could I be so stupid as to allow that to happen? Here I was, foolishly thinking that I'd earned their respect. Hell, Colton didn't even mutter a word throughout the whole health class. He just kept pushing himself harder in order to keep the bar too high for me to handle.

With no other choice, I'm left to walk straight out of the staff bathroom into a school full of boys wearing nothing but a towel, leaving my pride and dignity behind. My eyes begin to water as I try to hold my head up high but the further I walk, the louder the laughter becomes.

By the time I reach my target, I have strange boys all around me, each of them desperately trying to get a peek, hoping to the Gods above that I accidentally drop my towel. Hands reach for me, my ass and breasts are groped more than any woman should ever have to endure, and wolf whistles are heard from one end of the school to the other.

My fingers latch onto the towel with everything I've got as I step up in front of Colton and his band of douchebags with practically the whole school here to watch. Colton stands with his back to me but there's no doubt he hears the ruckus behind him, yet he refuses to turn around.

"Where are my fucking clothes?" I demand, forcing myself not to cry.

Colton slowly turns and as he takes me in, his brow raises in surprise and it hits me, this wasn't him. Anger pulses through his hazel eyes and I wonder if this has something to do with Spencer's comment this morning about me being Colton's to fuck around with. If that's true and Colton declared me his to fuck with, then someone has gone against their king. Right now, I couldn't give a shit. Right now, I just want my fucking clothes and to get the hell out of here.

I feel like a fucking rabbit among a thousand hungry foxes. There's no way I'm going to get out of this alive.

Colton studies my body, letting his eyes lazily drag up and down, silently reminding me that he has all the power here. "I don't know what you're talking about, but it sounds as though you need to take better care of your belongings."

"I know you know who did it."

"Of course I fucking know who did it," he says, stepping forward and crossing into my personal space like he had last night. Though last night felt somewhat intimate, this just feels all kinds of wrong. His voice lowers, only for me to hear. "I told you, if it's a war you wanted, then it's a war you'll get. You're not already backing out, are you? What a shame. I thought you had a little more fight in you. I haven't even had a chance to really humiliate you yet."

"Look at me, Colton. I'm standing in the middle of a fucking all-boys school in nothing but a towel. There's nothing you can do to me that's going to make me crack. I'm seeing this through."

I look over Colton's shoulder at Jude who's watching through narrowed eyes. I know it was him, after this morning's bullshit, it's fucking clear as day. "Did you think I was going to fold into a ball and cry on the bathroom floor until someone came to find me? Fucking weak. You want to make me look like a little bitch for not being able to walk through those doors in nothing but a towel, but the only bitch I see around here is you. You failed," I tell him. "Again. Who steals a woman's clothes anyway? That's so fucking lame. You're playing with the big kids now, Jude. If you plan on making an impression, then I'd suggest you up your game."

"Get out of my fucking way," A demanding voice cuts through the crowd, making me glance over my shoulder to see the top of Milo's head as he shoves and pushes his way through the gathered bodies. "Where the fuck is she?"

Milo breaks free of the crowd and almost falls when he reaches the center, but as he sees me standing here in nothing but a towel, his protective side comes out and for once I'm actually grateful for it. "Who the fuck did this?" he demands, glaring around the circle and coming to the same conclusion I had as he stops on Jude. "You're going to go down for this."

Jude scoffs, his lips pulling up in a sneer. "Fuck off, Rinaldi. This has nothing to do with you."

"She's my fucking friend and you just tried to humiliate her in front of five hundred horny teenage boys. What's your fucking game?" he demands, peeling off his shirt and handing it back to me. "You couldn't follow through on your sick plan to attack her last night so you hoped someone else would do it today? You're fucking pathetic, man. Grow the fuck up."

Jude launches forward and the closer he gets, the clearer his bruises become. "I told you to stay the fuck out of it," Jude snarls as Milo grabs my arm and tugs me away from Colton's cold glare.

"Or what?" Milo scoffs. "You can't fucking touch me and you know it. So what else could you possibly do? You've backed yourself into a corner. Are you going to go run to Daddy and hope he can help? But remember, to do that, you'd have to tell him exactly what it is you did."

Fury ripples over Jude's features and I watch as Charlie and Spencer subtly move in by his side, ready to hold him back if he plans on fucking shit up. "Oceania Munroe," my name is hollered, somehow heard loudly over the noise. I glance around and within moments, the crowd starts to part.

Dean Simmons walks through the bodies and when he reaches the front of the circle, he stares at me with a dangerous glare. "Get in my office now."

Well shit.

CHAPTER 9

Milo steps to the left, blocking Dean Simmons' view of me and quickly grabs his shirt from my hand as students begin scattering away. He bunches the shirt in his hands, finding the opening before slipping it over my head so I don't have to take my hands off the towel and risk it dropping to the ground in front of all these guys.

"Thanks," I murmur as I go to step around him, but he stops me as he takes my hand. With practiced ease, he drops a set of keys into my hand. "Get out of here. As soon as you're done with Simmons, take my car and go. Sticking around here isn't going to do you any favors."

My eyes meet his, searching for some kind of answers. Handing over your most beloved car isn't exactly something people do on the regular where I'm from, so to me, this is a huge fucking deal. "Are you sure? How will you get home?"

"I can hitch a ride back to your place to get my car after school," he says, squeezing my hand with an encouraging smile. "Don't worry about me."

"Oceania," Dean Simmons scolds, clearly not fond of being kept waiting.

I glance up at Milo one more time before letting out a breath and stepping away. Dean Simmons turns on his heel instantly, and I don't miss the way that Colton, Jude, Charlie, and Spencer all watch me stalk off.

Despite Milo's shirt coming down to my knees, walking through the school to get to Dean Simmons' office is still humiliating. Knowing that beneath this shirt is nothing but a towel and my nakedness is very off-putting. I'd do anything to be happily dressed in my usual school uniform with a bra and panties keeping all my bits warm.

I follow Dean Simmons right up to his office door where he stands and waves me through with a heavy scowl. "Take a seat."

I swallow back my fear. Why do I feel like I'm about to get in a ton of shit for doing absolutely nothing? Hell, I'm the freaking victim in this situation. I do as I'm told and drop down into the seat opposite his mahogany desk. "Is there something I can help you with?" I question, watching him stride through his ostentatious office toward his desk chair.

He doesn't respond for a while just stares with his brow cocked. "You've caused quite the drama in my school over the past two days."

My brows fly up and I struggle to keep the disdain off my face. "Umm … excuse me?" I say, unable to keep the incredulous laugh from bubbling up my throat. "You're going to have to explain that one to me because I've not done a damn thing wrong. I've been a perfect student."

Dean Simmons scoffs and it's a sound that grates on every single one of my nerves. "You have distracted my students. Since you started yesterday, there have been fights in the parking lot, one of my star students has a fractured arm and two black eyes, my coach is going to have x-rays done on his chest, and now I find you strutting around my quad in nothing but a towel. These boys are here to learn, not to be distracted by your sexuality."

I throw myself out of my chair and stand before him. "What a load of shit. First off, your star student is rocking two black eyes because he tried to attack me in my bedroom last night, and for the record, you'd be a fool to assume I could inflict that sort of damage. He came to me in the parking lot while also sending me death threats but I'm guessing that's just going to be looked over because I'm a female and around here that counts for nothing. Your coach is a fucking pervert along with the rest of your students and if I had the cash behind me, your coach would be held up in a sexual harassment case for so long he'd never see a field again in his life. Not to mention I'm still a minor so that's only looking worse for him. Besides, it's not my fault the dickhead can't catch a soccer ball."

"Watch your tone, young lady," he snaps, clearly not taking kindly to threats. "You're making a mockery of my school."

"You're doing that all on your own if you can't already see the issues lying within your school. It's you that chooses to do nothing. I wonder what Charles Carrington would think of that?"

Dean Simmons' eyes widen a fraction before the anger takes over. I smile to myself. That was a long shot, but it paid off. Charles Carrington is an important man around here, and judging by Dean Simmons' reaction, he either owns the place or is on the board. "Don't push me, Oceania. You're already walking a thin line. I have a 'three warnings and you're out' rule and today, you've pushed through two."

"That's bullshit. I haven't done anything."

"I've just sent my coach to the hospital for x-rays," he reminds me. "Did you or did you not kick a ball into his chest."

"I did."

"And are you not strutting around my school in nothing but a towel when I have over five hundred young men trying to concentrate on their studies?"

I see red. "My clothes and belongings were stolen from the bathroom while I was showering after PE. I can hardly be blamed for that. In fact, I want to report a theft. I still haven't received my belongings back."

"That's a tall story, Oceania," he growls, "and I will not put up with it. My students are outstanding young men of this community and do not take part in these ridiculous little stunts."

This is just getting absurd. No matter what I say, I'm always going to be the one in the wrong. Hell, I'm sure had Jude actually gotten his hands on me, that would have been my fault too.

I shake my head in astonishment and scoff at how pathetic this little meeting has been. "I'm out," I say, making sure Milo's shirt is pulled all the way down before abandoning the used towel on Dean Simmons' office floor.

I head for the door. "I am not finished with you, Oceania Munroe."

"Well, I'm more than finished here."

"I only accepted your admission because of your connection to Carrington. If you walk out that door I will not hesitate to terminate your enrollment."

Fuck that. I don't care if this embarrasses Charles, or if Mom has an issue with it, I'm not sticking around a second longer. I'm sure once Mom calms down and lets me explain, she'll be more than on my side. Most of the time, she's all about shutting up and doing what you have to do to get by, but sometimes the line of what's acceptable gets crossed and she'll never expect me to just take it like that. No doubt this means she's going to hear all about what happened with Jude yesterday and that's only going to worry her. She already has too much on her plate to worry about bullshit like that.

I can only imagine how Nic is going to handle this. Maybe it's best to keep this one quiet, after all, I said something yesterday and look how that escalated.

I hold my head high and walk out the door of Dean Simmons' office, making sure to slam it behind me as the anger pulses through my veins. How dare he blame all this bullshit on me. Okay, so yes, I kicked the ball at the coach, but he had it coming. Apart from that, I've done absolutely nothing wrong. This is complete bullshit.

I storm down to the student parking lot and don't miss the way the students stare as I go. It only manages to fuel my anger more. It's their lunch break and I'm distantly aware that I teased Charlie about some ridiculous lunch date that I had absolutely no intention of seeing through. It served its purpose of getting under Jude's skin and that's all I needed.

I drop down into Milo's Aston Martin and my emotions are too wild to even realize what I'm doing. This is one of those cars on my list and I'm about to drive it, yet right now, I couldn't care less.

I hit the gas and the Aston Martin peels out of the parking lot.

Within minutes, I'm shooting down the drive to the Carrington mansion and bringing the car to a screeching stop on the expensive drive, most likely leaving two thick rubber lines behind.

I fly up the stairs and push through the door into the huge foyer. I can't really remember all the ins and outs of this place just yet, but I'll be damned if I'm not going to do something about this. It's not right. I get that it's a boy's school but that doesn't mean the way I've been treated today is acceptable.

I find Charles' office and storm through the door. His head instantly whips up and at that moment, the similarities between him and his son are almost uncanny. There's a phone glued to his ear and upon taking in the look on my face, he lets out a frustrated huff. "I'm going to have to call you back."

Damn straight, he will.

Charles finishes up his call, not once taking his eyes off me as he hangs up and raises from his office chair. "Ocean, what is the meaning of this? That was a very important business call you just interrupted."

"Couldn't have been too important if you hung up to speak to me. You could have just told me to fuck off."

"What has gotten into you?" he demands. "Where is this attitude coming from and why the hell are you not at school? Where is your uniform?"

"My uniform was stolen from me while I was showering after PE and I was forced to walk around the school in nothing but a towel until I was offered a shirt."

"Excuse me?" he questions, looking shocked which I'm hoping is a good sign for me.

I continue, needing to get it all out before I go back and answer questions. I start pacing his office. "Yeah, this comes after that ridiculous coach demanded I strip down and change in the locker room with the eyes of thirty prying teenage boys watching me, and the kicker is if I refused he was going to fail me for Physical Education. I only got saved from that when Milo pointed out that it was a sexual harassment case waiting to happen. Can you fucking believe that? It was humiliating. Then he told me to sit out because I was only going to slow down the game. I mean, I might not be as fast as those boys, but I can still kick a fucking soccer ball up and down the field."

"Just take a breath," Charles says, walking around his desk and perching himself on the end. "Don't you worry. He'll be dealt with. Refusing to educate you is unacceptable behavior from a teacher."

"You haven't heard the worst of it," I grumble, skipping over the whole kicking the ball into the coach's chest thing. At least, for now.

"The worst?" he questions, raising off his desk as he begins getting agitated.

"Yeah, that stupid Dean Simmons has the balls to tell me that it was all my fault. That walking around the school in a fucking towel was some sort of stunt to distract the boys from their studies when in reality, it was nothing but complete humiliation. Do you know they don't even have a place for me to go to the bathroom? Imagine if that was Cora or Casey having to steal the key for the staff bathroom and sneak in just to pee?" I take a shaky breath, balling my hands into fists. "Then that ridiculous excuse of a Dean said that I was making a mockery out of the school, and although I was the one who was nearly attacked by one of his students, it's somehow all my fault. I've received death threats from that student, I've been discriminated against because of my gender, and I was sexually harassed by some dimwit pervert coach. I've never been more humiliated in all my life. I think he might have even terminated my enrollment, but I was too angry to stick around to know for sure."

Charles just stares, his mouth hanging open. "I, uhh … I don't even know where to start with all of that. This has all happened in the last two days?"

I nod and his face begins turning red with anger. "Where the hell was Colton during all of this?"

I let out a sigh. "Look, don't get me wrong, Colton is an A-class dickhead with a massive chip on his shoulder, but without him, I would have spent my night in the hospital doing a rape kit."

Charles brows furrow. "Rape? You said you were nearly attacked?"

I glance away, not feeling comfortable talking about it to Charles. "Yeah, Jude welcomed himself into my bedroom yesterday afternoon and tried to force himself on me. If Colton didn't walk by when he did … well, you know."

"Shit, Ocean," he says, his lips pressing into a hard line. "I'm sorry you had to go through that and under my roof none-the-less."

"Thank you, that means a lot."

"Now, about this coach and the Dean. Unfortunately, there's not a lot I can do about the boys stealing your belongings while you were showering. That is unfortunate and I can only imagine how that would have felt being the victim of that, let alone being the only female among all those boys' prying eyes. But you're tough, I see it in you. That's why I had you enrolled there. It's the best school with the best education and that's what I expect out of the children living under my roof."

I nod, wanting to agree but deep down, I'm not sure that I feel that tough.

"Was it Coach Sylvester?"

I nod again.

Charles groans. "I've had issues with that man for years. It'll be good to finally get rid of him."

"Get rid of him?"

"You don't think I'm going to let him get away with this, do you? Expecting you to change in front of a room full of boys is unacceptable and disgusting behavior for an educator. I'll be speaking with the other members of the board and I can assure you that he won't be a problem any longer. Now, Dean Simmons," Charles says with a grin slowly spreading across his face. "He's been another issue I've been meaning to deal with. Leave it to me. I'll put in a call to my lawyers and see what we can do about this. Bellevue Springs Academy has always had a stellar reputation and I won't stand for people like Simmons coming in and tearing it down. One school. United. Equal. That certainly doesn't sound like he's upholding our school code. I put him in that position and I can certainly take it away."

I watch Charles for a silent moment, my eyes beginning to fill with tears. "Thank you," I tell him, feeling the guilt start to creep up on me. "I don't think I've ever had someone be on my side like this before, but there is something you should know."

"Go on," he says, his voice low and his eyes narrow on me suspiciously.

"After I got dressed for PE, I sort of kicked a soccer ball into Coach Sylvester's chest. He was fine for the entirety of the lesson and even demonstrated things, but when I was with Dean Simmons, he said that it was violence against a faculty member and now Coach Sylvester has been sent for X-rays."

Charles lets out a sigh. "That makes things a little more difficult but nothing I can't handle."

"Thank you," I whisper.

"What did I tell you, Ocean? As long as you're living under my roof, you're considered family," he tells me, digging into his pocket and pulling out his phone. "Now run along and get yourself cleaned up.

Make sure you drop Colton's shirt into the hamper to be cleaned and pressed so he's not down a shirt."

"Oh, um … this isn't Colton's shirt. It's Milo's."

Charles' eyes darken. "Colton didn't offer you a shirt or something to cover up with?"

Whoops. Maybe I've said too much. "Nope."

Charles presses a button on his phone and holds it to his ear, looking at me as he waits. "If that is all, you need to get a move on. It seems I have some things to discuss with my son."

"Of course," I say. "Thank you."

"It'll be dealt with by morning," he assures me before speaking into his phone. "Colton. My office. Ten minutes." With that, he ends the call and I scurry away, feeling the weight of the world lifting off my shoulders. Not to mention, it sounds like Colton is about to get an ass-whooping from Daddy Warbucks and I don't want to be here when that happens.

I hurry up to my room and instantly dive into the over-the-top walk-in closet. I peel Milo's shirt over my head and grab a pair of sweatpants and a cotton crop. Being certain that Colton and his friends aren't here, I stride out of my closet and get myself dressed.

After a day like this, it would have been nice to be able to call Nic or one of the boys but with my phone currently in the hands of my clothes thief, I go without. Instead, I curl up in bed and try to forget that today ever happened.

It's only a few minutes later when I hear Charles' loud booming voice flowing from downstairs. There are too many walls between here and there, distorting his words beyond recognition, but from the sound of it, I'd say that Colton is here and getting the ass-whopping he so desperately needs.

The thought has a grin stretching across my face and with nothing left to do, I grab a textbook and try my best to catch up on my schoolwork.

By 3:30, Milo is standing in my bedroom doorway with an annoyed Harrison by his side. "Might I remind you about our guest list. It was put in place for a reason." I just stare at him as Milo silently laughs behind him which only serves to piss him off more. Harrison lets out a loud groan. "You'll do well to remember that I am not responsible for running around after you. If you are inviting friends over, you should answer the door yourself instead of wasting my time. I work solely for the Carrington's, not disrespectful princesses like yourself."

With that, Harrison zips his lips and walks out the door, leaving Milo to welcome himself into my room. "How are you feeling?" he questions, finding his discarded shirt on the end of my bed.

I shrug my shoulders as I reach for the keys of his Aston Martin on my bedside table. "Been better," I admit, tossing his keys across the room and watching as he effortlessly catches them. "The tub of ice cream helped a lot."

"Damn, that bad?" he murmurs. "Would hearing that Coach Sylvester was just arrested help?"

My eyes bug out of my head and I sit up a little straighter. "Bullshit. Really?"

"Yep, just before school let out. Cops pulled up and took him away in cuffs. They interviewed a few of the students from our PE class and they all had the same story so I guess you won't have to worry about that shit again."

I grin wide. "Wow. He really does work fast."

"Who does?"

"Charles Carrington. When I got back here I kind of went on a rant and told him everything that happened today. Dean Simmons was a douche and made out like I'd orchestrated the whole thing as some sort of attention-seeking stunt. Charles said he was going to handle it. He wasn't impressed."

"No shit. Charles is on the board for BSA and personally vouched for Simmons and a fuck-up like this reflects poorly on him. He's probably happy you went straight to him about it so he could handle it before word spread."

"Well, shit. I didn't think about that."

"Trust me, around here, everyone is in each other's pockets. It's hard to keep it straight sometimes," he explains before stepping toward the door. "Anyway, I wish I could stay and keep you company, but my father has requested my presence this afternoon."

"Is that a good thing or a bad thing?"

Milo presses his lips into a hard line. "It's too hard to tell. That man is unpredictable but if I have to take a wild guess, he's probably heard about what happened today. He's on the board with Charles so he would want to hear it directly from me."

I cringe, sending him all my good vibes. "Good luck."

"Thanks," he laughs. "I'll let myself out so I don't piss off your house bitch."

"Sure," I smile. "Thanks for letting me steal your car for the afternoon. I don't think I would have survived if I had to stay there a second longer."

"Anytime, babe."

With that, he steps out of my room, leaving the door wide open so I hear the sounds of the busy afternoon house. Judging by the loud, angry music coming from downstairs, I'd say that Colton is down there somewhere and is pissed. At one point, I hear Charlie and Spencer's voices from down the hallway, and I send a silent thanks up above when they leave without bugging me.

Mom comes in, no doubt having heard the gossip from the other staff about my day, and she demands answers. By the time I'm finally through explaining it all, It's time for dinner.

Just like yesterday, dinner is an awkward hour of sitting at a too big table with Colton glaring at me while Charles sits on his phone, unable to get out of a business call. Colton is up and gone from the table the second he can and just like yesterday, I avoid heading back upstairs by helping in the kitchen.

Time ticks by way too slowly, and after taking over Colton's media room for a few hours, I head upstairs to have a proper shower and go to bed. The shower I had at school was cut short and I hardly got a chance to wash properly before being rudely interrupted.

I stand under the hot stream of water, groaning with how my muscles ache from running around on the field for a good part of my day. My hand travels down my body and I do my best to rub my muscles, but truth be told, I'm probably going to be sore for a few days.

Grabbing my towel, I quickly dry my hair and wrap it around me, loving how warm and cozy it is. I didn't even know that heated towel rails were a thing, but apparently, they are, and I freaking love it. As much as I hate being here in this mansion, it certainly has its perks.

I step out of my bathroom and back into my moonlit bedroom as a yawn pulls from deep within me. I can't wait to climb into bed and find the peacefulness of sleep. I drop my towel at the bathroom door and stride across my room before slipping in between the sheets, not bothering to get dressed.

My head crashes down on the pillow and my eyes close with satisfaction, yet my mind still swirls with the memories of today. Apart from my dad's murder, it's been a long time since I've had such a shitty day.

Thoughts of Colton pop into my mind. This is all on him. I know Coach Sylvester would have still done what he did, but Colton has the power in that school. It's as obvious as the sky is blue. He would have just had to say one word and it would have been over. Same with the towel situation. Had he told the by-standers to fuck off they would have, but he didn't. He allowed it to continue.

God, I fucking hate him.

But those eyes, and the way he touched me when he came in here yesterday. His breath against my skin. The way he kissed me, so rough and forceful. I've never felt anything like it. He's powerful, and while it's scary as hell, it's also one of the most attractive things I've ever seen.

Goosebumps spread over my skin and I find my hand slipping down between the sheets and finding my center. I'm already so wet. Why does he have this insane power over me? What I wouldn't give to feel his hands on my body just one more time. I'm sure I'll get him out of my system after that.

His hazel eyes flash in my mind as my fingers rub slow, agonizing circles over my clit. I let out a low groan, not wanting to be heard. "God, yes," I moan, picking up my pace and wishing for something much better than my fingers.

A loud, amused scoff comes from the corner of my room and my eyes fly open. What the fuck was that? I fly up in bed, pulling the comforter with me to cover all the important bits to find Colton casually relaxed back into the armchair in the corner of my room, watching the whole fucking show.

Fuck. I just dropped my damn towel and strutted across my room then touched myself. Fuck my life.

What is his fucking problem?

"You're thinking about me, aren't you?" Colton murmurs, his voice dangerously low and tortured, almost as though he's struggling to remain in the armchair. "My hands on your body, my hard cock pushing up in between those sweet legs."

"Get the fuck out of here," I screech, climbing out of bed with the comforter heavily wrapped around me, getting more pissed by the second as I find him making himself even more comfortable. "Are you fucking insane? What kind of creep sits in the corner of a girl's room in the dark while she's in bed?"

His eyes blaze with lust and I watch as he raises his hand to find my phone between his fingers. "I came to give you this. Charlie dropped it off this afternoon but it's not my fault you decided to get naked and put on a show."

He spins the phone between his fingers and the backlight turns on, illuminating my room and showing off the hard column beneath his grey sweatpants, making my traitorous pussy clench with need.

I try to ignore the way his hard cock seems to be pointing right at me. "You've had that all afternoon?"

Colton shrugs a shoulder. "What can I say? I was waiting for the right time to give it to you, and it seems I found the perfect time."

"Give me my phone."

"Who's Nic?"

My eyes widen as frustration pulses through me. "You went through my phone?"

"Who's Nic, Jade? It sounds like he's got a real fucking hard-on for you."

My eyes drop down to the front of his sweatpants, not wanting to tell him a damn thing about my best friend. "He's not the only one."

Colton's gaze drops to his dick before trailing his eyes back up to meet mine, only now they're so much darker. Gone is the soft hazel, replaced with a seductive shade of forest green. His greedy stare promising more than he can offer me in words.

It's a fucking trap, Ocean. Don't fall for his games.

I hold my hand out, adjusting the comforter in my other so I don't accidentally drop it and give the guy another peep show. "My phone please."

"Why don't you come over here and then maybe I'll give you what you need."

His double meaning isn't lost on me and I hate him more for it. He wants to play a game. I see it in his eyes, but just how much am I willing to lose if this goes badly? There's no way in hell he's just going to hand over my phone and walk away. I have to take what's mine and considering how hard he got just watching me, it's going to be like taking candy from a baby.

Letting out a breath, I go for it.

The comforter drops to the ground and I watch as his brows shoot up. He didn't expect that. Victory shoots through me as I step out from the comforter at my feet. My eyes become hooded and I focus them heavily on his as I stride slowly across the room, swaying my hips and giving just the slightest bounce to my chest.

He swallows hard and adjusts himself in his pants.

Hook, line, and fucking sinker.

He can't take his eyes off me. He might hate me just as I hate him, but there's no denying that I'm under his skin. I'm an itch that he desperately wants to scratch, and that knowledge is going to be his downfall.

Reaching the armchair, I drop to my knees before him, still with my eyes locked on his. A low rumble sounds deep in his throat as I press myself between his knees. I slowly rise, brushing my body softly along his. I feel my nipple, brush along the fabric of his sweatpants only to feel his hard length beneath.

His fingers brush over my arm, leaving a trail of goosebumps in their wake. My hand slides up his body and over his wide chest until it's curved around the back of his neck. I hitch my knee up beside his hip and climb on until I'm straddled on his lap and can feel his cock pressed tightly against my clit.

I lean into him and close my eyes and his hand comes down on my waist then trails lower and grabs a handful of my ass. Why does that have to feel so damn good? My tits press against his chest and my lips come down on his neck. I kiss him, tasting his warm bronzed skin and breathing in that heavenly scent.

My phone is forgotten, and his other hand comes to my body as he presses his dick up against me. I grind on it, both of us groan, and I know that I'll more than likely leave a wet spot on his sweatpants.

Colton's hand comes up and threads into the hair at the back of my head. He grabs my hair and tears my head back until my tits are up in the air. He sucks my nipple into his mouth, flicking his tongue over the tight bud, sending my eyes rolling back into my head.

I'm helpless under his touch but then, so is he.

I roll my neck, pulling against his hold on my hair and he instantly lets go. My hand slips down beside his thigh and I wrap my fingers around my phone, keeping my body moving on his. My lips brush over his ear and he groans with need. "Do you want me, Colton?" I whisper, making his fingers clench against my ass.

"Fuck, yeah."

I let a moan slip through my lips and adjust myself on his lap, before kissing his neck once more. "Guess what?" I murmur, pressing my knee against his crotch and making his whole body stiffen like a board. I press harder and his eyes shoot up to mine and it's like having iced water tipped over his head. "You will never get this."

With that, I slip off his lap and grab the throw blanket on the dresser beside him and quickly wrap it around my body. "Now please," I say with a sickeningly sweet smile, my phone safely in my hand, and an epic female version of blue balls. "Get the fuck out. I won't be asking again."

He shakes his head, almost in shock, and I don't doubt that he feels like the biggest fool. He lost this round, and I can guarantee that now he knows exactly what lengths I'd go to; he won't be making that mistake again.

He stands before me and steps into my personal space, curling his hand around the back of my neck. His lips come down on mine just like they had yesterday. Bruising, forceful, and filled with power. "Game on."

CHAPTER 10

I sit beside Milo in the cafeteria, scowling at Colton from across the room. The more I watch him sitting on his tabletop surrounded by followers, the angrier I get. Everyone watches him eagerly as he speaks, all of them laughing even when he's not funny.

I try to tune him out but the only other thing for me to do is listen to the way Milo's friends go on and on about the cops showing up here yesterday and the board members filing into Dean Simmons' office first thing this morning. Apparently, it's all their gossipy mothers could talk about last night.

While yesterday was a shitty day with an even shittier ending, it means that now the guys at school have backed off. They now understand that I won't accept shit from anyone, and I'm not afraid of taking them down. Well, it mostly means that. I wouldn't have been able to do it without Charles Carrington and they know that.

Milo's elbow comes shooting into my arm. "What's up with you. You look like you're about to murder someone, or you're constipated. Seeing as though you have the best chefs in town, I'm going to go with option number one."

I press my lips into a tight line and my eyes involuntarily shoot across the room to Colton, only to find his glare already on me. I'm instantly reminded of how it felt grinding down against his hard cock and my thighs clench under the table, but of course, from where Colton sits across the room, he catches the movement.

Fuck. I hate him so bad.

"It's nothing," I grumble but Milo's wide grin tells me he knows exactly what it is.

"Why don't you just fuck him and get it out of your system?"

"No way. That's what he wants. I'll never give in to him like that. I'd rather watch him burn."

Milo groans and falls back into his seat, stretching his legs out wide under the table. "Ugh, thanks for reminding me why I go to an all-boys school. You chicks are so dramatic."

"And you dudes are dick heads."

"Shut up," he laughs. "You're such a bitch when you're horny. When was the last time you got dick?"

"Seriously?"

Milo continues as though I didn't even speak. "I'd offer you mine but you'd have to put a paper bag over your head and strap your titties down. I can't have them bouncing around and ruining my flow."

Realizing this is Milo's way of bugging me until I give in, I let out a frustrated groan and get it over and done with. "I had just taken a shower so I was walking around my room naked and got in bed, then you know …"

"You were spanking the monkey?" he supplies helpfully with a grin.

"Spanking the monkey?" I question. "What the fuck is that?"

"You know, jerking the gherkin."

"I don't have a gherkin."

Milo groans. "You know what I mean. You were getting off and from the way you can't stop scowling at the prick across the room, I'm assuming it was him you were thinking about."

Heat floods my cheeks and I let out a huff. "Okay, yes. I was getting off to the thought of Colton and I was just about to the good part when I realized he was in the room. He'd watched me strut around naked, climb into bed, and start going to town on myself and didn't say a damn word."

Milo howls with laughter. "You're fucking kidding me?"

"I wish I was."

"What did you do?"

"What do you think I did? I gave him the worst case of blue balls to ever exist and then told him to fuck off."

"You're my fucking queen," he declares, giving me a pathetic excuse of a bow while he remains seated beside me. "Personally, I would have just fucked him and called it a day."

"Yeah, well something tells me that when it comes to Colton Carrington it's never quite that simple."

"You'd be right about that," he tells me. "So, what are you going to do for revenge?"

"Revenge is such a harsh word. I like to call it returning the favor," I grin. "But so far, I don't know. I've been too pissed to even think about it."

"Well," he grins, spinning his phone between his fingers. "Maybe I could be of help until you come up with something good."

My eyes narrow at him and I watch as he unlocks his phone and pulls up a website. He starts entering details and a second later, puts the phone down on the table. "Watch," he smirks, looking pointedly across at Colton.

My brows furrow but I do as I'm told and watch as Colton receives a message to his phone. He reads over it, his eyes going big and then panic taking over. "FUCK," Colton roars through the cafeteria before grabbing his blazer off the table and stalking out.

I gape at Milo. "What did you do?"

"There's a site you can go to where you can anonymously send someone an alert saying that they need to go and get checked for an STI."

Laughter rattles me but my phone rings and I don't have a chance to tell him how freaking brilliant he is. "Oh," I say, spying Nic's name on my screen. "I've got to take this."

Milo nods as I push up from my seat and bring the phone to my ear. "Hey, Nic. What's going on?"

"It's your lunchtime, right? I'm just checking in. I didn't hear from you yesterday."

"Yeah, sorry about that. It was a bad day and my phone was gone."

"What do you mean gone?"

I let out a sigh and give him a quick rundown. "The pricks at school thought it'd be funny to steal all my things while I was showering after PE. There was all this bullshit that came after that. I don't know what happened to my clothes, but I got my phone back late last night when Colton snuck into my room and watched me getting off."

"WHAT?"

"Shit, dude. Calm down."

"Calm down? What the fuck is wrong with you?"

"I handled it."

"Oh, yeah? And how did you handle it?"

I go quiet. That's not exactly a story I want to be sharing with Nic. I can only imagine what kinds of shit he'd do. After all, the boys were more than happy to fuck up Jude the other day. If Nic found out the guy got a look at me naked and put his hands on me ... fuck. It'd all be over.

"Yeah ... that's what I thought," he says just as the bell sounds throughout the cafeteria.

I cringe, knowing he's not going to like this. "Hey, I've got to go. The bell went off."

"What? But I only just got you. Since when have you ever run off to class on time before?"

"I know, but this school is different. It's not like back home. I promise, I'll call you tonight when I have no distractions."

"Alright, O," he says reluctantly. "Bye."

He cuts the call and just like that, I'm left to suffer through the rest of the school day.

Two hours later, Milo hashes in the code for the gate at the Carrington mansion and after it peels back and he hits the gas, I find a very familiar beat-up old shitbox sitting at the bottom of the circle driveway, completely out of place.

A loud squeal pulls from deep within me and I can hardly contain my excitement. Milo jumps and shrieks beside me, surprised by my outburst. "What the hell, Ocean?"

"Hurry up," I demand, unable to keep still.

"Why?" he questions, eyeing the car which obviously doesn't belong. It stands out like an emo kid at a Taylor Swift concert. "Whose car is that?"

I don't respond as he brings his Aston Martin to a stop. I'm out the door before he can even say my name or demand another answer out of me. I race up the steps to the front door, huffing and puffing by the time I reach the top. I throw the door open and scramble through it. "Where is he?" I call out to Harrison as I race past.

"Don't run in the house," he calls after me.

"Where is he?" I repeat.

Harrison groans. "They're in the pool house."

They're? Plural.

I suck in an excited gasp.

FUCK YEAH! MY BOYS ARE HERE!

"OCEAN?" My name is hollered through the house from behind me. "What the fuck is going on?

I barge through the door of the staff quarters and race past mom who gives me a knowing grin, then I weave through tables, chairs, and the coffee cart. "I ain't slowing down, Milo. If you want in then you better hurry the fuck up."

"Language," mom scolds, but she's too late to do anything about it as I barge out through the back door and cut across the side of the house. I race around one of the three pools on the property until I finally find it. The pool house.

Milo remains heavy on my heels and I'm sure that by now he's probably caught onto what's going on. After all, I've spent the last few days telling him all about them. By now, he probably knows them better than I do.

The door of the pool house is propped open with a box and I race through it before quickly glancing around. I haven't been in here yet so this is all new, but right now, the furnishings are the last thing on my mind.

All four of my boys are making their way around the pool house, carrying boxes, and cleaning up the old housekeeper's things. To be honest, it looks like they're doing more harm than good but they have good intentions, whether they're selfish or not.

I don't dare stop, spying Nic in the kitchen. "There's our girl," Sebastian beams, giving Nic the slightest warning before I crash into him. Though, that warning could have also come from the squeal that tore out of me the second I saw my boys. I haven't gone this long without seeing them ... well, ever.

I throw myself up into the sky and he drops whatever is in his hands as he reaches out and catches me with ease.

My legs wrap around his waist as our arms curl around one another. His lips instantly come down on mine in a crushing kiss and I hold on with everything I have, kissing him back. He cuts the kiss short, knowing that anything more is going to set me off. "I fucking missed you," he grins, spinning me around.

I laugh as the other guys start making their way over, knowing that Nic and I needed this small moment together. "It's only been four days," I remind him.

"I know," he says, squeezing harder. "Four days too long. I've never gone this long without seeing you."

My heart flutters and I beam at him until Sebastian is there, slipping his hands around my waist and tearing me off Nic. "Come here, brat." He pulls me in tight and presses a kiss to my forehead and I feel my world finally beginning to right itself.

Eli is next and practically pulls me out of Sebastian's arms, only to dip me low and come at me with puckered lips. "Try it and your life won't be worth living," Nic warns, making Eli's lips pull into a wide teasing grin.

His head continues down toward me and he plants a kiss on my cheek, beaming down at me. "Hey, O. Missed you."

"Missed you too, turd," I smile as he helps me up.

Mr. Afraid Of Showing Emotion is next and I turn toward him

with a cheesy as fuck grin. "Hey, Kai."

He rolls his eyes. "Yeah, yeah," he grumbles under his breath, reaching for me and dragging me across the floor until I'm pulled into his wide arms. "Don't get all mushy on me, pretty girl."

I tilt my head, looking up and meeting his hard eyes. "Wouldn't dream of it."

"Who the fuck is this?" Elijah grunts, his tone taking on a dark edge, one that reminds me that these four guys are not just my best friends but also gang members, each of them with several kills under their belts.

"Is this Carrington?"

At the sound of the name, all four of them stiffen, becoming the lethal boys I know and love, more than prepared to teach Colton a lesson and deliver a not so subtle warning.

I glance back at Milo and as he takes in the four boys bearing down on him, I race forward, throwing myself in front of him before the guys can do any damage. "No, no, no," I screech. "You've got it wrong. This is Milo. He's practically been my lifesaver over the past few days."

"Milo?" Nic grunts, his eyes becoming suspicious. The other guys relax, the lethal look in their eyes disappearing, but I see the same suspicion reflected in all of them.

Kairo nods at Milo. "What do you want with our girl?"

Milo's face scrunches up. "Umm … nothing. She's a friend. That's all."

"That's all?" Sebastian questions, taking a subtle step forward. "I hear you're spending a lot of time with her. No one wants to be just *friends* with a chick and spends that amount of time with her unless he's trying to fuck her."

I roll my eyes and groan. "Knock it off," I say, walking back into Nic's arms and collapsing against his hard chest. "Milo's gay. If anything, he's been hanging around so he can get a good look at you four. I heard you guys have been considering a reverse harem since I've been gone, and Milo here has offered to be the girl in your sandwich."

All five of them look horrified by the idea while I grin with victory. Yeah, that got them to shut up.

"So, you're into dudes?" Elijah questions. "You don't want to get between Ocean's legs?"

"Look, I'm not going to lie. Ocean is sexy as fuck and if I were going to fuck a chick, she'd be the one I'd be trying to get with, but no. I'm not interested. I don't go to an all-boys school for the stellar education."

Nic scoffs a laugh and just like that, I know we're all cool. Though, maybe I should rephrase. My crew and I are all cool, while Milo looks like he's sweating bullets. These guys aren't exactly the clean-cut type of boys he's used to seeing around Bellevue Springs. My crew are the kind of guys who look like they belong in prison. All four of them are covered head to toe in tattoos and piercings, their gang colors hanging off them proudly, not to mention the guns I felt at each of their backs.

Milo will be alright though. If anything, from what I've seen of Bellevue Springs, he's safer here with these four gang members than the rest of this pretentious town.

I turn in Nic's arms and grin up at him. "What are you guys doing here?"

"Had to see you," he says. "I couldn't stand the thought of you living in that house with that prick. The first night that punk snuck into your room and tried to touch you and then Carrington crept into your room last night. I don't trust them and if this is as far away as I can get you, then you bet your ass that's what we're doing."

I beam up at him before looking around my small group of friends. "So you all came to help move the old bat out of here?"

"Sure fucking did, kid," Eli says.

"You know you guys are the best, right?"

Sebastian winks. "You can pay us back in sexual favors."

Nic reaches around my back and smacks Sebastian up the backside of his head. "Knock it off and get back to work. I want this done so we can spare an hour or two to chill with our girl before we have to get back."

"Really?" I beam. "Will you guys stay for dinner?"

"As long as it's your mom's nachos," Kai says.

I cringe. "Mom has been working around the clock so I don't know if she'll have time to cook but I can put it together. I'll just have to scavenge through the staff kitchen and see what I can steal."

"Fuck, yeah," Eli booms. "I fucking love those nachos. There's something about the way you and your mom make your nachos that makes it so much better than everyone else's."

"I know," I grin wickedly, catching Eli's eyes. "We lace it with laxatives and then watch as you guys stuff your faces and fight over the toilet."

He rolls his eyes, not believing me for a second. "In your dreams, babe. You would never do that to us. Your mom is too nice and you don't have the balls to follow through."

My gaze darkens. "Want to make a bet?" I question. "Just ask Milo about all the shit I've had the balls to do over the last few days. It's funny how tough you have to become when you don't have your crew at your back."

"Fuck," Eli murmurs, the laughter gone from his voice as Nic's hold tightens on my waist. "Is it really that bad?"

"Nah," I say, trying to reassure them. "I can handle it."

Milo scoffs from across the room. "Not that bad? There's already been attempted rape, death threats, and Jude got beat up ... but I'm starting to see how that happened now. A teacher has been arrested and the Dean might be losing his job. Add the bullshit you've been getting from Colton on top of that, and yeah, things are going just swimmingly."

I glare at my new friend. "Seriously?"

Nic and the boys look baffled. "Sounds like you've been holding out on us," Kai murmurs, annoyed that they've been kept in the dark.

Milo continues. "There's no point sugar-coating it, girl. Shit is going bad and you've only been here a few days. You could use the back up in your corner and they can't help you if they don't know what's been going on."

Nic nods. "I like this guy."

I groan. "No. You guys need to stay out of it and keep your asses out of Bellevue Springs unless it's to visit me. This place could get you guys in trouble. You've already got enough shit going on back home."

"Is that why you didn't tell us what's really been going on?"

"What can I say? I'm pretty good at bad decisions." On seeing Nic's blank stare, I roll my eyes and let out a sigh, more than ready to start defending myself. "Don't act like I haven't told you anything. I've told you the important bits."

Sebastian grunts. "But not all of it."

"No," I sigh. "Not all of it. This place isn't good for you. Don't act like I haven't noticed the staff watching you out of the corner of their eyes, assuming you're stealing all their shit. If one thing goes down while you're here, everyone is going to point their fingers at you because you're an easy out and they have the power to make it stick, no matter what evidence you have."

"We're big boys," Nic tells me. "We can take care of ourselves. It's you who needs to be looked out for." He waits until I nod and then continues. "Good, now, let's get you and your mom moved in so we can go and introduce ourselves to this Carrington kid."

I roll my eyes, grinning up at him. "I'm not introducing you," I laugh, glancing across at Milo with a knowing sparkle lighting my eyes. "Besides, I think he's a little caught up at the doctor's office, waiting for some results."

Sebastian narrows his eyes, flicking his gaze between me and Milo. "What did you do?"

Milo grins. "We may have sent an anonymous tip that he needed to get checked for an STI. He'll be shitting himself. An STI is a non-event for most people, but for people like Colton Carrington, an STI scandal is enough to have his face splashed across every news outlet in the world for months. It'd destroy his shiny reputation, not to mention what his father would do."

Well, shit. I didn't realize it was that bad.

Nic grins, pulling me in hard against his chest. "Okay," he laughs, indicating to Milo with a subtle lift of his chin. "You can keep him."

I beam up at him and he quickly spanks my ass, leaving it stinging for more. "Excellent," I laugh before glancing around the pool house and taking in the way the boys have been packing up the old house keeper's things. "Let's get this done, but first thing's first. I'm not a control freak, but you guys are doing it wrong."

CHAPTER 11

"Come on," Elijah says, his eyes filled with excitement as he speaks through a mouthful of nachos. "Let's go out. I bet they have the best nightclubs around here. You've still got that fake ID, right?"

I scrunch up my face as the other guys groan at the idea of staying out late and partying Eli style. I can't help but think of Milo. He went home a few hours ago but I'm sure if he were still here, he would have been on his feet and dragging Eli out the door, rattling off all the best clubs within a 50-mile radius.

"Sorry, I've got my Netflix pants on. I'm in for the night." He rolls his eyes as though he thinks I'm a bore, but we all know he loves me more than life itself. I glance across at Nic as he lounges on the couch with his third serving of nachos resting on his toned stomach. "Didn't you say you had things to do tonight anyway?"

He shakes his head. "Did. I fucked them off so we could hang out a bit longer. Dad can get some other poor loser to do his dirty work tonight."

"Are you sure?"

His eyes fill with emotion as he watches me, and a small smile lifts the corners of his lips. "Shut up and eat your dinner."

I grin down into my bowl and just as I go to respond, the door of the pool house flies open and mom steps through looking all kinds of exhausted. "Oh," she says, wide-eyed. "You boys are still here. How are you all? I feel like I haven't seen you in months when it's only been a few days."

"I know," Nic says, sitting up on the couch to make space, knowing her routine just as well as she does. "We're feeling it too."

Mom gives him a warm smile and despite all the shit she told me about spacing myself from the boys and trying to make other friends, she can't help but love them too. Sometimes families aren't the people who share our blood. Sometimes it's so much more than that.

No friends, only family.

Mom walks across the room while glancing around the pool house, stopping when she sees the framed photograph of us with my dad on the edge of the counter. Not being one to show her broken heart, she quickly covers the emotion and beams at the boys. "You boys did all of this just this afternoon? There must have been twenty of you to get it all set up so quickly," she says, dropping down onto the space beside Nic and kicking off her shoes.

Even though we all know there wasn't much to set up, the boys all grin proudly. I adore the way Mom likes to make them feel loved for doing something for us out of the kindness of their little overprotective hearts.

"It was no problem," Eli says. "You know we'd drop anything to make sure you guys had everything you needed."

Mom smiles across at him, her pride and love beaming through her eyes. "Thank you, sweetheart. I really do appreciate it. To be honest, I don't think the old bat was ever planning on moving out of here." She glances around, taking it all in before bringing her gaze back to me "It really is nice here. We've struck a good deal," she says. "Don't get me wrong, I absolutely loved my room in the main house but it's nice to have our own space to relax and be ourselves. Staying in that room for the last few days was so …"

"Hotel like?" I offer when she can't seem to find the word.

"Exactly," she says, pointing across at me. "In here, we get to be just us."

I smile across at her and it hits me just how much she's loving it here. She's thriving in her new job, loving the lifestyle, and making new friends. For once in her life, people other than her family are needing her, appreciating her, and valuing her time and she absolutely loves it. I just hope I'm not going to lose her to this world.

I slide my half-eaten bowl over to Kairo knowing he'll want to eat it despite the two bowls he's already chowed down. I push up from the table and make my way to the kitchen to dish up dinner for mom.

"How's the new job going?" Sebastian asks, sitting up on the kitchen counter.

Mom sighs, leaning back on the couch. "It's great. Better than I thought it was going to be but it's exhausting. It's got long hours and it's going to take me a little while to adjust to it. The Carringtons are great hosts. I was expecting them to be like the snobby rich people you see on TV, but Charles is great and a very generous man. He gives me a great rate and makes sure his staff are well cared for, Ocean too. I'm not so sure about Colton though, I haven't really had a chance to get to know him yet but I'm sure that will come. My feet though," she chuckles, leaning over and giving them a rub. "They've been aching with having to be on them all day long. I wasn't quite expecting that."

"I bet," I tell her, walking across the room and handing over her dinner. "Have you got the same shift tomorrow or do you get a break?"

"I've got a half-day tomorrow," she explains. "Charles is flying out at 4 am for a business meeting across the country and won't be requiring the staff on hand until the afternoon. Though the maids will still have to come in at their usual time and do their thing. After all, we have that big party to prepare for on Saturday. Friday is going to be insane with preparations. Maryne has been giving me the rundown on how it's all going to work."

"Wait," I say, my brows furrowed. "What party? I haven't heard about a party."

"Oh, you haven't?" she questions, her eyes beaming with excitement. "It's going to be amazing, like one of those grand parties you see in the movies. Apparently, it's some kind of tradition that Charles' ex-wife started some good ten years ago. They were so successful that even after she left, they've continued the tradition. There's a theme and all. This one is going to be black and white and I think they're planning a masquerade ball for next month's party. The best of the best are going to be there in gowns and tuxedos."

My eyes brim with wonder. "Are you kidding me?" I screech, hardly able to sit still as I picture an elegant party held in one of the ballrooms, complete with decorations, chandeliers, champagne, and everyone having an amazing time. "That sounds incredible."

"It will be but it's also going to be a massive job. Maryne has been going crazy with scheduling and event planning. I was thinking I could give her a hand in the morning. I've always been good with that sort of thing and it beats sitting around in here doing nothing while you're at school."

"Great idea. I'm sure she'll be grateful for any help she can get," I say, pressing my lips into a firm line and trying to work out how to word this next question. "So, this party …" I start. "Is it like, invitation only, or could I maybe … you know, sneak in?"

Mom's eyes bug out of her head. "You will do no such thing," she demands. "I can't have you sneaking in and getting in trouble. The whole drama with the school hasn't even started blowing over yet. You need to lie low, however, if Charles or Colton speak to you about the party and offer you an invite then I'd be happy to see you there and enjoying yourself, but under no circumstances will you be sneaking in or embarrassing us by trying to win yourself an invite." She looks around at the group of boys. "That goes for all of you. Ocean and I need me to keep this job. It's the only thing keeping us clothed, bathed, and fed at the moment. We can't be screwing it up. Not to mention, Ocean is currently receiving an education from some of the most sought out teachers in the country."

I nod, completely understanding where she's coming from. "Alright, mom. I'll behave," I tell her, feeling a slight pang of disappointment at the idea of not being able to attend the party, but then I guess I can always watch through the window and pretend there isn't glass sitting between me and the most expensive champagne I'll ever taste. "I promise. You don't need to worry about me."

Mom smiles up at me with love shining brightly through her big, blue eyes. "I know, love. I trust you," she murmurs, just for me despite the room full of boys listening in.

She gets busy eating her dinner and soon enough, the boys are crowded around her, catching her up on all the gossip that's been going on in Breakers Flats over the last few days. Spoiler alert, it's not much.

I get up and start cleaning up after dinner and smile up at Kairo when he silently gets up and starts helping me out. He's such a moody, quiet guy with the weight of the world on his shoulders. He looks like a hardened criminal yet deep down, he's a big softy with the sweetest heart. Apart from our boys and me, he'd never let anyone know.

"Alright, guys," mom says a little while later as a yawn comes up and surprises her. She gets to her feet. "I'm going to head off to bed. It was great seeing you all. Don't be strangers, okay?"

Nic stands with her. "You know we won't," he says, giving her a brief hug. "We'll chill out by the pool so you're not disturbed."

Mom gives him a warm smile and then says a quick goodbye to each of the guys before disappearing deeper into the pool house. Just as Nic had promised, the five of us get up and make our way out to the pool. The guys drop down into the sunbeds while I'm pulled down onto Nic's lap. Music is turned on, beers are found, and suddenly it's like any other night I've spent with these guys just with a different backdrop.

"How are you?" Nic murmurs in my ear, threading his arms around my waist as we watch Sebastian slip onto one of those massive blow-up pool floaties in the water. With a beer in one hand, he crosses his legs and props the other hand behind his head as though he belongs there.

"Better now," I tell him, leaning back against his wide chest and feeling more normal than I have in days.

"How are you really?" he questions, prodding for more information.

I let out a sigh and scrunch my face. "Kinda hungry, kinda tired, kinda horny, and kinda want another tattoo."

He sucks in a breath, knowing I only have the guts to get a tattoo when things are really fucking up for me. "That bad, huh?"

I shrug my shoulders. "It'll get better," I tell him. "As soon as Colton gets off my back, it'll be fine. The guys at school have eased up now that they see I'm not some pushover who's just going to accept their bullshit."

"Good," he murmurs. "You know I'd be here every day kicking those dickheads' asses but it's sounding more like a full-time job. As for the kinda hungry, tired, and horny part, you know I can help with that too, right?"

I roll my eyes and nudge my elbow back into his stomach, grinning as the soft 'Oomph' sails from between his lips. "Behave," I warn him.

Nic laughs and pushes a strand of hair back out of my face. The air is chilly but with Nic's warmth at my back, I hardly feel it.

The guys and I fuck around by the pool, all sense of time leaving us. Before I know it, we have a drunk Sebastian and Elijah on our hands, and I can't help but laugh when Eli gives Sebastian's pool floaty a push and he goes toppling into the water with a high-pitched squeal. Hell, it even manages to pull a smile out of Kairo.

Sebastian's head surfaces from the water and panic sets into the fine features of his face. He gasps, his eyes big and frantic as his hand dives down into the water and he digs through his jean's pocket.

"NOOOOO," he cries, producing all his joints from his pocket, now dripping wet and destroyed then trying his lighter only to find it waterlogged and completely useless. Though, if it were me, I'd be more concerned about the gun at his back which is probably now fucked, but judging by the look on his face, the gun is the furthest thing from his mind.

His bottom lip pouts out and if I didn't find it so damn funny I'd even feel sorry for the guy, but as it is, I struggle to reel in my laughter. "Oh, shit, man," Eli booms, not caring about hiding his amusement. "I didn't mean to do that."

Sebastian's gaze darkens as he turns his scowl on Eli. He slowly starts making his way out of the pool.

Eli's face drops. "Oh, fuck."

Sebastian takes off after him at a sprint, the idea of losing his weed managing to sober him up a little. Eli runs, crashing into things and launching himself over plants and garden gnomes.

This isn't going to end well but seeing as though we don't have much in the way of entertainment right now, Nic and Kairo don't do a thing to stop it.

"What the fuck is going on out here?" a loud booming voice demands, somehow managing to steal the breath right out of my lungs.

The boys instantly stop fucking around as my head whips to the back entrance of the main house. Colton fucking Carrington.

I should have known his douchiness was going to come down here and ruin all my fun.

His eyes rake over me on Nic's lap, taking in his arm secured around my waist. His eyes darken and I'm instantly reminded how it was his hands on me last night.

Nic stands, holding onto me as I slide to my feet. "Who the fuck is asking?" he demands despite already knowing exactly who this is, striding forward with the boys at his back looking like the baddest group of motherfuckers I've ever seen.

Colton's eyes travel over them with distaste and I cock a brow at how he doesn't back off. Everyone always backs off. It's like a silent rule. These four guys look as though they're ready to deliver death on a silver platter and Colton isn't even batting an eyelash.

Panic starts to surge within me and I hurry forward, squeezing myself between the boys. They stare over the top of my head and it's as though they don't even realize I'm here.

Colton's eyes narrow in challenge and chills sweep through my body. I've seen all sides of his douchiness, but I've never quite seen him like this. He looks just as lethal as my boys do, yet somehow he manages to do it without the tattoos, bandanas, or guns. Maybe it's the power that comes off him in waves or maybe it's all in my head and it's just this stupid attraction I have for him.

"You know exactly who I am," Colton says, easily pointing out Nic as the leader and making the other three straighten, their scowls deepening. "And you know exactly whose house you're in."

Nic's eyes travel up and down, sizing him up and mentally working out what it would be worth to beat the shit out of him. "Yeah, I know who you are, and I also know that you've been causing trouble for my girl."

Colton scoffs. "Your girl? If she was your girl, she'd be left satisfied and wouldn't need to take care of matters herself, but don't worry, Nic," he says with a slow grin, guessing who this is by the texts he read on my phone yesterday, "I'll take real good care of her."

Oh, fuck.

Nic goes to make a move and I slam my back up against Colton's chest so I can fight for Nic's attention. "Nic, look at me," I demand, pressing my hand on his chest and feeling the rapid beat of his heart beneath my palm. Nic doesn't dare cut his sharp gaze from Colton's so I push hard. "For fuck's sake, Nic. Look at me."

Reluctantly, Nic's gaze drops to mine, heated, wild, and pissed off. "Don't," I warn. "It's not fucking worth it. I've already made it damn clear that this fucker will never touch me."

"Maybe he needs a refresher course," Nic growls, his hands bunching into fists.

"Nic," I demand, reaching up and grabbing his face. "Time to go. You're not getting involved with this shit."

"The fuck I'm not."

"Please," I beg. "You heard what mom said. We *need* this."

Nic's jaw clenches and I feel the vibration of Colton's chest against my back as he silently laughs, making me want to cause all sorts of damage. Nic's eyes come back to mine and I watch in relief as the fight begins to leave him.

A silent message passes between us and as if sensing his resignation, the others back down. I close my eyes and the relief completely takes over but when I open them again, Nic's eyes are black as night and focused heavily on Colton's. "If you fucking touch her or even think about fucking with her again, I'll come for you and I'll fucking end you. Mark my words, Carrington. No one messes with what's mine."

Colton scoffs behind me and I silently beg for him not to mention what happened last night, otherwise, it'd be a bloodbath in here. Colton seems to understand that though and can clearly see that he's outnumbered. So, while he obviously has balls of steel, he's not fucking stupid.

Nic takes a step back and I go with him, peeling my back away from Colton's strong chest. We only get two steps before Nic pulls the gun from the waistband of his jeans and presses it into my chest. His eyes remain on Colton as he speaks to me. "He touches you. You take him out."

I swallow as I take the gun from his hands and nod. It's not a stubborn demand from an overprotective and jealous ex-boyfriend and best friend, but it's an order from the top, from the man who's going to be the leader of the Black Widows one day.

Nic leans in and presses a hasty kiss to my temple, one where I don't feel the love. "What have I always told you?" he questions, pulling back to meet my eyes.

I roll my eyes and can't help but feel some of the tension dissipating from within me. "Don't be the bigger person—slash their tires."

"That's my girl," he murmurs, looking broken at the thought of having to leave. This really isn't the goodbye I was hoping for but if he doesn't go now, I'm not sure how this night will end.

"Hey," I say, reaching up and slipping the bandana off the top of his head and bunching it between my fingers as I've done a million times before. "I love you."

His eyes soften. "Love you too, O. Call me when you can."

"I will," I promise.

I meet the boy's eyes and they all give discreet nods. Despite going against everything they know and challenging their most basic instincts to protect me, they walk away, leaving me here with an amused Colton at my back.

A shit storm brews inside of me as I turn a ferocious glare on Colton. My finger curls around the trigger, knowing Nic wouldn't be carrying an unloaded gun. This thing is more than ready to go, just like I am, but I'd never make a stupid mistake like that. I hold the gun down by my side with Nic's bandana scrunched in my other hand and I don't miss the way Colton's eyes flick down to it.

He's more than aware that he's crossed some invisible line and right now, he's ready to test the limits. "Fucking with me is one thing, but involving my boys is a low fucking blow."

"Don't know what you're talking about," he murmurs, his eyes dancing with the challenge. "I just came out to say hello."

I step into him, somehow managing to make my glare worse than anything Nic could deliver. When my boys are fucked with, I'm one pissed off bitch. "You need to back off, Carrington. You don't know what kind of bullshit you're getting yourself involved in."

"You don't think I know exactly who you are and what you're involved in? What the fuck do you think you're doing hanging out with trash like that anyway?" he demands, his lips pulling up into a disgusted sneer.

I scoff, smirking up at him. "Oh, haven't you heard? I *am* trash, just like them. They're my people, Colton, and if you fuck with my people, I'll fuck with you."

With that, I turn and walk back toward the pool house, dipping the gun into the waistband at the back of my jeans. "Hey," he calls after me. "Don't fucking walk away. I wasn't finished with you."

I turn back around but keep walking in the direction of the pool house, opening my arms out as I stare back at him. "What can I say? I'd love to stay and chat but this conversation is boring me to death and my survival instincts just kicked in. So, yeah … I'm out."

I give him a sickeningly sweet smile before flipping him off and disappearing into the pool house, hopefully somewhere that I won't be bothered by Colton Carrington ever again.

CHAPTER 12

Saturday night rolls around way too quickly.

Colton and I have somehow managed to avoid each other and completely stay out of each other's way so it's actually been an alright couple of days. To be honest, I didn't know Colton had it in him to leave me the hell alone. I guess I have my boys to thank for that. Had they not come and moved the old bag out of the pool house, I'd probably still be suffering the same old bullshit day in and day out.

Who knows? Maybe Colton's running scared, now that he knows what kind of power I have standing at my back. I'm not some bitch he can mess with whenever the fuck he wants. I'm the motherfucking bitch you want to stay away from.

I've only just started where Colton is concerned. He's damn lucky that he seems to have backed off, as I have a full arsenal of ammunition and I'm not afraid to use it. After all, messing with a chick who has nothing to lose is going to be the biggest regret of his life. Maybe the fucker will even learn a lesson or two, but then again, maybe I'm underestimating him. Yes, he's backed off, but maybe there's a reason why and he's getting ready to hit me in a big way.

I'd be a fool to assume the worst is over. Guys like Colton Carrington don't accept defeat, and the last time I saw him I had the last word. He might have won that round and got his way, but he saw it in my eyes, he'd barely scratched the surface.

Since that night, my four Black Widows have been in overprotective mode, especially since they witnessed Colton's antics first hand. I get at least two messages from each of them a day all randomly spaced out, so I never go long without hearing from one of them. I love them, but it kind of sucks. I know they love and adore me, but it'd be nice if they were messaging me just for the sake of saying hi, because they wanted to, not because they were waiting for something to go down. It doesn't matter how often I tell them that I can handle myself, they just keep messaging.

Nic is a different story though. He's still pissed about the whole thing and blows up my phone as much as he can. He calls before and after school then checks on me again at night. It's going to kill me when he finds his soulmate, but at the same time, maybe it will give him someone else to aim all that big dick energy at.

I try to take my mind off everything that's been going on this week and focus on me. Particularly my reflection in my full-length mirror. I can't even believe it's me.

My long dark hair flows in soft waves down my back, my makeup has been done to perfection, and the dress ... holy hell.

Charles had invited me to the party late last night after he'd overheard a few of the staff asking mom what my plans were for the night. They had wanted me to help out during the party, handing out champagne flutes and walking around with those expensive snack thingies with fancy names. Charles was on the doorstep of the pool house in no time. I was about to take my shower when I heard a knock at the door and to be honest, I was more than surprised to see him. It's his place and all, but I'd assumed he'd be the type to keep away from dedicated staff areas as though he was above it all.

He apologized for forgetting to extend an invitation and I beamed up at him as though he'd just handed me all my dreams on a silver platter. I was so excited about this party and when the invitation never came, I'd gotten used to the idea that I was going to have to watch through the ballroom window. Charles had explained that it was a big week and it had completely slipped his mind. He'd also assumed that I was just going to be there, invitation be damned. Honestly, I probably would have snuck in at some point despite mom's warning.

My excitement came off me in waves until I remembered that I didn't have anything appropriate to wear for the party. Thankfully, I was allowed to have free range of Cora and Casey's closets to find a suitable dress.

It was insane. I'd never seen anything like it.

I went through everything. I swear, there was more in their closets than in the whole mall in Breakers Flats. I spent two hours searching for something to wear and didn't even care that I could hear Colton's late-night activities in the next room. He was definitely having a good time, but no chick is *that* animated during sex. He was watching porn, or at least, I think he was. Either way, hearing him come through the wall got me so fucking hot but it was worth it. Hearing that low groan was sexy as hell but it didn't do anything for the whole stupid attraction to him thing.

Once I'd finally found a dress and returned to the safety of the pool house, I had no option but to finish myself off. I instantly cursed myself for thinking about him the whole time.

Today was a mess of people running around and I was annoyed to find that mom had given up the pool house for extra party storage. People were in and out all day long, making today perfect for exploring. With Colton out for the day and everyone else busy setting up for the party, I was free to search for every hidden bar and treasure in the main house.

It's no secret that I'm starting to make a reputation for myself in Bellevue Springs, some of it good, some of it so bad that I'm surprised people aren't coming after me with pitchforks and fires. Though, if anyone is lighting fires around here, it'll be me.

My fingers run back through my thick hair as my eyes sparkle. I feel as though I'm living a real modern-day Cinderella story, only the prince in this story is nothing but an entitled, rich turd.

My gaze sweeps down over the black dress which I borrowed from

Cora. It's absolutely stunning with a straight neckline that flows up to the thin straps which sit just off my shoulders. The fabric melts down my body, hugging my curves and making me feel incredible.

My thigh pokes out through the high slit in the floor-length gown, showing off my nude pumps which make me appear a million feet tall. I feel incredible which only serves as a reminder for how much I don't belong here.

Glancing up at the clock, I decide it's time to get a move on. I'm all for being fashionably late but there's a fine line between that, and being a rude dick.

I throw my phone down on my bed, touch up my maroon lips, and walk out the door like I'm on a catwalk.

This is going to be one of the best nights of my life. I can feel it in my bones. There's going to be all sorts of people here, celebrities, socialites, and the rich and famous. The best of the best will be here and somehow, that includes me tonight.

I walk out across the property and find people lingering around in fancy gowns, all of them laughing and having an incredible time sipping on their expensive champagne. My mood instantly begins to plummet. None of these women are wearing black gowns. All of them are dressed in white and look amazing.

I take a shaky breath, unsure of why I feel so damn nervous.

I walk through the crowds, feeling as though I have every eye on my back. They're probably wondering who I am, and the ones who already know are most likely scowling or gossiping about my misfortunes.

I try to put it to the back of my mind. I can't get inside my head like that or I'm going to ruin it for myself. If anything, these people have no clue who I am, and because my face isn't splashed over the front of some ridiculous magazine, they wouldn't give two shits about me.

I walk in through the back door and cut through the staff quarters. I get grins and adoring looks from the few members of the staff who I've come to know over the past week and naturally, there's a scowl from Harrison. He would have preferred that I stayed locked up in the pool house for the night, like Rapunzel up in her tower.

I cut through the massive kitchen and try not to get in anyone's way. There are at least ten chefs madly working at the hot stoves. Waitresses are busily filling glasses of champagne while waiters run in and out with trays of food.

I duck and dodge through them while scanning for mom. I haven't seen her since dinner last night so she still has no idea that I've been invited. I would have loved to show her my borrowed dress. She would have loved seeing me all dressed up like this, but I'm sure I'll see her at some point during the night.

I reach the back entrance to the ballroom and let out another shaky breath. Here goes nothing; my first elite party, and hopefully not my last.

The door swings wide and I step through.

It's like I'm transported into a different world, a freaking fairytale kind of world. It's enchanting.

The lights are dimmed while soft music fills the room with joy. People fill every corner while more pour through the main entrance.

Massive diamond chandeliers hang from the ceiling while the huge floor to ceiling glass doors have been opened wide to showcase the beautiful gardens.

There's a huge dance floor that's filled with loved-up couples in the most amazing outfits. Gowns don every woman, making them seem as though they've just made a stop here on their way to the Met Gala. The suits though … I've never really understood men and their suits until now. The men have brought their A-game tonight and for the first time in my life, I'm drooling over fifty-year-old men who look like they'd be fucking bosses in the boardroom and the bedroom.

I make my way around the room, taking in the black and white theme. There's not a splash of color to be seen yet somehow it just works. A waitress walks past me with a tray filled with champagne flutes, and I quickly scoop one off with a warm smile. She nods her head politely and I thank her before she scurries away. I take a mental note to learn her name later, feeling like we'll probably become good friends throughout the night.

I lift the champagne to my lips and resist pulling a face. "Holy mother of baby Jesus. What the fuck is this shit?"

This is definitely not the cheap fruity shit I'm used to drinking.

"That, my dear," comes a familiar voice from behind me as a suited arm slips underneath mine. "Is what we fancy people like to call expensive champagne."

I grin up at Milo, wondering where these people keep their Smirnoff's and Bacardi Breezers. "It tastes like expensive piss," I tell him.

"It's an acquired taste," Milo laughs and nods toward one of the waitresses who comes scurrying over to him. He plucks the champagne flute out of my hand and instantly hands it over to her. "Bring the lady something fruity," he tells her, "and keep them coming. She's not a big champagne drinker."

"Right away, sir," the waitress says, nodding and slipping away while making it seem as though she was never there in the first place.

"Well, well," I say, staring up at Milo like I'm seeing him with brand new eyes. "What happened to the Milo who wanted to be the cream in the middle of the gangbang sandwich?"

"Shut up," he says, rolling his eyes. "You need to learn the language of pompous ass if you want to fit in around here. It's kind of a requirement."

"It makes you sound like a douchebag," I laugh. "What are you doing here anyway? If I knew you were coming, I would have asked you to be my date and you could have escorted me in like I'm a big deal."

Milo scoffs under his breath. "My father would have loved that. He's been waiting for the day that I bring a girl to one of these bullshit events. In fact, come and dance with me. It'll get him off my back for at least a few months."

"At least let me get my drink first."

Milo shakes his head and takes my hand. "She'll find you," he promises. "Now come along so I can pretend to be straight for the night."

I follow along. "Is being gay that much of a big deal with your parents?" He scoffs and glances back at me as though I'm speaking another language. "In that case," I laugh, "I might even let you put your hand on my ass."

His face scrunches up but he laughs. "That's not a bad idea."

Milo gets me onto the dance floor and he instantly spins me around, collecting my body with ease and moving me across the floor. I can't help but laugh as my gown moves with my body, making me feel as though I've been taking dance lessons for years. "Wow, Mr. Rinaldi, you can take me out dancing any day," I tell him, knowing damn well that this effortless dance is coming from his expertise leading, rather than me fumbling around not knowing the difference between a foxtrot and the salsa.

"Shut up," he teases. "Any of the guys you've met at school could dance like this. They just choose not to show it because they don't have somebody to share it with. Trust me, even Colton could spin you around the floor and make you feel like a woman with his moves."

"Colton?" I laugh. "Yeah, right. He seems like the kind to trip over his own feet."

He shakes his head. "Not even close."

I look at him with an urgency to change the topic, not wanting to ruin my night talking about Colton. Milo's hand travels low on my back and I notice him glancing over my shoulder. "Your dad?"

"Yep."

I nod and press my body close to his and smother my laugh as his arm wraps tighter around my waist. "That should do it," I say, tilting my face to meet his eyes. "You never told me what you're doing here."

"Oh, right," he says as though my earlier question had completely slipped his mind. "I think I mentioned earlier in the week that my dad is on the school board with Carrington. They share a lot of business contacts. He hates parties like this but missing them would be a mistake. When his contacts are loose on alcohol and having a good time, dad always manages to close their business deals and open new ones."

"And you?" I ask, slightly impressed with his father's cunningness.

"Come on," he laughs. "Like you could keep me away from this shit. Have you seen the guys in their suits? They're like a walking wet dream. Not to mention, these parties are always off the hook. Just wait until all the old douchebags leave for their 10 pm bedtime and all that's left are the younger people. It gets fucking insane."

"No shit. Really?" I question, excited with the idea of having a wild night after all the classiness of the party disappears.

"Uh-huh. Fucking epic, bro. Just you wait."

Milo glances up once again and with a relieved sigh, he puts a little space between us and his hand raises to a much more respectable part of my lower back. "Oh, look," he says, coming to a stop. "The waitress is back with your drink."

Just as promised, a fruity drink waits for me on her tray and she happily hands it over after asking if there's anything else she can do for us. Once she hurries away to take orders from the other guests, Milo leads me off the dance floor and through the massive backdoors. As we wind our way through the beautiful gardens that Charles is so proud of, I loop my arms through his so I don't trip in the manicured grass.

"Did I mention that you look fucking delicious?" he asks.

"Me?" I scoff, gliding my eyes up and down his tall frame and taking in the suit that looks like it's been tailored perfectly to fit his body, though I'm positive that it has. "Look at you. You look like the best kind of treat. It's amazing you haven't found some guy to sneak into back rooms with and screw you until you can't walk."

Milo laughs, scooping up a glass of who the hell knows from a passing waitress. "I'm sure I would have if we weren't all hiding in our closets."

"Good point. What's the point of these parties anyway? Mom said it was some kind of tradition and as amazing as it's been so far, it just looks like some kind of excuse to show off how much money they have."

"Yeah," he says. "When it comes to Charles Carrington, it probably is, but from what I've been able to work out, Colton's mom used to be the one to host these elaborate parties. She was the big socialite around here. Everyone wanted to be her friend and attend the events that she went to. Her opinion meant everything, then when she left and took the girls, everything changed. That's when Colton turned into a douche by the way. I think deep down he wanted to go with his mom but the story is that Charles demanded he stay because he needed his son to take over the family business one day. Don't get me wrong, I'm sure Charles misses his daughters but in this world, his daughters won't offer him much except a pretty face to say good morning to, and an extra few faces to feed."

My mouth drops open. "Are you serious?"

He nods. "Welcome to my world. Where the wealthy are assholes and everyone else doesn't exist."

"No shit," I say. "I'm starting to see that."

"Yeah, anyway, so everything changed. He lost a lot of business when Laurelle left, so he kept on the traditions that she put in place and somehow that managed to help. The rumor is that he does it because he's still hung up on Laurelle and is hoping that the lifestyle might draw her back, but when it comes down to Charles, it's about business. It's always about business."

"Damn … the Carrington's are messed up."

"Understatement of the year," he grumbles as his lips pull up into a grin, just as amused by the topic as I am. He takes a sip of his drink and glances down at me. "So, the rest of your week seemed a little better."

I shrug my shoulders. "The whole week was pretty shitty," I tell him, "but there aren't any dead bodies and I didn't have to spend hard-earned cash on bail money so I guess it couldn't have been *that* bad. It definitely could have been worse."

"True," he says. "After all, you are finishing off your week at the most elite party of the month while wearing a twelve thousand dollar gown."

My mouth drops. "Twelve thousand dollars?" I shriek, struggling to keep my voice down. My gaze drops to the figure-hugging gown that's currently wrapped around my body like a second skin. Twelve thousand dollars? Holy fuck. The only time I've ever seen that kind of money was when I went on a job with Nic and it was either pay up or die.

"Geez," Milo laughs, discreetly looking around to make sure no one could overhear us. "Way to make it obvious that you're not from around here."

I roll my eyes. "Look at me, Milo. I'm not platinum blonde with fake boobs and a nose job. I have split ends and did my own freaking manicure, I think it's pretty damn clear that I'm not from around here."

"Good point," he says as we finish the loop through the gardens. "Let's head back up. You need another drink, and I'm starving."

My eyes drop to my glass to find it empty and my brows shoot up. How the hell did that happen? I hardly even remember sipping on it. Though for that to have happened, I must have liked it.

We return to the party a moment later and hardly get through the door before the waitress Milo had tasked to 'keep them coming' is there with a new drink to replace the old. I gingerly take it from her, feeling like some sort of princess. No one has ever gone out of their way for me like that. Is this really how the wealthy live their lives?

I've never been so jealous in my life. There's such a contrast from the way I've been brought up to how things are in this world. Every little thing is done differently. Just getting breakfast in the morning is different. I don't think I've had to make my own bed once since being here.

Milo leads me across the massive room, dodging all the people while being careful not to step on anyone's gown. He brings me to a stop in front of a long table that spans the whole length of the big room. Every little section of the table is piled high with food, all of which I wouldn't be able to name to save my life.

"Here," Milo says, handing me a plate with an excited gleam in his eyes. "Load it up. I have a feeling it's going to be a big night and you're going to need your energy."

Well, who am I to say no?

CHAPTER 13

My stomach aches with all the food I've eaten, and the thought of standing up from this table and having people assuming it's a baby bump protruding from my stomach is one of the scariest things I've ever felt. I don't know why though. I've faced down all sorts of shit. Having a food baby shouldn't be something that terrifies me but with all these elitist pigs at this party, one bad rumor could do a lot of damage.

I throw back what's left of my fifth fruity drink as Milo laughs at the way his father just left the table. He'd come over to introduce himself to Milo's special friend then Milo explained that I was Charles' niece from out of town, the same girl he'd heard all those stories about involving Coach Sylvester and Dean Simmons.

Realizing that I'm the only girl at school surrounded by five hundred boys, Milo's father grinned proudly, clapped his son on the back, and chuffed about the Rinaldi DNA being the best. After all, out of all those boys, it was his son I've chosen to spend my time with.

"Geez," I grin, pushing back from my chair and standing up, deciding that showing off my food bump is probably a better option than pissing myself in this gown. "He thinks you're some kind of stud."

"I am a fucking stud, babe" he laughs, digging a hand into his suit jacket that hangs on the back of his seat and producing four condoms. "He just slipped these in my pocket and reminded me that my grandmother is coming to town next week."

My brows furrow. "What's that supposed to mean?"

"He wants me to ask for the family ring. Apparently, the fact that you're part of the Carrington line and a woman, means you're suitable marriage material."

"The fuck?" I laugh. "Damn, he's got his wires crossed. He's going to be pissed when he realizes that I'm a nobody from Breakers Flats."

"I know, but it'll be worth it to see his face."

"Promise that I'll get to be there when he finds out?"

"Wouldn't have it any other way, wifey."

I roll my eyes knowing that's going to stick so I might as well go along with it. "Alright, hubby. I gotta pee," I tell him, indicating down to my empty glass. "If the pretty girl with the magic fruity drinks comes past, can you get me another?"

"Sure thing."

With that, I start scrambling. Why is it that the second you stand up after drinking you always feel like an absolute mess? The room is spinning a little and I swear, if I throw up on Cora's dress I'm going to be the joke of the town, considering I'm not already occupying that position.

I find mom across the room and she smiles brightly. She's been watching me all night with that proud momma bear look on her face. You know, after she nearly dragged my ass out of here assuming I'd snuck in and stolen a dress. She quickly realized that tonight might be the only time I'll ever get to play Cinderella, and she left me alone. But I'm not fooled, she's been keeping a sharp eye on me.

I somehow make it to the bathroom and find myself looking around in awe. Out of the millions of bathrooms in the Carrington mansion, this is one of the many I've never wandered into. It's flawless, absolutely stunning. I never really understood why people put so much money and effort into making luxurious bathrooms. I mean, do they realize that people use them for taking a shit? I have to admit though, it's kind of nice to have the heated toilet seat. Well, I'm hoping it's a heated toilet seat and not warmed by someone else's ass.

I hold back a gag as I finish my business and quickly wash my hands so I can get back to the party. I'm seriously having an incredible night. Milo has introduced me to a few of the girls from Bellevue Springs Private. Though he was quick to realize that I don't mix well with chicks. He also introduced me to some of Bellevue Springs' most eligible bachelors who don't strut around with poles up their asses, then he introduced me to the very opposite. The people he thinks I should stay away from are most likely the people I'd get along with; the wild ones, the ones who know how to hook me up, and the ones who wouldn't judge me if I got fucked up and woke up in a strange hotel room.

I walk out of the bathroom and as I go, I pass one of those girls with a tray of champagne flutes. Clearly having learned nothing from my mistakes, I bring the glass to my lips and take a nice long drink.

Fuck.

Yep, it still tastes like piss, though now that my mind is a little foggy with all the fruity yumminess I've been drinking, it's a little more tolerable. So because I like to punish myself, I throw back the rest of the glass and try not to choke on it. I'm a smart bitch like that.

I set the empty glass down on the edge of a stone statue in passing as I search for my new husband among the crowd. I wonder how many husbands I'm going to have before I get kicked out of Bellevue Springs.

"Yo, Help."

Chills run down my spine as I turn back to find my original Bellevue Springs husband staring at me, only it's not just Spencer, it's all four of them.

The second they get my full attention, eyes begin scanning up and down my body and I want nothing more than to smack the hungry expressions off each of their faces. This honey pot is not for sale, especially to douche canoes like this.

I can't help but look over them, and by 'them' what I really mean is

Colton. He looks incredible, he's practically oozing power and it speaks right to my soul. How can one person have such an effect over another without even murmuring a single word?

I wonder what would happen if I licked him right now? Nah, he probably wouldn't like that.

One part of me wants to high-five the guy and tell him to go get it while the other part wants to push every single one of the buttons on his expensive suit and see just how far I can push him.

His suit sits over his body just perfectly and it makes me so damn hungry. He looks sharp, demanding, and completely in control. That is until I notice the tiny little CC cufflinks at his wrist and realize that on top of looking like a fucking beast, he also looks like an arrogant asshat.

The other three look like children playing dress-up with Daddy's money while Colton Carrington looks like the fucker you don't want to be sitting across from in a boardroom meeting. Despite the smile across his handsome face, he looks dangerous. He fucking owns it and damn, it's the most attractive thing I've ever seen.

Colton oozes power and to me, nothing could be sexier.

Realizing I'm probably drooling, I pull on my game face and straighten my shoulders before his hazel eyes paralyze me. "What do you want?" I demand, my attitude coming out fast and thick as I stare down Spencer with a lethal glare.

His arm raises, holding out an empty tumbler to me and on instinct, I take it. "Scotch neat and make it quick."

I pull back, in confusion. "Excuse me?" I question as a slight smirk plays on Colton's lips.

Spencer stares as though I'm some kind of daft moron. "I don't make a habit of repeating myself," he says, dragging his gaze away from mine and rolling his eyes as he looks across at Colton. "I thought your dad only hired the best. His standards are slipping."

Hired? The fuck? Does this fucker think I'm working at this party?

My gaze narrows on him but before I get a word out, Jude thrusts his empty glass into my other hand, and I find myself flinching from his closeness. "I'll take a whiskey sour but go easy on the lemon."

Charlie grins, stepping into me and lowering his voice to a seductive whisper. "I'll just take whatever you've got on offer," he murmurs, as my eyes flick around the party to notice that the other waitresses are also in black dresses with a similar cut across the chest. Their dresses are all cocktail length with thick straps over their shoulders. Honestly, while they look great, their dresses have nothing on the gown that's currently hugging my body.

I guess on some level it makes sense for someone to mistake me as 'the help' but these four? No. They're just being pricks. They know damn well that I'm not working at this party.

Deciding to play their little game, I swivel my gaze to Colton. "And for you Mr. Carrington?" I question, adjusting the empty tumblers in my hands and staring heavily into his eyes, daring him to try me.

He doesn't respond, just stares with the challenge bright in his eyes. They narrow and I watch as his chin raises. I don't doubt he's weighing his options. The corner of his lip lifts and just like that, it's game time.

Excitement bubbles within me.

"Scotch neat," he murmurs in that low, domineering tone that makes my core rattle with desperation.

I grin and just as I go to leave, Jude raises his ugly head. "What the fuck are you waiting for, help? Get out of here and make it fast. You're not getting paid to waste my fucking time."

I scoff under my breath and walk straight through the center of them, barging my way between Jude and Colton's shoulders, regretting it a second later when I remember that I've drunk way too many of those magical fruity drinks to be making movements like that.

As I finally pass them, I hear Jude's disgusted scoff behind me. "Jesus fucking Christ. That chick is such a bitch. What does she think she's doing hanging around a party like this? Doesn't she realize she's the punchline in everyone's joke tonight."

His words sail right through to my soul and tear me limb from limb. It fucking aches yet somehow I keep myself moving. I'm a fucking joke. He's right. I'm the white trash playing dress up in a world I don't belong in.

Embarrassment sweeps through me. All night I've been shamelessly drinking and laughing with Milo. He's had his hand on my ass on the dancefloor, there have been drinks delivered one by one to our table with a stack of food higher than the ceiling and for a moment, I allowed myself to believe that I was just as good as the other fuckers in the room.

Charlie's voice comes murmured behind me. "Dude, she's going to spit in your fucking drink."

There's a sharp scoff and I hear the familiar tone of Colton's voice but his words are muffled by the music.

I keep myself moving while feeling like an absolute piece of shit. I bet all these rich party goers have been laughing behind my back all night. Here I was, foolish enough to assume the music was tonight's entertainment. They've probably had bets on when the trash was going to embarrass herself or cause a scene.

Well, I'll fucking show them.

I barge my way through to the kitchen and drop the glass tumblers down into the sink, not giving a shit about the people madly scrambling around me, trying to make the night go off without any issues.

I keep walking around to the bar and grab a tray before slamming four clean tumblers down. I can't even remember what they ordered, but I really couldn't give a shit. I mean, what the fuck is the difference between neat and sour, and what the fuck was Jude saying about lemon? It doesn't matter to me.

I grab the closest bottle which is a bourbon and freely pour into each of the glasses. No measuring, no fancy pour just straight from the bottle into the glass which was probably made of diamonds mined by child slaves. I give each tumbler an extra dollop of fuck you before slamming the bourbon down and scooping up the tray the same way the waitresses have been all night. After all, if I want to look the part, I have to play the part.

I walk back out to the party which suddenly doesn't seem so appealing. I spy Milo sitting at our table, looking around and probably wondering where his fake date has gone. I duck and dodge around the pretentious assholes who reach for the glasses on my tray.

As if feeling me coming, Colton looks back over his shoulder. His eyes narrow on me as he takes in the tray sitting firmly in my hand. He turns toward me and on cue, the other three stooges do too. "Took fucking long enough," Jude mutters beneath his breath.

I smile wide, ignoring the way they make me feel like the trash they always claim me to be, just like a good little waitress should.

I reach for a glass, knowing I'm going to have to make this quick.

"I tried to tell you," I say, raising my chin as my fingers curl around the tumbler. "I am not the fucking help."

My hand shoots out and the bourbon hits Jude right in the center of his douchey looking suit. A loud gasp comes sailing from his mouth but before he even has a moment to comprehend what the fuck is happening, the glass is slammed back down on the tray and replaced with another that's aimed for Spencer's chest.

"I am not fucking trash," I demand, slamming the second glass down and grabbing the third. It goes sailing through the air toward Charlie's chest. "And I'm not some fucking whore who's going to peel off my panties and let you fuck me over."

"The fuck are you doing?" Colton demands as Charlie is drenched in liquor.

Last but not least.

My glare snaps to their leader as my fingers curl around the fourth glass, more than ready to douse him in bourbon. "And as for you, you fucking pretentious asshole, you can suck my motherfucking, big ass dick."

The fourth shot of bourbon goes sailing through the air but after his three friends had already been covered in bourbon, he's quick enough to dodge out of the way and avoid his fancy suit being ruined. Unfortunately for them, Spencer and Charlie are hit with a second dose instead.

"You're going to pay for that," Spencer roars, barging past his friends, looking like he's more than ready to tear me apart, and not in the good way.

I give them a beaming smile. "Here's the fucking drinks you ordered," I tell them before slamming the tray of tumblers into Spencer's unsuspecting chest and spinning on my heels.

Holy fuck. What did I just do?

I race away as the familiar sound of shattering glass echoes through the ballroom behind me. Gasps of outrage are heard—Jude's being the loudest—and I expect a firm hand to wrap around my elbow and pull me back, but when nothing comes I pick up my pace and run out of here.

Fuck the party, fuck this stupid gown, and fuck them. Who are they to bring me down? Who are they to make me feel worthless? I'm a fucking Goddess. I may not have some fancy title or have a daddy with a swelling bank account, but I know what it's like to hustle. I know what it feels like to have to work for everything you've got, and these guys, they wouldn't recognize that shit if it bit them on their fucking entitled asses.

I storm out through the back doors of the ballroom and past the stupid gardens that you'd never see in Breakers Flats.

I want to go home. I'm over this bullshit. It's been a struggle since the second we moved in here. The boys tried to warn me that we didn't belong but I went ahead anyway, hoping for the best of a shitty situation. I should have just taken Nic up on his offer. He would have looked after us. He would have made sure we were alright. We just had to go and insist that we could take care of ourselves. Well, fuck that. I don't want to be some stupid idiot self-sufficient bitch anymore. I just want the world to open up at my feet and swallow me whole. I'm over this bullshit.

I cut around the back of the property, getting pissier by the second with how damn far the pool house is from the party. It was probably built for the sole purpose to keep the help as far away from them as possible. They wouldn't want their guests knowing they have trash living on the property.

Keeping my feet moving, I curse myself for deciding to wear these ridiculous shoes. They're absolutely beautiful but my feet hurt and I can't run nearly as fast as I want to. I turn the corner to walk around the side of the pool house and come to a startling stop when I find Charles Carrington with his dick in his hand and a blonde with her mouth full of it.

What the fuck?

My eyes bug out of my head and I'm like stone for the shortest second. So much for the theory of Charles being hung up on his ex-wife because it looks a little more like he's hung up on the chick with the fake titties, botox, and cock-sucking lips.

Charles leans back against the wall of the pool house, his eyes closed and euphoria over his face.

I hold back vomit. The dude is kind of hot for an old guy but still, that's not something I ever wanted to see. His hand is in the back of her hair, messing it up as he grabs chunks of her platinum extensions and forces her back and forth.

Fucking gross.

The sounds of her gags have me slipping back into the shadows and rushing around the other side of the pool house to the front door. The second I barge my way through it, I slam the door with everything I have, desperately needing some sort of outlet for my anger. Only as the door closes, it flies back open with a very pissed off momma bear scowling at me.

Mom hardly gets a word in before Harrison is there and all hell breaks loose.

He yells at Mom about keeping her daughter in line, Mom yells at me about keeping myself in check, and I yell at Harrison for having the audacity to come into this space that is ours and yell at my mother.

It's a whole clusterfuck but after a few minutes of back and forth bullshit, Mom and Harrison realize there's a party going on without them and scramble away, though Mom doesn't leave without a promise that this isn't over.

I drop down onto the couch while needing something … anything to help the anger fade from within my chest. I'd give anything to go back into that party and make them pay all over again. Hell, if I could just get my hands on them.

I've never been one for using a gun but knowing it's safely tucked into the back of my underwear drawer makes it incredibly appealing. I could just scare Jude with it a little.

The door opens and I glare at the wall "Fuck off," I yell over the couch.

"Well, that's no way to talk to the guy who could make it all go away."

My eyes bug out again and I throw myself off the couch and run into Nic's open arms. "What are you doing here?" I demand, crushing my face into his solid chest and hating the way my messed up emotions have tears streaming from my eyes.

"Milo called."

I let out a soft groan. "Of course he did."

"I was close by so … you know."

I nod my head against his chest, breathing him in and hoping his presence is enough to make the anger fade, but it doesn't work the way it has a million times before. I glance up. "You were close by?" I ask, raising a brow and knowing that means he had gang-related business around here but the question is what? What kind of people in Bellevue Springs would have business with a Black Widow?

Nic shakes his head. "You know, I really don't understand why you keep asking. I've never told you before, so why the hell would I start now?"

"Good point," I murmur, dropping my gaze.

"Do you need me to go and fuck up some rich boys?"

I let out a sigh. While the idea is appealing, they've already fucked up Jude and it didn't help to reel him in. Our usual tactics don't work with these people. They don't get intimidated the same way people back home do because they have nothing to lose. They will always have money at their back and that speaks so much louder than anything else.

Nic shuffles around and motions to a bag on his back. "Come on," he says with a familiar sparkle in his eyes that has excitement shooting through me. "I've got just the thing that would cheer you up."

With that, Nic takes my hand and pulls me straight back out the open door. He leads me around the back of the property and as we go, I can't help but notice Colton Carrington slipping out of the party and cutting though the gardens the same way I had gone.

I watch him as Nic pulls me along. Judging by the direction that Colton is walking, he's aiming for the pool house, but why? To make things worse? To check on me? To make sure I've been thoroughly punished? Who the fuck knows? I've come to learn that where Colton Carrington is concerned, it could mean absolutely anything.

As if sensing my gaze on him, his eyes snap up and zone in on mine.

I narrow my eyes as he stops in his tracks.

He watches, taking me in and scanning his heavy gaze over Nic's hand in mine and for a moment, I'd dare say he looked … jealous, but that can't be right. What the hell does he have to be jealous of?

Nic pulls on my hand and we fall behind the back portion of the mansion and as we do, Colton Carrington slips from my mind. I guess it's right what they say; out of sight, out of mind.

Nic walks a little further before coming to a stop and dropping the bag at my feet as he beams up at the back wall of the house. "Here," he says, opening his arms wide and grinning up at the wall. "A blank canvas."

My brows furrow but as I bend down and peer inside the bag, a wide grin cuts across my face.

Hell to the mother fucking yes.

CHAPTER 14

"G et up," a loud, booming voice demands just moments before something lands heavily on my stomach.

My eyes fly open to find my bag thrown across my bed and Colton Carrington staring down at me, very noticeably taking in the way my tank is glued to my body like a second skin and all twisted around from a night of restless sleep. "Get the hell out of my room, dickhead. You know, with how often you were bugging me, people will assume that you have a sick obsession with the help. They have people committed for that kind of shit."

"You fucking wish," he scowls. "Now get the fuck up. You're

coming with me."

"The hell I am," I demand, recalling what I did with Nic last night. I mean, if they're about to kick me out of here then I'm at least going to go out in style. I'll get up when I'm good and ready. Besides, I'll do anything to avoid facing my mother this morning. After all the bullshit of last night, I'm sure she's about to disown me and throw me out for the Black Widows to keep.

"Three fucking seconds or we leave without you."

"Leave?" I grunt, pushing up onto my elbows to see him better.

"Do I have to repeat everything I say when it comes to you? Are you fucking deaf? Get your bitch ass out of bed, grab your shit, and meet me out by the Veneno."

I narrow my eyes. It seems someone is still a little pissed about last night's shenanigans, but considering he hasn't mentioned the shenanigan with Nic, maybe he doesn't know. I'm not going to lie, my interest has been piqued and I'm desperate to know where the fuck he thinks he's about to take me, but then, my attitude shines brighter than any interest I might have. "And I thought I told you to fuck off. Hmm, funny. Maybe you're deaf too."

"Laying on the sarcasm a little thick, don't you think?"

I glare at the shithead. "But your personality gives me so much to work with. It'd be a shame to be wasteful."

He grabs my blanket and tears it off my bed, letting the cool morning air brush against my skin. I let out a shriek and my body instinctively curls in on itself. "What the fuck is your problem?" I demand, throwing myself to my feet and storming up to him, glaring into his damn gorgeous hazel eyes.

Colton's jaw clenches and it takes me a moment to realize that after too long refusing to get out of the gown last night, I fell asleep in a thin tank and panties. "I asked you nicely. We're going on a trip. You're either coming or you're not. I couldn't fucking give a shit."

"Trip?" I grunt. "What fucking trip?"

He turns and heads for the door. "You're down to two seconds, Jade."

I hate him. I hate him, I hate him.

Rage burns through me and I ball my hands into fists. He's so damn infuriating. "I was always taught to think before I act," I yell after him. "So, rest assured that when I beat the living shit out of you, I've thought about it and am confident with my decision."

I hear an irritated scoff before the sound of the pool house door slams closed.

Fuck. I really do hate him. I get it, I'm not for everybody. It takes a specific breed of man to be able to put up with my flavor of bullshit but there's a common decency us humans are expected to have around one another and he simply doesn't have it.

I go to reach for my blanket and as I turn to walk back to my bed, I find myself stopping.

A trip.

What kind of trip and why the hell does he want me to come along? This doesn't make sense. I cast my gaze out the window of the pool house to find the morning sun glistening off the pool, sparkling like New Year's Eve. It's a beautiful day. On days like this, people usually go to the beach, but rich people, they always step it up and it has my curiosity bursting at the seams.

Fuck, why am I so intrigued by this?

Before I even know what's happening, my bag is packed with my bikini and my high waisted shorts are firmly pulled into place. I stand in the bathroom mirror, run my fingers through my tangled hair, and brush my teeth.

What am I doing? I feel like I'm about to set myself up for torture yet I can't find the strength to stop. This is either going to be some ridiculous attempt at an apology and he's taking pity on me after my outburst last night or I'm walking into a trap, and where Colton is concerned, I'm going to go ahead and assume this is a trap.

I don't know, maybe I'm a glutton for punishment but one minute I'm contemplating what a bad idea this is going to be and the next thing I know, I'm dropping down into the sleek Veneno and watching out the window as Colton peels out of the driveway.

He drives for roughly half an hour and despite the music playing throughout the car, I've never heard silence so loud. The whole way to wherever we're going, I struggle with the need to either sucker punch him or climb on top of him and ride him like a cowgirl. There's something about the way a man drives a car, but the way Colton drives his Veneno … fuck. I'm screwed. It's the most attractive thing I've ever seen and it has my thighs clenching like a needy whore.

Five minutes later, Colton pulls into the marina, and my mouth drops.

Holy mother of sweet baby Jesus. Someone needs to fuck me in the ass and slap a little life back into me. This shit couldn't be real.

I stare out at the water where a long jetty or dock or whatever the fuck it's called stretches out into the water with massive boats on either side. I've never seen anything like it, not even in the movies. These boats are bigger than my old house. Hell, they're probably bigger than my old school.

This is the ultimate 'welcome to the billionaire's club.'

As I look along the water, I find a few jetty-dock things and see that each of them have at least twenty of these massive boats anchored at them. The center dock is the longest and is the one with the biggest boat in the ocean. Even without the obnoxious 'Carrington' written across the back, it's clear that's where we're heading. I doubt Charles Carrington is the type of guy to allow some other fucker to outshine one of his prized possessions. When it comes to him, he has to have the biggest house, the biggest boat, the biggest bank account. He's just that kind of guy.

Colton brings his Veneno to a stop right in front of the dock like some kind of asshole and I'm not surprised when a valet rushes in, desperate to adhere to his every wish and desire.

Colton leaves the car running and gets out so I grab my bag and follow suit, hurrying along as he rushes down the marina. I can't help but glance back as the valet takes off with the Veneno. A rush of jealousy fires through me. I'd give my right nut to drive that car, you know if I had a right nut. Maybe my right ovary then.

Colton reaches the end of the line and looks up at the massive boat with pride. I don't miss the way his eyes scan over the Carrington name on the back and wonder if maybe this thing is new. Music plays inside and my brows furrow. I hadn't seen any other cars here but then, why would I? The valet would have dealt with that. Either way, Colton and I are not alone. It gives me peace of mind that he isn't bringing me out here to kill and dump my body in the middle of the ocean.

He starts making his way up the stairs that lead into the boat and I follow, slightly panicked as I've never been on a boat before. I don't know if I can trust it, but then, if I'm going to try out this whole boating thing, it's probably best to try it in one like this rather than some piece of shit tin boat with rust and bullet holes like the one that's been stored in Kairo's backyard.

I get to the top and hardly have a chance to look around before Colton turns his dark stare on me. "The staff kitchen is downstairs. I'm sure you can make yourself comfortable down there."

I raise a brow. "Excuse me?" I demand with an amused scoff.

"I could hardly get staff on such short notice so unlucky for us, we're stuck with you for the day."

A piercing screech comes from across the boat. "Colton," some skank calls out. "You're here."

Colton looks back over his shoulder and I peer around him to see a group of at least ten girls in bikinis surrounded by guys that I recognize from school. "Give me a minute, babe," he says before glancing up and nodding to some guy in a captain's outfit.

Colton looks back at me. "First round of drinks served in ten minutes, then again every half hour but remain on the deck in case someone needs an extra refill. Once we're anchored, food will be brought out and hell, maybe after that, I might even let you enjoy yourself."

"Oh, fuck no."

I spin around and go to walk my ass back down the stairs only the boat starts pulling out. "Too fucking late, Jade," Colton says in my ear. "Get your ass down to the kitchen and make it quick. The clock is ticking."

I spin around and step into him, forcing him back a step. "Fuck you, Carrington. This is how it's going to go. I'm going to stay down one end of the boat while you fuck around on the other. You're going to stay out of my way and you're going to hope to whatever God you believe in that I decide to stay out of yours. I'm not your little maid bitch you can boss around. I'm not fucking employed by you nor will I ever be." I give him a sugary sweet smile. "Now, thanks for the invitation to your lame boat party, I'm sure I'm going to have a great time. Oh, and for the record, I'll take a vodka sunrise."

I barge past him deeper onto the boat and don't even bother looking around. I should have fucking known this was a bullshit game to try and humiliate me, but after the past week's worth of humiliation, it seems to be sliding off me like water off a duck's back. I guess there's only so much Colton Carrington can do to me, or maybe I've just lowered my expectations of the guy.

"Fucking bullshit, man," I hear Jude snap from the back deck. I look back over my shoulder to find Jude glaring at Colton with his arm outstretched, indicating to me. "Why did you bring that fucking bitch?"

Great. Now I have to spend my day with that douche too? Fucking perfect. And to think I could have been curled up in bed all day watching Netflix or chilling with my boys.

"Had no choice," Colton snaps back at him. "Shut the fuck up and have a drink."

Jude's eyes slice to mine and there's a dangerous warning, but what does it matter? It's not like I'll be going up there to spend my day with him.

I turn back and start heading down the stairs that lead into the main living area of the boat and find Charlie and Spencer. Charlie's face lights with excitement while Spencer scowls. He clearly isn't fond of me the way his friend is, but at least he doesn't look like he's about to tear me apart the way Jude did.

"Well, well," Charlie beams. "If I knew you were coming along, I wouldn't have brought Sara."

"You're kidding right?" I laugh, looking up at him. "You'll have better luck with Sara."

He laughs before jogging over and catching up with me. "I don't hold last night against you," he says. "It's nothing a dry cleaner can't deal with."

I groan to myself. "Oh, great, I'm so glad for you."

"It was an honest mistake," he adds, not getting the hint that I'd rather be left alone. "You know, your dress and all. It kinda looked like the waitresses and you know how us guys are with that kind of shit."

I turn on him, making him pull himself up. "You're just as bad as they are, Charlie," I say with a disappointed sigh. "Only, you might be worse because you're fake about it. Choose your side. Either be a dick with them or be chill, but I'm sick of this bullshit in-between crap you keep doing. Pick a fucking side and stay on it because right now, you're as fake as shit. At least the other guys are real with me."

Charlie's face falls and with that, I keep walking, pleased to find I don't have someone following along. I walk into one of the many bedrooms and look around. This is fucking insane. I hate how impressed I am by the Carringtons. The things they can afford to have never ceases to amaze me. I couldn't imagine a life where mom and I could ever be able to live like this.

I drop my bag down onto the bed and sit on the edge, needing a moment to come to terms with how shitty my day is going to be. I can't believe I let Colton play me like that, but he's fucking insane if he thinks he has even the slightest chance of getting me to play boat bitch all day to his entitled friends. I can't help but wonder what he meant with that comment he just threw at Jude.

'Had no choice.'

Why the hell wouldn't he have a choice? Everyone has a choice. Either storm into the pool house and wake me up or don't. It's as simple as that.

I let out a heavy sigh and decide that if I'm going to be stuck on a luxurious boat all day that I should make the best of it. Bad company aside, who knows when I could get an opportunity like this again.

I get up off the bed and turn around to start rifling through my bag. Just as I feel my bikini on my fingers, a hand curls around my neck. I suck in a gasp but within a moment, I'm thrown up against the hard wall with Jude bearing down on me.

"You think you can just get away with your bullshit and not be punished?" he roars, his breath smelling strongly of alcohol despite it only being eleven in the morning.

I suck in a breath as his hand tightens and begins restricting my oxygen. "You're a piece of shit. Get off me."

"You're not going to get away with this," he growls low getting right in my face so I can see the yellowing remains of the two black eyes Nic and the boys had happily given him earlier in the week. "You come into my world and start fucking shit up, well guess what? There are fucking consequences. You're a fucking nobody. If you went missing, would anyone even notice? I could do whatever the fuck I wanted to you out here and even if you squealed to the cops, I'd get away with it because that's just the way things are around here."

I try to stay calm, the same way Nic had taught me when faced with this situation. Though, there are a few other things Nic taught me about defending myself against dickheads like this.

I may be a glutton for punishment, but I learn from my mistakes and around here, I'll never go into any situation unprepared.

My hand curls around the cool metal at the back of my high waisted shorts. I tear the gun out and without hesitation, I hold it against his chin and get the biggest thrill out of the way his eyes bug out of his head and he becomes motionless.

His hand loosens on my throat and I lower my voice, mostly to sound somewhat intimidating but I'm pretty damn sure it's got a little to do with the fact that if I was to speak up, my voice would shake. "I told you to get your fucking hands off me," I remind him, pressing the gun harder against his chin.

Jude's hands drop and he remains silent, knowing damn well that I have the power. "You're wrong," I tell him, pressing up into him and letting my breath rush across his skin. "I have more people than you can count who would miss me and I can assure you, every last one of them would come looking." I tap my fingers against the bandage supporting his bad arm. "But I think you know that. Tell me, how many would come looking for you? How many of your boys would actually care?"

"What the fuck is going on in here?" Colton's low demanding voice questions from the doorway.

"We were just having a little chat, weren't we, Jude? Clearing the air and all that."

I feel his hard swallow against the tip of the gun and grin wickedly. Maybe it'll do me a little good if these guys knew just how fucked up I could get. Jude gives me a sharp nod and I wink before pulling back and watching as he all but races from the room. "Fucking bitch," he spits before walking out leaving me with Colton, studying me closer than ever before.

"What did he want?"

"What does it matter to you?"

Colton steps into the room, seeming to not care about the gun sitting heavily in my hand, almost as though he knows I'd never use it on him. "It fucking matters."

I watch him for a silent moment, both of us just staring and locked in each other's glare until I finally give in. "The loser was just trying to swing his dick around. He was trying to intimidate me and was in the middle of telling me just how easy it would be to get rid of me."

Colton lets out a heavy breath before nodding and stepping back. His eyes remain for a moment longer before he turns and stalks out of the room, leaving me gasping for breath.

I have to give myself a moment. I don't know what it is about that guy that makes such simple things so hard.

Once I've finally got myself under control, I get dressed and head up to the deck, determined not to let my day go to waste. Just as I had said to Colton, he stays at his end of the boat and I stay at mine and for some reason unknown to me, that's exactly what happens.

I sit at the bow of the boat feeling the wind slapping against my face and my hair blowing out behind me, my legs stretched out in the sun with my bag right beside me. After all, my gun can hardly be concealed in a bikini.

After ten minutes, the fight leaves me and I'm finally able to relax. Some random girl I've never met comes and sits with me for a while and offers me a drink and before I know it, all the girls are sunbaking on the front of the deck as the boat glides across the water like a skater on ice.

Luckily for me, the guys remain at the back of the boat, fucking around and doing what boys do. The anchor is dropped and suddenly it's a party in the middle of the ocean. The music booms through the open sea and bottles of spirits get passed around like a joint.

Needing to pee, I get up and make my way around the boat to find

Colton lounged back on a couch with a girl dancing over him. Her bikini top is nowhere to be found and up until I walked around here, she had his full attention.

His eyes snap to mine and as I walk across the back of the boat to the stairs, that's exactly where they stay. As the girl dances on him, he watches me and it's as though he's waiting for some kind of reaction.

He's right to wait too. He knows it bothers me yet neither of us can understand why. For some damn reason, he has my attention and I have his but I'm sure as hell not about to break. Without taking my eyes from his, I find my way to the stairs and start walking down.

I'll be damned if Colton Carrington ever gets the best of me again.

CHAPTER 15

olton's Veneno comes to a stop in the massive garage and I gawk as I glance around. I've never been in here before but it's just as I was hoping. It's piled high with collector cars. It's like a fucking showroom in here. Absolutely insane.

Dad would be in heaven, though he already is.

I get out of the car and seeing as though there's no other door out of his garage, I have no choice but to cut through the house to get out to the pool house and unfortunately for me, that probably means running into Harrison. I didn't see him this morning but I'd be smart to assume that he's still not moved past my little tantrum last night.

Mom though, I don't know how she's going to feel about this.

She's not one to hold a grudge and had said her peice last night, but this is a different world and we have more at stake now. I promised her that I'd be on my best behavior and in one easy go, I snapped that promise like a twig. Besides, while she'll never admit that she likes her job as a housekeeper for some rich guys, I know she really loves it here. She feels important in her role, needed, and appreciated. It's not a feeling that comes around often in Breakers Flats.

I follow Colton out of the garage and just like everywhere else we've gone today, it's done in absolute silence. "Where the hell have you been?" Charles roars the second we step out of the foyer, making me wonder if he'd been sitting here waiting all day when in reality he probably just had Harrison notify him when the Veneno came through the front gates.

Colton spins around and I stand in the opening of the foyer as awkwardly as possible. "Took the boat out," Colton says factually.

Charles raises a brow and a vein appears at his temple, the only sign that he's about to blow. "You did what?" he roars. "You knew what today was. Do you have any idea how incompetent you made yourself and this family look?"

Colton scoffs. "Fuck this family and your goddamn board. I don't want to take over your stupid business and I couldn't give a rat's ass about your fucked up business meetings. Leave me the fuck out of them."

Charles looks taken back but it's clear this isn't a new argument. "When I schedule you a meeting with the board, I expect you to be there. I don't care what you want in life. You will take over the business and you'll do it with a fucking smile on your face."

I gape at the man who, up until now, has always seemed so incredibly nice. He's always been hospitable, caring, and welcoming, but right now, I'm seeing a completely different person. It's as though the Charles I met during the week, the one who helped me with the stupid sexist school doesn't even exist. Was it all an act? Because this man right here, this is the real Charles Carrington, the arrogant rich asshole I was expecting him to be all along. So why the act? Why try and get mom and me on board with the Mr. Wonderful routine?

Colton scoffs and goes to walk away but when Charles steps toward him, Colton flinches and my back straightens. What the fuck was that about?

As if remembering that he's bigger than Charles, Colton raises his chin and narrows his eyes. "Find someone else to take over your precious business."

"Keep talking like that and you'll be finding some other rich bastard to fund your luxurious lifestyle."

Colton narrows his eyes at his father but it doesn't last long as Charles' rage turns on me. "Is this your doing?"

"My doing?" I question, throwing my hands up in innocence.

"Your little outing with my son," he demands, stepping toward me. "Don't think I didn't notice your scandalous behavior at last night's event. Dancing with that Rinaldi boy all night and then trying to make a fool of my son by pouring drinks all over him and causing a scene. Don't act like I don't know about those boys you have coming and going from the pool house all the time."

"I…"

"ANSWER ME?" he roars.

Colton steps in front of me, stealing his father's attention and saving me from his scrutiny. "She had nothing to do with it. I took her because I knew you were going to be like this."

All I can do is gape at him as the fear runs down my spine. Who the fuck is this man? Who the fuck are both of them? But more importantly, did Colton just protect me from his father? I don't understand it. Ever since I've gotten here he's tried to intimidate me, bully me, threaten some bullshit war, but when it comes down to it, he does this? If anything, he should be throwing me to the wolves, but one thing is for sure, Colton's 'had no choice,' comment from earlier is starting to make sense.

"You had no right," Charles demands.

"No right?" Colton scoffs. "No right to do what? Take the girl on the boat? She's not your property, father."

"Isn't she?" he asks, his eyes flicking over his son's shoulder to take me in. "She lives in my home rent-free, I pay for her schooling, she eats my food. It certainly sounds like she's my property."

"The fuck?" I demand, going to step around Colton. I'm no one's property. I don't care what the circumstances are, I don't care how fucked up things are no one claims me as their own. Only I get to do that.

Colton's strong arm snaps out and slams against my chest, leaving me breathless. I don't get another step before he forces me back behind him once again, promptly shutting me up. "It's that kind of bullshit you used to say to mom and the girls that made them leave. You're a fucking arrogant asshole, dad, and you're running everyone out of your life. You think the people who have stayed are here because they like you?"

Charles steps into Colton and the gun in my bag starts feeling incredibly heavy. "You watch your tone, boy."

"What are you going to do about it? Hit me? I dare you. You know you haven't been able to land one on me for years."

Charles' eyes flare with the challenge but he's not stupid, he knows Colton is right and from the look of it, it seems like that theory has been tried and tested. He pokes a finger hard into Colton's chest. "This isn't over," he demands. "I'll be rescheduling that meeting and you'll be showing up with a fucking smile on your face even if I have to get you there myself."

The threat sits heavy in the air as Charles walks away and I'm left standing behind Colton's wide frame staring after him in shock.

"What the fuck just happened?"

Colton looks back at me, his eyes narrowed but not glaring like he usually does, they just look … deflated.

He lets out a breath and without another word, starts walking away. I stare after him. Like father like son, I guess, only that's not right. Colton just spent the last ten minutes practically arguing against that very point and for some reason, I want to believe him.

I need answers and I need them now.

Not waiting another second, I race after Colton.

I get to the stairs and look up to find him lost at the top. "Hey,"

I call out though it comes out as more of an order than a subtle suggestion to get his ass back down here. Colton glances back and scoffs before continuing to the top and grating on my nerves.

That fucker.

I sprint up the stairs, taking two at a time and as I reach the top, I find Colton halfway down the hall, just passing the room I used the first few days I stayed here, the very room where the douche watched me almost get myself off, the same room where I rubbed my body all over him and felt him come alive beneath my fingers. Don't get me wrong here, I hated living that close to him but at the same time, I kind of miss it. How fucking wrong is that?

I reach Colton just as he pushes the door open of his bedroom and I sneak in behind just in time for it to slam behind me.

He lets out a frustrated groan and turns on me but before he can tell me to get out of his room, I demand my answers. "What the hell was that?"

"None of your fucking business," he snaps, reaching for the door.

I throw myself in front of it, blocking his way. "No. It is my business. I live here too and if I'm going to have some psycho maniac screaming at me that I'm his fucking property, then yeah, it is my fucking business and I deserve answers."

Colton just stares and I clench my jaw. "I will stand here for the rest of the day if I have to, and I swear to you, you won't enjoy it."

He backs me up right against the door and in a flash, slams his hands down on either side of my face. "I said it's none of your fucking business."

I raise my chin to meet his eyes. "You don't scare me, Colton," I say, lowering my voice. "Where I come from, you're nothing but an arrogant prick with a chip on your shoulder just like your daddy. If you wanted to hurt me, you would have done it already and if you really wanted to go to war, you would have made a move. You're chicken shit, Colton Carrington."

Fury blazes behind his eyes and he hesitates for just a moment before pressing into me and crushing his lips against mine. He kisses me deeply. Not rushed and forceful like the two times before and my body instantly wakes up.

My hands fall to his chest and slide up behind his neck, tangling in his hair as his drop to my ass. He lifts me and uses his body to keep me pinned against the door as my legs wrap around his waist.

What is this? Why does it always set my body on fire?

Colton grinds against me and a moan slips from between my lips. The sound is like a drug to him and his kisses become more hungry, needier, but I'm already there meeting him with that same desire.

My hands become a tangled mess in his hair and I want nothing more than for him to strip me bare and pound into me, giving us both what we've been craving since that very first touch, but I can't. Despite the fact that I made a point that it will never happen, this is Colton Carrington, the biggest douchebag I've ever met. He could get any girl he wanted. In fact, I don't doubt he has them lined up just waiting for him to give them a chance. So, what is he doing with me?

He's playing me like a puppet and every single time, I fall into his trap. Hook, line, and sinker and it won't be long until I give him exactly what he wants. Who'd be the fool then?

Fuck.

The thought is like having a bucket of ice water thrown over my head on the coldest day of the year.

My hand tightens in his hair and I tear him away from me. "No," I tell him. "You can't keep doing this to avoid talking."

His eyes narrow on mine and he dips his face dangerously low and even though his lips were just on mine, something seems so much worse now, so much darker. "If you don't want to fuck, Jade, then leave."

"No."

Colton moves back just an inch and it gives me space to move, but it also means I'm no longer pinned to the door and I fall back against it, hastily unwrapping my legs to catch my fall. I keep myself pressed to the door. "Nowhere to run, Colton," I taunt, knowing that whenever he kisses me, he flies straight out the door. "You can't keep doing this."

"Doing what?" he questions, moving to his bed and flopping down as though he's not raging on the inside that I currently have him trapped.

"Playing dumb doesn't suit you, Carrington," I snap, knowing that one would sting.

"Yeah?" he questions. "Well playing the victim doesn't suit you."

"When have I ever played the victim?"

He raises a brow. "When haven't you? Running to Dad when you couldn't handle people at school, running your mouth to your boyfriend every time Jude even looks your way. There's a whole fucking list of things. Though, speaking of your boyfriend, I wonder how he's going to feel to learn that you can't keep your fucking hands off me."

"You're kidding, right?" I laugh. "First off, you've kissed me every single time, and second, he's not my boyfriend. I'm free to do whatever the fuck I want to do." He scoffs and I get him back on track. "Just tell me what the fuck that bullshit downstairs was with your dad and I'll happily leave you the hell alone."

Colton groans and sits up but I see no signs of him giving in. "He used to hit you didn't he?" I ask, watching him closely. His elbows rest against his knees and he drops his chin against his hands, slicing his eyes across to me, silently warning me that this topic is not up for discussion, but his silence is confirmation enough.

"Did he put his hands on your mom?"

"How is that any of your business?"

"It's why she left, isn't it? And she took your sisters because he was hurting them too."

"You don't know what you're talking about."

"But I do. I saw it in the way you flinched when he stepped toward you. It's like you were a defenseless kid again before you remembered that you tower over him now."

Colton's gaze falls back to the carpet of his room and I take his silence as another confirmation. Growing a pair of balls, I walk across the room and take his chin between my fingers and lift until his eyes are on mine. "Why did she leave you behind?"

Something changes behind his eyes that catches me off guard. It's like a waterfall of emotions. Sad, happy, hurt, pain, and sorrow. It's as though they soften while hardening all at the same time. "She didn't," he tells me, briefly making me wonder why the hell he's allowing me to do this, even more so why he's answering. "He hunted us down and took me back. He doesn't care about them. They're all there for show and every time he proved it, it gutted my sisters. Dad married solely for the reason of having a son to continue the family business the traditional way. Mom was never supposed to fall pregnant with the twins."

"And me?" I question. "Downstairs before you blocked him. Would he have hit me?"

His brow flinches. "He thought about it but once he realized you had my protection, he wasn't willing to see it through."

"Why did you do that?"

He shakes his head. "Next question, Jade."

I let out a sigh. There's so much I could ask and I should be hitting him with it but one more wrong question and I'll be sent out of here without another answer. I need to tread carefully. Something tells me he's only letting his walls down because of the bullshit with his dad. Any other time and I'd have been kicked out of here before I got to taste his lips on mine.

"Why has your dad been putting on the nice guy act for me and my mom?"

Colton shakes his head again but this time it's not because he doesn't want to answer, it's because he's just as clueless as I am. "I don't know," he says, his eyes going far away as his hand moves to my waist. He pulls me in between his knees and it's almost as though he hasn't even realized he's doing it.

Our eyes are at the same level but he doesn't look at me, he just keeps staring off out his bedroom window, deep in thought. My hand falls to his shoulder and on instinct, slides up around the back of his neck and it's like his body calls to me.

"Why are you friends with Jude? You realize he's a dick, right? I mean, you're a dick, but he's like on a whole different level of dick. You belong as some domineering, arrogant CEO in a boardroom, swimming in pools of cash while he belongs behind bars, convicted on rape charges."

Colton presses his lips into a tight line and while he's not agreeing, he's also not disagreeing and that speaks volumes.

Silence falls between us and for once, it's peaceful. It's not the awkward, irritated silence from this morning or the frustrated and confused silence from the ride back home. It's just kind of nice … it's right, that is until he looks back at me and stands. "You should go."

It's like flipping a switch and for a moment I wonder if both he and his dad suffer from bipolar disorder. I stumble back a step and in doing that, both our hands fall to our sides, killing anything that was lingering in the air between us.

I meet his eyes for a short moment. Neither of us say a word, it's just silence until I turn and walk straight out his door, my heart, body, and soul a complete mess.

CHAPTER 16

I walk into my math class just in time to hear Mr. Weathers' sarcastic booming voice. "Alright, guys. Congratulations. Your disastrous behavior last week has earned you all a seating chart. Check the chart and take your seats. These will be your designated spots until the end of your senior year. Learn it, love it, live it."

The fuck? No.

Everyone looks horrified as Mr. Weathers stands at the front looking as proud as punch. We all look around at one another, wondering if we take a stand what kind of action would be taken against us. There are too many personalities within this classroom, all of which don't mix well.

Knowing better than to try and fight the system a second time so soon after the first, I reluctantly make my way over to the whiteboard and begin searching for my name.

"Get a move on, guys. We've got a lot to get through today," Mr. Weathers says, earning a loud groan from the students. He smirks to himself before saying in a singsong tone, far too pleased with himself. "If you were going to be salty, then you should have brought the tequila."

I smother a laugh. Despite how much I'm cursing the guy for giving us a seating chart, I also think he's kind of awesome. It's only the first day of my second week and I haven't really had a chance to get to know him as a teacher, but so far, he's made a good impression. His tequila comment goes a long way in helping me forgive him for the seating chart. Who knows, he might have seated me with Milo.

With the boys all piling in behind me to get a look at the chart, I make it quick.

My eyes scan over it, searching out my name and when I find it, my stomach sinks. Colton fucking Carrington. How is it possible for one infuriating human being to ruin every little aspect of my life?

The guys start shoving behind me and I make quick work of squeezing out of the crowd, annoyed that my ass was grabbed in the process. I glance up and find that the ass grabber was Charlie and for some reason, it doesn't annoy me as much as it should. Charlie is cute and while he's a bit of an ass, he's also fun and flirty and I know he doesn't mean anything by it. He's just living life, trying to enjoy himself and in doing that, he chooses to bug me, but in a good way, not the infuriating way Colton does.

Had it been Colton grabbing my ass, he would have lost his right nut, had a fist to the jaw, and then a little public humiliation just to make me feel better about myself. You know, assuming it wasn't like the night where I practically put my ass in his hands. I was more than asking for it then and had he pushed me just a little further, I know I would have ended up a victim to his charm. After the bullshit he pulled with Nic during the week and the whole yacht bullshit, he won't ever get that close to my body again.

I make my way over to my new designated seat and drop my ass down while watching the boys try to work out the simple seating chart. They see their name on the chart but actually working out the corresponding table for them to park their asses seems a little harder. Honestly, I expect better from boys who've apparently had an elite upbringing with the best education money can buy.

Colton moves in to check his name and I grin to myself as he works out that he's stuck with me. He turns, his eyes instantly zoning on me, and boy does he look pissed. I guess we're going to pretend that the whole makeout session in his room didn't happen yesterday. Though, I shouldn't be surprised. So far, we've been acting like the whole naked and grinding on his lap thing didn't happen either but if we're going to be technical, that was a different situation altogether.

He stalks toward me as though it's somehow my fault that he got stuck sitting beside me, but truth be told, he's the luckiest motherfucker around. Any other of these guys would be thrilled to be the one who got to sit next to the only person in the school with a hot rack, perky ass, and doesn't smell like a dirty gym bag.

Colton steps right up to the table and leans over it. "Move. You're not sitting here."

I smile, looking up at him as I cross my legs and lean back in the chair, making a show of getting comfortable. "Really? I'm not? Because it sure as shit looks like I am."

His eyes darken, irritated with having to deal with me. "Move."

I raise a brow and grin up at him, loving nothing more than getting on his nerves. "That'd be a negative, Ghost Rider."

His eyes flame and I watch in amusement as his jaw clenches. Maybe this whole seating chart thing will be better than I thought it would. "Colton, take your seat," Mr. Weathers booms as the students around us get seated. "What's the matter? Does the pretty girl have cooties?"

"No. The pretty girl has a death wish," he mutters, his eyes never once leaving mine as he responds to our teacher.

Charlie leans forward from the space behind me, his voice thick with lust. "Don't worry, man," he murmurs, meeting my eyes and winking. "I'll deal with those cooties for you."

Ugh. please. This guy seriously needs to get laid.

Mr. Weathers lets out a frustrated groan, clearly done with this morning's bullshit. "Take your seat, Colton. You're wasting my time. She's not going to bite—"

"Careful," I say, "I just might."

Weathers continues as though I didn't just interrupt. "And Charlie, sit your ass back in your seat and mind your damn business."

Charlie runs his finger across his lips, pretending to zip them while Colton drops down beside me. His arm brushes against mine, sending a wave of electricity pulsing through my body that sets me on fire. I'm in so much trouble when it comes to this guy. Sometimes it's hard to tell if I want to hate him or try to see the best in him. Hell, maybe I just want to fuck him.

Why couldn't he have been some kind of saint? That sharp jawline, perfect body, and sun-kissed caramelized skin is wasted on him. Those eyes though … fuck.

Mr. Weathers starts his lesson and I open my textbook knowing damn well that I won't be able to keep up in this class. I haven't been able to keep up in many of the classes actually. What these guys are learning is a huge step up from the basic bullshit we were being taught at Breakers Flats High.

There's no doubt about it that this is an elite education and to be honest, throwing me straight in the deep end was more than likely an epic fuck up on a gigantic scale. I'll never be able to catch up to these guys and I sure as hell don't have the will to. It'd be a fail across the board purely for the fact that I'm so behind. I'm not one of those academically minded kinds of girls. I've never had to be, and suddenly having all this school work looming over me … yeah, it's a bit intimidating. The fact that I don't understand any of the gibberish that's coming out of Mr. Weathers mouth, well that's just downright humiliating. I've never felt so stupid. All these guys are my age and are easily following along while I feel completely out in the dark.

It didn't happen often at Breakers Flats High, but when it did, my go-to coping mechanism was pulling out my phone and giving up until the lesson was over. I don't have that option here and for the first time ever, I think I actually miss that stupid school.

Colton's arm brushes past mine again and goosebumps sweep through me. I'm slammed back into yesterday afternoon when he had me pressed up against his bedroom door. He'd lowered his walls and let me in if only for a minute, but that minute was enough to tell me that this whole douchebag, arrogant prick routine is just that. He actually has a heart buried under all the coal and my gut tells me that it's damaged. You don't escape a childhood like that without a few scars.

Mr. Weathers finishes with his lesson on whatever the fuck I just blanked on and requests us to turn to page 84 in our textbooks. I get busy scanning through the pages when a bang at the door has everyone's heads shooting up.

I look over just in time to see Spencer storming through the door. His eyes are stormy and his brows are drawn with a hard, pissed off line. There's practically steam huffing out of his ears. I'd hate to be the guy who pissed off Spencer Vanderbilt. His eyes scan around the room and within seconds land on our table.

Oh, fuck. What have I done now?

My heart rate kicks up a notch and I feel the need to cower behind Colton's large frame. Maybe If I disappear, he'll forget I'm here. Don't get me wrong, I can handle guys coming at me constantly, but being in the dark and not knowing what it's about? Yeah, I'm not a fan. I like a little preparation to ensure a thorough ass-kicking. Nonetheless, I don't hide.

Colton accused me of playing the victim and I'm determined to prove him wrong. I can handle my own shit. I don't need someone coming in and saving me, but in reality, that's what Nic and the boys have always done. I hadn't even realized that I'd been using them as a crutch and just claiming that I was tough shit. How wrong have I been?

Mr. Weathers flies to his feet and storms forward, realizing something is about to go down but Spencer evades him like some kind of ninja and forges on. "Spencer," Weathers roars. "Out. Now."

It's as though he didn't say a damn word.

He reaches our table and his hand shoots out. I wince, preparing to be struck but his hand curls into a fist around the front of Colton's shirt. He tears him out of his seat and I watch with my mouth hanging open at his sheer strength to be able to do that.

Spencer pushes past me and slams Colton against the wall at my back so hard that I feel it vibrate with the pressure. "Spence," Charlie yells from the back of the room. "What the fuck, dude?"

"Is it true?" Spencer growls, leaning into Colton and getting right in his face, making me panic that Spencer is going to cause some damage. After all, to mess up Colton's face would be a damn shame. It's so fucking pretty, but on the other hand, watching these two fight would have me coming so hard. I wonder how they'd feel about sharing. Spencer has that whole rich, playboy, dangerous vibe going on and it's kind of sexy. Add that to Colton's bad boy mystic and it's a sandwich I'd be a part of any day.

Colton doesn't take his eyes from Spencer for even a second. "Is what true?"

"Your old man with Jacquie."

"The fuck are you talking about?" Colton demands, getting his hands up between them and giving Spencer a hard shove, his hand flailing in the process and whacking me across the face.

"Ah, fuck," I grunt, slapping a hand over the sharp sting on my face but neither of them seem to notice as they're too stuck in their stare-off. Weathers certainly notices though and does his best to get between them, however, he doesn't get far.

"My dad's not fucking your cousin," Colton roars, pissed off to be put in this situation. "That's bullshit. Where the fuck did you hear that crap?"

"Don't fucking lie to me, man," Spencer demands, trying to grab him again, the two of them constantly bumping into the side of my chair and making me rock around.

"I'm not fucking lying. He's not screwing your cousin."

Getting tired of being rocked around, I slam my chair back into Spencer's hip and fly to my feet. "Who's your cousin? Platinum blonde, fake titties, and big cock-sucking lips?"

Spencer tears his eyes from Colton and his glare is sharp enough to kill. "Yeah. What the fuck do you know about it?" he growls as I feel Colton's eyes raking over my face and zoning in on the red mark covering my cheek.

A grin rips across my face. I could break the news to him nicely, but he's been nothing but a cocky prick since I first met him, not to mention that he offered to marry me for a payday. I'm assuming the wedding is off now that he's probably worked out that I'm not related to Daddy Warbucks.

"Yeah," I tell him, not sugar-coating it and making sure it comes across as bitchy as possible. "I saw them getting freaky during the party behind the pool house. It was right after I gave you fuckers matching suits. How was your bourbon by the way? It looked like you really enjoyed it. Personally, I'm not really into dark spirits."

Spencer's jaw clenches and fury ripples off him in waves, especially now being reminded of the fun I had during the party. "You're lying."

I shake my head, struggling to hold back my laughter. "Just ask her. A girl like that would probably tell you all about it. He was practically choking her, his dick was so far down her throat. I swear you could see the tears glistening in her eyes in the moonlight. It was so romantic especially with the gardens in the background." I turn to Colton. "Those flowers really get your dad hard, you should be proud."

Turning my gaze back on Spencer, I grin wide and hammer the last nail into the coffin. "Damn Spence, that cousin of yours, she really knows her way around a big, hard cock. It was a two hand job. I could practically see it sliding down her throat."

Charlie chokes on a laugh as Spencer grabs me and slams me up against Colton's chest, having no other wall space unless he was to walk around the next table. "What the fuck did you just say?" he spits as Colton grabs my waist, trying to hold me up to lessen the blow.

"You heard me, pretty boy. She was loving it, though anyone would if they thought they were about to get a big payday out of it."

"My cousin ain't no fucking whore, bitch."

"Come on, now," Weathers says from over near his desk with

absolutely no care in his voice. Clearly, he's given up on trying to break this shit up and is going with the 'boys will be boys' option and letting them sort it out themselves. Though when it comes to these guys, that's probably a good idea.

Charlie clears his throat from behind us. "Actually, man," he says awkwardly, scrunching his face as he looks across the room at Spencer. "I did see them walking out of the party around that time. She could be telling the truth, and besides, what does she have to gain by lying about it? Don't act like she wasn't offering to bend over for my old man six months ago for a business deal."

"Fuck," Spencer roars, curling his fists tighter against my upper arms and slamming me back against Colton again.

Colton releases my waist and snaps his arm out around me, punching his best friend high on his chest, forcing him to release my arms. "Back the fuck off, man. I know she's a fucking bitch but she's still a chick. Stop being so fucking rough."

Spencer's eyes flash down to me and as if only now realizing that he's been throwing me around like a ragdoll, he releases me, though I'm not fooled, he doesn't look a damn bit sorry about it. It's not something I'll be losing sleep over though. After all, I'm determined not to be a victim.

Spencer backs off a step and it's just enough space for me to slip past him and to be met by Milo who checks me over and holds a cold drink bottle to the side of my face.

"What are we going to do about this?" Spencer asks, staring down Colton as though it's his fault that his dad decided to fuck a 22-year-old skank.

Colton shrugs his shoulders. "I don't know. Fucking leave it, man. He'll get bored of her and fuck her off in a month or two. In the meantime, he gets his dick sucked and she gets to go shopping on his credit card. Hell, if she lasts three months, he'll even give her a nice check to keep quiet."

Spencer drops a shoulder and a loud roar comes tearing out of him as he slams into Colton's stomach. The two of them go slamming into the wall and put a big hole in the drywall. Fists start flying and I thank whoever lives above that I was able to slip out of there before this bullshit went down.

Shit quickly gets out of control. "Fuck," Charlie grunts, loosening his tie and going in after them. "Why's it always me who has to break it up?"

And just like that, he dives in and the rest of the class crowds around, ready for the show.

CHAPTER 17

I walk out of the school watching as Milo pulls away to go to whatever business meeting his father had planned for him to sit in on this afternoon. I have to admit, I feel kind of sorry for the guy. Since our performance on Saturday night, his dad has been all over him like a rash. Now that he's confident that his son is as straight as an arrow, he's suddenly proud and while Milo loves his father's attention, the reasons for it are heartbreaking.

I can't understand why people on this side of the world have such a hard time adapting to the LGBTQ community. It's not as though it's just sprung up out of nowhere. Hell, most of the celebrities they're inviting to their fancy parties are gay so why should it matter if one of their own is too?

It makes me so angry for Milo. He deserves better. In this day and age, he shouldn't be forced to hide in the closet. He should be loud and proud of the man he is.

I let out a deep sigh as his car fades from view. He practically ran out of here the second the bell sounded but I get it. No matter who your father is, sometimes you just need his attention. Hell, I know I'd do just about anything to spend time with my father right now. If I knew my time with him was limited, I would have been sure to spend every waking moment by his side.

Damn, I hope he knew how much I loved him.

I start making my way down to the student parking lot. I'm most likely setting myself up for a fail here, but if I just happen to catch Colton in a good mood, he might just let me catch a ride with him. My chances aren't great seeing as though he and Spencer went at it in Math class today. I'm sure both their parents have heard about it which could only mean that Charles is waiting for him in his office, and hell, we know how their 'discussions' usually pan out.

"Sup, Jade?"

What the fuck? That isn't Colton.

I whip my head around at the sound of the guy's voice with my senses on high alert. No one calls me Jade except for Colton and he only does it because he knows how it annoys me and refuses to stop. Hell, I still haven't worked out why he calls me Jade but right now, that's not my issue.

Five guys come and hover around me while the one who had

called me by Colton's irritating name comes right up into my personal space and throws an arm over my shoulder. I don't know these guys but I've seen them around school. They're complete douchebags and what's more, they completely idolize Colton.

Just fucking great. This couldn't be good and seeing as though no one here is aware of the strange little thing Colton and I have got going on, this could only mean bad news.

The guys smell of grease and judging by the dirty hand that's dangling down by my left tit, I'd dare say these guys have just come from shop class. Though, if I were to put my money on it—not that I have any—I'd say these guys didn't learn a damn thing while in their shop class. I've spent years around boys fixing up stolen cars and Harleys and these guys wouldn't know the difference between a hammer and a wrench.

"Get your dirty as fuck hands off me," I say, pushing the dickwads hand off my shoulder and scowling at the black marks left on my white blouse. I clench my jaw. Maryne is going to give me hell for that.

"Come on, *Jade*. Play with us," the guy says as his friends move in closer. "We just want to have a little fun."

I let out a groan. Judging by the way he keeps emphasizing the name 'Jade' I'm going to go out on a limb here and say that whatever bullshit plan he has in place is a crime of passion. He wants to impress Colton and by doing that, it means getting at me. "If you want to have fun, then go home and find the inflatable doll hiding under your bed. The five of you could gather around and take turns. It'll be like your very own gang bang."

"We'd rather chill with you."

Fuck this. I'm only a couple of meters away from the student parking lot. I just have to get to Colton's car, find the douchebag in question and hide out in his Veneno then it'll all be over. They're insane if they think I'm about to entertain their bullshit. "You know, I just checked my schedule and unfortunately, you're shit out of luck. I'm actually super busy right now. We'll have to do it another time."

"Come on, babydoll. Don't be like that," one of the guys to my right says with a sick tone to his dark voice as I start weaving through cars. "We just want to play."

I stop by Charlie's cherry red Ferrari and turn on them, only they keep coming and my back is pushed up against the passenger's side door. "What the fuck is your problem?" I ask, scanning over all of them. "How specific do I need to be? But don't worry, I'll use small syllables because clearly, your understanding is lacking. Here goes. Are you ready?" I glance around, laying the sarcasm on thick. "You. All. Need. To. Fuck. Off."

I find Colton making his way down here and surprise, surprise, his eyes are already locked on my situation but with the lazy way he strides toward the parking lot, he's not going to be much help. I wouldn't be surprised if the fucker pulled out a box of popcorn and got comfortable for the show. Charlie is there though and at least he shows a little concern, but it's not like he's making a move to help me out.

I don't need them anyway. As Colton said, I always play the victim, and as far as I'm concerned, that bullshit is a thing of the past.

"Now, now, *Jade*," the guy says, forcing my attention back to him and making a scowl appear on Colton's face as he hears his nickname for me being used. "There's no need to be like that. I see how this looks and I swear, our intentions are good."

It's the oldest fucking trick in the book. Declaring your good intentions is about the same as saying 'Hey, I'm here to fuck things up.'

I push up off the edge of the Ferrari and take the Colton wannabe by the shoulders before slamming my knee up into his junk. "Maybe I wasn't clear enough for you," I yell as he buckles over and howls in pain. "I asked you kindly to fuck off. You don't want to see how I demand shit."

The guy's head is down by my crotch and despite having spent a good portion of my day watching Spencer and Colton have it out, this takes the prize of being my favorite moment of the day. "Fucking bitch," he growls low before turning to his friends. "Fucking do it."

Do it? Do what?

My head whips to them to find them all moving in closer and crowding me against the Ferrari. "Get off me," I scream, having absolutely no idea what they plan on doing.

"HEY," I hear Charlie's voice booming, still too far away.

"Not so fucking tough now, are you, princess?" One of the guys murmur right against my face as I feel one of them scrambling around. A sick laughter comes from one of them and I hastily look around for some way out but they have me trapped.

I find Charlie jogging down toward us and Colton still lazily heading for his car in the distance. Stupid fucker. "What the fuck are you doing?" Charlie hounds only a few meters away now. "Get the fuck off my Ferrari."

There's movement to my side and I flick my gaze across to watch as one of them pulls out some kind of bottle. It's dirty and the smell coming off it is enough to make me want to hurl. The guys all press into me, keeping me pinned.

I start flailing around as their plan becomes clear. The guy with the bottle uncaps it and meets my eye with a sick grin. He reaches up and in one quick pour thick, black grease drops down over my head, tangling into my thick hair.

I squeal as Charlie's booming anger tears through the parking lot. The grease drips down onto my skin and it instantly starts to burn.

This isn't just regular grease. They've put something in it.

I curl into a ball as the last of the bottle is tipped over my head. Their laughs and snickers are so fucking loud but I barely hear them over the sound of my fucking heart racing.

It hurts. It fucking hurts so bad.

Charlie starts hauling guys off me and as they're pulled off and my body is freed, I fall to the ground in a heap of mess. I expect Charlie to come after me but when he starts looking after his cherry red Ferrari, it becomes clear what his desperation was about.

Seeing the anger on his face, the five guys start running but it's the last of my problems. There's some kind of acid in this grease and if I don't move fast, I'll end up with burns covering my skin.

Shakily, I get to my feet, leaving my bag laying on the dirty ground in a heap of grease. I start rushing toward the staff bathroom, pulling at my clothes and not even giving a shit that I don't have something to change into. I have to get in a shower and I don't fucking care if it means walking home in nothing but a towel. I'll be okay as long as I can get this acidic grease off my skin.

The acid starts to really burn and I find myself glancing back for those fucking guys as I run. They're all out of sight but I do find one set of eyes burning into me. Colton stands by his Veneno with the scissor door open wide and seeing that he's caught my attention, he gently shakes his head and drops down into his car, dismissing me.

I don't know what it is about Colton or why it bothers me so much. Maybe it's because of the bullshit I just suffered through with those guys in the hopes they could get Colton's attention for even a second or maybe it's all the shit I've had to deal with since moving to Bellevue Springs. Whatever it is, it has tears springing to my eyes and violently falling in waves.

I crash through the door of the bathroom as a sobbing mess and race through to the showers. I throw myself in, clothes and all, turning the taps on as hard as they can go, desperate to get this shit off me.

The water comes down hard and it stings against my already raw skin, but I suffer through it knowing how badly I need this. Without it … fuck. I can't even imagine.

I start tearing off my ruined clothes, leaving me in my underwear that mostly seems to be okay. Thick chunks of grease start rolling off me, but a lot of it sticks to my body like a second skin and I'm forced to scrub against my tender skin.

The tears continue rolling down my face and I find it hard to breathe through my thick sobs. I'm a fucking mess.

Once my skin is free of acidic grease, I start on my hair and find myself broken as chunks of my long luscious hair break off and pool at the bottom of the shower. I scrub furiously, desperately needing it gone. The longer it's in there, the worse it's going to get.

It takes half an hour of washing my hair and scrubbing my body and by the time I finally get out, I'm a fucking disaster. It was impossible to get all the grease from my scalp and as I wrap a white towel around my body and it moves around, I find grease hiding in places that I didn't even know I had.

My hair is destroyed and my skin is patchy and red but as long as the burn is gone, I'm going to be alright.

I stare at my reflection in the mirror of the staff bathroom.

How did it come to this?

I thought things were just starting to ease. Colton had declared early on that he was the only one allowed to fuck with me. When the hell did that shit change? Had it changed? If anything, I thought that the fucking with me thing was over, especially after yesterday.

I scan over my red, splotchy face. My eyes stand out just like they do every time I've been crying. They're the brightest blue, but when I've been crying, it's like they glisten and shimmer, or maybe it's just the red puffiness surrounding them that makes them look this way.

My hair hangs by my side and it looks like a mess. It's in knots and every time I touch it my hand comes out slimy with the remaining grease and filled with strands of hair. There is no saving it from what I can see, pulling a Britney and shaving it off might be my only option.

There has to be a better way.

I search through the cupboards and find a plastic bag to shove my destroyed uniform in before finding a bathrobe and pulling it around my pained body.

I walk out into the school, pleased that it's the end of the day so I can avoid repeat performances. Apparently, walking around an all-boys school practically naked is frowned upon by the staff.

I walk down to the parking lot to find it mostly empty but more importantly, my bag sits in a dirty pile, completely destroyed. I rifle through it for my purse, phone, and keys, and decide the rest of it can go and fuck itself. Screw my homework and screw the textbooks. They can all suffer like I have.

With Colton and the boys long gone, I start the agonizing walk home and keep my gaze glued to the sidewalk. Cars fly past me, beeping in outrage at my lack of clothing and all I can do is cry.

From the very first step until I'm pushing through the massive door of the Carrington mansion, tears stream down my face. I've never felt anything like it. I've been attacked by guys before but never like that. Usually, they stick with taunts and call me a whore for preferring to hang out with my crew rather than bitchy girls. My boys would deal with it straight away and then I'd be free to continue as I was.

There was that bullshit with Jude and of course Colton, but it was nothing like this.

I've always valued my hair. I'm not one of those girls who is obsessive over makeup. I don't need to look perfect every second of the day, but I've always loved my hair. It was long and beautiful. It fell in thick waves and tickled the top of my ass. It was my signature thing. When people mentioned my name, the first thing they thought of was my long, dark hair.

Now it's a rats nest and falling out in chunks.

I get into the mansion and I listen out. The first thing I hear is the sound of the vacuum and I follow it, knowing it's bound to be my mom. The closer I get, the faster I walk as the devastation seems to harden against my soul.

I break through to the massive kitchen and find mom in the media room, vacuuming her life away as though she doesn't have a care in the world.

I run to her.

I throw open the door of the room and seeing me in her peripheral vision, her head whips around. She takes me in and as she does, her eyes widen in shock but she doesn't have even a slight moment to ask me what happened before I crash into her and she curls me into her arms.

I cry into her shoulder as she holds me tight. "Oh, honey," she says, heartbroken. "What happened to you?"

"They ... they ..." I struggle to get the words past the rapid sobs and I give up. I'll try again once the pain has begun to ease.

"Shh," mom soothes, running her hand up and down my back, no doubt able to smell the grease wafting from my hair despite the bucketloads of shampoo I've already scrubbed through it. "It's going to be okay. Calm down, sweet girl."

I rub my already sore eyes against her shoulder and despite the pristine way she's expected to keep her uniform, she doesn't pull away.

"I thought this week was going to be better," I cry.

"I know, I thought so too," she says, moving her hand to the back of my head and then pulling back with furrowed brows. "What is this in your hair?" she questions, horrified by the slimy feel coming off on her hand then gasping when she sees the missing chunks. "Who did this?"

I shake my head as she draws back to see me better. "A group of guys," I say, dropping the bag with my destroyed uniform to the floor. "They cornered me in the student parking lot and tipped grease over my head. They'd put acid in it and all my hair started snapping off and my skin …" I take a sniffly breath. "It burned, mom. My skin is all red and sore and my hair … it keeps snapping off."

Fury fires from her eyes. "This school has been nothing but trouble since you first started," she says, beginning to pace the room, her arms flailing around. "I'm going to have a meeting with that … that … dean first thing in the morning. Those boys are going to see justice. They will not get away with this. Acid? ACID! Who does that to a young woman?" Her head starts shaking as the outrage builds within her. "I should call the police. Their whole futures will be taken away from them in seconds. That'll teach those privileged little bastards."

I drop down onto the wide couch and watch as mom continues to pace. "'What am I going to do? I've already washed my hair a million times and every time I touch it, more hair snaps off. It's not coming out."

Mom stops pacing and looks back at me, looking just as lost as I feel. She lets out a heavy, broken sigh. "I don't know, honey. I wish I had the money to send you to a salon. Maybe after my shift, I could have a look and see what can be salvaged."

I drop my face into my hands knowing that's our only option.

My phone burns a hole in my robe pocket. I'd do anything to call Nic and have him come and handle this. He'd drop everything and be here in no time, but his version of helping will result in bloodshed and I'll still be left looking like this. While it'll help me feel a little better, it'll do nothing to fix the devastation left behind.

Mom steps into me and I feel her hands in my hair. "I wish I could do more for you, sweetheart."

"I know," I murmur, knowing this is killing her just as much as it is for me. After all, a direct attack on her daughter is a direct attack on her. I stand up and she instantly pulls me back into her arms. "I think I'm just going to go get dressed and then I might just chill out with you while you work. Is that okay or do you think that might cause shit with Harrison?"

"Harrison can go and play with the shark for all I care. If my baby has had a bad day and wants to hang out with her momma, then that's exactly what my baby is going to get."

I give mom a tight smile before slipping out of her arms and rushing off to the pool house. I quickly get dressed while avoiding every mirror in this place and before I know it, I'm snuggled up on the couch with a blanket while mom does her thing around me.

She's just about finished when I see Colton out in the kitchen. He drops his keys on the kitchen counter and starts rifling through the cupboards for something to eat then walks down to the living space that overlooks the ridiculously insane pool.

As I watch him, I can't help but feel that this is all on him. He could have stopped it. He could have had control over his little followers, and he sure as hell could have at least asked if I was alright.

The more I think about it, the angrier I get and before I even know what I'm doing, I'm out in the living room, storming toward the cocky fuck. His head snaps around, hearing me coming and I watch as his brow raises. I know he sees how fucked up my hair is and I don't doubt he can see the redness around my eyes and covering my skin. I look like a fucking mess.

I walk right up to him and hold my hand out, not breaking my stare for even a second. "Wallet," I demand, taking note of all the cuts and bruises left behind from his brawl with Spencer.

He grins at me in amusement before relaxing back against the couch, spreading his arms out along the top. "You're fucking insane if you think you're about to get your grubby hands on my wallet."

"So help me God, Carrington. Give me your goddamn wallet right fucking now before I tell this whole damn town that you've been fucking around with the help."

His eyes narrow just a fraction as he watches me and I feel myself beginning to break. My eyes start watering and I silently scold myself and hope to God that I can hold it together long enough to get what I need. After that, I'm free to break but I refuse to let it happen in front of him.

"Why?" he questions, studying me, and drawing it out, realizing that I'm on the edge and all it would take is a slight push to break me.

"Because I need to fix what you broke."

"Me? I didn't do shit."

I scoff and resist pulling out my claws. "You could have stopped it, and to me that makes you just as guilty."

The hard edge in his eyes begins to fade and as if finally realizing the broken desperation filling every inch of me, he takes pity and slips his hand into his pocket. He pulls out a brown leather wallet and reluctantly hands it over.

I take it from him, feeling my fingers brush over his warm skin. With his eyes focusing heavily on every little movement, I flip it open and quickly scan through everything in it before finding what I need.

I slip the platinum credit card out of its spot and hand Colton his wallet. "Thank you," I murmur so low that I don't even know if he hears it.

Something passes between us but I don't wait around to figure it out. I turn and walk back out through the kitchen and hear as he gets up behind me. He heads in the opposite direction and I let out a breath. Why does dealing with him always leave me a mess?

I find myself stopping by the counter and I can't help but notice the keys he'd left here earlier.

He's going to kill me.

I can't … but ...

Fuck it. After the day I've had, I deserve it. Screw him. It's not like I'm going to hurt it.

I slip the keys off the counter and rush out into the garage feeling the adrenaline beginning to pulse through my veins and somehow managing to heal something within me. I unlock the car and slip in while trying my best not to make a sound but the second I turn on the engine, he's going to know.

I have to make this fast.

I hit the button for the garage door and check the gate is open then knowing I have an unobstructed ride through the property. I kick over the engine and high tail it out of there.

The Veneno purrs beneath me and I all but come in the seat. The smooth finishes and flawless drive make me want to squeal with delight. I can't believe I'm driving this.

I do my best to keep my head off the chair while my phone blows up in my pocket, though I'm more interested in the shiny little credit card that's buried in there with it.

All too soon I pull up at the salon and I reluctantly get out of the car. Maybe on the way back, I'll take it for a little joy ride, but first, I need to deal with me.

I walk into the salon and the moment the lady behind the counter takes me in, her features break. "Oh, honey. Come on through. We've got you."

CHAPTER 18

My hair flows in soft waves down my back and while it's not as thick and now a little shorter with some new layers, it's a million times better than it was before. Well, for what Colton just paid, he'd want to hope it was fucking perfect. I nearly died at the cost but I guess that is what you get for coming to a salon in Bellevue Springs. I could have driven to the salon back home but there's no doubt in my mind that the Veneno would have been stolen by the time I was done.

I spent two hours with the hairdresser slowly massaging the shit out of my hair. She had to use some heavy-duty stuff but in the end, it started to come out and when it was all gone, the desperation within my soul finally began to dissipate until I was feeling normal again. Well, normal isn't the right word. I'm far from normal and come tomorrow at school, I'll be fucking those five boys up. Hell, I bet I could even get Charlie on board, you know after I kick his ass for caring more about his precious Ferrari.

The hairdresser gave me some products—courtesy of Colton of course— that will help to strengthen it back to its former glory. I threw in a little makeup, some nail polishes, and some styling products for mom to top it off.

To be honest, I feel a little bad about stealing Colton's credit card and charging over eight hundred dollars to it, but I can't find it in me to regret it. Besides, I doubt eight hundred dollars is really going to break the bank. Charles' business probably earns over a million dollars per hour. Though, that still didn't stop me from gawking at the hairdresser when she told me the price. I nearly died, but with a swipe of the card, it was all over.

After receiving my millionth call from Colton, I turn off my phone and drop back down into his Veneno. At least this time I will actually enjoy my ride.

I turn on the car and feel the purr of the engine. It's perfect. I'd give my world to own something like this one day but unfortunately, my world isn't going to be enough.

I drive through the streets, taking my sweet ass time and feeling the anger slipping away. An hour passes before I pull back into the driveway of the Carrington mansion and come to a stop right by the front stairs.

I've hardly stepped out of the car before Colton is flying through the door and storming down the stairs while looking over his Veneno in a way that suggests he doesn't trust me not to break it. "You stole my fucking car," he hollers, his voice echoing over the massive property.

I walk up to him and place the keys gently into his hand before stretching up onto my tippy toes. I press a feather-soft kiss to his cheek that has him rearing back from me. "Thank you," I murmur, offering him a warm smile.

His brows furrow and I step away before quickly hurrying back and pulling the credit card out of my back pocket. "Here you go. I'm done with this."

He looks at me as though I'm some sort of alien but I leave it in the past as I waltz up the sixty-six stairs leading to the front door. By the time I'm reaching for the door, Colton is by my side and pulling me to a stop. "What the hell was that?" he demands. "You can't just take my car whenever the fuck you want. I was calling you."

"Oh," I say, wide-eyed, throwing in the sarcasm that I know is going to grind under his skin. "That was you? Sorry, I didn't realize."

I go to walk through the open door but he pulls me up again. "Seriously? That's all you've got to say?"

I look up at him. "What do you want me to say? Yeah, I stole your car and your damn credit card but who gives a shit? It's not like you didn't know where I was. You could have come and got it. Besides, I didn't crash it, I didn't scratch it, I didn't even breathe funny in it, though I might have adjusted the seat to reach the pedals but that's it. I got my hair fixed and now everything is alright in the world. Chill the fuck out. You can go back to being the stubborn asshat that you usually are and I'll go back to pretending you don't exist."

"Ahh, no," he scoffs. "That's not how it's going to go."

"Oh, so you don't want me to pretend like you don't exist. That's fine, I can let the world know that you have a little issue keeping away from me. Though, think of what they might say. Colton Carrington slumming it with the staff. Damn, that won't look good."

"You know that's not what I mean."

"Then please, enlighten me, oh wise one."

His eyes darken and he steps into me, backing me up against one of the many pillars that wrap around the mansion. "You're going to march your bitch ass back down those stairs and wash my fucking car until it's sparkling and then you're going to beg me not to kick you out of here. My Veneno is off fucking limits, especially to people like you."

"People like me?" I scoff, pushing hard against his chest and forcing him back a step. "You mean 'the help.'"

"No, Jade. I mean people like you. People like Oceania fucking Munroe who think that they can come in here and piss over everything that you've worked for."

"Worked for? You haven't worked for anything a day in your life. You've had everything handed to you on a silver platter. Oh, no, poor rich boy has to share his multi-million dollar home because Daddy hired more staff to help wipe his ass. Heaven forbid he has to get his own breakfast in the morning or wash his own damn clothes. I'm so sorry, Colton, I didn't realize how hard your life must be."

"Don't underestimate me, Jade."

"For the last fucking time, the name is Ocean, you daft cunt. Learn it."

I turn around, ready to storm through the house and cut through the staff quarters to the pool house but I come up short when Charles Carrington blocks my way. "Colton," he demands. "I've just had a call from the bank. There was unusual activity at a hair salon. Did you lose your credit card? Do I need to cancel it and report it stolen?"

Oh, shit. This isn't going to go well.

"No," Colton says with a heavy sigh, his eyes slicing back to mine. "It was me. It's the only salon that stocks what Cora and Casey use for their hair. They called and asked me to make a stop."

The fuck?

I narrow my eyes on him. Why would he cover for me like that? I'm starting to lose count of how many times he's saved my ass around here. But why? It doesn't make sense. If he hates me so damn much, why not use the opportunity to throw me under the bus?

"Oh," Charles says, pulling himself up and losing the attitude while acting as though they didn't almost have a fight right by this very foyer only yesterday. "Very well then. How are your sisters?"

"Fine," Colton says, keeping it short. "They were thinking of visiting next month."

"That'd be nice." Charles nods. "Now, what happened to your face? Who do I need to make a check out for this month?"

Colton shakes his head. "It was nothing. Just Spencer pissed because he found out that you're screwing his cousin ... or screwing her over. Either one."

Oh, shit. Shots fired.

"Cousin?" he questions and I stare between the two, waiting for the shit to hit the fan like it had yesterday.

"Jacqueline Vanderbilt. You had your dick shoved halfway down her throat during the party."

"Oh, that's right. Was she a Vanderbilt? Eager young thing she was, but that Spencer. He needs to learn to control his emotions." A shiver runs down my spine at how quickly he dismisses the topic. I mean, the girl gave him the ride of his life while deep-throating him. She deserves a little more respect than that. At least, I think she does. She had some skill.

I resist scowling and then fix whatever expression may be on my face when Charles looks down at me. "Ocean. I trust you're settling in at school. There haven't been any more issues with the faculty?"

Wow, he just skipped over the whole beaten and bloodied son standing before him thing. Not even asking if he was alright before dismissing that too. Though, it's not as though I've even asked if he was okay. When I first saw him after school, the first thing out of my mouth was a demand for his wallet and that must make me as bad as Charles.

I raise my chin and realize that to get anything across with Charles, it needs to be quick and factual. Straight to the point. "No. Just teenage boys who are about to learn what it means to deal with Ocean Munroe."

Charles' face darkens and he turns an accusing scowl on Colton before licking his gaze back to me. "It wasn't Colton and his friends retaliating for Saturday night, was it?"

"No," I say bluntly as Colton scoffs behind my shoulder. "I've already handled the backlash from that."

"Handled quietly?"

I think back to yesterday on the boat with the gun jammed under Jude's chin and nod. He won't be squealing about that anytime soon. "Yes," I tell him. "It won't be an issue."

Charles grunts. "Good. I will not accept you dragging the Carrington name through the mud. If there's an issue, it gets dealt with quickly and in private."

Sir. Yes, sir.

I nod while wondering what the hell happened to the douchebag I was introduced to yesterday. He's kind of a strange mix between the Charles from day one and the Charles who silently threatened to beat the shit out of his son yesterday. Though, after seeing him with his pants around his ankles and a 22-year-old gold digger attached to his dick, it's a little harder to take him seriously. Which reminds me, the Carrington name has already been dragged through the mud today. After Colton and Spencer's fight, all the students could talk about was Charles Carrington dropping his pants for some random slut. The rumors that followed were just the icing on the cake.

Charles looks back to his son. "I'd like to see you in my office in ten minutes," he instructs before turning. He goes to walk away when Harrison steps in from the side room with the guy who I'm pretty sure is the gardener, but what can I say? I haven't really paid that much attention to who's been running sound with a pair of garden scissors.

I step through the threshold of the house with Colton at my

back and start making my way to cut through the staff quarters when Harrison's voice stops us both. "Mr. Carrington, I need to report that Enrique here has discovered some vandalism to the property."

"The fuck?" Colton murmurs behind me.

Uh-oh.

"Vandalism?" Charles grunts, looking to the gardener. "What is he talking about? What did you find?"

Enrique looks like he's going to be sick for being spoken to directly but he holds his shit together. "Sir, there is graffiti covering the back wall of your home and it is rather … uh. Unpleasant."

Colton's eyes slice to mine. He knows. There's no doubt, he knows. He saw me and Nic walking around there the other night. At the time, he probably assumed we were sneaking around there to fuck. We should have been more careful.

"Show me," Charles snaps.

Oh, shit.

Despite not being invited, Colton and I follow along and the walk to the back of the property seems to go on forever. Colton stands right beside me the whole way. "It was your boyfriend, wasn't it?"

I scoff under my breath. "I don't know what you're talking about."

He mutters low. "Right."

We walk around to the back of the mansion and I prepare myself for my downfall, struggling to hide the grin as I look up at the work of art splashed across the back wall of the house. It's just as amazing as I remembered it.

Colton's face drops as Charles goes red. "This is unacceptable,"

Charles roars as he takes in the very clear image of him being spit-roasted by Colton and Spencer while Jude and Charlie stand back with their dicks in their hands, holding up scoreboards. To be honest, I think Charles' outrage comes more from the fact that the cartoon Jude and Charlie only scored him a three and a four.

"I want whoever did this found and dealt with," Charles demands.

"Yes, sir," Harrison says immediately. "I believe it would have happened during the party on Saturday night. Perhaps we should discuss stricter security measures for the next event."

Charles just stares, shaking his head. "No. This bullshit just doesn't happen around here. We have been doing things a certain way for over ten years and we're not going to change now because of one delinquent."

"Yes, sir."

"I bet it was that Rinaldi kid," Charles continues, looking to Colton for confirmation. "You saw how oddly he was behaving during the party. Not to mention his father barely made 500 million last year. No wonder he's acting out."

"No," I rush in. "It wasn't Milo."

Charles turns to me as Harrison watches me through suspicious eyes and I curse myself. That was too fucking obvious and judging by the look he's giving me, he knows too.

"How do you know?" Charles demands.

My eyes flick around and come to a stop on Colton, desperately wishing for help but I know better, he's more than happy to throw me to the wolves. "I, uh … I was with him all night. He didn't do it."

Charles steps forward, narrowing his eyes. "You were with him?"

"Yes."

"You left the party after destroying my son's suit."

I nod. "I did," I say, knowing what I'm about to say is taking a risk. "He came to check that I was alright and we hung out in the pool house until his father came to take him home."

Charles watches me for another second before his chin raises and the tension dissipates, and just like that, I'm off the hook. "Right," he says, looking back to Harrison. "Get onto the surveillance and have it dealt with. I want it gone by the end of the day."

Charles walks away and within seconds, Enrique scurries away. I go to leave too but Harrison steps into my way. "You have two choices," he says, bearing down on me and not giving a shit that Colton is here watching him scold one of their house guests. "You can either clean it yourself or I can take the cost of paint out of your mother's paycheck. What's it going to be?"

Fuck.

"I'll clean it."

Harrison pulls his lips into a tight, smug line. "That's what I thought."

I roll my eyes and just as I go to throw shade back at him, he turns on his heel and scatters off, probably to go and make one of the staff cry. I let out a heavy sigh and after looking back at my masterpiece one more time, I cut across the lawn and head for the pool house.

I search in cupboards until I find a big bucket and fill it with warm soapy water then get something to scrub with. This isn't exactly my first time scrubbing graffiti off a wall, but it's the first time I've done it without a police officer breathing down my neck.

I haul the bucket around to the back of the house and as I turn the final corner, I find Colton sitting back in one of the sunbeds from the pool with his feet up and beer in hand. "What the hell do you think you're doing?"

He winks but for once it does not affect me. "Came to watch the show. After all, if someone went to all the effort just to draw a picture of me, it'd be rude not to at least appreciate it while I can."

"You're an ass," I grunt, walking up to the wall and dropping the bucket at my feet.

"And you're a spoiled brat."

"That's rich coming from you. Tell me, how was the caviar that was served on your thirteen birthday? Or what about the million-dollar deposit to your bank account that you received for your tenth?"

Colton narrows his eyes at me. "You know nothing about my life."

"Look around you," I say, waving my hand around the massive, luxurious property. "It's certainly comfortable. You wouldn't know how it feels to not be able to walk from one end of your street to the other without being shot at, or what about getting home at night to find the electricity and gas has been turned off. Do you know what it feels like to be hungry?"

Colton's eyes drop away and just like that, he gets it, but he'll never understand it. Not unless it's something he experiences for himself, but he won't. He'll never have to.

Getting nothing from him, I dunk my scrubbing brush into the water and get to work. I try to ignore his presence at my back but it's impossible. Why is he there? Is he just bored and wants to chill out? Maybe he's lonely in this big house and has no one to talk to, but if he felt like that, he could hang out with one of his friends. I don't understand him and it's driving me insane.

When it gets too much, I look back over my shoulder to find him watching me. "Why are you here, Colton?" I ask quietly, letting him know the fight is gone.

His eyes trail up my body to meet mine and I watch as confusion flickers across his face. "Honestly, I've got no fucking idea."

I nod and dunk the scrubber back into the water, feeling just as confused as he looks. "Okay, then. Why did you cover for me with your dad before? You could have thrown me under the bus and told him that I stole your credit card."

"But you didn't steal my credit card. You stole my fucking Veneno. You came to me, you asked for what you wanted, I gave it to you and I let you walk away without putting any limitations on you. That's on me. You could have spent whatever you wanted and it would have been on me. You shouldn't get in trouble for something that I allowed to happen, though if you touch my fucking car again, I'll end you."

I keep my focus on the wall, positive that if I actually looked at him, he'll shut down and I won't get another word out of him. "Speaking of things that you allowed to happen," I say, skipping over the whole 'I'll end you' comment because we both know that I'll always win. "Why didn't you do something at school?"

"What do you mean?"

"With those guys? You could have stopped them."

"It's not my job to fight all your wars, Ocean," he murmurs, using my name and sending shivers shooting down my spine.

"They'd put acid in the grease. It burned my skin and snapped off chunks of my hair. I was lucky that I didn't end up in the hospital."

Colton is silent for a moment and I refuse to look back as I continue scrubbing. "I didn't know that," he says. "I wouldn't have allowed that. I'd never allow anyone to cause you harm, Jade."

I don't respond as the heaviness of it all begins to cloud my mind. This whole situation is getting frustrating. Twice now he's let me in and when he does, he's kind and shows that deep down, he has a heart but the second he can, he flips the switch and we return to enemy territory.

I can't help but wonder what seeing this graffiti would have felt like for him. Had I known what I now know about Colton's childhood, I probably would have chosen another image to humiliate him with. Seeing this was probably a kick in the gut and I can't help but feel like shit about it, but then, he's also an ass so there's that.

Minutes turn to an hour where I work in our comfortable silence and then all too soon, the wall is clean and dread sinks heavily into my stomach. Why don't I want this to end?

I look back at Colton and lean against the sparkling clean wall as he looks down at his phone. "You knew they were going to pour that grease all over me."

A grin pulls at his lips as his hazel eyes raise to meet mine. "Baby, you didn't think I was there by accident, did you? I wasn't about to miss the show."

I narrow my gaze and lift the bucket of dirty water from my feet. "You're a real ass, you know that, right?"

He shrugs his shoulders as I go to walk past him and in the blink of an eye, I throw my arm out, sending dirty water cascading over the billionaire douchebag.

My eyes bug out of my head as I realize what the hell I just did.

Oh, fuck.

We both pause, looking at each other in shock but upon realizing that I'm wasting precious moments, I run faster than I've ever run in my life.

Colton comes bounding behind me and just as I spy the door to the pool house, his arm curls around my waist, and in seconds, we go crashing down into one of the many pools littered across this insanely perfect property.

CHAPTER 19

I lean back against the headboard of my bed, staring at the TV while not actually taking any of it in. I've had Netflix on for the better part of the night and after realizing that I wasn't going to find sleep tonight, I completely gave up.

Staring at my ceiling didn't cut it, so on went Netflix and that's how I ended up watching the first season of Lucifer, and to be honest, I wasn't expecting to like it quite so much but there's something so exciting about the devil. Maybe it's a bad boy thing … or a British accent thing.

My eyes are heavy and my body is screaming for sleep. It's well past four in the morning but for some reason, I can't seem to switch off. It's been a beyond shitty day with the whole acid grease shower I took and the whole getting sprung for vandalism thing. Not to mention Colton throwing me in the pool completely messed with my new hair and after the torture my hair has been through today, I wasn't willing to destroy it more by washing and drying it again.

So, here is where I've sat all afternoon and night with damp hair and a heavy scowl. With nothing else to do, I pull out my phone and send a quick text, knowing Nic is usually only just getting home at this ridiculous time.

I attach a selfie I took of me standing against the graffitied wall with my scrubbing brush.

Ocean - Sprung!!!!

He texts back almost instantly and I smile to myself. I've been missing him over the past few days.

Nic - Oh, shit! Did you get in trouble? What are you doing awake? You should be sleeping for school tomorrow.

Ocean - Long story! Didn't get busted. Colton and the douchey butler kept it quiet, but scrubbing that wall for over an hour was punishment enough.

Nic - Shit, O. I'm sorry. That's on me.

Ocean - Don't be stupid. If it wasn't spray paint, I would have found another way to fuck with them.

Nic - Good point. Go to bed, babe.

I roll my eyes at his usual bossy nature. Some things will never change. I could be apart from him for years, I could be married with kids and still get messages from him telling me to go to bed. It's one of the many reasons I love him. No matter what the circumstances, he will always be there for me, always protecting, and always taking care of me.

Knowing he's bound to drive over here and kick my ass if I don't do what he says, I let out a sigh and scoot down in my bed.

Ocean - Night.

Nic doesn't respond but I didn't expect him to. He's not the kind to send sweet little goodnight messages. He only gets emotional when it's important and seeing as though it's well into the middle of the night, he's probably more interested in taking some girl home and having his dick sucked until he passes out.

I pull the covers up over my chest and try to get comfortable. I turn off the TV and try my hardest to sleep but it's impossible. No matter what I try, I can't seem to find that sweet unconsciousness.

I stare out the window, watching as the soft breeze sweeps across the top of the pool and makes the smallest ripples in the water. The morning staff has already arrived so there's a glow over the backyard from the staff quarters and without that, I wouldn't be able to see the figure cutting through the backyard.

I sit up, feeling a chill shooting down my spine. This shit used to happen all the time in Breakers Flats. It's not exactly new for me, but here? No, this shit isn't supposed to happen here.

I watch the figure move, narrowing my eyes at the pained way he slinks through the yard. There's something … familiar about him.

The guy moves closer and I fight the urge to sound some kind of alarm. I don't know what it is but my gut tells me to keep quiet.

I watch him as he moves closer to the main house, letting out a breath of relief when he sails straight past the doors of the pool house–doors that are most likely unlocked.

The closer he gets, the more light that shines upon him and as he crosses the window of the pool house, I see his face.

Colton.

I suck in a gasp, taking him in. He got fucked up fighting at school today, but this is worse. So much worse. He looks like he's just taken a few rounds with a professional MMA fighter.

I throw myself out of bed and race through the living room, skipping over my suitcase which I've neglected to put away since the boys first moved us in here. Reaching the door, I tear it open and throw myself out of it, unsure why I seem to care so much.

"Colton," I hiss through the night as he goes to reach for the back door of the main house.

He whips around, surprised to see me awake at this time of night but in doing that, he shows me exactly what his night has been like. "Go to bed," he demands, mimicking the last words I got from Nic, only from him, they don't seem quite so sincere.

I trail my eyes over his face and body. Someone tried to fuck him up but judging from his bloodied and bruised knuckles, Colton might have been the one doing the fucking up. "What happened to you?"

He shakes his head so slightly that for a moment, I wonder if I'd imagined it. "It's nothing."

Colton turns back and reaches for the door handle but I race after him, determined not to let him get away with this. "It's not nothing,"

I say, moving in beside him and reaching the handle before he can. "You're hurt."

"Don't worry about me, Jade," he says as I swing the back door open.

I step through the door first, making him wait his damn turn before looking back and ushering him through. "Sit your stubborn ass down. I'll patch you up."

Colton's eyes come to mine and they narrow in suspicion, but what does he have to be suspicious about? It's not like I'm purposefully going to poke and prod him harder than necessary. Though, now that the idea has wriggled it's way inside my brain … damn.

I couldn't possibly be that mean, could I?

Seeing I'm not about to give him any other choice, he walks through the door and I follow him through to the bathroom. He walks right up to the sink and shoves his hands under the cool water. He sucks in a hiss and I watch through the mirror as his face scrunches in pain.

I hand him a towel and cringe as he pats his hands dry, leaving blood all over the white, expensive towels. If I'd done that back home, mom would have whooped my ass, but it's a different world here, and replacing a towel isn't even something to blink at.

The towel gets dropped into the basin and I watch as he reaches over his head and shrugs out of his shirt. The fabric trails up his skin and I try not to get turned on by the raw emotion on his face. He's in pain but goddamn, that body. Every time he puts it on display, the need to touch him intensifies.

Colton looks over his injuries in the mirror and I watch as his eyes scan over his body. He takes in his bruised jaw, his bloodied hand, the grazes, and red marks across his ribs. I watched him fight Spencer at school and he was amazing. He could even rival some of the Black Widows, so for him to end up looking like this, it must have been a bad fight. Maybe a few guys tried to jump him or the other guy had something over him. All I know is that for him to get injured this way, he wasn't fighting with his head in the game.

His eyes come back to mine and there are so many emotions there—rage, pain, desperation, and hurt. Every one of them tear me apart and it confuses me more than anything I've ever known.

"Come on," I say, trying to distract myself from the confusion clouding my mind. It must be a lack of sleep, otherwise, I'd be perfectly fine. I take his shoulders and push him back to sit on the edge of the marble counter. My fingers burn against his skin but I put it to the back of my mind. I'm surprised he's allowed me to get this far and if he's actually going to let me patch him up, then I need to concentrate.

Once he's seated, I start going through all the cupboards and drawers until I find the first aid kit. Not wasting a second, I dump it down on the counter beside him and start rifling through it.

I start with his face and damn it, it's so hard to concentrate.

Why do I want to kiss him so badly? I should be hating him. I should be curled up in my bed letting him suffer in here on his own. Instead, I'm being as gentle as I possibly can, hoping to God that his handsome face doesn't scar.

The only noise that fills the bathroom is the sounds of me going back and forth to the first aid kit. He lets me concentrate and I'm grateful. My mind is already a mess of confusion. The last thing I need is his chatter to make it worse.

Once his face and hands are bandaged, I move down to his ribs. My fingers brush lightly over his skin and he sucks in a sharp breath. "Why are you doing this?" he murmurs, asking the very question that I haven't been able to stop asking myself.

I shrug my shoulders, not having a proper answer for him. "Someone had to," I tell him, refusing to meet his eyes. "And something tells me you're the kind of guy who would have just gone straight to bed without giving this a second thought."

A soft chuckle slips from between his lips and the sound pulls at something within me. "You might be right about that."

"I'm right about a lot of things," I fire back at him.

Colton's lips pull into a tight line and I do my best to keep my concentration on his ribs, ignoring his strong abs and pecs that stare back at me, begging to be touched. "How'd you learn how to do this?" he questions, catching me off guard, though I can't figure out why. It's a standard question, but it's something personal, and Colton and I strictly don't do personal … except for the other night in his room, but that was different.

"I have four best friends in a gang," I say, choosing to entertain his question. "Knowing how to patch up dickheads with big egos is kind of a requirement."

"Do they get in fights a lot?"

I nod, feeling a soft smile pulling across my lips. I've missed talking about them. "Kairo's a loose cannon. He's had a rough life and holds a lot of anger so if you even look at him wrong he'll beat the shit out of you."

"And Nic?" A flash of something appears behind his eyes but is gone before I have a chance to figure out what it means.

"Nic's the smart one," I tell him. "He's the one you don't want to cross. He's calculating and deadly, and when it comes to protecting what's his, there's no standing in his way."

"Is that supposed to be some kind of warning?"

I meet his heavy gaze and there's so much there but I ignore it, unsure what any of it means. I shrug a shoulder and look back at Colton's ribs. "Take it how you want."

His voice is low, inquiring, and curious. "What's the deal with you two?"

My walls shoot up. I don't like this. Why does he want to know? Why does he *need* to know? I'm used to being the one who's fishing for answers, not the other way around. Is this some kind of trick? Get me to open up and then use it against me in this ridiculous little war?

Reluctance pulls heavy within me yet I find myself eager to please him. "There's nothing going on. He's my best friend and he broke my heart. That's all there is to it."

Colton scoffs. "It seems like a shitload more than just that."

"It is, but that's between me and Nic."

"Got it," he says, raising his hands in surrender. "None of my business." I rub some antiseptic cream into his ribs and just like that, the topic of Nic is dropped. "So, what about the other two?"

"Elijah and Sebastian?" I ask. "They're my world. The four of them are. Sebastian is a flirt, kind of like Charlie actually. He's the go-to guy if you want to party, and the majority of the time he's getting stoned. Elijah is the one with the big heart. He'll never admit it though."

"You guys sound tight."

"We are."

Colton reaches up and brushes his fingers over my shoulder and past my tattoo. "What would they say if they found out about this?"

I shuffle over, watching as his hand falls from my shoulder. "There's nothing for them to find out," I tell him. "Any of it. If they knew you snuck into my room and saw what you saw, they'd kill you without hesitation and if they knew that you've been doing everything in your power to make every day for me a living hell, they'd have you by the balls. There's no winning for you in this situation. You're fucked either way. It's better to just keep your mouth shut."

"If that's the case, then why haven't you said something? You say they're so fucking protective and lethal, you could have squealed and all your problems would have disappeared."

I look away and make sure to press a little harder against his rib which only manages to pull a wicked grin out of him. "You don't want to get rid of me, do you?" he questions, reaching out for my waist and pulling me between his legs. "You love it. You crave the attention and the adrenaline."

"I don't know what you're talking about."

He scoffs. "Don't bullshit me, Jade. I see the way you're always searching me out in a room. You're drawn to me like a moth to a flame.

Even after I tear you down, you keep coming back because you crave it. You want my touch just as badly as you want the fight."

I shake my head. "You're wrong."

His hand brushes over my cheek. "I'm right and you know it, but it's okay, Jade. I like your kind of fucked up."

"You're wrong," I repeat. "I don't like you. I don't even like you a little. You're a fucking arrogant prick, you treat the people around you like shit, and you wouldn't know the first thing about enjoying life. I despise you, Colton. You and I will never be on the same page."

Colton leans in, ignoring the way the movement is bound to tear through his ribs. His lips brush gently over mine. "I couldn't agree more. You're trash and you'll never be on the same page as me let alone the same level."

"If I'm trash, then why do you keep covering for me? Why do you keep coming back for more, and why the hell can't you keep your hands off me?"

He shakes his head, his eyes flaming with desire. "I've got no fucking clue."

He holds my eyes for a moment longer and when it gets too much, I step out of his hold and grab the bandage. "Put your arms up."

He does as he's told and I make quick work of wrapping his ribs, desperately wanting to get out of here. This whole thing is getting to be too much for me to handle. There are so many lines being crossed but in reality, I have no idea where those lines even lay.

I like things black and white and right now, there's a whole lot of grey. Hell, there's a whole fucking rainbow in there and I have no idea what any of it means. I've never been so confused in my life. I have this growing need to touch him while at the same time, I want to punch him in the junk and watch him cry.

God, he's a fucking ass and with each word he says, I only want to hate him more. Only, then he has to go and hit me with moments like this afternoon when he sat with me as I cleaned the wall, and the day before when he opened up about his father's abuse. It doesn't make sense and I'm starting to get whiplash.

There's something building between us, something big and it's scaring the absolute shit out of me.

I finish off Colton's bandages and give him a forced smile. "You're all good," I tell him, already retreating to the bathroom door.

I push my way out and am just about safe when his voice rings out behind me. "Wait."

Shit. So fucking close.

I stop in the doorway and look back at Colton, silently waiting. His eyes meet mine and there's a strange vulnerability shining back at me. His gaze lingers on my new haircut before it drops to his bandaged knuckles. "You don't need to worry about those guys hurting you again."

"Guys?" I question. "You mean the dickheads from school?"

He nods and just like that, I know exactly where these cuts and bruises came from.

I step back into the bathroom, pulling the door closed behind me and feeling the tension rise in the room. "You beat them up? All five of them?"

He nods. "They hurt you. They took it too far."

Emotion swells inside of me. Maybe it's the lack of sleep or the confusion that's been intensifying day by day, but one second I'm hesitating by the door, and the next I'm crossing the bathroom and curling my fingers around the back of his neck.

My lips press against his as his hands sweep around my waist, pulling me in tight against his exhausted body. He holds me tenderly almost as though I'm some kind of valued possession, the same way I'd imagine him to hold the love of his life, and despite knowing what a bad idea this is, I can't bring myself to stop.

It's not like the forceful, domineering kisses we've shared over the past week, this is something different, something more and it terrifies me.

Colton Carrington should not have that kind of hold over me but clearly, he does.

Not allowing myself to get drowned in his trap, I pull away, refusing to meet his eyes before scrambling through the door like a terrified little bitch.

CHAPTER 20

"**A**nd then ... and then," Milo howls, slapping a hand on the table as we wait for Mr. Hall to arrive at our Economics class. "Then he showed me the ring and made a point that he was going to keep it in his safe for when I was ready to pop the question."

"Are you kidding?" I laugh as tears fill my eyes and I try my hardest to wipe them away, only they come straight back again. It's hard to believe that the black and white party was only three days ago. It almost seems like it's been a lifetime since I poured bourbon all over the four famous shitheads of Bellevue Springs. I'm seriously experiencing life at fifteen what the fucks an hour. I wonder if every weekend is going to be so full on or if this past one was just special because Colton had a point to prove.

Today has been a bit wild for a Tuesday. Not only were there rumors going around claiming that the five grease monkeys that attacked me were involved in some sort of gang mugging last night, but they've also mysteriously been suspended after I saw my mother slipping into the back of one of Charles' many cars, leaving the school grounds.

I can only imagine how that meeting with Dean Simmons would have gone. Mom was fuming about it all night. The second she finished with her shift, she let it all out and it's clear that it's all she could think about all afternoon. I'm scared of my mother on a good day, but to be on the end of her anger after someone hurt her only baby in an environment where she's supposed to be protected, I can guarantee that Simmons would have been shitting his pants. That woman knows how to get what she wants and she's not afraid to take it with both hands.

"I wish I was kidding," Milo says. "Mom couldn't stop gushing about how my wedding day was going to be the best day of my life."

"Anyone who thinks their wedding day is the best day of their life clearly has never experienced the joys of having two candy bars fall out of the vending machine at the same time."

"Where the hell do you come up with this shit?"

I raise a questioning brow. "You can't deny that I have a valid point."

"Maybe," he says. "But to be honest, none of the idiots around here would know that feeling. We don't have vending machines."

"Oh, that's right. You guys have butlers and maids that fetch your candy bars for you."

"Damn straight, wifey," he grins widely. "Now, do you want to hear about our wedding or not?"

Milo continues with his story but my attention is drawn away as Colton walks into the room with Jude and Spencer at his back. Just like always, his eyes come to mine first, and just like always, I can't tear my gaze away.

He scoffs and looks away as though having my attention is a humiliation that he can't stand to have and it grinds on my nerves. He's more than happy to have me patching him up all night, he's more than okay to jump to my defense and beat the living shit out of five boys he's most likely known his whole life, and he's more than on board with the idea of kissing me at four in the morning, but having the rest of the world know that he has my attention is a no go.

He's infuriating.

I clench my jaw, wishing I could march right over there and smack the smirk off his face.

Colton is a completely different person when we're at home. It's as though in the comfort of his own home he has a soul that's kind, caring, and filled with confusion—it's not so bad. Here at school, it's as though I don't even exist. He treats me like the trash he always claims me to be, and soon enough my patience is going to wear thin and I'm going to snap.

Patience has never been my strong suit. Just ask Mia Bodegraven from third grade who was on the receiving end of my most iconic tantrum yet. She didn't think I was cool enough to be invited to her stupid pamper birthday party and told the whole school that I had boy germs because I prefer to hang out with them. I showed that bitch. I stole mom's phone and texted all the parents of the kids she'd invited and told them the party had been canceled and then I had my own party, and guess who wasn't invited? I like to think I was a conniving kid and it's only helped me to become the baddest bitch these fuckers have ever dealt with. Oh, not to mention that I might have also punched her in the nose when my mom found out and demanded I apologize to the little cow. That was also my very first suspension. I was so proud of myself.

Colton drops down into his desk chair at the back of the classroom as other students begin to gravitate toward him, all wanting his attention, all wanting to hear what he has to say and then claim it to be gospel.

A quick thirty seconds pass before Mr. Hall finally walks in and breaks up the gag-fest at the back of the room. Milo hushes beside me but refuses to finish his story until every last word is out. Apparently, our wedding will be set in the Hamptons during spring on his father's holiday property. He already has a caterer and photographer in mind, though the ceremony part has to be in a church otherwise Milo's grandmother would die of embarrassment, and we couldn't possibly have that happen, especially on our wedding day.

Mr. Hall gets started on today's lesson while I try to ignore the growing presence at the back of the room. My whole body screams to turn and look at him, just to see if he's as aware of me as I am of him.

Maybe I could drop a pen and sneak a peek.

Shit. What is wrong with me? I need to get a grip and pretend he's not even there. Out of sight out of mind. Yeah, that's a load of bullshit. Whoever came up with that stupid saying clearly never had a spider disappear in their bedroom.

A loud screeching tears through the room and sends chills down my spine. My head whips around as every student in the classroom sits up a little straighter.

It's an alarm.

Fuck.

Panic sits heavily in my bones as silence falls across the room.

No, no, no, no, no. This can't be happening again.

"What are you doing?" I yell at Mr. Hall who stands at the front of the room doing absolutely nothing. In fact, no one is making a fucking move. They should be diving into the corners of the room, away from windows.

This is the real out of sight out of mind. This is the ultimate fucking test.

I look around in horror before it becomes startlingly obvious. These guys have never had to deal with a threat like this before. They probably just assume this is the kind of shit that only happens in movies but for me, it's all too real.

I fly across the room so fast that I don't even remember moving. "Get down," I yell, diving against the classroom door and slamming it shut while simultaneously closing the blinds on the little window at the top of the door.

After turning the latch I look around in a panic to find all the guys watching me in confusion while slowly rising to their feet. "Oceania," Mr. Hall scolds. "What do you think you're doing? Get off the floor and move out of the way."

"ARE YOU FUCKING INSANE? Why aren't you doing anything? Can't you hear that alarm? There's a fucking shooter in the school and you're screwing around, wasting time. You're going to be responsible if one of these fuckwits get shot—"

"Miss Munroe."

For fuck's sake. This guy is a joke. He should be doing something to help. All this time I thought this school was so superior and it turns out they don't even have policies and procedures in place to deal with these kinds of emergencies. Back in Breakers Flats, we were running these drills every two weeks after Shawn Landers brought a gun to school and opened fire at his history teacher. He missed by miles and was tackled to the ground by a senior student then promptly knocked the fuck out, but I'll never forget the fear that rattled through my bones. Hearing random gunshots around Breakers Flats isn't exactly a new thing, but having it inside the school that was filled with innocent lives was terrifying.

I fly to my feet, scrambling around the room. "Someone help me get all the blinds down," I demand, knowing we're all going to be safer if we can work together and get ourselves hidden. I wonder if this classroom has some kind of storeroom.

"Ocean, babe," Milo's voice cuts through the noise and I look to him with fear. "No one has a gun. It's the fire drill alarm. There's no shooter here."

I look to him in confusion, because I don't believe what I'm hearing. "What?" I question, my heart still pounding in my chest.

Milo nods, but it's not until I look at Colton at the back of the room and see the concern lining his hazel eyes that I finally start to get it. He nods so discreetly that no one else would be able to see it and in that moment, relief washes over me, taking the fear of my memories with it.

I notice the faces of the students around me. A fuck up like that should have them all laughing, but all I see are somber expressions and for the first time since being here, I think they might just understand the type of world I've grown up in.

I take a shaky breath, looking back at Milo. "It's just a fire drill," I murmur to myself, almost as though I need to hear the words repeated over and over again to make it more real.

"Yes," Mr. Hall demands with a sour tone to his voice. "It is a fire drill and you've made us appear incompetent of clearing the classroom in a timely manner. Now, please unlock my classroom door and promptly file out of the room and make your way to the designated meeting area."

Well, shit.

I nod and turn on my heel, feeling like a fucking idiot.

I hightail it out of here, not giving a damn that I have no idea where this designated meeting area is. All that matters is getting out of here before someone has something to say about my little performance. Standing in a towel in front of the whole student body is nothing compared to being confronted and questioned about one of the scariest days of my life.

"What the hell was that about?" Milo demands, quickly catching up with me.

"Nothing," I rush out. "Just a startling reminder of how different our worlds really are."

"Did that shit used to happen a lot back home?" he questions, his voice low and full of concern.

My eyes drop to the floor, not wanting to discuss this. "More than you'll ever know."

Milo picks up on my hesitation and drops the topic, choosing to slip his hand into mine and pull me along to the gymnasium where the whole school is lined up in alphabetical order, far away from the main buildings of the school. Milo explains what's going to happen and ten minutes later, I'm standing with the rest of the M's waiting for my name to be marked off.

Ten minutes pass and then twenty before I lean over to the guy beside me. "What's taking so long?" I ask, trying not to laugh at the horror on his face as I speak to him.

"Oh, um…" he starts, stumbling over his words. "They like to be precise. They have faculty checking every classroom, storage room, and bathroom to make sure they have everyone accounted for. There are always a few kids who disappear during this shit to get us out of class."

No shit.

"In that case," I say with a smile. "I'm out of here."

I slip through the crowd as I hear his voice trailing behind me. "Wait, no. You can't."

I lose him in no time and start making my way around the gymnasium. There are teachers everywhere, most of them lingering by the main entrance so if I want to get out of here undetected, I'm going to have to go exploring.

There's only one door that's mostly out of sight and I quickly duck through it to find a back hallway. I have no other choice but to follow it and then find myself laughing as I walk right through to an Olympic sized swimming pool. I should have known there was one of these here. I wouldn't even be surprised to find this thing heated. The good news is that a pool like this is bound to have a proper entrance that I'll be able to freely walk through, assuming it's not locked.

I start walking around the massive pool and find myself gawking up at the grandstand. They must be able to fit at least two thousand spectators in here. Why the hell would they need this much seating? Is rich boy swimming *that* popular? Who would have known?

I get halfway around the pool when a voice calls out from behind me, so close behind me that it sends chills sweeping across my skin. "Seems we've got a stray."

I whip around to find Jude hovering with a nasty, smug grin, watching me like a hawk. I roll my eyes as a show of annoyance even though it's something very different that I feel rushing through my veins. "Fuck off, Jude," I say with an irritated groan, discreetly taking a step away from him.

He walks with me, meeting me step for step. "No gun today?" he questions, eyeing me up and down. "Damn, baby. You don't seem so tough now."

"I'm warning you, Jude. Back the fuck off. If you touch me, I'll fucking ruin you."

"Touch you?" he laughs. "Look at you. You're nothing. I'd fuck anything with a heartbeat but I wouldn't waste my time with you. Maybe at the start I considered it, but your putrid low class has me rethinking. You're the kind of bitch to purposely get pregnant and try to dig your claws into my money, but I'd fucking bury you before that happens."

I give him a sugary sweet smile. "In order to insult me, I must value your opinion first. Nice try though."

Jude's features darken. I'd dare say the guys of Bellevue Springs aren't the type who are used to women fighting back.

My face scrunches as I look at him with distaste. The guy seriously thinks he's a fucking prize. He's the kind who thinks every woman wants him but he couldn't be more wrong. Sure he's attractive, but the second he opens his mouth, he ruins his chances. I turn and walk away, only the fucker follows me. "You are the reason why there are directions on shampoo bottles. What didn't you understand? Leave me the fuck alone."

"I'll leave you alone once I've finished dealing with you," Jude scoffs.

I spin around, no stranger to a threat. "What the fuck is that supposed to mean?" I demand, getting in his face and throwing him off guard.

Jude's grin twists and becomes wicked. "It means you're a fucking problem."

His arms snap out with a speed I wasn't prepared for. Nails dig into my skin and panic rises in my chest. He moves to the side, blocking me from getting away and using his body to force me toward the pool. "HEL—"

A hand is slammed down over my mouth and I try not to panic. There's no doubt that I'm going in this pool but panic is only going to make it harder to get out of it, that's assuming he's going to let me out.

Jude gets his hands around me and I'm lifted off the edge of the pool. I claw my nails against his skin, desperately trying to inflict as much pain as possible.

"Yo, what the fuck are you doing?" a voice comes from somewhere around the huge room.

"Fuck off, Spence. This is between me and this bitch."

I push against him, desperately trying to free myself. "Let me go."

"Leave her alone, man," he says sounding bored, almost as though he isn't going to do shit about this. "She's probably going to squeal the second she gets a chance. You're only causing more problems for yourself."

"I'm fucking solving one," he spits back, grunting as I fight against him. "This bitch won't be a problem once I'm through with her."

Oh, fuck.

Jude gets my hands trapped in one of his and I know it's game over. I can't get out of this, not without getting thrown into the pool.

"I'm going to fucking kill you," I screech.

"Not if I kill you first," he promises just moments before he throws me hard, sending me hurtling toward the deep water.

I suck in one last desperate breath just as my body crashes down hard against the still water. Panic creeps up on me. I'm not a great swimmer. I was lucky the other night when Colton tackled me into his pool that his arms were around me and we were mostly in a shallow part of the pool, but this water must be at least eight feet deep.

The momentum from Jude's throw has me diving nearly all the way to the bottom and I try to remind myself to keep calm. Panicking isn't going to help my ass get back to the surface. My momentum slows and I find myself concentrating on getting to the surface.

It's just like taking a swim at the local swimming hole. I've done it countless times before. This is nothing. I can handle this.

The panic begins to seep out of me and as my feet come under me to push up off the bottom. I find myself opening my eyes and looking up through the water. Jude hovers above the edge of the pool, looking down and watching the show and while I can't make out his feature, it's damn clear that he's intent on causing as much harm as possible. I bet he's counting on the fact that a poor girl like me wouldn't have taken swimming lessons as a kid. He'd be right, but that doesn't mean that I'm completely hopeless.

If he wants to play, then we'll play.

I have enough oxygen in my system to make him doublethink his tactics. I should have filed a report against him when I had the chance. An attempted rape case would look good beside his attempted murder one, but he won't be getting the best of me.

A few seconds pass and I use my arms to roll myself onto my back. My arms spread out at my sides and I have to gently sway my feet to keep me below the water. I'm not surprised when Spencer comes rushing in beside Jude and with the water beginning to calm, it's easy to see the panic on his face.

It's only a moment after Spencer arrives that the whole group is there. Colton and Charlie step up to the side of the pool and it makes me wonder where the hell they came from. For them to be here so soon, they must have been here while I was struggling against Jude, meaning they saw and didn't do a damn thing about it.

I look up at Colton and somehow this goes from some kind of bullshit war between Jude and I to a challenge between Colton and I.

Who will break first?

Colton's face remains cool, calm, and collected and I watch as the four of them talk among themselves, the only sign of his distress being his fisted hands at his sides. He never takes his eyes off mine.

My oxygen slowly begins running out, but I know my body. I know my limits. I can play this out for a little while longer.

A fifth body appears at the opposite edge of the pool and my eyes break Colton's hold to find Milo staring down in horror. I watch as he goes to jump but Colton's loud, booming "NO. Leave her," is heard, even through the water.

Milo hesitates and his eyes flick to mine. I don't doubt he's questioning if I'm actually alive down here, so I move my arm back and forth, trying to ease his mind enough to take a backseat.

I look back at Colton. Time is running out.

Will he break, or will I?

It's a risky fucking game, but I wasn't taught to take the easy way out. I was taught to fight for what I believe in, though I have a feeling that mom wouldn't quite be pleased to find that this was the way my young mind interpreted her lesson.

It's fucking stupid is what it is. Trust me, that knowledge isn't lost on me.

I've been down here for at least thirty full seconds and common sense would have him knowing that I can't last much longer. The question is am I stubborn enough to allow myself to pass out down here or does he blow his 'I don't give a shit' facade and come in here after me?

It's a fight for dominance and right now, neither of us is willing to relent.

I'll give myself five more seconds and then the game is up.

Five.

Four.

Three.

Colton jumps.

He dives in after me, swimming down into the deep waters and quickly grabbing at me. He scoops me into his strong arms and pushes up off the bottom of the pool with everything he's got.

We break the surface within sheer moments and I discreetly suck in a deep breath as I hear Colton doing the same. I flop my body heavily against his as he swims to the edge of the pool.

Charlie and Spencer are there and grab my arms. They haul me out and lay me on the dirty ground.

"Is she fucking breathing?" Colton roars as I hear a rush of water, telling me he must have pulled himself out of the pool.

"I don't know," Charlie replies, a little too close to my face as the other two remain silent.

"MOVE."

I feel hands on my body, cold and wet just like mine and I know it's Colton.

"Ocean?" Milo calls in a panic, sending a wave of guilt coursing through me, but I don't respond. I'm going to see this through. If Colton wants to insist on fucking with my head, then I'm going to do the same. "If your little fucked up game has killed her, I'm coming after you, Carrington. All of you fuckers will go down for this."

"If we go down, you're fucking coming with us," Jude spits at him. "You could have dived in, but you didn't. If she's dead, then that's on you too."

Fuck. My poor Milo.

He'll forgive me, he has too.

"Shut the fuck up," Colton roars. "I have to give her CPR."

I feel the heat of Colton's lips hovering above mine, ready to start saving my life and I decide that enough is enough. For him to think that he's about to start CPR means that I've taken this far enough.

My eyes spring open and I grin up at him. "Well, who would have known that you cared so much?"

His face drops, realizing that he's just been played. He rears back from me. "That's fucked up," he roars and I hear Milo's breath of relief. "I can't … FUCK."

Colton flies to his feet and within moments, he's slamming his way out the door with a pissed off Charlie right on his heels. Spencer meets my eyes and shakes his head before following and then I'm left with Jude staring down at me.

He doesn't say a word, just starts walking away as though he never did a thing. "This isn't over," I call after him, glad that he's just witnessed how fucking crazy I can be. "I'm going to take you the fuck down, Jude, and when I do, you're going to wish you never met me."

He slams through the door but I know that he got my message loud and clear.

"Colton was right," Milo says, dropping to his knees beside me. "That really was fucked up."

"I know," I say with a cringe. "I'm sorry. I didn't want to scare you like that, but I'd already started and I wasn't going to back down."

"Scared?" he laughs. "Girl, I wasn't scared. That was all acting. I saw the breath you took the second you broke through the water. You made a fool of him, but you better be armed, he's going to come back swinging and when he does, you better be prepared."

CHAPTER 21

I sit cross-legged on the sunbed while looking down at my stupid math textbook. It's been yet another shitty week. The sun has just set on Saturday night, taking my boys away with it, though I shouldn't have been surprised. Saturday nights are their time to shine. It's when the Black Widows come out to play and they can hardly do it while chilling out in Bellevue Springs. I mean, who would scare the teenagers into obedience if they're not there to do it? It's not like Nic's father is actually going to go out and get the job done. He'd rather send his son into shitty situations.

God, I hate that guy. It's hard to believe someone so vile could be related to Nic. The only thing they share is their looks, everything else is completely different. He's the type who would willingly throw his men under the bus just to save himself. He's a real asshole.

I bring my attention back to the textbook. I've only been staring at it for fifteen minutes, but it's been a long fifteen minutes. Usually, my struggle to concentrate comes from my lack of interest in the work, but tonight, it's Colton.

Lately, it's always Colton.

He's having a party in the main house and all of Bellevue Springs must be here. There are people lingering everywhere. It's so not my scene. My idea of a fun Saturday night is chilling with my boys back at home. We've always kept away from the party scene. Bad shit always went down at parties and the more people at a party, the more witnesses there were. In our town, witnesses meant jail time.

Music thumps heavily through the property and despite how badly I'm itching to go over there and take a quick peek, I keep my ass parked on the sunbed. Hell, I don't even care if I actually read one damn word in the textbook tonight. It's open on my lap and that's all I need. It's my distraction, and if someone comes creeping out here, I have all the right to tell them to fuck off and to quit disturbing me. Though in all honesty, the textbook is more of an excuse. Without it, I'd just look like a jealous idiot who didn't get invited to the popular guy's party.

Tune it out. Tune it out. Tune it out.

I don't care about a stupid party.

I'm a big girl. I can handle a night of resistance. Besides, Colton has gone out of his way to make my life a living hell. Especially in the last few days since the whole pretending to drown thing. Let's just say he's a little put off that I was able to pull one over on him. He makes such a show of not caring, especially in public and when that facade was challenged, he wasn't happy. Since then, it's like he's been Colton 2.0. Everything is more. More scowls, more hate, more taunts. I've never heard 'the help' or 'Jade' so much in my life.

Colton hates me, that much is clear, but there's also a small part of him that cares and it drives him insane. He doesn't know why he cares and quite frankly, I don't know either, but it makes for great entertainment.

"There you are," comes a familiar voice sailing high over the noise of the party. "I've been looking for you all night. No way did I expect you to be hiding out here."

My eyes snap up from the textbook to Milo and take in the way he sways from left to right. "Dare I ask where you thought I was hiding?" I question. "And for the record, I'm not hiding out. I'm studying."

Milo laughs, a real belly laugh that has him stumbling forward and wobbling by the side of the pool. "Keep lying to yourself, babe," he says, striding toward me. "You're hiding out so bad that you might as well climb in the closet with me. It's a tight fit in there, but I can make some room. Rent ain't cheap though."

I roll my eyes as he collects the textbook and drops it onto the floor then promptly steals its spot on the end of the sunbed. "Do you mind? I was reading that."

"No you weren't," he scoffs. "But just to be clear, I thought you were more exciting than this. I checked all the upstairs bedrooms, hoping to find you in the middle of a gangbang sandwich. When I couldn't find you, I thought maybe you'd be handcuffed to your bed and was stuck. I only came down here because it was my last option and I'm sorry to tell you, babe, but finding you sulking out here with absolutely no dicks flying around your face is really killing my Ocean Munroe is a bad bitch vibe."

My brows pinch. "I am not sulking."

"You're right. You're not sulking. You're butthurt and jealous."

"You better take that back before I give you a gangbang sandwich with my fist, then trust me, you'll be the one butthurt."

A crooked smile stretches across his face and my eyes are rolling before he even gets a word out. A lousy chuckle pulls from within before a hiccup comes up and surprises us both. "Damn, Ocean. You know, I think I might have had just enough to drink to let you try it, but serious question though", he says, leaning forward and taking my hand. His thumb runs over the top of my hand before curling my fingers into a fist. "How soft are your hands and just how pointy are your knuckles?"

I tear my hand out of his grip and scrunch my face as I glare. "Stay away from my hands, you creepy perv."

Milo shrugs his shoulders. "Then don't offer to shove them up my ass. Now hurry up, I need you at this party so I can finally start enjoying myself. You're my entertainment, you know that, right?"

I shake my head. "I'm really not feeling a party right now. I'd rather just stay here."

"Stay here and mope? God, you're so boring. When a man adopts a girl from the hood, she's supposed to be fucking wild. You're letting me down, Ocean. You're giving all the girls from Broken Flats a bad name."

"It's Breakers Flats," I say with a snobby groan.

"I don't care if it's Pervert Hills, you're coming to party with me. I'll keep you away from Carrington, pour shots down your throat, and encourage bad decisions. Besides, Jude is already passed out and Spencer is finger fucking some skank from BSP in the spa."

I raise a brow. Why do I want to see that so bad?

My eyes slide up to meet Milo's, and on seeing those big puppy dog eyes and pleasing smile, I cave. "Fine, but just know, if he comes at me, I'm not holding back."

Milo grins wider and throws himself to his feet, grabbing my hand and hauling me up behind him. "Good. Now, you're going to need a bikini."

Fuck me.

Half an hour later, I sit around the pool with hundreds of bodies partying around me and I have to admit, I'm kind of having a good time. There are too many people that Colton hasn't been an issue for me, and just as Milo had promised, Jude is passed out while Spencer is grinding against some chick in the spa.

Milo has already managed to shove two shots down my throat. I hadn't even finished dressing and he'd already found a bottle of Vodka. I thought he was drunk when he came to get me, but it turns out I didn't really understand the true meaning of the word because now he is absolutely wasted. I mean, damn. He's a mess, but a good kind of mess.

He goes off to who knows where and I realize that despite his many promises about partying with me and encouraging bad decisions, I'm probably not going to see him for the rest of the night.

A girl who looks vaguely familiar walks up beside me and drops down onto Milo's vacated sunbed and instantly falls into a chatty conversation. I don't hear a word she says as all I can think about is how I know her. She seems so familiar. Usually, in these situations, I like to say that I probably know the person from school but in this case, I really can't. You know, considering that she has the most perfect pair of tits staring back at me. It's not fair. I mean, mine are great. I absolutely love them and wouldn't change them for anything, but hers are … wow!

She's been here for nearly ten minutes chatting before it hits me— the boat. This was the girl who came and chatted to me and made that day just a little more bearable. It's crazy to think just how much has happened since that day.

Now confident that I know who she is, I'm able to relax back into the sunbed and listen to her chatter and just like on the boat, I find that she's really not too bad. It's a shame I can't remember her name but when I think about it, I'm not sure she ever offered it and after all this time, it'd probably be considered rude to ask for it now. I'll check with Milo later.

Soon enough, girls start gravitating toward us and for some reason, they're all fawning over the tattoo that sits over my shoulder. I guess in their clean-cut world, seeing a girl with visible tattoos isn't something they come across every day. They're always covered or hidden away. I don't doubt that a handful of these girls are hiding little tramp stamps and love hearts.

One girl tells me how she wishes she could get one and before I know it, I'm racing through the massive house, collecting a bowl of things and showing them all how to DIY tattoo, doing the good old stick and poke with India ink, thread, and a needle.

Hours pass before my stomach begins growling and I go searching for food. I still haven't spoken to Milo but I've been keeping an eye on him. It's impossible not to. He seems to be everywhere. He's so damn loud, but I don't care because it makes watching him a shitload easier.

I wander into the house, following the smell of pizza and grin as I find the many arrays of boxes spread out over the kitchen counter. All my favorites are here and as I dig in, I'm happy to find them still warm.

Taking a bite, my eyes roll into the back of my head. This is life right here. Whoever made this pizza deserves a fucking medal. Knowing I won't be going anywhere for a while, I grab a plate and load it up before jumping up onto the kitchen counter and watching the party as I eat.

I'm halfway through my third slice when the douche squad comes rolling through the kitchen and I groan to myself. It's all four of them and I silently curse the stupid bitch who woke up Jude, though he seems content with ignoring my presence which I'm more than alright with. Spencer looks over me with interest while Colton just glares, looking as though he's about to have some kind of tantrum because I had the nerve to show up at his party uninvited.

Charlie's eyes instantly fall to my bikini top and instead of walking straight past, he pulls himself up and gives me a flirty smile. "I was wondering if you were going to make an appearance tonight."

I can practically hear Colton's eye roll, but knowing how much it annoys him, I play along. A flirtatious smile tears across my face and for a moment, Charlie looks dumbfounded. "What are you talking about?" I say with a fake giggle, lightly smacking his chest. "I've been here for ages, silly."

His jaw drops a fraction and I take all sorts of satisfaction out of it, watching how a guy like Charlie who would have girls constantly throwing themselves at him is affected by the one chick his parents wouldn't approve of. Don't get me wrong, that thought sucks and only serves to remind me how I don't belong here, but it's also kind of thrilling.

"You have? Nah, it's not possible," he says, dropping his eyes over my body again. "I would have noticed you the second you walked through the door."

I lean forward and trail my fingers over the front of his shirt before twisting them into the material and pulling him in. He steps in between my legs and his hands instantly fall to my thighs. "You see, that's just it," I whisper into his ear, my breath tickling against his neck. "I came through the back."

Colton turns his back on us and focuses on grabbing a slice of pizza. "Don't fall for her bullshit, Charlie. She's just playing you."

His eyes linger on my mouth and I watch as his tongue pokes out and trails over his full bottom lip, completely enraptured by me. "Nah," he says, his voice low and tortured, choosing not to believe his friend when in reality, he'd be smart to. "She wouldn't do that. Look at her eyes. She's down."

Colton turns and watches the show while Spencer pushes up onto the counter beside the pizza boxes. A lazy grin plays on his lips as he watches his friend about to strike out while Jude happily sulks and walks away, making life a little easier for us all. Though hopefully, he's not about to go and search out some poor girl to assault.

I can't help but look up and meet Colton's eyes across the kitchen. Why are they always on me? They burn so dangerously. It's so intense and alluring and if Charlie wasn't standing between my legs right now, I'd be clenching my thighs.

Charlie raises his chin, welcoming me in and I find myself dipping my face down toward his. Knowing Colton's watching closely has my courage skyrocketing and I brush my lips over Charlie's. He catches them in his and kisses me deeply, but allows me to take control. My tongue pokes out as my eyes close in satisfaction.

Damn, this boy can kiss but I refuse to get carried away. I'm not starting something with Charlie that I won't be finishing. I pull back, keeping my lips hovered right over his. "Colton's right," I whisper. "I'm not down for anything except to fuck you over."

His eyes blaze with need. "Please fuck me over."

Colton's scoff has my eyes shooting back up to see raging jealousy that seems to disappear the second my eyes land on his. Confusion sweeps through me but Spencer quickly steals my attention. "Come on, man," he says. "You're all fucking talk. Look at her, she needs a fucking man to keep her satisfied. You've seen the guys she's used to hanging out with. You couldn't cut it."

Wait. When did Charlie see my boys?

Charlie looks back at his friend and flips him the bird before stepping out of my legs and sitting up on the counter beside me, still keeping his hand on my thigh, though it doesn't go unnoticed that Colton can't stop staring at it. "Trust me," Charlie says with a cocky grin, looking at Spencer. He squeezes his hand on my thigh and trails it a little higher, making a desperate thrill sweep through me. When was the last time I got laid? "I can give her exactly what she needs."

"Please," Spencer scoffs, meeting my eyes. "You ever want a real man to show you what's up, all you have to do is call."

I raise a brow as tension seems to roll off Charlie in waves. I didn't take him as the possessive type but then I guess I don't really know these guys. What I do know is that Charlie thinks that he has some kind of claim on me and that shit is not about to fly.

I keep my gaze pinned on Spencer and gently lower my finger to my thigh. I watch as he zones in on it then I slowly begin sliding it up toward the promised land. I feel Colton's heated gaze, just as heavily focused on my thigh as his friends but I don't dare look away from Spencer. This game is too much fun. "You think you can handle me?" I murmur, my voice low and full of seduction.

Spencer licks his dry lips as his eyes become hooded. "I know I can," he says. "You won't be able to walk after I'm through with you."

I bite my bottom lip just to be a tease then open my legs wider. "Then what are you waiting for?" I whisper, knowing damn well these three boys can hear me perfectly well. They're desperate for my every word. "Come and get it."

Spencer's eyes go wide as his brows shoot up. Hesitation filters through his features and I laugh under my breath. Charlie's hand tightens again while Colton's eyes seem to darken even more.

I scoot to the edge of the counter which has Charlie's hand falling off my thigh then jump down. I cross to the other side and walk straight into Spencer's open legs. His hands instinctively fall to my waist and I grin up at him. "Your hesitation tells me everything I need to know," I taunt. "You're all talk, but what's more is how easily affected you are. I didn't even touch you and I had you eating out of the palm of my hand. You're weak, Spencer. Charlie might be willing to make a fool of himself and get screwed over in the process but at least he went for it. He didn't hesitate."

Charlie howls with laughter as Spencer's eyes darken in rage. He likes showing himself up. He likes being the guy who can do no wrong but being called out for his bullshit … no, that doesn't sit well.

"Watch it," he growls deeply.

I shake my head. "No, you watch it. The next time you come promising a girl that you have what it takes to make her scream, make sure you can follow through with the goods. There's nothing worse than getting into bed with a guy to find out he has absolutely no idea what he's doing and I'm sorry to tell you, Spencer, but you just proved in less than two seconds that you're exactly that guy."

I give him a sweet smile then push up onto my tippy toes and press a feather-soft kiss on his cheek before he has a chance to tell me to fuck off. "You're sweet though, so there's that."

With that, I turn and walk away but not before stopping at Colton and resting my hand against his chest. "Same goes for you, big guy," I murmur, capturing his deep gaze and holding it hostage. "All talk."

Something flashes in his eyes but I don't hang around to find out what because there's no doubt in my mind that given the chance, he'll be the one to follow through and if he did, it would destroy me.

CHAPTER 22

Colton's thick fingers push up into me, making me groan deeply and hold onto him with everything I have, desperately needing more. They plunge deep, reaching me in places I never even knew about.

In. Out. In. Out. It's the best kind of torture.

Why have I waited so long for this? I should have just let him have me that first time in my room.

My hand curls up around his back until my fingers are knotted in his messy hair. His thumb presses against my clit and starts making slow, painful circles that have my orgasm creeping up on me. He's barely touched me. How is it possible to be so close to the edge already?

Colton's hand grabs the base of my neck and tightens. I suck in a breath and meet his heated gaze. Hazel pools of desire look back at me and I want to drown in them, swim in their depths until he completely claims me.

Yes. Fuck. This is everything.

My chest presses up against his and he stretches out his fingers against my neck, his thumb pushing up against my jaw and forcing my head aside. His full lips instantly take advantage, kissing me below my ear and turning every nerve ending into a writhing mess of elation.

His tongue starts working over my sensitive skin as his fingers pick up their pace. He adds a third finger and a loud, guttural groan is pulled from deep within me.

"Colton," I pant. "Yes."

My orgasm creeps closer. I feel it there, so desperate to let it go. It builds higher and higher and every touch has me needing more. It's torture. Sweet, sweet torture.

Freezing water begins to pool around me and my eyes fly open only to find myself staring up at the starry sky. What the actual fuck. I go to start looking around and find my mattress completely soaked and quickly sinking into the pool.

A loud gasp tears out of me and I throw myself to my feet on top of the mattress. The cool air of the night quickly hits my skin and freezes my wet body. I have to jump. I'm right in the fucking middle, but more importantly, how the fuck did I get here? I might have drunk way too much at that party but I can guarantee that I didn't drag my mattress out here and decide to sleep in the middle of the fucking

Se

pool.

Laughter catches my attention and my head snaps up.

My fucking question is answered.

The four fucking douchebags of Bellevue Springs sit around the pool with a fire burning watching my struggle. Without a doubt, I know that they snuck into the pool house and somehow lifted my mattress off my bed with me sleeping on top of it.

Fucking pricks.

Chills sweep through my body. I hadn't minded so much when it was Colton sneaking into my room while I slept. Yeah, I was vulnerable but for some stupid reason, I trusted him not to hurt me. Spencer and Jude in my room while I sleep? Yeah, that's different.

"Were you having a sex dream?" Charlie yells out, laughing and making the others snicker even more.

Fuck. Please don't tell me I said anything in my sleep that I'm going to regret.

I look at Colton and from the smug look in his eyes, it's damn clear that I had and they know exactly who I was dreaming about. Shit, I might as well own it. I look back at Charlie with a cocky grin. "So, what if I was? It's not like it was about you."

His face falls and just as I go to celebrate my win, the mattress completely submerges and I fall deep into the cold water.

Oh, fuck. Fuck, fuck. It's freezing in here. What the hell happened to it being a heated pool? Where's the fucking hot water when you need it?

I break the surface and suck in a deep breath. The party-goers are well and truly gone and seeing as though it's not completely pitch dark out here, I'm going to assume that it's creeping up to six in the morning.

I trudge out of the pool and glare at each of them. "I fucking hate you pricks."

"Don't worry, Jade," Jude spits, using Colton's name for me and somehow making it sound like degrading trash in the process, but judging by the scowl on Colton's face, he doesn't appreciate it. "We don't like you either."

"Speak for yourself," Charlie mutters, getting up and meeting me with a towel in hand.

I take it from him without so much as a thank you and quickly wrap it around my freezing body. Desperately needing to warm up and not wanting to wake mom, I huddle around the boys' fire. Soon enough, I find myself being pulled down beside Charlie, who doesn't seem too put out by the fact that my sex dream wasn't about him.

It's not as though I'll be able to get back to sleep after that, even if I did have a bed to sleep in. I swear, Colton better have it replaced by tonight otherwise I'll be taking his bed and he can sleep on the mattress at the bottom of the pool.

The boys talk among themselves almost as if I'm not here and a strange comfort takes over me. It's kind of like being back home and chilling out with my crew. For the first time I don't want to hate these guys, though every time a drop of water falls from my hair and splashes against my knee, the anger rises back up.

I hate that I feel so comfortable here. I should be tearing my hair out, desperate to get as far as possible, but the thought of getting up and leaving doesn't sit well with me. There are a million other options I could have taken to dry up and get warm. I could have gone inside and stood under a hot shower, I could have cranked up the heating, yet here I am, sitting out in the cool early morning with a bunch of dudes who have all declared their mutual dislike for me.

What the fuck is wrong with me? Maybe I'm a glutton for punishment. I can't deny the way Colton has me all pent up after every time he tries to humiliate me. Every time his harsh words hit my chest, I'm left in a puddle of desire. Every time his sharp glare turns my way, I need to touch him. Whenever he looks down at me, I'm desperate to show him what he's missing. There's got to be something wrong with me because that shit isn't normal.

That dream though … that felt so damn real. I wonder what the real thing is like?

Charlie knocks his knee against mine, distracting me from my torturous thoughts and making me realize that I've been subconsciously staring at the guy sitting across from me. "You okay?"

I raise a brow and look up at him. "You actually care?"

"Of course I do," he murmurs, keeping our conversation private. "I may be a flirt and enjoy watching you get your ass handed to you, but I'm not a complete dick. I have a heart buried inside here somewhere."

"Could have fooled me," I laugh.

"Ah huh," he grins. "So my plan is working."

I roll my eyes and nudge him with my shoulder. "You're such an idiot," I tell him before pausing a moment. "Why are you so nice to me? These other guys are pricks and go out of their way to make life hell, but you … I don't know. You're different."

Charlie considers my question for a moment before shrugging his shoulders. "What can I say? I like to be unpredictable." I give him a blank stare, not pleased with his bullshit response. He lets out a sigh and starts over. "I don't get off on hurting beautiful women like they do. It's as simple as that. I'm all about love, not war and right now, the bullshit between you and the boys is creeping dangerously close to war."

"I think it's already there."

He shakes his head. "No, it's not," he says, glancing up and looking at Colton who hasn't taken his eyes off us since I first sat down. "Things are … changing."

"What's that supposed to mean?"

"I don't know," he murmurs, deep in thought. "Colton isn't hurting you for the sake of being a dick. There's something there and it's thrown off his game, and when Colton is off, the whole of Bellevue Springs is off."

"What kind of bullshit explanation is that? I'm more confused now than before you said anything." Charlie grins wide and his smile blows me away so I move along before I do something stupid. "What about the other two? Why do they need to be pricks? Are they that far up Colton's ass that they need to impress him with their douchey skills?"

Charlie barks out a sharp laugh that has Jude and Spencer looking our way, but they're a little too far away to hear what's being said. "No," he says. "That's just them. Jude is just a fucking prick. I would have warned you to stay away from him but he tried his usual bullshit on you before I got the chance. Unfortunately, I think you learned that lesson the hard way and Spencer … Spence is just your usual brand of arrogance. He likes getting the upper hand and the fact that you shut him down so epically during the party is a big part of why you're still sitting here and not being burned at a stake. I don't know how but what you said has somehow earned his respect."

"Bullshit. Really?"

Charlie shrugs his shoulders again. "It seems that way. Had it been me, it would have just pissed me off, but Spencer finds respect in people who demand it."

"And how am I meant to earn Colton's?"

"Baby, you got that the second you showed up."

My eyes narrow as my brows pinch in confusion. Surely this guy is talking shit because there's no way I have Colton Carrington's respect. It's just not possible but the way Charlie is looking at me with honesty in his eyes, he's telling his truth.

"Come on," he says when I don't respond. "Enough of this heavy bullshit. Let's go inside. I'll make you a coffee to warm you up."

I nod and allow him to pull me along while feeling the heat of Colton's gaze on my back.

This whole thing is confusing me. One minute Colton hates me and the next he's protecting me from his father. He sat with me while I scrubbed the wall, opened up to me in his room, he gave me insight into his life, and even let me steal his credit card to fix my hair when my heart was crushed. What's happening here? There's an intense sexual tension between us and every time another guy even looks my way, he looks jealous as hell. So, why does he act the way he does? Why tear me down? Why stand above the school pool and watch me below the water, testing my limits? Why call me the help and make me feel small?

I'm not too daft to realize that he's interested. That's just common sense, though it's probably just my body he's interested in. Is it his precious reputation he's trying to protect? Will his world come crashing down in burning flames if people were to realize that he was nice to the help?

I don't understand this world, but more importantly, I don't want to. To understand it would mean to be one of them and that's something that'll never happen. My roots are back home and that's where I belong, even if it makes me trash.

Charlie leads me into the kitchen and instantly grabs my waist to hoist me up onto the counter. He silently works around me, setting up the fancy as fuck coffee machine that I've been avoiding since being here. It's far too complicated for me but Charlie handles it like a pro.

"You're really not a bad guy, are you?" I question, watching him work.

He shakes his head and looks back at me with a sparkle hitting his eye. "Nope. I just like to pretend. You know I heard girls are into bad boys."

I laugh and gently kick out my leg, hitting his hip. "Girls love a bad boy, but you're not one of them."

"So, I don't have you fooled?"

I laugh, finding him more endearing than I should. "Not in the least."

"Damn," he mutters, pulling the coffee mug free and handing it over.

I take it eagerly and groan as the heat from the mug seeps through to my cold hands. Damn, that feels good. Unable to help myself, I raise the mug to my lips and take a quick sip, closing my eyes as the satisfaction rocks through me. I let out a soft sigh. "Shit, that's good," I murmur, opening my eyes to find Charlie standing right in front of me, his eyes heated as he watches the elation on my face.

"Fuck, I didn't realize that I could get hard over coffee."

Charlie steps into me and I feel him pressing up against my core, sending my mind into overdrive. My legs curl around him, holding him there as he stares into my eyes. The coffee mug is plucked from between my hands and placed down on the counter beside me.

He grinds against me and we both groan. The need within me spikes and turns into a desperate desire. It's been over six months since I was with someone, and the last few times I've tried to get off I've been rudely interrupted.

Charlie slides a hand dangerously high on my thigh and I let out a breathy pant. If only he would touch me just to take the edge off. His lips drop to my collar bone and start pressing tortuous kisses up toward my ear. "I want you," he says, his voice low and gravelly, filled with all sorts of need and desire.

I curl my hands around his back and slip them up his shirt, feeling the tight muscles beneath his skin. He's so warm and inviting. I want to feel his body all over me, inside of me.

"If you don't want this, you need to tell me now," he warns.

I groan and tighten my legs around his waist, pressing him harder against my center. "Don't stop."

"Fuck, baby. I want to fuck you so bad."

It's like music to my ears.

"Only if you promise to be rough."

A low guttural growl pulls from deep within his chest as his hands find my ass. He picks me up off the counter as though I'm as light as a feather, not once taking his lips from my neck. Charlie starts walking and right now, I don't even care where he takes me. Hell, if the guys weren't sitting right outside the door with a perfect view of the kitchen, I would have demanded he fuck me right there on the counter.

At the thought of the guys, I can't help but raise my eyes over Charlie's shoulder. Colton watches us with a raging fire burning brightly behind his hazel eyes. If looks could kill, Charlie would be dead but he can't do anything about it. If he treated me well, this might have been him. I would have happily rode him all night long. I would have blown his shallow little mind, but he wants to play games and because of that, I'm about to fuck one of his best friends and I'm going to enjoy it.

Charlie pushes through to the den and I silently thank him as the four walls around us mask the jealousy and confusion radiating off Colton, allowing me to concentrate on the fine piece of man meat wrapped between my legs.

He kicks the door closed behind him and the sharp 'bang' of the door closing has my world ready to detonate. It's just me and Charlie with a million possibilities and a silent promise of the time of my life.

His hands fall to my waist and I reluctantly unwrap my legs just in time to be thrown down on the big couch.

I look up at him and there's a fire burning so intensely that it speaks right to my core. Holy hell. He's ready. More than fucking ready.

His shirt is pulled over his head and I watch as it's discarded on the floor before his hands find the button of his jeans. He stalks toward the couch and I bite down on my lip.

Fuck, yes. I need this so bad.

Charlie's jeans drop and I'm not at all surprised to find him going commando. His cock springs to attention and it's almost as though it's staring right at me; large, powerful, and in charge. This thing is going to be my undoing and if he doesn't slam it deep within me soon, I think I might scream.

I scramble up on the couch so my back is up against the backrest and as he looks down at me, I feel everything clench.

"Strip."

Oh, holy hell. Who is this guy? This isn't the fun-loving Charlie who grins about girls liking bad boys, this is a fucking man ready to claim what's his and for that, I will bow at his feet and let him take it, all of it. There's nothing worse than getting a guy in bed to find he's an incompetent, nervous wreck. I like someone who will take charge, dominate me, and make me feel like a goddamn woman. A guy just like Charlie.

I peel my damp shirt over my head to find my bikini still beneath. I never bothered to get dressed after the party, just pulled my pajamas over my bikini. My shorts are twisted and cold but I make quick work of them too.

I get to my feet and stand up on the couch in my red bikini, putting us eye to eye.

Charlie reaches out to touch me and I slap his hand away. "Wait your turn," I demand.

His eyes blaze but he refrains from touching me like a good boy should. I reach up behind my neck and tug on the bikini string, slowly releasing the knot at the base of my neck.

His hand falls to his hard cock and I watch as he slowly pumps up and down.

My bikini top falls to the couch and I run my hand over my tits. My nipples are hard from the cold, wet bikini, only making them sensitive to my touch.

I palm my breast, squeezing it hard and watching as he mimics the movement on his cock then grins. "Fuck, baby. You're perfect but I need to touch you. Taste you."

"You will," I promise.

I release my breast and pull on the two knots on either side of my bikini bottoms just as slowly as I had with the top. The flimsy material falls away and I slide my hand over my hip and down between my legs, feeling my wetness staining my fingertips.

I gently circle my clit, not once taking my eyes off Charlie.

He looks pained, desperate and I decide not to torture him any longer.

Knowing I won't make it if we fooled around first, I glance down at his discarded jeans. "Do you have a condom?" He gives the slightest nod and I sigh a breath of relief. "You're going to need to put that on."

A seductive grin crosses his face and within seconds the foil wrapper is between his hands. Not willing to release the hand on his dick, he raises the condom to his mouth to tear it open with his teeth and I pinch it from his fingers. "Let me."

Charlie steps closer to me and as I tear the little foil packet open, his free hand falls to my waist before running up and down my skin. I take hold of his large size and slide the condom over his impressive length, loving the way his eyes flutter closed at my touch.

I grab hold of his shoulders and push him down to the couch. He instantly looks up at me, his eyes burning with lust as I remain standing. I step over him, a foot on either side of his thighs, showing him everything that he gets to play with before sinking down over him.

I line myself up with his cock and drop down over him until he's fully seated inside of me. My head falls to his shoulder, my eyes closed as I get used to his size. "Shit, Charlie."

He groans low, taking my hips to hold me still. "Take your time, baby."

I start rocking back and forth, getting used to him until I'm ready to go. I pull back and meet his eyes. "I'm good. I need to move."

His hand spanks down on my ass and we both groan. "Fuck, yes."

I start moving, riding his cock like a fucking cowgirl at a rodeo. He meets me with every thrust while he sucks my nipple into his mouth. His fingers tighten on my hips and up until now, he's let me take control but I know he's dying to take charge. While he's down with being fucked, he wants to fuck me and he wants to do it right.

Without missing a beat, he scoots down on the couch and the new position has his cock slamming against my G-spot and making my eyes clench. "Yes," I scream, panting with need, knowing damn well that the boys can hear me out by the pool.

"Don't you dare fucking come. Not yet," he growls, not even close to being finished with me.

Charlie's arm curls around my waist and within the space of two seconds, he flips us over until my back is pressing against the soft cushions of the couch. He doesn't skip a beat and picks up my rhythm right where I left off, only in this position, he's able to dive so much deeper.

My leg is hitched up over his hip as he slams into me and I hold onto him, begging him not to stop. Charlie presses his hand down between us and starts rubbing lazy circles against my clit, making my orgasm build like never before.

I'm right on the edge and when his hand spanks down on my ass once again, my orgasm tears through me. Charlie doesn't stop moving and I clench down around him, loving the ecstasy on his face as he watches me come undone.

My leg falls from around his hip but when he grins down at me, I know he's not nearly done. He flips me over until I'm on my knees with my back against his solid chest and his hard cock firmly against my ass. He pushes me down, pressing my chest against the soft cushions leaving my ass high in the air, ready and waiting.

His groan is nearly enough to have me coming again, but something tells me that I don't have to worry about that. Charlie isn't the kind of guy to walk away, leaving a woman with only one ground-shattering orgasm. If he's going to tear it apart, then he's going to make sure his job is thoroughly done. What can I say? I love an overachiever.

He takes my hips and rocks me back toward him. "You said you wanted it rough," he comments, his voice low and dangerously addictive. "Are you sure you can handle it? I don't want to hold back."

I wiggle my ass, letting him know I'm ready. "Fuck me, Charlie."

Just like I'd said to Spencer, Charlie isn't the kind to need to be told twice. He slams into me hard and fast and I scream out while trying to fist my fingers into the material of the cushions. I can practically feel him in my throat, and damn it, I'm going to be feeling him with every step I take for the next few days.

His fingers clench and I know it's going to bruise yet that only has me pushing my ass back into him, wanting more.

My hand slips down beneath me and I rub my clit as he tortures me with his cock. His hand roams over my ass and down past my crack until his fingers are lightly pressing against my hole.

I suck in a breath. I've never been wild enough to explore with that but the small amount of pressure he's giving me has me desperately rethinking. This is fucking good.

He pushes a little harder and picks up his pace. His other hand at my hip squeezes and just like that, we both come hard until we're crashing down on the couch, completely and utterly spent.

CHAPTER 23

"I heard he fucked her on Carrington's kitchen counter."

"Really? I heard she took it in the ass like a desperate little slut."

"Bullshit. That's not what happened. She sucked him off all night, rode him real fucking hard, and let him come all over those big tits of hers."

"Damn, I can't wait to fuck that little bitch. I'll show her what it's like to really fuck."

"Wanna double up? I bet a kinky bitch like that wouldn't mind a little sharing."

What the actual fuck? I knew I shouldn't have come to school today. I had a bad feeling about this.

I step out from behind Milo's massive frame and take a look at the three juniors standing behind us. They're fucking skinny little computer nerds. I don't doubt that these guys are referring to me and Charlie but what's funny is that if these guys even tried to fuck me, I'd probably break their fragile little bones in the process.

"The fuck did you just say?"

All three pairs of eyes snap to me before widening in fear. "Oh, shit," the one in the center gasps.

Damn fucking right.

I don't hold back and luckily for me, Milo has my back just as I knew he would. I go for the guy in the center and shove my hands into his chest until his back slams against the brick wall behind him.

The fucker looks as though he's about to piss his pants and secretly, I hope he does. It will serve as a lesson that nobody is going to get away with talking about me like that. Not to their friends, certainly not to me, hell, not even to themselves. If my crew had overheard that, the three of them would already be in the ground, but as Colton pointed out, I have an issue with leaning on them when I should be handling my problems myself.

Milo grabs the two others and easily restrains them. He probably loves being a part of a boy sandwich but truth be told, these boys probably aren't his type. I bet he's more of a muscly, golden pretty boy type … say, someone like Spencer.

I press up into the guy, putting my hand around his throat the same way Nic had taught me. Nic actually taught me a whole lot about bringing a man to his knees and defending myself against dickheads like this. He kind of got off on it. There's something about violence that gets him worked up and I can't deny that I'm finally starting to understand it. I'll have to tell him all about it. Not the part about why I had to do it of course because that will be classified as running for help and I can't have that.

"I know you weren't just talking about me," I say, giving the guy's throat a little squeeze and watching the way his eyes bug out of his head with fear.

"I wasn't. I swear."

"You swear?" I question, narrowing my eyes.

He tries to nod and I give him a sweet smile, refusing to let up on my hold. We both know he's lying, just like we both know that I'm not squeezing hard enough to cause any damage, just a little discomfort. "Then please, fill me in on the gossip. Who's the kinky bitch that's about to be double-teamed? Wait … what did you say she did? Got fucked on the kitchen counter after sucking the guy off all night and letting him destroy her ass?"

The guy looks to his friends who are too shit scared to say a word before looking to Milo for help, but they should know better. This is my show and I'll run it the way I see fit.

He looks back at me. "I … I don't know. I just heard tha—"

"You heard wrong," I tell him. "Who the fuck has been talking shit?"

He looks back over my head at Milo who scoffs. "I'd hurry up and tell her what the fuck she's looking for before you really fuck up and piss her off. Trust me, this is tame. You don't want to see this bitch when her claws come out."

The guy panics and takes a deep breath before meeting my eyes. "Fine. Charlie was boasting about it during health but half of the guys already knew."

"What was he saying?"

"Just that he sealed the deal with you and that you were fucking wild."

I push into him harder, not sure if I should be happy about the wild comment or fuming that he was stupid enough to tell the world about it. "How did the other guys already know?"

"I don't know," he groans, his eyes beginning to fill with tears. "I just heard them talking."

I roll my eyes and let out a frustrated huff. "If I ever hear you or any of your scrawny little friends talking about me, or any woman, like that again, I'm going to tear off your good for nothing balls and then feed them to you. Got it?"

He nods viciously and after a silent pause, I release my hold. The guy runs with his dickhead friends trailing behind, every single one of them tripping over their own feet in their desperate need to escape.

I turn to Milo.

"Are you okay?" he asks before I get a chance to start ranting.

I start storming toward the cafeteria. "I'm going to kill him."

"Oh, okay. We're really doing this?" he rushes out, hurrying after me while digging into the pockets of his expensive school blazer. "Hold up. Let me get my phone first. I need to record this shit."

I ignore him as I continue toward the cafeteria. Milo's legs are twice the size as mine and in his desperation to see Charlie Bryant get his ass kicked, he'll probably beat me there.

As I storm through the hallway, unwanted attention falls on me. Hands start reaching out, my tits are grabbed, my ass squeezed, and then come the comments.

"How much?"

"Wanna fuck?"

"I'll tap that sweet ass for you."

Fury tears through me. How fucking hard is it to get through one goddamn day at this school without being sexually harassed?

This bullshit was starting to settle down until Charlie had to go and open his big fucking mouth. Now every bastard here thinks I'm some cheap whore who will drop her panties for anyone.

This is humiliating. He turned a great night into a fucking nightmare.

Just as expected, Milo gets to the cafeteria a slight moment before I do and slams through the double doors like a fucking queen, taking away the moment for me. I'm going to have to speak to him about this. There's nothing better than being the one who gets to slam through the doors and make a dramatic entrance. That freaking spotlight stealer.

All eyes shoot our way and it's as though I have a sign above my head saying 'I'm down for a gang bang.' They all start heading my way and within seconds, I have fifty horny teenagers crowding around me, touching, groping, feeling.

Comments are thrown my way, my hand is grabbed and rubbed

against someone's dick and then to top it all off, a fucking hand shoots straight up my skirt.

Panic rises within me. I have to get out of here.

What the fuck is this?

Their laughter and taunting is so damn loud that I can no longer make out a single voice let alone my own terrified scream.

Milo starts pushing guys away but there are too many of them and he's quickly overpowered. More people join while others try to help but it's not until Colton's loud "LEAVE HER THE FUCK ALONE," comes tearing through the cafeteria that the chaos ceases.

Students start getting pulled away from each direction as Milo continues pushing guys away from the inside of the circle. It's like I'm a tiny little bunny that's been thrown in the hungry lion's den. It's absolute bullshit.

I've never seen anything like this before and it makes me wonder why. There have been comments like that thrown around about me since day one, so why the insane chaos now? These guys see girls every weekend at parties. Why would they all of a sudden come at me like this? It doesn't make sense … unless someone put them up to it.

Fuck. How blatantly obvious. How could I have not seen this straight away?

Realizing that their fun is over, the guys slowly begin slinking away but it doesn't stop the few last stragglers from trying to feel me up. They get pushed aside and soon enough, it's me standing in the middle of a small circle with five boys protectively crowded around me; Colton, Milo, Charlie, Spencer, and Jude.

The last two confuse me. I don't know why they would help but I'm grateful.

Colton's eyes roam over my body, checking that I'm okay, but all my attention is on Charlie. I ball my hands into fists and keep them glued to my side, resisting the urge to break his nose. "You just had to go and open your big mouth," I yell with tears filling my eyes. "What the fuck was that, huh? I told you to fuck me, not to fuck me over."

Charlie's mouth drops. "I don't … what do you mean? I only told the boys."

"Bullshit. You were just boasting about it during your health class. What the fuck, Charlie? This is all on you. How would you feel if this was your mother, or your sisters, your cousins? I shouldn't have to be scared of being sexually assaulted every time I walk into this fucking school. It's already bad enough as it is and now this? Are you fucking insane?"

"What are you talking about?" he demands, making the anger bubble up inside me which only pisses me off more. I've never had a guy make me regret climbing into bed with him until now. "I didn't put them up to this."

Jude scoffs. "Sexually harassed? They were just making crude comments and getting in your face. I'd hardly call that sexual harassment."

I turn on him as the others seem to shut the hell up. "Are you kidding me? Unsolicited demands to get on my knees and suck someone's dick is the definition of sexual harassment. Not to mention that in the last two minutes, my tits have been grabbed by fifty different hands, my ass has been squeezed, hands have slipped up my skirt, pulled on my underwear. What is the fucking matter with you? Oh, hold on. It only counts as sexual harassment with you once the deal is done and the cops are called."

Colton steps in closer. "What are you talking about? They were just getting in your face."

I shake my head but it's Milo who speaks up. "Nah, man. It was fucking bad. You probably couldn't see it from outside the circle but nearly every fucker in this goddamn cafeteria just copped a feel. It was fucking wrong. Someone put them up to this."

I glare at Charlie who looks as though he's about to be sick, but I couldn't care less. His big mouth put me in this position and because of that, whatever we may or may not have shared over the weekend is long gone. "This is all on you."

"Babe, I …"

He doesn't get another word out before Colton's large fist slams across his jaw. I duck, narrowly missing Charlie's flailing arms as he falls back against Spencer. Colton keeps coming for him but Charlie isn't one to sit back and take a beating—whether he deserves it or not.

Spencer and Jude quickly jump in though it's unclear if they're trying to break it up or land a few blows just for the hell of it. What I do know is that I need to get the hell out of here before I get nailed in the face and end up needing plastic surgery that I can't pay for.

Milo grabs my wrist and yanks hard, pulling me away from the boys. "Come on," he says, pulling me along toward the cafeteria door. "You need to get out of here before Dean Simmons finds a way to blame this shit on you."

Fuck. He's right.

I hurry out with him and after making a quick stop at my locker, I find myself down at the student parking lot with Milo's Aston Martin keys firmly in the palm of my hand.

I drop down into the car and within seconds I'm peeling out of the parking lot, pissed at myself for being so upset that I can't even take pleasure in this sweet ride. The same thing happened when I stole Colton's Veneno. Why is it that every time I'm in an expensive car, it's because I'm running?

This is bullshit.

I shouldn't be running. I shouldn't have to run. I did nothing wrong and because I'm a female, I'm going to be torn to shreds. Who cares if the boys send each other to the Emergency Room, who cares if the students thought it was appropriate to touch me, who cares if there's a fucking brawl at the school? It's all going to be pinned on me.

I need to get out of here but I have no other options. Though … that's not entirely true. Nic would take me with open arms and he'll give me the best kind of life that he can give. I should be thankful. I should be grabbing hold of that with both hands and not letting it go. After all, he loves me. I'm sure I'll eventually be able to move past the whole cheating thing, but what happens when he takes over his father's gang? That puts him right at the top with a target on his back. Hell, it would put a target on mine too.

That's not a way to live.

I have to do something. I have to break free without breaking mom's heart. I have to get out of here, but how? I have nowhere to go, no money, no car. I'm useless. I'm stuck.

I need a plan, but what?

Not graduating just seems stupid. Maybe I could hang around for the next few months, keep my head down, and try to get through high school. If I somehow manage to graduate, that already puts me higher than 50% of the kids back home. But what do I do then? Where will I go? I don't have the cash to take me anywhere and the thought of going back home kind of hurts. I love it there and my crew, but I want to be better, I want more for myself. Especially now after seeing what else is out there. I can be better. I will be. I refuse to sell myself short.

I need a job and to be honest, the answer is staring me in the face, but I've been too stubborn to do anything about it. I'm too proud, and too ashamed.

I have to meet with Charles Carrington and I won't be walking out until I get what I need.

I guess now Colton really will have a right to call me 'the help.'

CHAPTER 24

I race up the stairs of douchebags' headquarters and fly through the front door. Ever since my plan wriggled it's way into my brain it's all I've been able to think about. I have to do this. I have to stand on my own two feet and prove that I can make it in this cutthroat world.

Sure, I may never be some billionaire in a fancy mansion but I'll be happy and proud of what I've accomplished—assuming I actually accomplish something. I will though, I have to. There are no other options for me. I don't want to be some gang leader's forgotten wife and I don't want to be living off someone else's money. I need a little independence and if *Destiny's Child* taught me anything, it's how to be an *'Independent Woman.'*

I bypass Harrison in the foyer who's putting on a good show of being busy when we both know it's all an act. The only reason he ever comes into the foyer is when there's someone at the door and I highly doubt that he'll be here to open it for me. He's come to learn Milo's Aston Martin over the past couple of weeks and usually makes a point in not answering the door. The fact that he's standing here right now means he's curious. He wants to know why the hell I'm here and not at school and whatever reason it is, he's hoping he can use it against me one day.

Men are so stupid. One day they'll learn not to play with fire but until then, it'll be fun watching them get burned.

With Harrison trailing slightly behind me, trying to keep far away enough so I don't notice he's actually following me through the house, I make my way to Charles' incredible home office. Though the second my target becomes obvious, Harrison slinks away into the shadows almost as though he was never there to begin with.

As I reach his door, I find it slightly ajar and I poke my head through the gap while knocking for his attention. Charles stands by his massive floor to ceiling windows, staring out over his property, deep in thought.

My intrusion startles him and I cringe as his head whips around with a speed not safe for a man his age. "Sorry to interrupt you," I say politely. "May I come in?"

His brows pinch in concern before he nods and sweeps his hand toward the chairs opposite his wide desk. "Of course," he says, striding toward his desk. "What can I help you with? Has something happened at that school? Is it Dean Simmons again?"

A slight excitement lights his eyes and I realize that he's hoping for me to say yes. He wants Dean Simmons out and is using me to make it happen. How could I have not seen this? I guess the first time I came in here asking for help, I was so blinded by shock, rage, and distress that I mistook his little game for kindness.

"Yes, something has happened, however, it's nothing that I can't handle," I explain, wanting to give him a little to work with in order to soften him up.

Confusion filters across his features as he slowly raises his chin. "Then what can I do for you, Ocean?"

A chill runs through my spine at his use of my name which is ridiculous but I try to ignore it and continue. I swallow my pride and hope to God that what I'm about to say isn't going to fuck up anything for my mom. "I want to start by saying how grateful I am for everything you've done for mom and I. Without your help, I don't know where we would have ended up."

His eyes shine with pride but I'm not stupid enough to mistake it as goodwill, a mistake I surely would have made upon first meeting him. No, this is the look of a man who thinks that his act is paying off and knows how it must make him appear as a generous man among his rich friends. "Of course," he says with a nod as an impatient flare shoots through his features. "What is it that you need?"

"A job."

"A job?"

"Yes, sir."

"Might I ask why?"

I raise my chin, trying to keep my pride but it's quickly breaking away. "Sir, I mean no disrespect but after graduation, I need to learn to stand on my own two feet. Mom and I have no money saved up, no car, nowhere to live apart from your pool house and I don't expect your generosity to continue after I finish school, so I'd like to prepare myself for that. Breakers Flats is my home, it's where I grew up and I have so much love for it, but if I can avoid going back, I will. I want to better my life and if I have to mop and scrub every room in this house, I will. I want to be better. I don't want to be that girl who falls down a destructive path, gets pregnant, or forgotten. I want to succeed and I didn't realize how badly I wanted that until I came here and saw how much more there was to the world."

Charles looks speechless for a moment and I watch as he gathers his thoughts. "I admire that," he says, shocking me. "That's one of the many reasons why I set you up with such a prestigious school. Having graduated from Bellevue Springs Academy on your resume will help open doors for you. Have you considered college?"

"College?" I laugh in shock. That's certainly not a question I've been asked before. "No, college isn't exactly something kids like me are taught to aspire to. Most of us are just hoping we can make it to the end of high school without being shot in a gang war, getting pregnant, or jumped in. All I want to do is save up some money so when that uncertainty after graduation comes, I'll be able to land on my feet and have a little something there to keep me going until I can find a home and a job where I won't have to sell either myself or drugs."

"I see," he says, his eyes narrowing in thought. "So, why come to me? Surely you must realize by now that Harrison is head of my staff. He deals with employment applications."

"With all due respect, Sir, Harrison is a dick and would laugh me off before I even got a sentence out. Besides, this is your home and you hold the power. Why speak to Harrison when I could go straight to the top?"

A sparkle hits his eyes and I realize that I've said the magical words. Charles considers me a moment before finally nodding. "Alright, you may work weekends and after school once your homework is complete. You'll need to report to Maryne and she will tell you where she needs you. However, Harrison is still your superior and you will show him respect."

I nod. "Yes, sir."

"Right," he says, looking down at his watch. "It's too late to return for the rest of your school day so you might as well get changed out of your uniform and get started."

I nod again. "Thank you," I say graciously, feeling ease settle over me knowing that I now have a shot at making it out of here. "I won't let you down."

"Good, now unless you'd like to start explaining why this couldn't wait until you had finished your schooling for the day, I suggest you run along."

My eyes bug out at the thought of having to explain to Colton's father that I slept with Charlie on one of his many couches and then was humiliated because I rocked his world so greatly that every fucked-up student at school was passionately demanding a slice of heaven too. No thanks, I'll pass on that one.

I get up from the desk chair and silently thank Charles once again before scurrying away so he doesn't get a chance to change his mind. I thought for sure he was going to tell me no or he'd make me work a little harder for it but it all came together and now I actually have a shot at survival after graduating.

Elation fills me as I skip around the house, heading for the back door. I make my way into the pool house and just as Charles had requested, I get out of my school uniform and find the comfiest sweatpants and tank that I own. My sweatpants aren't actually mine, they're Nic's that I stole and refused to give back so I have to roll them at the hips a few times just to keep them up. My white tank also isn't mine. I'm pretty sure Kairo gave me this after he found it in his room. It's tight and cropped and I absolutely love it, you know, after I washed it a million times. It's the benefit of having a bunch of guy friends. After they sleep with a chick and kick her out the next morning, they usually leave something behind and that something is always given to me. I'd like to claim it as a token of their affection but the reality is that they don't want to give the girl a reason to come back.

Knowing that Maryne is going to make me earn every cent, I grab Nic's red bandana and tie it around my hair to keep it off my face. The last thing I need is my hair falling into the toilet or accidentally getting sucked into a vacuum cleaner. God knows my dark locks have already suffered through hell.

Ready for my first day on the job, I make my way into the staff quarters and report for duty. Maryne is busy rushing around as usual but she finds the time to stop and help me out. "Alright," she starts giving me a cheesy grin. "I heard that you're my new protege."

"News travels quickly," I laugh, having only walked out of Charles' office less than five minutes ago.

Maryne shrugs her shoulders. "What can I say? We like to be on the ball here. Now, I don't have a uniform your size but I'll get some ordered. Until then," she says with a pause, looking up and down my body with a frown, "this will have to do."

I don't know whether to be offended or not so I put it to the back of my mind and follow her as she starts leading me through the staff quarters, going over the same introduction that mom had gone through with Harrison. Though I don't know why she bothers, I know where I am and what's going on. This is my third week here.

"Okay," she says, twenty minutes later. "I don't have a list of jobs set out for you just yet but for now, you can start by taking a few things off your mother's list. She's been working around the clock making sure everything is perfect. She's worth her weight in gold."

"She is," I smile, proud of mom for doing so well in a job that she seems to really be enjoying.

"Why don't you start with the formal dining area?" she questions. "The room needs to be cleaned, swept, mopped, and dusted. Charles is having a business dinner there tomorrow evening so it needs to be in pristine condition. I'll choose the table settings while you're cleaning and once you've finished that, you can set the table and have it ready to go.''

I nod, my eyes wide as I realize just how much preparation goes into one dinner, and that's not even talking about the menu or entertainment. Her job must be ridiculously busy. It's no wonder she hasn't had time to have kids of her own.

Wanting to impress her, I scurry away and find everything I need to get started. I make my way into the formal dining room and look around. The room is huge, but I can handle it. It's not like it's littered with crap. It's already in pristine order like the rest of the house but things get missed and I'm determined to make sure that it's absolutely perfect.

I walk around the massive dining table and put each of the chairs up so I can get right under the table as I clean. I get halfway through before realizing that something is missing. I pull my phone out of my pocket and press play on my music.

Delacey fills my ears with *'Cruel Intentions'* and I can't help but get lost in the music as I get back to work. I dance and move while gliding the broom along the marble floor. This really isn't so bad, in fact, it's oddly soothing. After my shitty day, I feel like I finally have control. I feel like some part of my life is dictated by me and me alone and no one can take this away from me. This is me finally stepping out and making something of myself, setting up a future that I can be proud of.

I finish sweeping and get halfway through mopping when footsteps sound on the marble floor behind me. I whip around to find Colton striding through the dining room, his eyes on me, no doubt having just seen me dancing.

He walks straight over the wet floors, smirking and knowing just how much it would be getting under my skin. Maybe I set my expectations too high. Colton is going to make this hell. How could I have not even considered that before begging for this?

His eyes rake up and down my body and despite knowing that I look damn cute, he makes me feel like trash. His lips pull up in a disgusted sneer and although it's not the first time he's looked at me like this, it's the first time he's actually truly made me feel this way. A scoff comes tearing out of him. "I guess you're nothing but the help after all."

"What do you want?" I demand. "You're ruining the floors. I'm going to have to start again."

He steps in closer, so close that I can feel the heat coming off his body, making my fingers itch to touch him. "Stay away from my friends."

I raise my chin and grin up at him, knowing just how much my cockiness irritates him. "What's the matter, Carrington? Jealous I let Charlie get a little too close? He didn't even have to try, unlike you who can't seem to stay away."

"You fucking wish," he snaps. "You acted like a whore and you got what was coming your way."

"You mean a mind-blowing fuck-fest with your best friend or the whole school assaulting me? Come on, Colton, don't tell me you're one of those arrogant assholes who blame the victim. 'She asked for it.' 'She wanted it.' 'If her skirt wasn't so short …'"

"Fuck off," he snarls, clearly not fond of that accusation. "Your behavior is embarrassing the Carrington name. What happened today was unacceptable. Everything you do reflects on me."

"Hold on a second," I say, obnoxiously studying his face. "Forgive me, Charles. I thought I was speaking to your douchebag son."

His eyes harden. "Don't."

"Don't what, baby? Don't call you out on your bullshit? Don't get under your skin? Don't make you want me so bad that you can't resist getting in my face every moment of every single day?"

"You're fucking kidding yourself if you think I want you," he spits. "Sure, you're fucking hot and I'm down if you want to fuck, but with a girl like you, that's all you'll ever be. A means to an end. Just another whore begging for a little attention. That's the way it was with Charlie, right? He fucked that tight little cunt and all but forgot you existed. He couldn't wait to go bragging, sealing the deal so you'd never come running back for more."

"Fuck you," I growl, unsure why his words cut so deep. "You don't know what you're talking about. Charlie isn't like that."

"Isn't he?" Colton laughs. "You've known him for two fucking seconds. I've known him my whole life. You're a fucking game and he played you just how he wanted."

No. I refuse to believe it. It wasn't like that with Charlie. I know boys. I can smell their bullshit from miles away and Charlie is a genuine guy despite his many flaws. He wouldn't intentionally hurt a woman like that … I don't think at least.

Shit. Maybe I have been fooled. Have I been looking at this the wrong way?

I feel like such an idiot and the fact that it's happening right in front of Colton just seems to make it so much worse.

Seeing the realization on my face, he laughs. "That's what I thought," he tells me. "So maybe now you'll listen. Stay the fuck away from my friends."

Not willing to back down despite knowing that I've already lost, I narrow my eyes at him. "Have you ever stopped to notice that your friends are the ones who are always coming at me, not the other way around? Maybe they're the ones who you should be warning to back off."

He laughs. "If they want to come at you for an easy fuck, that's their business, but they're smart enough to see through trash like you. You won't be getting a fucking dime."

Hurt seeps through my chest. I know at the very start he'd accused me of being just like all the other girls who hang around these guys, desperate for a payday, hoping maybe they can get themselves knocked up and claim a bucket load of cash. If he thinks I'm anything like that, he's got me all wrong.

I raise my chin, hating that he can see the hurt in my eyes. "I think it's time for you to fuck off now."

He tsks me. "Is that any way to speak to your new boss?" he questions, reaching out and pulling the bandana out of my hair. He pinches it between two fingers as though it is drenched in filth. "This isn't part of your uniform, trash," Colton says, dropping the bandana into the dirty mop water. "I expect a higher standard from my help."

With that, he walks away, tracking dirty footprints through my freshly mopped floor, making everything inside of me ache.

CHAPTER 25

After finishing off a few extra jobs for Maryne, I start making my way back to the staff quarters. The start of my shift was freaking awesome. I was actually enjoying myself. It was relaxing and knowing that this was the start of the rest of my life went a long way in making me forget that Colton was my boss and I was officially the help. I'm making my own cash now and one day, I'll have enough to get me the hell out of here and away from Colton freaking Carrington.

His words though … fuck. They tore me apart and killed my vibe in a big way. I don't know why I allowed him to get to me like that. They were just empty words. It's always empty words with him, but for some damn reason, his opinion matters.

I hate that. I want to be stronger than that. I've grown up in a town where the horrible things people say are a million times worse, yet when it comes from Colton Carrington, it cuts me down.

I guess what he said wasn't all that horrible compared to other things he's said and done over the past few weeks, you know, except for suggesting that Charlie played me. I don't understand why that doesn't sit well with me. It's not as though I was hoping for something more with Charlie. It was just a little fun to scratch an itch, we both knew that. There's never been anything more than innocent flirting between us, but I guess I just assumed that Charlie was a little more honest, maybe even a bit of a gentleman. I didn't peg him as the type to screw someone over and then brag about it to the world. I thought he was classier than that.

I bet Colton was waiting all freaking afternoon to get home and rub it in my face that the whole school thought that I was an easy, cheap whore. There are a few things that aren't adding up and it's been plaguing my mind all afternoon. Why did the boys all come to my rescue and save me from the mob and why did Colton punch Charlie if he didn't care about defending my honor?

Colton claims that he doesn't give a shit about me. He's called me trash, the help, and now a whore so why punch his friend over me? What Charlie did was something I'm sure every guy does. Hell, I'm sure Colton is even the type to brag about the girls he fucks, so why is this any different? Truth be told, I don't think Charlie was the one behind the students crowding me like that. He seems too honest, too sweet. That seems like something either Spencer or Jude would have orchestrated and seeing as though Spencer has half a brain, I'm going to guess it was Jude.

Though, could it have been Colton? He has the darkness within him to do it and he certainly has the will, but he seemed too surprised and was also the first to tell everyone to get away from me. Why does he keep saving me like this? Does he think I'm some kind of damsel who needs his saving? Yes, okay, so today's situation wasn't going to get any better by me throwing a tantrum. I was close to losing it and curling into the fetal position on the cafeteria floor. Milo couldn't hold them all off on his own so Colton's presence really was needed but the credit card thing, the way he's always blocking me from his father's scrutiny. I just don't get it.

I put everything away and clean out all the things that I've been using during my shift just like I've seen mom do when she's done for the day. I stop by the laundry room and scoop Nic's red bandana out of the washing machine and start making my way back to the pool house.

I think a shower is in order and then I'll be more than happy to collapse into bed and stay there until the sun is streaming in through my bedroom window.

I walk out through the backdoor and go to cut across the pool area when I come up short. A pair of hardened hazel eyes stare back at me while a guilty pair of blue ones are practically screaming for forgiveness. Colton and Charlie sit out by the pool, both of them leaning forward onto their knees and looking as though they'd rather be anywhere but here.

Obviously, the two of them are sorting out whatever bullshit went down between them at school. Why else would they both look as though they'd rather be dipping their balls into a pool of acid?

Neither of them strikes me as the apologetic type, but then, neither of them struck me as the kind to let some weird bullshit with a girl get between them. To be serious, I still don't understand how I got between them today, and judging by the confusion on Charlie's face, he's been struggling to figure it out too.

Why does Colton care that the guy was bragging about sleeping with me? It's not as though he didn't know it happened. He was sitting in the next room, listening to me scream Charlie's name. I wonder if my moans got him hard. I know he liked it when he caught me that night in bed. Hell, there are a lot of things Colton Carrington has caught me doing that he insists has no effect on him, but the proof is always there by the heated desire in his eye and the rock hard cock that presses against the zipper of his jeans, begging to be freed.

I pick up my pace, desperate to get out of here. Colton already has my head messed up after his bullshit in the formal dining hall and after everything that went down at school, this is really the last thing I want to deal with.

They watch as I pass and I can't help but feel the heaviness of their gazes on my back. Colton looks as though he's trying to make me disappear out of thin air while Charlie looks as though he's ready to say something.

I keep walking, hoping I can get out of this unscathed. Just a few more steps and I'll be alright. Just a few more steps to freedom.

"Wait."

Fuck.

"What do you want, Charlie?" I question, continuing to walk away only to have him get up and follow me while Colton lets out a frustrated groan from behind us.

"Can we talk?"

"Haven't you done enough talking today?"

"Come on, babe. As if you didn't tell Milo about it. Why am I being punished for something that you did too."

I stop walking and spin around to glare at his pretty face that looks like freaking sunshine. "Are you serious right now?" I demand as I spy Colton over his shoulder watching us like a hawk and no doubt listening to every word that's about to be said. "Yeah, I talked to Milo. I told him how fucking great it was. I bragged about how you gave me exactly what I asked for, how it was freaking incredible, but you know what I didn't do? I didn't make you out to be some kind of cheap whore, my actions didn't lead to you being sexually harassed at school, and I didn't make you feel humiliated for being with me. Fuck you, Charlie."

I turn and walk away when I hear Colton's scoff behind me and I fly back around, already on too much of a roll to stop. "And fuck you too, Carrington. All four of you bastards are the worst kind of people. Arrogant assholes like you wouldn't survive in the real world. I'd love to see where you would all be without Daddy's money. Hell, I know Jude would probably be in jail."

Colton steps forward, his eyes burning into mine. "What do you know about that?"

My brow shoots up. Did I just touch on something real? I've suggested something like this before but never got a response out of him. It was just an assumption, an educated guess at what Jude's future will hold but Colton's reaction is saying so much more. He doesn't need to know that though. My lips pull into a knowing smirk and I watch with satisfaction as his face begins to fall in horror. Hell, even Charlie looks fucking nervous.

I hold his glare and see true panic behind his eyes. Without a doubt, I'll be calling Nic and asking him to look into this. The way he keeps warning me away from these guys suggests that he might even know something. I wouldn't be surprised. Nic is the type to do his homework, but if there really is something there that I should know, I can guarantee that I will find out. I want to know every last dirty secret about the people who I'm around. When it comes to Jude Carter, I have a feeling there's a lot to learn. Hell, the way Colton hasn't stopped looking at me has me wondering if he's involved in whatever shit is going on here. What I do know is that it's bad.

I turn and keep walking back to the pool house, my senses on high alert. I can't hear them following me and just as I let out a breath of relief, Charlie comes hurrying to catch up. "Wait. We didn't actually solve anything."

"Charlie," I groan in frustration, thankful that Colton has stayed away. "There's nothing to solve. You ran your mouth to the world and blew your shot."

"Shot?" he questions with a raised brow. "I actually had a shot for something more with you?"

"I … no. That's not what I meant."

"Then explain."

"I just … I don't know. Maybe I would have done a few repeat performances until I got bored, but not anymore. Not after the bullshit that went down today."

"Come on, babe," he says, grabbing my hand. "You know I'm not like that. Sure, I like to fuck around but I swear, I only told Colton, Jude, and Spence and it's mostly because they already caught the sound effects from the main event. I didn't tell the whole fucking school like you think I did and I sure as hell didn't get them to attack you like that."

"Some kid during lunch said that you were boasting about it during health class, saying how fucking wild I was."

"Babe," he says with a soft sigh and an apology in his blue eyes. "I don't take health on a Monday. He lied. Someone put him up to it."

My brows furrow. That doesn't make sense. "Who would do that?"

Charlie's eyes harden and he glances back over his shoulder to find Colton already staring, still listening intently to our conversation. He nods to Charlie, having some kind of silent conversation, and just like that, they know exactly what happened today and who was behind this whole clusterfuck, and if I had to take one guess, I'd say it was Jude.

Charlie turns back to me with a promise shining behind his eyes. "We'll handle it."

I shake my head. "I can handle myself, Charlie. I'm not a damsel that needs your saving."

"I don't care. I'm going to handle it," he says. "And trust me, I know you're not some weak damsel who can't take care of herself. You're a fucking queen who deserves their respect, no matter what Colton likes to say."

At the mention of his name, I can't help but look back at him to find his glare hardening on his friend. He didn't appreciate that comment but I sure as hell did. "You better not be trying to sweet-talk me back into bed, Charlie Bryant."

A cheeky as fuck grin stretches wide over his face as his eyes sparkle with mischief. He sucks in a shocked gasp, feigning outrage. "I would never."

"You're an asshole, Charlie," I tell him. "And just know that your chances of getting back between my legs are practically non-existent, but you're charming as hell and because of that, I might just forgive you."

His eyes narrow and he appears deep in thought. "Practically non-existent or non-existent? Because practically non-existent means that there's maybe a sliver of hope for me."

I roll my eyes and can't help but smile. "Non-existent, Charlie," I lie, knowing damn well that if he was to come at me again with that goofy as hell, charming smile that I'd be a goner. After all, I'm only human and have absolutely zero self-control. Except when it comes to Colton of course, with him, I'm all over the place. Sometimes I have the self-control of a saint and other times … well, other times, I grind my naked body all over him, silently begging him to make the move we both know we want to make.

Charlie steps into me. "Okay, I get it but just tell me that you don't hate me. I fucked up, I shouldn't have said anything to the boys but you were so damn good. I haven't been able to stop thinking about how damn addictive it felt sliding in between those sweet legs, but I swear, I'll respect your privacy and keep my mouth shut from now on. Just tell me you're not going to hold it against me for long because baby, not being able to do that again is a fucking tragedy."

"I can't make any promises," I tell him, feeling as though what he did wasn't really that bad considering I did the same thing with Milo. It's not his fault that his so-called *friend* decided to take what he said and use it as a tool to try and destroy me. "I'll think about it."

His arm curls around my back and he pulls me in before pressing a kiss to my forehead. "I'm sorry, Ocean. You deserved better than that. What happened at school should never have happened. We're going to make it right even if it means beating an apology out of every last fucker who put their hands on you."

"You really have this whole knight in shining armor mentality about yourself, don't you?"

He grins wide and releases my waist before walking backward toward Colton. "Can't help it. When I see a pretty girl, I'm putty in her hands."

I roll my eyes and turn back to the pool house. "Get lost, Charlie," I call over my shoulder, feeling his flirty gaze on my ass. "Go be putty in someone else's hands."

His laughter flows through the yard and just as I push open the door of the pool house, I hear his voice murmur to Colton. "Dude, how the fuck have you resisted that? You see that ass, right? Fucking perfect."

Colton's muttered reply comes low and tortured and if I wasn't listening so hard, I probably would have missed it. "Resisting Oceania Munroe is the hardest fucking thing I've ever done."

CHAPTER 26

The week goes by way too fast and by Friday night as I stand on the familiar doorstep, I can't help the wide grin that stretches across my face. I grab the door handle and give it a twist before shoving my hip into the wood, knowing how the door sticks.

With a hard shove, the door swings open and I find my boys lounged around Nic's small apartment as though they're part of the furniture. The suddenness of my arrival has each of them flying to their feet with their hands flinching for their guns, that is until they get a good look at who stands before them.

"Pretty girl," Kairo cheers, racing forward with Sebastian by his side. Nic hovers in his kitchen, leaning back against the sink with a grin on his face as Eli awkwardly drops back down on the couch.

"What are you doing here?" Sebastian demands, scooping me into his arms just a split moment before Kai can. "Is something wrong? Did something happen?"

I laugh as I hold onto the turd with both hands, squeezing him tight. "What hasn't happened?" I say with a low groan. "But no, I'm perfectly fine. I just wanted to visit my boys."

"That's more than alright with me," he says, squeezing until I can't breathe and lifting me off my feet.

"Put me down, moron," I say, whacking his back. "You're going to make me pass out if you squeeze any harder."

"That's the plan. If you pass out, you won't be able to get back," he laughs, giving me a wiggle as he looks up over my shoulder at Nic. "Does this place have a basement? We could keep her locked down there."

"Sorry," Nic grumbles. "The basement is being used as my sex dungeon, though I'm sure you'll find plenty of handcuffs and ropes down there to keep her here. Actually, on second thought, go right ahead and put her in my dungeon. I'm sure I could find a few uses for her down there."

I flip him the bird despite not being able to see his face, though I don't need to see it to know that there's a mischievous sparkle lighting his dark eyes and a grin stretched wide across his face. I'll get him back for that dig later, as for now, I have a few more boys to say hi to.

As if reading my thoughts, Kai grabs me and pulls me out of

Sebastian's hold, though thankfully allowing me to actually keep my feet firmly planted on the ground. He pulls me in hard and presses a warm, inviting kiss to my temple. "Missed you, pretty girl," he murmurs. "Have they been treating you alright?"

I shrug my shoulders. "They've been treating me exactly how you'd expect arrogant billionaires to treat their staff."

"Staff?" Nic questions from across the room. "Are you working there now?"

"Nothing in this world is free," I remind him. "Charles lets me work afternoons and weekends as long as I've got my homework up to date. He keeps reminding me how important it is for me to graduate but I think it's more about how it would look back on him if I were to fail after he made the effort to get me in."

"With people like that, a reputation has the power to either make or break them," Nic mutters, telling me something that I've already come to learn over the past few weeks of living in Bellevue Springs, but he can tell me it a million times if it means dropping the whole working there topic.

Sebastian scoffs his agreement behind me. "No wonder they have so many skeletons locked up in their closets."

A chuckle pulls from deep within my stomach as I recall the few skeletons I've already discovered of Charles' but I don't get to think about it long before Kai is stealing my attention again. "How'd you get here? Did you take one of those rich prick's cars? Which one? Something we can lift?" He looks up at Nic. "How much can we get for parts on an Aston Martin or Ferrari? Wait. Did you take that kid's

Lambo?"

I roll my eyes and slam my elbow into his ribs. "First of all, I took the bus right after school and it took forever," I start, watching as his face falls with disappointment. "And secondly, even if I did take one of their cars, I'm not about to let you steal it and strip it for parts."

"Babe, just think about the payday. I thought you had our backs? Do you know what kind of money we could make out of cars like that? Those pricks wouldn't even miss it."

"Not going to happen, Kai," I tell him. "And for the record, I do have your backs, more than you know which is exactly why I could never let you do that. Their cars are more important to them than their kids. Not to mention that every single part probably has a tracking number on it."

"We'd deal with that shit, O. It's not my first rodeo. They'll never catch us."

"Knock it off," Nic grumbles from the kitchen. "She said no. Respect it."

"Fine." Kai groans and slumps over to the couch before dropping down beside Eli with a frown the size of the car he wants to steal. He should consider himself lucky that I took the stupid bus. I've never witnessed it before but something tells me that no one gets away with stealing from Charles Carrington, especially guys like my boys. He'd use them as an example and completely ruin their lives.

With Kai busy sulking and Eli staring at his hands, I go for Nic next and he welcomes me with open arms. I fold into him as though I belong there and despite the pain that rockets through my chest, I can't help but feel like I'm home. "Where have you been, baby girl?" he murmurs into my hair. "I've missed you."

"I missed you too," I whisper against his strong chest, refusing to let go.

His lips press softly against my temple for the slightest second and the urge to raise my head and capture his lips with mine tears through me. I miss what we had so bad. The past six months since we've been apart have really sucked but when it's not right, it's not right. I deserve a man who is going to be faithful to me and although he hates it, he completely agrees.

Nic picks me up and slides my ass back onto the counter before stepping into my open legs. "Where have you been?" he questions, repeating his unanswered question. "I was expecting you to make the trip home weeks ago."

"I know, I just … it's been busy with school and now I'm working."

"School and work?" he questions. "You sure that's it? Nothing else is keeping you there?"

He watches me with curious eyes and I don't know how, but something tells me that he knows everything that's been going down in Bellevue Springs … including Charlie. I let out a sigh, not being one to lie to him, but wanting to protect him from the truth if it's going to hurt. "Nothing that's worth it," I clarify, knowing he will understand my unspoken message.

"You're going to get hurt," he murmurs, keeping our conversation private. "Guys like that … to them, you're just the help. Be careful."

His words are like a shot right through my soul. I don't know if he'd used that phrase on purpose or if it was just a coincidence but either way, it speaks enormous amounts of truth, so much that he could never understand. "I'm a big girl, Nic. I can take care of myself."

He shakes his head. "You're not, O," he tells me gently, pressing a finger to the side of my head. "You're a big girl in here," he says before moving those fingers to my chest and hovering them right over my heart, "but in here, you're just like everyone else. You're not incapable of being hurt, Ocean. No matter how much you guard yourself and keep those thick walls up, every day they're being chipped away, and eventually, one of those pricks will hold the power to destroy you, whether you want them to or not."

My mind instantly flashes to Colton and the way his words have the ability to tear me down. Nic might be onto something, but I refuse to believe it. Colton Carrington will never have that power over me, I won't allow it, no matter how much I have to hold myself back. I will not break.

"They won't," I tell him adamantly, knowing he can read the lie on my lips just as easily as I can. "Besides, I won't be hanging around there long enough to allow it to happen."

"What's that supposed to mean?"

"Why do you think I asked Charles if I can work there? I want to have options after I graduate. I can't stay there and live off their money, no matter how enticing it is. I'm better than that and I want to make my own way."

"So come back home then. You can move in here with me."

"And your mom," I say, finishing off his sentence.

"Come on, you know I'm only here because I can't bear to leave her alone in this town. She's too outspoken. It's dangerous for her here."

"She's Kian's ex-wife and the mother of his only child, I doubt anyone would be stupid enough to make a move against her."

"On the contrary, mom and I are the only things that they can use against him. We've been targeted for years."

My eyes bug out of my head. "What? Are you lying? You've never told me that before."

Nic shrugs his shoulders. "It never came up."

I stare at him as though he's just taken a trip to the other side of the universe. My hand slaps hard across his glorious chest and he does his best to catch it before I can do it again. "Are you insane? Like seriously, are you? How can that just never come up?"

"Chill out," he says as the others start looking our way. "It's not a big deal. Mom has been a target ever since she got together with dad back in the day. She knew it was a part of getting involved with the head of the Black Widows and they both knew the risk of bringing a kid into the world. It's just the way things are around here and it's going to be the same when I have to take over for him. Fuck, babe. I thought you would have realized that by now."

"I just never really thought about it in that way. Your parents are divorced so I figured she was safe and you, well, no one is stupid enough to go after you."

"He divorced her thinking the same thing but it didn't exactly work out that way, and as for me, I can handle myself. If they want to come at me, then let them."

My hand smacks out again. "Don't say that, asshole. I can't live in a world where you don't exist."

His eyes meet mine as he moves in a little closer. "Yet here you are forcing me to do the same."

Something breaks within me and I struggle to work out if it's my heart or my spirit. "That's not fair," I murmur, pulling my hands back from him. "It's not like I'm choosing to be away from you guys. This is just the way it has to be. Mom and I have no other choice unless we'd prefer to be on the streets. You know what would happen to us here. Two unprotected women, we wouldn't be safe."

"I could look after you. I told you I would. You'd have my protection and the protection of the Widows. You know the guys would never let anything happen to you." He grabs my hands and forces my eyes to remain on his stormy ones. "You're safer here than you are with those rich pricks. This is your home, O. Come home to me."

"Nic," I sigh, trying to pull my hands free. "Mom and I need to do this. We need to learn to stand on our own two feet without dad, and besides, mom is thriving in Bellevue Springs. She feels valued and important. What she does fills the void and gives her something to think about apart from missing dad. She's been hurting so much, but there ... she's happy. I won't take that away from her just so I can be close to my friends."

"Friends?" he scoffs, offended. "*No friends, only family.*"

"You know what I meant, Nic."

"Yeah," he says, pulling back and averting his eyes and crushing me in the process. "I can understand your confusion. It really does feel like just friends lately."

My glare hits him hard and fast. "You want to start on that shit?" I demand. "You're the one who made me feel like just a friend first. Hell, you made me feel like a lot less than that, or have you forgotten the reason why we're not together anymore?"

"Don't bring that old shit up," he demands, stepping into me and grabbing my chin.

I tear my chin free. "Then quit trying to use a bullshit guilt trip on me to bring me home. I made my decision. I'm living in Bellevue Springs until I graduate and then starting a life for myself. I'm breaking free of this town and building something that I can be proud of. Why can't you get on board with that? There was once a time where you would have jumped at an opportunity for me to get out of here."

He shrugs his shoulders, leaning back against the sink just as he was when I first arrived. "I'm a selfish bastard, and that was a long time ago, way before I fell in love with you."

"You're not in love with me, Nic. You just want to be because it's the easiest option. If you were in love with me, the idea of sleeping with another woman would have made you sick, just like it did to me."

"Don't you fucking tell me what I'm feeling."

I clench my jaw and watch him as his chest rises and falls with rapid movement. There's a storm brewing behind his eyes and if I keep pushing, I'll see the man his father has always pushed him to be— demanding, relentless, and forceful. Don't get me wrong, he'll never hurt me, but he sure as hell will put me in my place if he feels the need.

I've never had a problem with it because I always give it right back, but that's not what I want for my night here.

I jump down from the counter and step into him with a heavy sigh, putting my hands at his waist. "I didn't come here to fight. Can we just have a good night together? I missed you guys and wanted to see you after another big week."

Nic watches me for a silent moment before giving in and pulling me to his chest. His arms wrap around my waist as his lips press to the top of my head. "I know, I'm sorry. I don't want to fight either. Having you so far away all the time and surrounded by those people just gets to me. It's driving me crazy not having you close. I like to keep a close eye on you and that's not so easy anymore."

"Hey," Elijah's voice comes tearing through the small apartment. "Can I remind you that you haven't even brought that sweet ass over here to say hello yet, so wrap up your bullshit. I have a question."

I look up at Nic. "A question?"

A wicked grin spreads across his face. "You know when you first walked in here and said that you had our backs?" I nod, narrowing my eyes in suspicion and he quickly continues. "Well, now's your time to prove it."

Fuck. I don't like the sound of that but either way, I'm grateful as the small distraction seems to have helped take the tension out of the air so that Nic and I can get on with our night and actually have a good time, rather than waste the night with scowls and snappy comments.

I pull out of Nic's arms and walk my so-called sweet ass across the room until I'm dropping down heavily on Eli's lap. "OH, FUCK," he growls, pushing me off his lap so hard that I go flying across the room and slam into the wall.

"What the fuck, man?" Sebastian demands, somehow already by my side and helping me up as Kairo's heavy fist slams hard into Eli's arm, only he doesn't seem to notice as all his energy is focused on his junk.

There are tears of pain in his eyes and I instantly forget that the fucker just launched me across the room like a bitch who's claiming he's her baby daddy. "What's wrong?" I demand, walking back over to him.

Eli meets my eye and there's nothing but embarrassment there. "I need to ask you something and you can't say no because all these fuckers already have. You're my last option."

My brows pull down as I try to start putting the puzzle pieces together. "What are you talking about?"

"I have to show you something."

My eyes drop to his groin, where he's still clutching tightly, and judging from the pain on his face, it's not hard to work out that something's wrong with his junk. I shake my head so fast that I fear it might come wobbling right off. "No. No way. I'm not looking at your dirty junk. I can't. If I see that, I'll never be able to look at you again without thinking about it."

"Please, babe. I'm desperate. There's something wrong and I just need to know what it is before my fucking dick falls off."

"You know there are doctors for this kind of shit, right?"

His eyes harden and I resist laughing. "I'm not about to drop my pants for some strange doctor when you can just tell me what's wrong. What if it's something simple and I can just get a cream for it?"

"What if it's not and I guess the wrong thing and it gets worse? You need a doctor."

"Please."

I look at the other guys. "Come on, why can't you guys do this? You guys would know more about STIs and dicks than I would."

Sebastian scoffs. "Seriously? I'm not about to get up close and personal with his cock, especially if he has some kind of disease. Besides, you're a chick. You'll take this more seriously than we would and not to mention, you've already seen Eli's dick up close and personal. It's nothing new for you."

My eyes instantly fly up to Nic's at the reminder of the one drunken mistake I made with Eli nearly two years ago; the one I desperately try to forget and the one Nic is still sore about despite us not having been together then. "Really? You just had to go and bring that up?".

Sebastian grins while Kai looks at me. "You know, left untreated, his dick will probably fall off, right?"

Eli's eyes bug out of his head. "The fuck? My dick's going to fall off?" He demands, looking back to me and begging. "Please, babe. Just look real quick and tell me what it is and I swear, I'll never ask you to do anything like this again. I'll make it up to you. I'll … I'll … fuck, I don't know what I'll do, but I swear, whatever you want, it's yours."

His desperation has me caving like a little bitch. "Get me some gloves."

Eli's head falls back to the couch with relief as Nic's laugh is heard all over the apartment. He ducks down under the sink and a second later, a box of latex gloves is sailing through the air. Sebastian's hand flies up and catches it with ease before throwing them down beside me.

"Lose your pants," I tell Eli while pulling a pair of gloves out and struggling to get my hands into them.

"Why?" he demands, awkwardly getting to his feet. "You're not going to touch it."

"I have to. I have to see all of it. I can't just look at the top. What if it's worse underneath and we miss it?"

He groans and I watch with amusement as his face breaks. "Fine."

Despite how desperate he is for me to check it out and tell him what the hell is going on, he's also reluctant, knowing this is a step neither of us ever wanted to take in our relationship, but apparently, it's a must.

His jeans come off and I can't help but notice the way the three other guys shuffle around to get a good look even though they all refused to be the one to look. I guess when you're curious about something, nothing will stand in your way.

Elijah's boxers come down and the three guys instantly jump back in horror as my eyes bug out of my head. I instinctively try to move back but if I don't check this out, Eli could end up in serious trouble.

"Fuck, man," Nic gasps from way, way across the room. "How could you let it get like that?"

"I woke up like this, bro," Eli insists. "It's not like I've been letting it fester."

Sebastian shivers his voice a low groan. "Don't use words like 'fester,' man."

Embarrassment floods Eli and for a moment, I feel kind of bad for him until I realize that he's only in this position because he fucked some dirty bitch and didn't use a condom.

Wanting to put him out of his misery, I pull on my big girl panties and move in close. "This isn't good, Eli," I murmur, really getting in there and studying every angle.

"Just … tell me it can be fixed."

I release his dick and pull the gloves off before walking into the bathroom and washing my hands, then arms, and my face just for the sake of it. By the time I walk back out, his pants are back on and he's pacing the living room. "Well?" he asks, clearly annoyed that my hand washing took too long.

"I need to google it," I say, dropping down onto the couch and pulling out my phone. Nic sits beside me and his hand instinctively falls to my thigh as the boys start talking among themselves.

I get busy googling and after ten minutes of being as thorough as possible, I look up at Eli. "There's good news and bad news."

He finally stops pacing and turns to me with wide eyes. "What? What is it?"

"The bad news is that you have Syphilis and you're going to have to go to an actual doctor, but the good news is that it looks new and can be treated with a cream … I think."

Relief has his whole body sagging against the wall "Seriously? So, my dick isn't going to fall off?"

"Not tonight," I tell him, always loving to be the one to deliver good news. "But you need to find a doctor, like now before that shit gets any worse."

His face falls and he lets out a deep sigh. "Fine," he says, walking forward and plucking his car keys off the table with absolute devastation, making my heart break for him.

Sebastian groans and gets to his feet. "Wait up, man. I'll come with you."

The two of them walk out the door and not a second later, Kai is getting to his feet too. "Sorry, pretty girl," he says, leaning down and pressing a kiss to my forehead. "I have shit I need to deal with tonight."

I nod, understanding all too well what kind of shit he's talking about and just like that, the fun night I was supposed to have with my boys is completely gone, though I can only hope that they'll all be back later. For now, it's just me and Nic and when his arm falls over my shoulder and he pulls me into his side, I can't help but be okay with that.

CHAPTER 27

The sound of the shower on the other side of the wall has my eyes springing open to find that I'm still in Breakers Flats, at Nic's apartment, and curled up in his warm, familiar bed.

Fuck. I fell asleep. That wasn't part of the plan but after having dinner and catching up with Nic's mom when she returned from work, I was exhausted. I didn't even realize that I'd fallen asleep halfway through the movie, and to be honest, I'm kinda pissed. That was a good movie.

My hand rubs over my eyes and by the time I sit up in bed, the shower is cutting off. It's only a minute before Nic comes striding back into his room, dripping wet with a towel around his waist. He starts getting dressed and I can't help but watch the show.

I've never quite understood why guys do that. They get out of the shower and instantly wrap the towel around them. What's the freaking point of using the damn towel in the first place if you're not going to use it to mop up the water that's rushing over your skin? It infuriates me to no end, even more so when Nic pulls his shirt on and the beads of water left on his skin instantly soak into his shirt. I couldn't do it. I'm one of those girls who needs a thorough drying after my shower.

"What time is it?" I ask, watching as he pulls on a pair of jeans. Nic usually isn't one to get up and dressed first thing in the morning. He usually sleeps till late in the afternoon and fucks around in his sweatpants until his father is demanding his attention, so watching him dress now tells me it's time to get up and get my shit together.

"7 am," he mutters, making my heart break. Who the hell wakes up at 7 am on a Saturday morning?

"Come again?" I sputter, dropping back down against Nic's warm pillow. "Come back to bed. It's too early."

"As much as I'd love to climb back in bed with you, we have to go. I have business this afternoon and I want to drive you home first. I don't want you to take the bus again. Too many dodgy fuckers around here."

My bottom lip pouts but I can't help but like his plan. The bus ride would take me nearly four hours, but if Nic's driving, he will have me there in two. I reluctantly sit back up, bringing the blankets with me only to realize that it's not necessary. I'm completely clothed and I let out a small sigh of relief. I don't think I've ever woken in this bed with clothes on before, but I guess there's a first for everything.

"Worried that I took advantage of you while you slept?" Nic scoffs, diving through his closet for his shoes.

I roll my eyes and peel myself out of bed, ignoring his comment. I know he'd never take advantage of me like that. I walk straight through to the bathroom and roll my eyes at the way the bathroom mirror is fogged up with steam. Is it really that hard to use the bathroom fan? Boys will be boys, I guess. Some habits die hard.

I take care of business and as I step out into the hallway, I find Nic emerging from his bedroom. "You good?' he asks, looking me up and down to make sure I'm ready.

"Yeah, but we're going to need to stop for coffee on the way."

He rolls his eyes which is as good as a yes. Nic isn't a coffee drinker and honestly, I don't get it. What kind of person isn't a coffee drinker?

Soon enough, I'm riding in the front of Nic's car as he speeds down the highway. Music fills the cab while heaviness sits on my heart. I'm not ready to go back. If I could stay just another few hours, maybe another day then that need to be with my boys might ease just a little, but I can't. I'm supposed to be working and if I'm late, mom will never …

Fuck. Mom.

I suck in a gasp and start rifling through my things for my phone. "What's wrong?" Nic demands, struggling to keep his eyes on the road.

"I didn't tell mom that I was staying out yesterday. She would have worried all night."

"Chill out, O," Nic soothes. "I called her last night when you passed out on the couch and let her know I was driving you home this morning. She's good. She knows you're safe."

Relief settles through me and I relax back into the seat. "Thanks," I say with a grateful sigh, looking out at him to watch the way he handles his car with ease. "Did you hear from Eli last night? Is he good?"

"Yeah, He's fine. There was a hold up at the doctor's office so it took longer than he anticipated but he got his antibiotics and will probably be popping pills all fucking day. The poor fucker can't get his rocks off for at least two weeks."

I laugh, imagining the way his heart would have broken hearing that advice. "So, no cream?"

"Apparently not."

I nod, feeling sorry for the guy when I remember one of the reasons I wanted to see Nic in the first place. "Can I ask you something?"

His brows furrow, knowing I never ask if I can ask something. It's simply not something that I do. He looks over at me and narrows his eyes. "What?"

"You're not going to like it."

"Spit it out, Ocean."

I press my lips into a firm line, trying to work out the right way to word this when I fuck it all to hell and go for it. Nic isn't easily offended and despite knowing that he's not going to want to discuss this, I can't go back to Bellevue Springs without knowing the truth. "I need to know what you know about Colton and his friends. I know you've done your homework on them," I tell him. "I'm not stupid. I know that you dug into their backgrounds and I know it wasn't exactly done legally which means that you have all the dirt you need on them, and I need to know it."

His fingers tighten on the steering wheel. "Can't you just be satisfied with me telling you to steer clear of them?"

I shake my head. "I need to know what situation I'm about to walk back into. They all have skeletons in their closets."

"Do you understand what kind of position you're putting me in? This information was given to me in confidence. If word gets out that I spilled information, we'd lose our contact and it'd be my head on the firing line."

"I won't tell anyone," I promise. "I just need to know what to look out for."

Nic is quiet for a short moment before letting out a pained sigh. He doesn't want to break his contact's trust but at the same time, my safety will always come first where Nic is concerned. "Alright," he finally says, "But I swear to God, O. If this gets out and it's traced back to me, it's my fucking balls on the line. Do you understand that?"

"Yeah, I got it," I tell him. "You can trust me."

Nic's eyes slice across to mine and seeing the honesty shining back at him, he nods. "The four of them were all involved in some sort of rape allegations," he starts, making me suck in a sharp breath. "The whole thing is a fucking mess and I'm amazed by how they were able to get out of it. I'm telling you, O. If this shit happened in Breakers Flats, there'd be jail time and fucking heads blown off."

"What happened?"

"It was nearly two years ago and there was some kind of party at Carrington's place. Colton had his boys over, you know, the same ones who have been hanging around now."

"Charlie, Spencer, and Jude?"

"Yeah, that's them," he says. "There were two girls involved and from what I read of one of their statements, she and her friend were invited to party with the four boys and they willingly went. One thing lead to another and they were fucking around and having a good time. That was the last thing the girl remembered."

A bad feeling settles into my stomach and my mind instantly takes me to Jude. The three others are good guys despite their stubborn and douchey attitudes. "What happened?"

"About a week after the party, the girl received a recording of her being fucked along with a message, blackmailing her and her family. She had no recollection of being fucked but the evidence was there. What she does remember is that there were four boys at the house, four boys partying with them, and only four boys who could have been the one filming her being raped."

"Fuck," I breathe.

"Yeah, naturally all four of them denied any wrongdoing and as it was a week after, there was no DNA evidence. The other girl didn't remember a damn thing either and because of that, it was impossible to press charges."

"How is it that nobody knows about this?" I question feeling absolutely sick for the poor girl, especially after Jude came at me the way he did over the past few weeks. I guess on the bright side, she's lucky to not remember it, but now she's seen the evidence and I'm sure it's burned into her brain.

"You really think Daddy Carrington was going to allow something like this to get out? He stepped in and had all their lawyers sort out a deal. It was settled in private and all parties were paid off and told to keep quiet. They all signed confidentiality agreements and that was the end of it. One of those boys is a rapist, Ocean, and the three others know and haven't said anything which makes them just as fucking bad."

I can't help but agree and as I turn to Nic, I see the anger pouring out of him in waves. "It's Jude Carter," I tell him, feeling it in my gut.

"How do you know that?"

"I just know," I say, cringing with the truth that's sat heavily on my shoulders. "That time he came into my room, you know, right at the beginning … that wasn't an isolated incident. He's come at me a few times since then."

"WHAT?" Nic roars as the car swerves off the highway. I gape at him as I struggle to keep myself from rocking around in the car. "Did he fucking touch you? How long has this been going on?'

"Calm down. He hasn't fucking touched me. He just … *tried* a few times, but I had your gun and I was fine, besides, I think he's given up now. He's more interested in making me pay and giving me pathetic death threats. I can handle it, Nic. I've been handling it."

"What do you mean making you pay?"

Fuck. I knew I should have left that part out. "He belittles me every chance he gets, tries to humiliate me, and then there was the time he threw me into the pool with the promise of never letting me out. It's just stupid shit like that. He has no game and honestly, he lacks originality. I've seen you do worse … so much worse."

Nic's knuckles whiten on the steering wheel and he goes dangerously quiet. "Say something," I beg him, hating the unease of not knowing how he's going to react. Usually, I can read him like a book, but right now, I'm getting nothing.

"I fucking trusted you to be honest with me."

"It's a two-way street, Nic. I was honest with you until you beat the shit out of Jude and made everything worse. I told you that I could handle it and you didn't trust me."

His hands slam down on the steering wheel and in the blink of an eye, he pulls back out onto the highway, driving faster than ever before. "This is so much more than petty high school bullshit, Ocean. This is real world shit. How can you not see that? You can't handle it. You're just a kid."

"Oh, so now I'm a kid? Fucking perfect. I wasn't so much of a kid when you were wanting to fuck."

"Don't you bring that into this bullshit. You're coming home. I won't allow you to stay there."

My eyes bug out of my head. "Allow me? You're not my fucking father, Nic. You're not even my boyfriend. I'm staying there and there's nothing you can do about it."

"Over my dead body," he spits.

"Stop the fucking car, I'm getting out." He rolls his eyes and the rage builds up within me. "You lost the right to tell me what to do.

You need to back off, Nic. I love you but right now, you're being an impossible jerk. I can't handle your bullshit. I'm not going back to Breakers Flats. For now, Bellevue Springs is my home and I'll deal with the bullshit that comes along with that on my own terms."

"That's fucking bullshit, Ocean."

"I don't care what you think it is, but I'm not throwing away my chance for a proper future just so you can feel better about yourself and play the part of a top-dog alpha. I won't do it, and you shouldn't even ask."

His hand slams down on the steering wheel again. "You're so fucking infuriating."

"Try dealing with you on a daily basis."

Nic rolls his eyes and starts muttering under his breath the same way his mom does when she's pissed but nonetheless, he drives me back to Bellevue Springs. We sit in silence and it's awful. I hate leaving things like this with Nic but by the time he pulls up in front of the massive mansion, there's resentment bubbling within me.

The car comes to a stop and we sit there, neither of us wanting to leave it like that but both far too stubborn to be the first to make it better. "I know what happened at school on Monday," he says. "And I know about Charlie."

Fuck.

Nic scoffs seeing the look on my face. "You have five hundred horny teenagers at your school. Finding out what's going on with you wasn't that hard."

I look out the window, refusing to meet his eyes. "It was handled."

"Handled?" he spits. "By who? How?"

"I …" I cut myself off, thinking over the week and realizing that I don't exactly know how it was handled. On Tuesday morning, Jude didn't show up for school and then again on Wednesday. The same thing happened until the end of the week and I just assumed it was handled just as they promised. "The boys fixed it."

"The boys?" he laughs. "The same guys who kept quiet about him raping that poor girl? The same boys who've allowed him to come at you time and time again? The same fucking boys who treat you like trash? Call you fucking trash?"

"I … I … I don't know, okay. They said they were going to handle it and then he was gone. So yeah, they did handle it."

"No, Ocean. I fucking handled it. Your fucking precious boys let him get away with it. They walked out of there and left that fucker breathing. I. Handled. It."

My eyes bug out of my head as I suck in a sharp gasp. "You killed him?"

"No," he snaps, "But I fucking should have. Unfortunately, the fucker is going to live."

"Nic …"

"No," he says, cutting me off. "Just go. Go be with your new crew in your big fucking house with your fancy fucking cars and expensive school." He looks away as a tear rolls down my cheek. "You've changed, Ocean. I don't even know who you are right now."

Nic kicks over the engine cutting our conversation short, and with nothing else to say, I push open the car door and get out before watching as Nic disappears up the long driveway, leaving my heart an absolute mess.

CHAPTER 28

The weekend passes uneventfully and then Monday quickly turns into Thursday. I've never had such a bad week here. Nothing has even happened. Colton has left me alone, there's still no sign of Jude, and Milo has kept me smiling, yet the heaviness in my heart from leaving things so shitty with Nic has killed me. Hell, I think I'd prefer having the whole school groping me than having to deal with this.

I make my way down to the parking lot after another painful day and lean against the passenger's side door of Milo's Aston Martin as I watch the students filtering out of school.

I hate it here but the fact that I've chosen to stay tells me that Nic was right. I have changed, or at least, maybe I'm changing. Right now, I can't work out if that's a bad thing or a good thing. All I know is that he shouldn't be pissed at me for wanting more out of life.

I see Milo walking out of the front gates and a smile pulls at my lips until I really take him in. He's walking out of the school like his ass is on fire and the look on his face is telling me that something is wrong, very wrong.

My brows crease as he storms down toward me and I notice a shitload of students calling after him. My stomach drops.

"Get into the car," Milo demands as he reaches me, whispering low while filled with desperation.

"Wait. What? Why?"

"Just … please. They know I'm gay. It's like a witch hunt up there. They're all coming after me and if they catch me, I'll be fucking dead in seconds." he indicates down his body. "This shit doesn't fly here."

"That's fucking bullshit," I demand, standing my ground and refusing to move. "Don't let them. Stand up for yourself."

"You don't get it," he urges. "I'm as good as fucking dead. Being gay is not acceptable here."

"I understand that. I don't accept it, but I get it, trust me, I do. But I'm not going to stand here and have you running scared. It's not fair. If you don't want them to know, then we do something about it. You want back in the closet, then that's where you're going to go."

"What?" he grunts. "You're fucking insane. Once you're out of the closet, you can't go back in. It doesn't work like that."

I grin wide, strutting over to him. "You want a bet?"

His brows furrow in confusion and the closer I get to him, the hungrier my expression becomes. My hands fall to his chest and I force his back against the car while pressing my body against his. "What the hell are you doing?" he panics, flicking his eyes up toward the angry mob that's making their way down here.

"I'm going to kiss you, Milo, and it's going to be fucking hot. Your hand is going to squeeze my ass and you're going to grind into me until you have those guys questioning themselves. I don't care if you have to picture me as Jason Momoa, but you're going to do it and you're going to pretend that you love it. Got it?"

"You just got done having all these pricks calling you a whore. This isn't going to help."

"I don't give a shit about that. This is more important."

I don't give him a chance before my lips press needily against his. I close my eyes and kiss him as though he's my whole fucking world and I hold back a laugh at the way his body stiffens. I feel his stare on the side of my face and I don't doubt he's trying to hold back a gag, but I'm doing this and I'm giving it my all because I'd prefer Milo to be hidden in the closet, where he's happy and safe, then being out and having to hide in terror.

He'll reach the point where he can proudly come out of the closet one day and when he does, it'll be for him and not because someone else has forced it on him. And when that day comes, I'm going to be his biggest cheerleader, until then, I'm going to be his beard girlfriend.

Milo's body starts to relax and while there's still a heavy hesitation, he quickly gets on board with the plan. His arm curls around my back and holds me tight before it trails down to my ass. He gives it a firm squeeze and I make sure to press my chest harder against his, showing just how desperately I crave his touch.

His other hand slides up the inside of my shirt, brushing along my skin until his fingers are cupped around the curve of my breast. We look like a couple of horny teenagers and judging by the silence of the crowd staring at us, I'd suggest they're starting to second guess themselves.

My hand curls into the back of his hair and I fist my fingers into it, grabbing hold and upping the intensity. Milo has been putting on a show of being a straight guy ever since starting high school and today is his best performance yet. I should get him a trophy. Hell, if he was straight, I might even be into this.

He pulls back ever so slightly but keeps his hands moving on my body, making out as though we're still unable to pull away from each other in our desperation. "Shove your filthy little whore tongue in my mouth again and I'm going to bite it the fuck off," he murmurs against my lips.

I tighten my hold in his hair and in response, he squeezes my ass to the point of pain. "Watch it, Milo," I whisper, my lips moving against his as I talk. "Just be lucky it's only my tongue. I'm more than happy to throw you down and sit on your face to prove you're straight."

He gags. "Stop. You're going to make me hurl."

"What's wrong? The idea of running your tongue over my clit and making me come on your face is not appealing to you?"

"Shut up," he grumbles, grinding against me again before squeezing my breast. "I think I understand the beauty of tits now though. These things are so soft and squishy."

"Alright, perv. Time for the big finale."

"Big finale?"

I roll my eyes. "Haven't you watched any romantic movies? You're going to have to lift me onto the hood of your car, step between my legs, and take control in a big way."

"No fucking way. You'll scratch my hood."

"You want to sell the straight story, then act like a straight guy."

"For fuck's sake."

Within the blink of an eye, Milo's hands slip under my ass and he lifts me onto the hood of his car. His hands fall to my thighs and he pushes them wide before stepping between them and lining his dick right up with my center. He grinds against me as his hands find my jaw and force my face up to his.

He kisses me deeply and holy hell, it's fucking hot.

I shouldn't be turned on but damn. This boy has skills. I'm sure if he was straight, he'd be as much of a man-slut as Charlie. I wonder what he'd be like in bed …

No. Ocean. Do not go there. Milo is off-limits. This is already pushing the friendship.

He pulls back and looks down at me as though I'm the most desirable woman he's ever had the pleasure of looking at. "Was that the big finale you were hoping for?"

I grin up at him. "Damn straight. You nearly gave me a big finale there."

His face drops. "Tell me you're lying."

"Sorry," I say with a shrug. "What can I say? You were grinding all over my lady bits like a damn pro. Hell, Charlie didn't even get me that close so fast."

"Okay," he says, taking my waist and helping me down. "I need to get in the car so I can hurl in private."

He walks me back around to the passenger side door and as we go, something has me looking up. The crowd of pissed off homophobes has vanished without a sound, but there are two sets of eyes staring at me, one filled with a look of pissed off jealousy while the other just looks turned on.

I tear my gaze away. At least I know our little plan worked. If Charlie and Colton are fooled, then I'm damn sure that the rest of the school is too.

I drop down into the Aston Martin and soon enough, Milo is pulling into the driveway of the Carrington mansion. He comes to a stop in front of the mansion and after thanking me for acting like the whore they all think I am, he drives off, leaving me to race up the stairs and get stuck into my homework. After all, the quicker my homework is done, the sooner I can get to work, and the sooner I get to work, the more I'm able to get paid.

After racing to the top of the stairs and struggling to catch my breath, I barge through the big double doors and come to a screeching halt when I find Harrison standing at the door waiting for me. He looks down at his watch and then back to me. "Miss Munroe. You are due home from school at promptly 3:45 pm. It is now 4 pm."

"Ah, I see you've discovered time. Congratulations."

I go to keep walking but he stops me. "Homework can wait today," he says, making my brows draw in confusion. My homework was the one main certainty that ensured I was able to work. "You are to meet with Maryne immediately in the dining hall."

"What? Why?" I question, going over everything I've done since being here and trying to work out where the hell I fucked up. There's only one reason why my presence would be requested like this and that's if I was about to get fired. "I haven't done anything wrong. I've been a perfect employee. I don't even scowl at Colton when I'm working."

Harrison sighs, looking frustrated at having to explain himself. "You are not in trouble Miss Munroe, however, your version of being a perfect employee varies from my version. You've been satisfactory at best."

I cringe and look up at him. "Then what's going on?"

"Mr. Carrington has been called to attend a business meeting in the Maldives for two weeks. He will be leaving on Sunday morning. Due to …"

"The Maldives for two weeks?" I scoff, cutting him off just because I know how much he hates it when I do. "That hardly sounds like a business meeting to me. Sounds like he's going on a spontaneous vacation with some money-hungry gold digger and if you were to ask me, it's probably that cousin of Spencer's. What was her name again?" I pause a moment before it comes rushing back. "Oh, that's right. Jacquie Vanderbilt. Did you see what those two were getting up to at the black and white party? Though, he did suggest that he'd only just met her so I guess it may be someone else …"

Harrison's glare sharpens to a point where I fear he's going to snap, but unfortunately, he holds himself together like a true professional. "Mr. Carrington's business meetings are none of your concern," he tells me. "You have no place scrutinizing his actions or questioning his motives. If he has said he is going away for business, then that is all you are required to know. Nothing less, nothing more. You are here to work. Is that understood?"

"Yes," I sigh, not willing to push it. He's clearly not in the mood for our little banter. Though, something tells me he doesn't classify this as banter. "Understood."

"Good. Now, with Mr. Carrington unavailable for the next two weeks, the Masquerade party that was planned for next week has been brought forward to this weekend so Mr. Carrington can attend. He will be flying out on Sunday morning."

Well, that perked me right up.

"The Masquerade party is this weekend, like in two days?"

"Yes, keep up, Miss Munroe." I roll my eyes and he continues. "Now, with such short notice, we're going to need all hands on deck. Maryne is busy in the dining room finalizing all the party details with your mother and they could use some help. The whole house is going to have to be cleaned from top to bottom so it's going to be a late night. I suggest you take tomorrow off from your schooling duties to do your part."

"Um … okay," I say slightly confused but more than happy to take the day off from Bellevue Springs Academy.

"The party is starting promptly at 7 pm sharp and due to short notice and being understaffed for the event, anyone working the night will be paid double time. Maryne will have a dress rush ordered for you so that you may work at the party. Are there any questions?"

My brows pinch. "Umm … double time?"

"You will be paid twice your usual rate."

My eyes bug out of my head. "Woah," I laugh. "I am so down for that."

"Good, because you didn't have a choice."

"No," comes from a demanding, familiar voice behind me, instantly stealing Harrison's full attention.

"I'm sorry, Mr. Carrington? No?"

Colton steps in beside me, refusing to look at me as he addresses Harrison's confusion while also leaving me wondering how the hell he managed to sneak up on us. His Veneno isn't exactly quiet. "No, Ocean will not be working at the party. She will be attending as my guest."

Harrison's eyes widen a fraction but he does his best to reign in his surprise. Me, however, I'm not that practiced. "The fuck?" I screech, finally gaining his attention. "No way in hell. I'm not attending as your guest. Are you insane? You've hardly spoken to me in two weeks and when you do, it's to remind me that I'm trash and a whore, so thanks, but no thanks. I'll be joyfully declining your bullshit offer."

Harrison looks horrified that I had the nerve to speak to a Carrington like that and goes to reprimand me when Colton looks back at him. "Are we clear?"

Harrison nods. "Yes, sir. Miss Munroe will attend as your guest. I will have her added to the list."

The fuck? Am I mute or are they both deaf?

Colton nods dismissively. "Thank you," he says, then walks away.

"Oh, hell no," I yell, racing after him. He gets away from me but I'm determined to say my peace. He turns into the massive kitchen, most likely on his way to lock himself in the den so he doesn't have to deal with me, but after a few weeks of living in this place, I've learned a few tricks.

By the time Colton is walking through the door of the den, I'm already there, staring at him and waiting ever so impatiently. His eyes widen in surprise before he narrows them at me with his usual tough-guy act.

"What the hell is your problem?" I demand. "You don't get to make those kinds of demands. I'm not going to the party with you. Besides, Harrison said it was double time and I need the money."

"You're going to the party."

"You're right, I am because I'll be working at it."

"You're not fucking working at the party. If you need the money so badly then you can help with preparations and with the clean up on Sunday. Besides, Harrison never lets the staff do both the party and the cleanup."

"But …"

"No. You're coming."

I stare at him, my brows pinched with confusion. "I don't understand you," I tell him. "Why do you want me there? Every chance you get you're pushing me away. You're usually desperate to have me anywhere but near you and now this? You're giving me whiplash. I can't keep up with you."

Colton lets out a frustrated sigh and runs a hand through his messy hair as his eyes soften and he lets go of that hard-ass exterior. "Just ... please."

My brow raises. I did not just hear that correctly, did I?

"But why? Why do you want me there?"

He shakes his head, silently begging me not to ask him that question. There's strange desperation behind his eyes and something tells me that he's just as terrified of the answer as I am, so for once, I do him a favor and leave it.

My eyes drop to my hands. "Even if I wanted to go, I can't."

His voice is low and grumbly and at this moment he seems like a complete stranger to the already confusing version of Colton Carrington that I've come to know. "Why not?"

"I don't have a dress or a mask so I'd look even more out of place than what I do now, and in case you haven't noticed, being different around here is cause for humiliation."

"You know the guys at school are only dickheads to you because they want you and know that they don't stand a chance."

I raise my chin and meet his eyes. "And you?"

Colton sighs and dips his fingers into the pocket of his school slacks before pulling out a familiar little card. He hands it to me and I take it in confusion. "Buy yourself a gown and anything else you need."

I look down at the card in my hand before trying to hand it back. "I can't do that. It's not my money to spend."

"You can and you will," he murmurs, his voice impossibly lower. "Someone as beautiful as you should not be in a borrowed dress. You deserve the most expensive gown at the party."

With that, he turns and walks away, leaving me gaping after him, unsure why my heart is racing so fast, but needing to put it to the back of my mind before I race after him and throw myself into his inviting arm, I pull out my phone.

It rings twice before Milo's voice comes hollered through the phone. "What's up, bitch?"

"The masquerade party just got put forward to this weekend and guess who was given a Carrington credit card to go and buy the most expensive gown she can find?"

"No way," he screeches, excitedly. "WE'RE GOING SHOPPING!"

CHAPTER 29

The Rinaldi's limousine pulls into the long driveway that leads down to the Carrington mansion and stops by the gate, marking our names off the guest list.

Butterflies swarm through my stomach. I've never officially been on a guest list like this before. I mean, I guess I kinda was for the black and white party but that doesn't really count. Charles added me on as an afterthought for that one and I felt as though I was playing Cinderella going to the ball, but tonight, I feel as though I belong here.

My white-gloved hands trail over my silk gown and I catch myself glancing down at the golden material as it frames my body just right. I feel like a fucking princess.

Milo hired a hair and makeup artist to come to his place and do me up like some kind of barbie doll. I usually hate other people doing my makeup and touching my hair, but it was done to perfection and gives me chills every time I look in the mirror, which just happens to be a lot.

The driver hits the gas again and we start making our way down the drive. I find myself gawking out the window at the mansion. I live in this place yet I've never seen it lit up like this. Lights line either side of the driveway and although I've seen them there every time I'm forced to walk up and down this long beast, I've never witnessed them actually turn on while the moon briefly lights up the night sky.

It's simply stunning.

Tonight could turn to shit from here on out and I'd still have the audacity to say that it has been one of the best nights of my life. This world finds new ways to amaze me every single day and today, it's this party.

I haven't even gotten inside and I know it's going to be incredible. Just as Harrison had requested, I took yesterday off school and helped get the house ready for the party. I watched as trucks arrived and started unloading decorations while a sound team came in to hang speakers and set up audio equipment. I listened as they did their soundcheck and fell in love while the room turned from a plain ballroom to a venue fit for the biggest party of the year.

The limo comes to a stop and the driver hurries around to open the door. "Alright," Milo's mom says, giving Milo and I a warm smile while still assuming that we're an item. "Masks on."

My gloved fingers trail over the soft lace of the mask sitting in my lap and I pick it up. It's amazing. Milo and I had spent all Thursday night searching for this mask but when we finally saw it, it spoke to me and I knew it was the one.

I place it over my face, making sure not to ruin my makeup in the process and just as I go to fasten it at the back, Milo leans over. "Here, let me." I beam at him and turn my head, knowing he'll fasten it the way the hairstylist had suggested as to not ruin my hair. "There, perfect."

I straighten up and pull the small mirror out of my purse and take a look.

It's like a complete stranger staring back at me. My plum lips stand out with the black lace mask, but my blue eyes are so bright that they're stealing the show. I hate how obnoxious that makes me sound, but tonight, I'm going all out and I don't care who it offends.

Milo's parents scoot out of the car and Milo quickly follows, knowing there's bound to be a line of cars piling up behind us. Milo stands at the open door and offers me his hand. I graciously take it as I slip my leg out of the car.

The high split of my silk gown shows off my thigh but I quickly hurry out of the limousine and raise to my feet beside him, covering my legs before I go ahead and show off the goods.

Milo's parents are long gone so we start making our way up the sixty-six steps to the front door. His hand falls to my back, leading me up the stairs like a true gentleman and I'm thankful knowing that I was bound to fall in these stiletto heels.

Milo's hand brushes against the skin of my back, reminding me just how dangerously low it dips. If I was to make the wrong move, every guest at the party would get a good look at my lacy thong covered ass. Hell, without the Hollywood tape, I'm sure they would have already seen it.

The closer we get to the front door, the higher the nerves rise within me. I don't understand why though. I shouldn't be nervous. It's just a party in the place I've been calling home, yet for some reason, I can't wait to find Colton and show him just how amazing this gown really is. After all, he just paid 10k for it.

My feet are already hurting in these heels by the time we reach the top, but I'm determined not to let that ruin my night. I'll stumble back to the pool house with bloodied feet if I have to. I won't give this night up for anything. Besides, the funny little butterflies in my tummy keep whispering that tonight is going to be different, that Colton is going to be different. After all, he invited me here as his guest and that has to mean something, right? Maybe he's ready to put the worst behind him or maybe he's ready to tell me whatever it is he keeps holding back from me.

All I know is that Nic's warning hasn't stopped going through my mind and that's probably because we still haven't talked. I hate it. I don't think I've ever gone a week without talking to him. Not even a simple text, but that's what you get when you mix two people with stubborn as hell attitudes.

Soft music flows outside as Milo's hand tightens on my lower back. "Are you ready?"

I look down, and quickly adjust the gloves that sit high above my elbows then follow the line down the soft golden silk that brushes gently along the ground. "Yeah," I tell him, forcing the butterflies out once and for all. "I'm more than ready."

We walk through the door and are instantly welcomed by a host who takes Milo's jacket and asks if she can check my purse. I hold on to it and thank her anyway simply because I don't think a complete stranger has ever been so kind to me before.

We get three more steps before a woman with a tray of champagne flutes comes walking by. Milo stops her and takes two glasses, handing one to me before sending her on her way. I instantly take a sip and notice it's not the bitter champagne that I hated at the last party, but the sweet, fruity one that I had drunk instead.

Half the glass is gone before we even walk out of the foyer and into the main ballroom. We step through the doors and I'm surprised to see so many people already here. It's only 7:30 pm but I guess when Charles Carrington is throwing a party, you want to soak up every last second.

I find myself looking around and can't help but feel like tonight is an old school Taylor Swift song. It's sparkling and enchanting. It's everything I hoped from a fairytale night.

Milo and I get halfway across the floor when I find him.

Colton Carrington.

As if sensing me, his hazel eyes turn my way and they send electricity shooting down my spine. He wears a light grey three-piece suit with a white dress shirt that fits him perfectly. He looks like he's just been pulled out of either a James Bond movie or a GQ magazine.

His eyes never break from mine. He looks hungry, and from the way he starts making his way toward me, it's clear that tonight he won't be holding back.

I swallow my nerves and notice that as he gets closer, his metal, gold-plated mask perfectly complements my gown and I'm left speechless. Surely that wasn't on purpose … right?

Why do I feel so nervous around him? Why am I so desperate for him to take my hand and kiss me as though I'm the only girl in the world? This is the guy who declared he was going to make my life a living hell, he's the guy who stood back and watched as five guys poured acidic grease all over me, he's the one who's made me feel small ever since I got here, yet he's also the one who has gone out of his way to protect me, stand up for me, save me.

My world is quickly beginning to revolve around him and it scares the ever-loving shit out of me.

Colton steps up in front of me, tall, dark, and oh so fucking handsome. His eyes roam over my face while mine mimics his movements. I swallow hard, feeling my mouth begin to dry. I need to feel my lips on his. It's been way too long since he kissed me last and I'm quickly beginning to realize that his kiss is my drug and I'm deeply addicted.

As if on instinct, his hand reaches out to mine and I take it willingly, both of us watching with shallow breath as his fingers lace through mine.

What is this?

A throat clears beside us and both our heads whip up to Milo. His eyes are cautiously on mine, a secret message within them asking me what I want to do when it occurs to me that Colton and the rest of the room think that Milo and I are together.

I go to pull my hand free but Colton tightens his grip. He's not letting go, at least not for the rest of the night.

Colton looks to Milo and somehow it turns into a pissing contest but it doesn't last long because Colton is a Carrington and he's been taught from a young age to take what he wants and don't relent.

Milo bows out while slipping my purse from my hand and I want to curse him while also thanking him but I can't do either because the second he's gone, all that exists is Colton.

He tugs gently on my hand and I fall into his side, allowing him to lead me through the room the same way Milo had been doing. His hand falls to my bare back and the heat that comes from his touch is enough to leave my skin burning and desperate for more. The champagne flute is plucked out of my hand and swiftly delivered on to a passing waitresses tray and before I know it, we're heading for the dance floor.

Colton walks in silence, neither of us knowing what to say. When we reach the dance floor, he spins me into his arms and my hand instantly falls to his wide chest, taking possession as though it was mine to claim. Colton's arm curls around my lower back and just as he had done earlier, claims me. Our hands find one another's and just to add a little more confusion to the mix, he pulls me in tight to his body.

I don't understand this. All this time I thought he was afraid to show the world that there was something—however minimal—between us, yet here he is, displaying it for the world to see. Every one of the wealthy bastards in this town are here tonight and Colton is flaunting the trash their family brought in. It doesn't make sense but for tonight, I think I can try to forget.

Maybe it's the masks acting as armor, and making us brave.

My eyes close for a brief second, inhaling and smelling his manly scent that drives me wild. I've never smelt anything like it. It's so naturally him with a splash of greek God.

The music flows through the room and Colton is quick to pick up the rhythm, leading me just as easily as Milo had done at the Black and White party. A million questions rush through my mind but I put each of them aside, refusing to ruin this moment with talk. After all, Colton and I seem overly compatible except for when it comes time to communicate.

As we dance, Nic's warning comes back to haunt me. He said I was going to get hurt and I think he might have been right. Colton Carrington has all the power here. I'm putty in his hands yet for some reason, I'm allowing it to continue.

Colton's hand travels up my spine and pulls me in tighter so that my face hovers just by his. If I didn't have these heels, I'd be squished into his chest, which really isn't a problem for me, but this just adds to the perfection of my night.

"You're so fucking beautiful, Jade," he murmurs so low that I wonder if I heard him correctly.

My heart races as I pull back and look up into his deep, hazel eyes. I don't think I've ever seen them quite so dark before. I'm completely captivated by him. Every tiny little move he makes is written on my soul and it scares me like never before.

I can't be feeling like this when it comes to Colton Carrington. I should be wanting to tear him apart for making a comment like that. Why is he making this so much harder?

I tilt my chin, needing to see him properly. "Don't do this," I beg.

His brows furrow as his eyes pierce right through to my soul. "Do what?"

"Make it so damn hard to hate you."

"Maybe I don't want you to hate me, not anymore."

Those fucking beautiful words. I don't think he understands the power they hold because if he did, there's no way in hell he'd be uttering them to me. Surely this is some kind of game and just when I think everything is falling into place, he's going to pull the rug from under my feet. So, why does it feel so damn real?

"I don't think you know what you want," I whisper, watching the way his gaze focuses heavily on mine.

"You might be right about that," he says as his hand slides down my back, trailing over my spine and making goosebumps rise over my skin. "But I know what I want right now."

Oh, holy hell. This isn't good.

He moves into me and everything goes weak. All that exists at this moment is him.

Why do I need this so bad?

Colton gets closer and closer and his intentions become startlingly clear. He's going to kiss me and I'm going to love it, need it, crave it but most of all, it's going to end me. I don't know if I have the strength to keep hating him after this. Our first few kisses were different. They were hungry and spoke from a part of us that we couldn't control, but this … this is so much more. This isn't just our bodies speaking, this is our hearts and that's where it gets dangerous … complicated.

His arms tighten around my body and I'm a fucking goner. I know I should tell him no. I know I should try to stop this, but I can't. I need his kiss more than I need my next breath. Come tomorrow, I can curse myself and go over all the reasons why this was such a horrible mistake, but for now, I have no choice but to make the mistake and make it damn good.

His face comes right in front of mine and he stops, waiting for me to close the last inch between us.

This is it. My final chance at escape, my very last shot at saving myself the heartache that is bound to come after this, because there's no doubt in my mind that he's going to break me, but what's more, I'm going to let him.

Putting my heart and sanity on the line, I raise my chin, closing the gap, and finally feel his soft lips press against mine.

My knees go weak and if he wasn't holding me up, I'm sure I'd be some kind of puddle at his feet. My brain screams at me, telling me how wrong it is but as his lips start moving against mine, every last thought turns to mush.

He holds me tight while at the same time, his touch is feather soft. It's as though I'm precious to him, something worth valuing. I know Nic loves me in his own distorted, over-protective way, but he's never held me like this. Colton and I don't have a history or even a proper relationship between us and already the connection I feel between us right now is stronger than anything I've ever had with Nic.

He makes my heart race, my palms sweat, my breath catch in my throat. He's somehow everything to me while also being absolutely nothing at all. It's the most confusing and infuriating thing I've ever felt. Every moment of every day, I need to know where he is, I want to be in the same room as him, while desperately needing to get away.

I've never felt such confusion. I need some sort of clarification from him. I need him to tell me what the hell is going on here and why I feel the way I do, but deep down, I know he's just as confused as I am. He has no fucking clue and is going off instinct, but come tomorrow when the gown is gone, the music stops playing and the party fades away, we'll be back to square one and that knowledge sits heavy on my chest.

His tongue sweeps into my mouth and I welcome it with a desperation I wasn't aware I was capable of. My hand slides up his chest and wraps around the back of his neck, holding him tight and silently begging him not to stop.

That delicious scent of his cologne wraps around me and I get lost in time. I don't know how long we stand here in the middle of the dance floor fused to each other, but my mind slowly begins to come back.

Milo is here somewhere and I remember that I'm supposed to be playing the role of his doting girlfriend but I guess that didn't last long. My mom is also making her rounds through the party and I cringe at the thought that she's seen me getting too close to her boss' son. I can only imagine what she's thinking right now.

The thought sobers me and I reluctantly pull back from the sweetest thing I've ever tasted. I can't help but meet his eyes and when I do, I find them filled with lust. So dark and wanting. My hand slips back down to his chest with my fingers splayed across the material of his soft grey suit. "What is this?"

He shakes his head before dropping his forehead softly against mine and finding my hand. His fingers lace through mine just as they were before we reached the dance floor and the butterflies in my stomach go nuts all over again.

"Don't ruin this by putting labels on it," he finally says. "All I know is that for some reason, I can't stay away from you."

My voice lowers to the softest whisper. "I don't want you to."

His intense gaze remains on mine, neither of us knowing where to go from here. I'm in unchartered territory and I've never felt so lost. Any move I make could have this all falling apart while at the same time, I'd be smart to stop this now.

"This doesn't make any sense," I murmur. "I'm 'the help.' I'm trash. Why suddenly change your mind?"

"Look at yourself, Jade," he says, his voice thick with something I can't quite put my finger on. "Do you look like trash? You may be the help but you've never been trash. You belong here with me."

I shake my head though I have no way of knowing if it's out of confusion or because I simply don't agree. "I … I don't know."

His hand tightens on my waist. "What's the deal with Rinaldi? Are you together?"

"No, we're just …"

"That's all I needed to know, Jade."

This is dangerous for us both. His reputation might not withstand the rumors of getting together with the help, while my heart couldn't handle the torture of people's scrutiny. I can just imagine what they would say about me and it sounds a lot like the comments that fly through my mind every time I think of Jacqueline Vanderbilt. Though one thing is for sure, Colton has already publicly flaunted his desire to get something from me, and while one night with the help won't hurt him, having a relationship with me would.

Disappointment flares through me and I push against his chest, pulling myself out of his arms. "We shouldn't do this," I tell him, feeling myself begin to break. "Even if it is just for tonight, it's not going to end well for either of us."

He steps into me, trying to capture me once again. "It'll be fine," he promises.

"I just … I can't," I say, stepping out of his reach. "I'm sorry, I need to think about this."

I walk away before he has the chance to change my mind and I curse myself for being so stupid. I should be dancing in his arms and living my Cinderella fairy tale. I should be taking a risk, giving it my all and seeing where it gets me, but I can't because I know how hard it's going to hurt when he changes his mind.

I wasn't meant for this world, no matter what he thinks. It's just a dress and a little makeup, apart from that, I'm still the girl from Breakers Flats, I'm still the girl who grew up surrounded by gang violence and living day to day not knowing if I was going to eat.

This world isn't me and despite how sparkly and tempting it is, I can't let it claim me. It will chew me up and spit me out. It'll destroy me.

CHAPTER 30

My shoulders slam into other guests as I try to navigate my way through the crowd. I still can't believe how many people showed up here tonight, but that's the least of my worries.

I somehow make it to the back door and I push out into the fresh air, taking a deep breath. I hadn't realized how desperately I needed that.

I start making my way down to the gardens but after the rainfall we had during the week, the ground is soft and my heels quickly begin sinking into the grass. I turn and hightail it back to the mansion. I'm all about taking a stroll through the gardens on a fresh evening like tonight dressed like some kind of princess, but not at the risk of looking like an awkward baby duck trying to make its way through thick mud. I've already made a fool of myself too many times, I won't be doing it again.

I get up to one of the many outdoor entertaining areas and as I look back inside the floor to ceiling glass wall, I find Colton standing with Charlie in deep conversation, both their eyes trained on me.

I look away, unable to handle the jealousy in Charlie's and the intensity from Colton. I need to think this through. I need a plan, or at least an idea of how I should handle this. I need to call Nic and tell him that he was right. I need things to be okay between us again and I need my world to stop feeling so alien.

Knowing that if I walk around to the pool house, there's a big risk of me hiding out and pretending my problems don't exist. Not wanting my night to be over, I walk out by the main pool and stand at the side, listening to the sound of the waterfall raining over the deep end of the pool.

It's simply stunning. It's the best pool in Bellevue Springs and that's saying a lot, though I've come to learn that when dealing with anything on the Carrington property, it's usually the very best money can buy. That's just the way that Charles likes it.

With my feet hurting from the heels, I lift the bottom of my gown and slip out of my shoes, groaning with the pleasure of having bare feet. I lift my gown a little higher and drop down beside the pool before dangling my legs into the water and being extra careful not to let any of the golden silk fall into the pool.

This dress costs more than I could make in a year and the thought of having even an inch of it destroyed by pool water makes me want to hurl. Hell, I feel awful about the price tag on this thing. If I can, I'll be heading right back to the store and checking out their returns policy. Besides, it's not like I can wear it to another event. I'd be the laughing stock. Rewearing a dress around here is as good as committing a crime.

It's so damn beautiful out here. I don't understand why I spend so much time locked up in the pool house. I should come out here more often and enjoy the mansion before this fairy tale comes to an ugly end.

"What are you doing out here?" a familiar voice asks.

I look back over my shoulder and find Spencer slowly making his way toward me. Things between us have been better since that night sitting around the fire and when he had helped to save me from a mob of horny teenagers. I think at some point, I might have even earned his respect.

I shrug my shoulders and look back toward the water. "I'm just taking it all in," I tell him. "It's not every day a girl from Breakers Flats gets to attend a party like this wearing a ten thousand dollar gown and stilettos high enough to reach the fucking sun."

He laughs and drops down onto the edge of a sunbed, keeping a respectable distance as let's face it, our friendship hasn't quite developed enough for him to get any closer. "I didn't think of it that way. Parties like this are just kinda the norm for us."

"Not for me," I say. "It's like being in some kind of fairy tale."

"And is nailing prince charming part of that fairy tale?" he questions, making me look back to find his brow cocked in curiosity.

"I'm sorry?" I question, ready to jump on the defense.

"I'm sorry," he says, holding up his hands to show innocence. "I didn't mean that as some kind of attack. I was just referencing how close you were with Colt on the dance floor."

"Oh, I … umm …" I panic, turning back to the water, trying to prepare myself for the 'you're not good enough for my boy' speech that's about to come. "It's nothing. Just a little kiss is all."

"That wasn't just a little kiss," Spencer argues. "He's into you. Colton doesn't make a habit of claiming women publicly."

Claiming me? What the fuck is he talking about? I'm not someone who can be claimed that easily. Hell, Nic's been trying to claim me for months and isn't even close to sealing that deal again. My brows furrow and I find myself looking back at Spencer. "He didn't claim me. It was just a kiss on the dance floor. It meant nothing."

"Uh-huh," he says with a scoff, easily reading the lie as though I had it written across my forehead. "You keep telling yourself that, but what it comes down to is that you don't know Colton the way that I do. You're good for him."

My eyes bug out of my head. "I'm … what?"

Spencer bounces his brows and gets up from the sunbed. "Just think about it, okay? I can see you're into him and he needs someone like you to keep him grounded. Especially now that his mom and sisters aren't around. It couldn't be easy dealing with his old man every day. The kid is lonely and for some reason, your arrival here has managed to wake him up."

Surely I'm not hearing him correctly.

Spencer turns to walk away but stops when a waitress appears by my side with a tray of champagne flutes and offers me one. "Miss," she says with a polite nod of her head.

"Oh, thank you," I say, taking it from her and lifting it to my lips, knowing I'm going to need more than a few of these to make it through the rest of my night. The girl stops by Spencer and offers him a glass but he respectfully declines and sends her on her way.

"Look," he says, once we're alone again. "You two would drive each other fucking insane and I'm not going to lie, you'd get a lot of hate from … well, everybody, but it would work."

"Colton doesn't strike me as a relationship kinda guy."

"Oh," Spencer laughs. "He's not, but sometimes the best things to happen to us are the ones we didn't know we needed."

With that, he turns and walks away, leaving me to stew over every last word he just said. It also doesn't go unnoticed that he offered no apology for the bullshit he's put me through along with his friends since I came here but for some reason, I don't seem to care. It seems so in the past now that it hardly matters. We've all moved on and are now entering this new stage of confusion.

I throw back what's left in my glass and look back around me, searching for the waitress again. I could use a few more of these drinks, maybe a bottle would be nice.

I catch the eye of a waiter through the window of the staff quarters and hold up my empty glass. He comes rushing out with a new one and I thank him before asking him to keep them coming.

An hour passes when I decide it's time to face the music. I still don't know what I want to do but what I do know is that to miss this awesome party because I'm too busy sulking outside would be a tragedy.

I get to my feet and the second I straighten myself up, my head starts to spin.

Woah. I was not expecting that. How many of those fruity drinks did I have?

I look around for a towel to dry off my feet so I don't ruin my dress and make it a pain to get my heels back on. I start walking toward the main part of the house, knowing there's bound to be something in there but with every step I take, my head grows dizzier.

Why is it that you always feel extra drunk when you stand up? I have the same issue with tequila, though that's usually after I've found the bottom of the bottle. I don't think I drank quite that much though. I would have only had four glasses and it's the fruity shit, nowhere near as strong as tequila.

I get to the back door and practically fall into it before struggling with the handle as my fingers begin to feel numb. What the hell is this? I keep trying, spying a chair just inside the door. If I could just sit for a minute, I'll be alright. I just need this to pass. Maybe a few glasses of water and a little food will help sober me up. I just want to go back to the party even if it means avoiding Colton and spending my night pretending to be Milo's girlfriend.

My eyes grow heavy and my knees become weak as I finally get the door to work, I pull it open and find myself stumbling through the open door. This isn't right.

I crash into the wall and have to hold a hand against it to keep me on my feet. What's happening to me? "Help," I say weakly, needing to press my whole body against the wall as my head continues to spin.

I try to take a step and feel my body sliding down the wall. knowing that once I hit the ground, I won't be able to get up again. I desperately try to right myself, only my attempts are laughable.

"About fucking time," comes a voice from behind me.

No. No, no, no. I didn't think he was here. He's been MIA all week.

I try to spin around but the movement only has my mind spinning and my feet twisting awkwardly beneath me. I start to fall but Jude rushes in and slips a hand around my waist while pulling my arm around his neck.

I try to push him away but his grip only tightens and I finally start to understand what's going on and even in my fucked-up state, I'm more than aware that this is a situation I don't want to be in.

"Is everything alright in here?" a passing waiter asks on his way back to the kitchen, eyeing me warily.

"Yes," Jude is quick to say, giving the guy a charming smile. "She's just had a bit too much to drink. I'm going to take her upstairs to sleep it off before the other guests see her like this."

"Of course," the waiter says with a polite nod.

"Wait … no, no…" I say, my voice barely recognizable.

"Now, now," Jude says, speaking over me. "Let's get you to bed, sweetheart."

No, no, no, no, no. This can't be happening.

I keep trying to fight against him, dig my nails in and kick at his feet but it's as though I have the strength of a newborn kitten. "Keep trying," he laughs in my ear. "Nothing is going to stop me from taking what's mine."

"Nic's going to come for you," I slur. "They all are."

"Let them fucking try. Your little gang bangers have already fucking tried and failed. They're going to wish they had killed me by the time I'm through with you, but beware, when they come for me, I'll be waiting and this time, they won't be walking out alive."

We reach one of the many staircases and he easily sweeps me up into his arms then starts up the stairs. I try to wriggle free, not even caring if it means, dropping to the floor and tumbling down the stairs. I'd do anything if it meant getting out of here.

"Help. Someone help."

My voice comes out as barely a whisper and Jude's loud booming voice instantly drowns me out. "You've got Colton wrapped around your little finger but he'll see after this that you're nothing but a whore. Can you hear that, trash. No one is coming for you. No one cares about you here."

Tears begin filling my eyes as he reaches the top of the stairs and dives into the first guest bedroom. All my hopes of getting out of this begin to plummet and all I'm left with is the knowledge that my boys are going to kill him. There's no getting out of this. I'm going to be left to endure it. Endure the pain and endure the dirty memories that will plague me for the rest of my life.

The door is kicked shut behind him and the panic rises in my chest.

My heart beats rapidly and I start searching the room for anything that can be used as a weapon. There's a lamp on the bedside table but seeing as though I could hardly open the back door, I doubt I'm going to be able to lift it let alone smack it hard enough over the top of his head to do any damage.

I'm fucked.

Maybe this is what Nic meant by his warning. Maybe he wasn't referring to my heart getting hurt at all, maybe he was meaning something a little more physical. Either way I look at it, he's right. I should have gone home with him. I should have let him take me and then I would have been safe. I wouldn't be having to deal with this. I'd be happy and know that no matter what, I had four boys at my back.

Why am I so fucking stupid? This is all on me. I'm going to be raped and there's not a goddamn thing I can do about it. I thought I was strong enough to handle this.

Jude throws me down on the bed and my head slams against the wooden headboard. I hear a sickening crack but the sound is drowned out by the pain that rocks through my body. He starts striding toward me, looking at the way the split in my dress is open and drawn up, showing off my lace thong.

He licks his lips while pulling on his tie and loosening it. His dress shirt is freed from his pants and his hand falls to his belt. "I'm going to enjoy this," he says hungrily, his eyes full of a darkened desire. "I'm going to fuck you so hard that everywhere you go, you're going to feel me. You'll never forget where I've been."

No, no, no, no. Please, no.

"Beg all you fucking want," he spits, grabbing my leg and tugging me down the bed, making me realize that I'd said that out loud. "Do you know what kind of shit I've been through ever since you got here? You fucking owe me, bitch."

He pulls me until my legs dangle off the end of the bed then grabs the gown where the split meets. He tears it hard and the silk easily comes apart under his grip, revealing my body to him.

The material lays discarded at my side and as he reaches for my bra, I use every last ounce of my strength to bring my knee up and slam it against his balls. Jude yells out, gripping his junk as he doubles over. "Fucking bitch," he grunts.

I try to roll away and get only an inch before he's back. "You're going to pay for that," he demands as his hand cracks out and slaps hard against my face. The sound vibrates through my cracked skull but the pain has nothing on the incessant throbbing at the back of my head.

Jude pulls me back to him and holds my legs tight, learning from his mistakes as he uses his other hand to unzip his pants and pull out his dirty cock. I struggle against him, wishing that darkness would hurry up and claim me. If I have no choice but to endure this, then I'd rather not remember it. This is the kind of shit you never come back from, never fully recover. The wounds may heal but they always leave scars.

My thong is ripped down my legs before they're curled around him. He spits, his cold, wet saliva dripping down against my pussy. Jude doesn't waste a second rubbing it against my opening, knowing damn well that a disgusting rapist like him could never get me wet.

He lines himself up with my entrance and in one hard thrust, he slams deep inside me. His fingers tighten on my waist, hard enough to leave bruises and I cry out despite knowing I can't be heard, as silent tears track down my face..

He goes again. Twice, three times, a fourth.

The door flies open. "Ocean, where ar … the fuck?"

My head whips to the door as Jude roughly rips out of me and spins around. Colton stands gaping for a moment, trying to figure out what he's actually seeing. There's fury in his eyes as he looks at his friend but as his gaze slices to me, it turns to hurt.

"Help me," I try to say but my words fall flat.

"Get the fuck out," Jude roars but Colton doesn't take his eyes off me, instead he looks at the blood smeared across the bed, the blood matted in my hair, the red handprint across my face, the torn gown, and my desperate tears.

The door has barely finished swinging open by the time he completely comprehends what's going on.

He rushes forward and Jude has just enough time to release my legs before trying to stop Colton's fist from flying at his face. My legs drop heavily and I roll off the side of the bed, going down with a hard bang.

Tears stream down my face as I try to find the strength to get myself up and out of this damn room, but I can't. My body is lifeless and all I'm able to do is watch the way that Colton tears Jude apart. They begin to blur as I feel the darkness beginning to creep up on me.

My eyes grow heavy watching punch after punch. Blood soaks Jude's face while Colton's knuckles turn a deep shade of red, his face filled with a darkness that I've never seen before.

With one heavy blow to the temple, it's lights out for Jude but Colton doesn't stop, completely overtaken by his rage.

Desperately needing help, I call out to him. "Colton," I cry, fearing my words are gibberish on my tongue. "You're going to kill him. You need to stop."

Colton instantly stops what he's doing as his head whips around to take me in. He looks back down at Jude and his eyes widen in understanding.

He climbs off him and races to me, effortlessly scooping my lifeless body into his capable arms. He practically races out of the room, curling me into his chest. My head lolls against him as I feel the darkness creeping closer, sneaking up on me like a wave. I don't know how much longer I can hold on before it crashes down over me.

Colton kicks through his bedroom door and drops down on his bed, refusing to let me go. "You're going to be alright, baby. Just hold on. I promise you, he'll never hurt you again."

My eyes close and his arms instinctively tighten around me. "Please be okay, baby," he whispers into the dark room like a chant. "Please be okay."

I feel movement beneath me and am jostled around but unconsciousness claims me as I feel the vibrations of his voice against his chest. "Spence," he says, his voice thick with raw desperation. "I need your help."

CHAPTER 31

Hands grab at me and my eyes spring open in fear. I try to pull away but the grip only tightens. "Shhhh, O. It's me," Nic's melodic voice whispers through the room. "You're safe, baby. You're safe."

My body relaxes against his and I let him hold me before realizing where I am. It's my room in the pool house, but how did I get here? The last thing I remember is passing out in Colton's arms, so how the hell did I end up in Nic's?

"What are you doing here?" I murmur, nuzzling my face into his chest and hoping that his familiarity can help me to forget the nightmare of last night.

"Carrington called and said you needed help," he says with an edge in his voice that has my stomach sinking.

"You know, don't you?" I ask, my voice breaking as the tears begin to fill my eyes.

"Of course I fucking know," he grumbles, holding me tighter and making the tears spill. "I should have never let you stay here."

I shake my head, silently telling him that this is not his fault. If anything, it's on me. I was the one who made the stupid decision, I was the one who insisted I stay, and I was the one who had to be difficult about it, but there's no use saying that to Nic because he will never hear it.

"I'm so sorry, O."

His words kill me and have the few tears on my face turning into a fucking stream. "I tried to make him stop," I cry. "I wasn't strong enough and I couldn't move or see properly. My head kept spinning. I'm sorry, Nic. I should have fought harder. I should have stayed at the party."

"Shhhh, baby. This isn't on you. You don't need to explain it to me, I know."

"You know?" I question, raising my head to meet his dark eyes. "How?"

"Do you really think I was going to let Colton leave it at 'your girl needs help?' I got every last detail out of that fucker, but don't you worry, O. I'm going to make this better. I'm going to make that bastard pay."

"I know," I tell him, knowing damn well that Jude won't be living to see the end of the day. Seeing as though it was me who was hurt, Nic might make it last. Either way, it's a face I will never have to worry about seeing ever again.

Nic scoots down in bed, bringing me with him and running his hand up and down my back when it occurs to me that in any other situation, he would be out looking for the fucker and the fact that he's still here is speaking volumes. He cares so much about me.

I'm instantly flooded with guilt over everything that's happened over the past few weeks. I've been kissing boys, showing off my naked body for Colton and grinding against him, sleeping with Charlie— all things that would have him breaking yet he's still here, more than willing to defend me against dickheads like Jude Carter.

"I love you, Nic," I whisper against his chest, feeling his arm tighten around me. "I'm sorry that we fought. You were right and I was too stubborn to see it."

"You don't need to apologize, O. I was an asshole. There was no need for me to yell at you like that but you know how I get when I feel your safety is in question. You're my girl even when you're not and you should know by now that I will go to the ends of the earth to protect you."

"Don't think for a second that I don't know how lucky I am to have you."

His phone ringing between us cuts our little moment in half and he pushes me aside to get into his jeans pocket. We both look at the screen of his phone to see Kai's name looking back at us.

Nic hits speakerphone. "Kai. You better have good fucking news for me."

"How's my girl?"

"She's *my* fucking girl," he scolds, spoken like a true possessive asshole.

"I'm fine," I tell Kai, ignoring Nic's alpha douchiness. "A little banged up and I feel a little drowsy from whatever was slipped in my drink, but I'll be okay."

"You better be okay," Kai tells me. "I swear, we're going to get him for this. I've got you."

"Kai," Nic snaps, done with our conversation. "Tell me you got the fucking kid?"

"Nope. The fucker's gone missing."

"Missing?" I question. "Who? Are you talking about Jude?"

Nic nods but it's Kairo who responds. "Yeah, pretty girl. Carrington said he left him in the guest room last night coz he was pretty fucked up but he wasn't there this morning. I've checked his place and his parents confirmed that his car was still in the garage. He couldn't have gotten far."

"Fuck," Nic roars, sitting up in bed, the sound penetrating my head and making it pound, though all I can think about is the terror Jude's parents must have felt at being faced with someone like Kairo when he's looking for answers.

Nic looks at me as I place a hand over my face, trying to dull the ache. "Do you know where he could be? You knew the fucker better than us."

My lips twitch at the way Nic already refers to him in the past tense. I shake my head. "No, I only ever saw him here or at school," I explain, leaving out the whole boat thing though I think it's obvious that he isn't hiding out on the Carringtons' boat … though is it really such a long stretch? "Check the marina," I tell Kai. "There's a shitload of boats out there. He could be hiding out in one of those. He'd be stupid to think you guys weren't coming for him. I told him that much."

"Alright, pretty girl," Kai says. "I'll call you when I've got something."

The call goes dead without so much as a goodbye and I'm left watching Nic as he slides out of bed. "If the fucker is running, I need to go out and help the boys find him," he tells me. "Will you be alright here? I'll come back as soon as I can."

I nod, knowing that at some point today I'm going to have to get out of bed, find some pain-killers and go and thank Colton for saving my ass yet again. "Yeah," I tell him, knowing he's not about to walk out that door if I give even the slightest hint that I need him. "I'll be fine. I want to shower and I need to go up to the house and see Colton."

Darkness seeps into Nic's eyes. "I'd prefer if you didn't."

"Didn't what?" I question. "See Colton?"

He nods and I narrow my eyes waiting for an explanation. Nic sighs and turns away, collecting his keys off my set of drawers. "You're into him, O. I see it all over your face so forgive me for not wanting my girl to go and throw herself at the guy who brought that fucker into her life."

I stare at him, not sure what to say. "I'm not your girl anymore. It's okay for me to be into someone else."

Nic walks up to me and leans down on the bed until his face is hovering just in front of mine. "Baby, just because you say something, doesn't make it true. You're my girl and one of these days, you're going to come to your senses and come home to me."

"Don't hold your breath," I grin.

Nic rolls his eyes and drops a feather-soft kiss to my lips before turning and walking out of the room. "I'm glad you're alright, O," he calls as he walks out through the pool house. I listen out as he walks away and I hear the familiar sound of the door shutting behind him.

I let out a soft sigh as I'm left with nothing but my thoughts. I have to get out of here. If I sit in bed for much longer I'm going to drive myself insane. I know Nic is going to find Jude and put an end to my suffering. It's a fact. It's as true as saying that the sky is blue or that I have a stubborn streak, but it doesn't change the fact that it happened and it certainly does nothing to ease the torturous memories that have continuously sailed through my mind since I first woke up.

I peel myself out of bed and get up to my feet. I'm not going to lie, it's not the first time I've been drugged but that time was by accident and possibly a little self-inflicted. Sebastian and I were screwing around with some pills that we'd found and apparently, it wasn't the good stuff. I'd taken the wrong one and Nic, Kai, and Eli were quick to let Sebastian know what they thought of that. The poor guy couldn't walk for a week.

I was taken care of and in safe hands, nothing at all like what happened last night. The next morning had sucked. I was wobbly on my feet and my mind was foggy until I could sleep it off and I'm assuming today is going to be the same.

I push up to my feet and hold onto the wall. My legs feel like jelly but for the most part, I think the drug is out of my system. I slowly start creeping toward the bathroom, silently thanking whoever lives above that Nic decided to go. I don't want him to see me like this. He would have stayed and insisted on helping me with every tiny little thing.

Holding onto the glass of the shower, I somehow manage to lean in and turn on the taps and after stripping off my clothes—clothes that certainly don't belong to me or Nic—I search through the bathroom drawers for some pain-killers.

As I stand under the hot water and scrub the feel of his hands off my body, my mind wanders. It doesn't make sense to me that Jude has run, not after the beating he took from Colton last night. He must be some kind of superhuman to have woken early and run out of here before Nic found him. From the sound of it, Nic's been here all night and if Jude was there when he arrived, he wouldn't be out searching for him now. It's a two-hour drive from Breakers Flats and assuming Colton called him right after I passed out, that gives Jude two hours to regain consciousness and make a run for it.

Not fucking possible. Not after that beating. Jude would have been out for hours.

Something doesn't add up here.

My mind takes me back to the fogginess of last night. I remember Colton coming and looking for me and I remember the way his eyes had locked onto mine, the fury, the jealousy, the rage. I remember it all.

He nearly killed him and then he took me away from my nightmare. He held me in my arms and murmured, begging for me to be okay, but then he said something else just as my world was fading to black.

'Spence, I need your help.'

They know something. They know where he is. It's the only thing that makes sense.

I fly out of the shower and pull Colton's shirt back over my head before curling my hair up into a big clip. Underwear and sweatpants go on and a second later, I'm storming out the door to the huge mansion that still baffles me.

The clean-up crew is here and busy and resentment settles within me. I was supposed to enjoy that party and I was supposed to earn a shitload of cash helping these guys clean it up. Instead, I'm cleaning up a different mess entirely. A mess that should never have been made.

By the time I reach the stairs that lead up to Colton's bedroom, my legs are starting to feel the burn. The pain-killers and the hot shower certainly worked their magic but there's only so much they can do, but I'm not stopping. I don't even care if I have to sit at the top for ten minutes before slamming my way through Colton's door. I will be getting answers and I don't care how I have to get them.

It's some kind of miracle that I get to the top and find the will to force myself to the end of the hallway until I'm standing in front of his door.

I don't wait.

I barge through the door, throwing it open, much like Colton had done last night. I fly into his room just a moment before his ensuite door opens and he strides out in nothing but a white towel wrapped dangerously low around his defined hips.

He comes to a standstill, staring at me in shock, clearly not having expected me to come barging in here first thing on a Sunday morning. "What ar–"

"What did you do?" I demand, cutting him off.

His brows crease and I try not to get distracted by the drops of water that slowly trail down his strong body, dripping from his hair, and making his skin look good enough to eat. "What the fuck are you talking about? I didn't do anything."

"Jude," I snap, watching as he walks around the room as though I'm not even here. "I know you stashed him somewhere so Nic couldn't get to him."

Colton stops walking and turns to face me, his eyes hardening at my accusation. "Get this straight, Ocean. I don't give a shit what happens to the mother fucker after he put his hands on you. Dominic can have him for all I fucking care."

I swallow at the intensity of his stare but it doesn't go unnoticed that he didn't exactly answer my question. I can't stop staring. It's never made sense why he cares so damn much but there's something real there, something honest and downright raw.

I swallow my pride and walk toward him and with each step I take, the intensity grows until I'm standing right before him. Instinct has his hands falling to my waist as I claim his bare chest just as I had last night on the dance floor.

My skin burns under his touch despite the thin shirt that acts as a barrier between us and I can't help but wonder if I'm about to be met with the overprotective amazing guy I was with on the dance floor last night or if I'm about to see the Colton that tears me down, the one I've become so accustomed to over the past month of being in Bellevue Springs, the one I've learned to despise.

"Why did you want me at that party, Colton?" I murmur, letting him see the real me, the one who has been plagued with this question, the one who won't dare stop fighting for answers.

He watches me, his eyes roaming over my face as though I'm some sort of mythical creature that's completely bewitched him. "You've showered," he comments. My brows pinch in confusion but he's quick to explain himself. "You put my shirt back on."

My eyes drop to my body. To be completely honest, my morning has been a little too fucked up to think too much about the shirt but now that I see it for what it is, I can't help but like the way it feels on me and the way it screams of possession. My chin raises and I meet his eyes again. "Colton," I whisper. "The party?"

His chest drops as he exhales and I find myself spreading my fingers out over his damp skin. His eyes soften and I watch the exact moment as he decides to finally be real with me. "There's something about you, Jade. It drives me in-fucking-sane but when you're not around, I crave it. I need it more than you could ever fucking know."

"Then why are you such a dick to me?"

He shakes his head, not prepared to answer that knowing that a question like that is a ticking time bomb just waiting to explode. "Hearing you with Charlie … fuck, babe. You'll never understand how fucking close I was to storming in there and tearing that mother fucker off you but I knew you wanted it even though I know a part of you was only with him to get at me."

My lips press together and although I don't say a damn word, it's the clarification that he needs.

"Understand something about me, babe. I don't get jealous, but hearing that … I've never been so fucking jealous in my life."

"But …"

He continues as though I didn't say a damn word, desperate to get it out before this moment passes or one of us fucks it up again. "After Charlie, you pulled away. The snarky comments stopped, the attitude started to fall away but I craved it. I needed it from you and so I pushed you and it only pushed you further away."

"So, what? The party was just some desperate attempt to reel me back in?"

"No, Jade. The party was a desperate attempt not to lose you. I saw you in the parking lot with Milo and I'm not even going to try to understand that shit, but I can't watch you move on to another guy and fall further away."

He falls silent but words are lost on me. I haven't got a clue what I'm supposed to say to that but I feel it right down in my gut. The pull between us is too strong, too real.

I push up onto my tippy-toes and as I do, his face drops and our lips meet in the middle. His arms curl more securely around me as mine wrap around the back of his neck, holding him close and refusing to let go. The kiss is short, nothing like the one we shared last night but it's so full of power that it cripples me.

I pull away and drop back to my feet, needing a moment to collect myself and as his forehead drops to mine, I'm reminded of that perfect moment on the dance floor before the night turned to shit. "I shouldn't have walked out last night," I tell him. "I was safe with you."

Colton's fingers come up and brush the hair off the side of my face before his fingertips gently trail over my skin. "You're always safe with me, Ocean," he says, his voice thick with emotion. "Even when it doesn't seem like it, you're my priority. Since the second I first saw you."

His words are my undoing and I can't help but raise my chin and brush my lips over his once again. "Thank you for last night," I whisper. "For everything. Saving me, the party, the gown. It was perfect until it wasn't."

He doesn't respond, just nods and to him, that's as good of a 'you're welcome' as I'm going to get. My eyes drop and I focus heavily on his wide, tanned chest. "He destroyed my gown."

His fingers tighten on my body, holding me closer. "I'll buy you a new one."

I shake my head. "No, please don't do that," I tell him. "I don't want any more reminders of how he tore it from my body. I just …"

"It was your first gown." I nod, loving how intune he is with me. "Are you okay, Jade?"

"No …" I say, looking up. "I don't know. Maybe. I haven't really had a chance to process everything."

He watches me for a moment before slipping his hands down

my body and lifting me. My legs automatically wrap around his waist, holding on as he strides across his bedroom. He sits down on his bed with his back pressed up against the headboard and my knees on either side of his thighs. "You're strong, Jade. You're going to be alright."

I pull back and rest my weight on his legs while refusing to release my hold from around his neck. "Why do you call me Jade?"

A soft smile pulls at the corners of his lips and it blows me the hell way. "Have you ever seen a sky blue jadeite crystal?"

I raise my brow, wondering how a guy like Colton knows anything about crystals. "Do I look like the kind of girl who's seen a sky blue jadeite crystal?"

He laughs and raises a hand, brushing his fingers over my brow and circling under my eye. "It's the same color as your eyes."

My mouth drops as butterflies sweep through my stomach and make my heart race. "So, all this time I've been pissed with you for calling me the wrong name when in reality …"

"It's the perfect name."

"You should have told me."

His soft smile turns into a wicked grin. "As if I was going to do that. Do you have any idea how entertaining it is watching you get your panties in a twist over things you don't understand?"

My hand smacks out but his reflexes are on point and he catches it with ease. "You're an ass."

Colton tugs on my hand and I fall into him. He catches me so that I don't crash headfirst into his chest but a part of me kinda wishes I had. My face hovers in front of his and I catch my breath, feeling the tension rising between us.

"Tell me something I don't know," he murmurs low, his eyes glued to mine.

I can't resist him a second longer and fuze my lips to his. The hunger builds within each of us and he curls a strong arm around my back and pulls me in close. My body plasters against his and every last thought, every problem, every insult flies out the fucking window. All that exists is him.

I rock back and forth over him and feel him harden beneath me. After the night I had, sex should be the furthest thing from my mind. I should be running for the hills but the need continues to grow within and if I don't do this now, I might not survive.

I need Colton Carrington and I need him now. I don't know when I might ever get a chance like this again.

He reads my body and reaches for my shirt, pulling it over my head and dropping it to the bed beside him. His lips fall to my neck and I turn my face away, giving him as much room to explore as I possibly can all while his hands roam over my bare skin, trailing over my back and claiming every inch of me.

His hands find my jaw and he forces my gaze back to his. I see nothing but a pure, raging desire and I know he sees the same reflected in mine. "Are you sure about this?" he questions reluctantly as my chest rises and falls with rapid movements. "I can wait …"

"But I can't."

His gaze heats and his lips come straight back to mine. My underwear and sweatpants are ripped down my body as the towel around his narrow waist is pulled off.

The hunger intensifies and his fingers dig into my hips, moving me exactly where he wants me. I flinch at his forceful nature and know that any other time, I would love it but not now, not so soon after …

"I need you to give me control," I tell him, panting heavily and dropping my head back as his lips return to my neck and fingers trail over my nipple, lightly pinching and sending bolts of electricity shooting through me right through to my center.

His hand curls back around my neck, bringing my eyes to his again. He shakes his head. "I don't give up control."

My eyes sharpen and for a brief moment, we fight for power, we fight for control, and we fight for our place in this twisted relationship. The need within him takes over and just like that, I see that he wants this more than his need to be in control and I know he will give me what I need even if he doesn't know it himself.

A grin pulls at my lips and I raise my chin, showing him who holds the power here. "You can and you will," I tell him before reaching down between us and curling my hand around his hard cock.

My hand pumps up and down and the low groan in the back of his throat is enough to set me on fire. I've been craving this exact moment since the second I first walked through the doors of the Carrington mansion and laid my eyes on him and finally it's here and I know it's going to be so much more than I ever imagined it could be.

His hand trails down my body and just as his warm finger presses against my aching clit, a sharp knock sounds at his bedroom door just moment's before it's thrown open and Harrison comes rushing in, not waiting for an invitation or respecting any of the sacred rules he put in place, and that could only mean one thing—something is wrong.

"For fuck's sake," Colton mutters under his breath. "I can't catch a fucking break."

"Mr, Carrington," Harrison says wide-eyed, completely ignoring the fact that we're just seconds from having the fuck of a lifetime. His voice shakes and the terror coming off him in waves has me forgetting everything that's just happened in this room. Something isn't just wrong, it's really wrong. "You must come with me immediately."

CHAPTER 32

H arrison instantly steps out of the room, leaving the door wide open and turning his back as he waits for us to dress.

I scramble off Colton's lap and as our eyes meet, I see the wall starting to slam back down. His hand whips out and a second later, the shirt he'd just peeled off my body slams into my chest. I hastily pull it over my head as he grabs his discarded towel and covers his junk.

Colton crosses his room in the blink of an eye, he's in a pair of sweatpants with a loose tank that I've seen him wearing in his home gym.

He walks to the door and looks back at me, silently telling me to hurry the fuck up.

I hurry after him and he holds the door for me as I pass. I stop and turn to Harrison, waiting to see what the hell is going on. "Miss Munroe, please return to the pool house and remain there until the police have taken your statement."

"Police?" I grunt, looking up at Colton who looks just as confused. His eyes meet mine and for a second I wonder if this has something to do with last night but Colton hardly seems like the type to call the cops and press charges. He'd prefer to take matters into his own hands which is exactly what he did. The last thing he wants is cops coming to sniff around and find out that he beat the ever-loving shit out of him and it's not like Nic would have called …

Shit. Nic.

What's he done? If anything, he found Jude and took care of the issue, and now someone has found the body.

Fuck. FUCK. Nic can't be that stupid. He's always so careful with this shit but this time his emotions are riding high. He could have fucked up.

Shit. This can't be happening.

"Miss Munroe," Harrison snaps, irritated. "Get moving please."

"No. She stays with me," Colton steps in.

"Mr. Carrington, I must advise against that," Harrison says. "This is a family matter of extreme importance. Oceania should be sent back to the pool house to await the police's arrival."

"I've spoken," Colton snaps. "She stays with me. Now, what is going on, and why the hell are the police involved? I should have been notified. You know the procedure for when dad is out of town. *Everything* goes through me."

Harrison shoots a nasty glare my way before looking back at Colton and nodding. "Sir, of course, I understand the procedures, however, this is a timely circumstance and it prudent that we act fast."

Colton gets frustrated with Harrison dancing around the topic and narrows his glare. "What's going on, Harrison?"

"Sir, I think you should see for yourself."

Realizing that he's not going to get the answers he needs, Colton nods and allows Harrison to lead the way. Colton takes my hand and pulls me along, keeping up with Harrison's fast, long strides. "It's cool," I murmur as Harrison practically flies down the stairs. "I can go back to the pool house and wait."

"You're staying with me," he snaps in a tone that suggests an ass-whooping if I was to argue the point. "If this has something to do with Jude and the police have been called, then I can guarantee that you're not safe. They're going to take one look at you and assume that the poor girl from Breakers Flats is in the wrong. You'll be carted away in handcuffs without even a chance to fight your case. You're staying right by my fucking side."

My eyes bug out of my head and I find myself clutching his hand even tighter, terrified of being taken away. I see it happen all the time in Breakers Flats and I refuse to be one of those statistics. "But I didn't do anything wrong."

"It doesn't matter. It's just how things happen around here. Jude's family will go to extraordinary lengths to hide their son's indiscretions, no matter how fucking wrong they are. They'd rather drag an innocent woman through the mud than their reputation."

"Just like they did with that blackmail video of Jude raping that poor girl."

Colton's gaze snaps to mine. "How did you ..." he cuts himself off with a heavy sigh, deciding that now isn't the time to figure out how I could have found out one of his many secrets, but it won't take him long to work out that Nic would have been the one to share it with me. "Look, it could be something else entirely but whatever it is, you don't speak to the cops without me there, got it?"

"Yeah, got it," I grumble, hating being spoken at but keeping my mouth shut and deciding to fight him on that later.

We reach the bottom of the stairs and Harrison turns to the right, heading down the hallway that I've only ever gone down while looking for Charles' office.

I feel the tension rolling off Colton in waves and as Harrison comes to a stop in front of the familiar door, Colton eyes him down. "What's the meaning of this?" he questions. "You know you're not to be in dad's office while he's out on business."

"Sir," Harrison says, ignoring his stab and eyeing me again, clearly not pleased that I'm still here. He looks back at Colton. "You need to prepare yourself."

Colton's face scrunches in confusion but he doesn't get a chance to ask again before Harrison twists the door handle and pushes the door wide.

Colton steps through and I follow behind but come to a startling stop as I crash into his Colton's strong back. A sharp gasp comes tearing out of him as he pulls me behind him, protecting me from whatever secrets this office holds.

My hand presses against his back and I try to prepare myself for what I'm about to see, but nothing can prepare someone for this.

Charles Carrington lays over his massive mahogany desk staring up at the ceiling, his eyes wide and terrified as an old silver dagger protrudes from his chest.

Blood is soaked through the dress shirt he'd worn to the party and is pooled over the desk and puddled on the marble floor beneath.

My heart begins to race as I take in the intricate design on the dagger, the exact same as the one that ended my father's life. Flashbacks cripple me, walking into my small family living room to find my dad laying on the ground, drenched in blood with an ancient, intricate designed silver dagger pierced through his chest.

How can this be happening again? It can't be the same dagger. It was taken away by the cops, locked up in evidence, and never to be seen again.

My breath comes in short, jagged gasps as the need to run sails through me, but I don't. This isn't my father who's just been murdered, it's Colton's. What would he think of me if I was so weak as to run?

No, I need to endure the memories and stand by his side, the same way I wish someone had done for me all those months ago. Remembering the pain, the grief, and devastation I felt, finding my father like that has my hand slipping back into his, letting him know that whatever he needs from me is his and he instantly clutches onto it like a lifeline.

"He's dead," Colton murmurs beside me, looking like a lost little boy who's just found out that the world is a dangerous place. The need to say something sails through me, but the shock of seeing Charles and *that* dagger has me unable to find words and I feel as though I'm failing him.

"Sir," comes from Harrison as he discreetly steps into the office. "He is. From what we can gather, this happened as recently as the early hours of this morning. I need to know how you want to proceed?"

Colton's head whips around to Harrison. "What?"

"This is yours now," Harrison replies, sweeping his hand around the room. "You are the head of this family. The Carrington fortune is yours, the businesses, the assets. *Everything*. From this moment on, you are being watched by your competitors, your family, and the people who would do anything to take it all away. Your father has been preparing you for this moment all your life. How you respond to this is how you will start your reign as the wealthiest heir this town has ever seen. What you do from now on matters. Every move, every step, *every mistake*."

I look up at Colton and watch as his gaze darkens. He soaks up every word Harrison says and as his hand slips out of mine, I feel the world crashing down around me and combusting into flames.

Colton strides toward the desk, his back straight and shoulders strong. He walks around it until he's staring down at his deceased father, the dagger reflecting in his eyes. A moment of silence passes before he leans over his father and trails his fingers over his open eyes, closing them for the final time and silently saying goodbye to the man who made his life a living hell.

Something changes in him and I watch as he goes from the sweet boy I was dancing with during the party to a tortured man. In that split second, that boy ceased to exist and all that's left behind is a shell of a man who I thought I was just beginning to know.

Colton's hand curls around the hilt of the dagger, hiding its intricate details below his palm. His jaw clenches and he pulls it out slowly. Every inch of the silver, bloodied blade that appears has his eyes darkening further until they're as black as night.

He looks at me and what little connection we had dissipates and burns before my very eyes, tearing me apart, just as Nic warned me he would.

He's no longer Colton Carrington; popular billionaire playboy with a need to torture me, he's the new prince of darkness.

Colton spins the bloodied dagger in his fingers before slamming it down on the desk, making the silver clatter and echo in my ears. His piercing stare shoots to Harrison—dark, dangerous, and lethal. "Find whoever did this," he demands, and at that moment, he looks nothing like the guy I've come to know. The guy who protected me from his friend and nearly beat him to death is gone, the guy who brushed hair back off my face and kissed me as though I was every dream he'd ever had no longer exists.

This man before me is a stranger and he looks just like his

father.

Cold.

Deadly.

Un-fucking-touchable.

Sheridan Anne

Rejects Paradise Series Playlist

Game of Survival - Ruelle
I'm Gonna Show You Crazy - Bebe Rexha
Nightmare - Halsey
Never Tear Us Apart - Bishop Briggs
Bird Set Free - Sia
Helium - Sia
Dusk Till Dawn - Zayn feat Sia
Heaven - Julia Michaels
Graveyard - Halsey
Bad Bitch - Bebe Rexha
Love Drug - G-Easy feat Halsey
Hurricane - Tommee Profitt
Unloveable - Delacey
Power - Isak Danielson
Cruel Intentions - Delacey feat G-Easy
Not Afraid Anymore - Halsey
Unstoppable - Sia
Monsters - Tommee Profitt
Can't Help Falling In Love - Tommee Profitt
Angel Cry - G-Easy feat Devon Baldwin
Bad At Love - Halsey
Creep - G-Easy feat Ashley Benson
In The End - Tommee Profitt
Wicked Game - Daisy Gray
Haunted - Beyonce
Gasoline - Halsey
I Feel Like I'm Drowning - Two Feet
Twisted - Two Feet
Wild Horses - Bishop Briggs
The Fire - Bishop Briggs
Killer - Vallerie Broussard

Thanks for reading!

If you enjoyed reading this book as much as I enjoyed writing it, please consider leavinge a review.

www.amazon.com/dp/B089XTWKYL

For more information on Rejects Paradise, find me on Facebook or Instagram –

www.facebook.com/SheridanAnneAuthor

www.instagram.com/Sheridan.Anne.Author

Other Series by Sheridan Anne

www.amazon.com/Sheridan-Anne/e/B079TLXN6K

Young Adult / New Adult - Romance

The Broken Hill High Series (5 Book Series + Novella)

Haven Falls (7 Book Series + Novella)

Broken Hill Boys (5 Book Novella Series)

Aston Creek High (4 Book Series)

Rejects Paradise (4 Book Series)

New Adult Romance

Kings of Denver (4 Book Series)

Denver Royalty (3 Book Series)

Rebels Advocate (4 Book Series)

Urban Fantasy - Pen name: Cassidy Summers

Slayer Academy (3 Book Series)

Sheridan Anne

Printed in Great Britain
by Amazon

38877271R00253